A Snapshot of Murder

Frances Brody

Plus

Kate Shackleton's First Case

(a complete story)

piatkus

PIATKUS

First published in Great Britain in 2018 by Piatkus

1 3 5 7 9 10 8 6 4 2

A CIP catalogue record for this book
is available from the British Library.

ISBN 978-0-349-41432-4

Typeset in Perpetua by M Rules

Printed and bound by CPI Group (UK) Ltd, Croydon, CR0 4YY

Papers used by Piatkus are from well-managed forests
and other responsible sources.

Piatkus
An imprint of
Little, Brown Book Group
Carmelite House
50 Victoria Embankment
London EC4Y 0DZ

An Hachette UK Company
www.hachette.co.uk

www.littlebrown.co.uk

To Julie Akhurst, Ann Dinsdale
and Steven Wood

One

The Gentle Art of Photography

The first whisper that all might not be well in the world of photography came in the spring of 1928. It was just a few days after my niece Harriet and I had travelled to London, with a photographer friend, for a rally outside Parliament to mark the second reading of the Equal Franchise bill.

At the very next Photographic Society meeting, the idea for a weekend photographic expedition was floated. Our destination would be Haworth, timed to coincide with a momentous event in the world of those of us who love the work of the Brontë sisters.

On the first Saturday of August, a wealthy benefactor, who had purchased Haworth Parsonage, would present the deeds of the parsonage to the Brontë Society for the benefit of the nation. The new Brontë Museum would be declared open.

Seven of us went on that photographic outing. Six of us returned.

The story begins on a fine day in April.

*

Sunlight burst through my bedroom curtains. There would be no going back to sleep. What wakened me was the call of the first cuckoo; 1928 had started well.

I slid from my bed and went to the open window to look out at the garden and the small wood beyond. Golden light, tinged with the red of sunrise, brought clusters of daffodils into sharp focus. The cuckoo continued its call, chiming with cooing doves and the song of a blackbird, though it remained out of sight. It is the thing you can't see that you most want to spot.

This felt like a good morning to be alive.

The cat stirred as I went into the kitchen, raising her head from her bed in the carton lined with a battered cushion and an ancient woolly.

She watched me fill the kettle and light the gas jet. She climbed from her bed and stretched. I opened the door for her to go out. Sookie has grown old. Birds have no fear of her.

Ten minutes later, I put on my coat, carried my cup of tea into the wood and sat on the fallen log to drink it. Just for now, the world was mine.

A gentle breeze set daffodils nodding to each other. After a stroll around the wood, I went back inside to continue the task abandoned the night before – sorting photographs. The dining room is also our office and I keep photographs in the sideboard. There is a carton, unmarked, containing my husband Gerald's photographs. After a decade of Gerald's absence, I can still only look at a few photographs at a time. Some were still in the box that my housekeeper, Mrs Sugden, had marked: Mrs Shackleton – Photographs.

One day soon I would put them in albums, in some kind of order.

For now, I needed to remind myself which ones I had chosen to show to my fellow snappers at our photographic society meeting tonight, so that I could plan my commentary.

Spreading out my collection of pictures, I felt like a Tarot reader who has been given too many packs of cards.

Certain patterns emerged. A clutch of images portrayed men and women by gates and in doorways. Mrs Sugden posed by our back gate. Lizzie Luck, a weaver, leaned against the frame of her cottage door, proudly showing her handiwork, a piece of wedding lace. Richard Morgan, wearing trousers that ended above his boots, a Capuchin monkey perched on his shoulder, stood by the stable door where he houses a much-loved pony.

What I liked about these photographs was not just the light and shade, but the question mark. My subjects might be about to bar the way to their abode, or smile a welcome. I placed these together – people, their entrances and exits, rooted to the place they made their own. Was home a refuge or prison? Did they find themselves there by default or design?

My most recent doorway picture, one that I would treasure, was of my photographer friend Carine Murchison. During our recent trip to London, Carine went to the door of number 10 Downing Street, raised the letterbox and peered in. She wanted to see if the prime minister happened to be standing in the hallway. The burly policeman on duty studiously ignored her.

While she had her nose practically through the letterbox,

I snapped her picture. Our members would laugh at this one. Carine had made extra copies for me, and tinted some of them.

My train of thought was broken by the sound of my niece tramping down the stairs. Harriet has been staying with me for several months. She has a few daytime hours' work in a town centre café and an evening job at the local cinema.

'Auntie Kate, what a lot of pictures!'

'Too many.'

'Have you chosen?'

'Of course! My talk is this evening.' My niece has a habit of going to work without as much as a slice of toast inside her. 'Mrs Sugden will be up by now. There'll be tea in the pot and porridge on the stove.'

Mrs Sugden's annexe has a door to the kitchen. I leave her to her own devices in the morning, so as not to be in the way.

Harriet pulled a face. 'I'll get something at the café.' She went to the oak sideboard and looked at herself in the mirror, tilting her cloche at the jaunty angle she prefers. I am amazed her hats stay on. 'I do like this sideboard.'

'So do I.'

It's odd how we take the furniture and fittings of our life for granted and then, just occasionally, some item seems to demand attention.

Harriet ran her finger across the decorative diamond-shaped strip above the drawers and cupboard. The maker had not settled to one type of decoration. Tiny squares and oblongs embellished the sides and the inset of the cupboard doors. Embossed swirls graced the sideboard's low back. Doors and cupboards boasted anchor-shaped brass handles.

4

Its real secret attraction is a flattering mirror, but Harriet commented on its mad legs. 'It has square feet, ankles shaped like double egg cups and twisty legs.'

A few years ago, when Harriet saw her young face in the mirror, she asked if she could have the sideboard when I die. 'Ask me nearer the time,' I had said. She asked me an hour later.

Her attraction to sideboards, which she regards as posh, is endearing. What worries me is her almost Victorian pre-occupation with death. She and her younger brother Austin found their father's body at the quarry where he worked. It was Saturday afternoon. Ethan Armstrong's fellow workers had gone home. The children walked through the deserted quarry, carrying their father's dinner. He was a talented stonemason, working on a slate sundial, a man with enemies as well as admirers. My sister Mary Jane married again. I don't believe that Harriet and Austin will ever get over the loss of their dad. That is not something a child will ever fully recover from. Yet Harriet is cheerful and resilient. Having left school, she wasted no time in finding work, showing a great reluctance for more sitting at a desk.

Now she came to look over my shoulder at the doorway and gateway photographs.

'So these are for your magic lantern show?'

'Carine has helped me with it.'

Harriet was impressed. 'She does the slides for the picture house. When the screen shows the "Ladies please remove your hats" or the song sheet for the children's matinée, her studio name appears at the bottom of the slide. I wish I could do that.'

'Have a studio?'

'No! Make slides.'

'Well you could. You can do anything if you put your mind to it.'

'Do you think she'd show me?'

'I'm sure she would. Ask her.'

'Will you ask her for me? She's your friend.' She looked over my shoulder at the next batch of photographs.

'I'll mention it, but you must learn to ask for yourself.'

If the first selection of my photographs could be called 'Home', the next would be 'Work'.

A maid reached to take a sheet from a line, clothes pegs clipped to her apron, shadows from the washing creating dark shapes in the cobbled yard.

A group of dye workers in caps and mufflers, with shirt-sleeves rolled and ragged trousers tucked into their boots, screened their eyes against the sun. All except the small man in the middle with lined skin and a challenging stare.

'You're going to a lot of trouble, Auntie.'

'It's my turn to be the entertainment.'

Harriet picked up a picture of my father in his West Riding Constabulary police superintendent's uniform, and my mother in her finery on the day of a garden strawberry tea party.

'Aren't you including family?'

'No.'

'Why not?'

The photograph of my birth mother, Harriet's grand-mother, had slid under a picture of me as a baby. I call my birth mother Mam, as do my many siblings whom I hardly know, apart from Mary Jane, Harriet's mother. I had taken this picture of Mam outside her little house in

Swan Yard, Wakefield, opposite the railway station, one of those places that the sun gives a miss and where the dirty breeze turns washed sheets grey. Mam was an old woman, old before her time.

I brought it alongside the picture of my mother and father, who adopted me.

'Think about it, Harriet. Would you want to see portraits of the Photographic Society family members?'

'Certainly not! And I suppose nosey parkers would ask why you have two mothers.'

Harriet picked up a studio portrait of Gerald, in uniform. 'Is this my Uncle Gerald?'

'Yes.'

'I wish I'd met him. He's so handsome.'

'I prefer this one.' I showed her the photograph that I had taken on the cliffs at Whitby. It captured Gerald's heart, his soul, his smile and the checks of his shirt. The man in uniform was a man who would never return. The man on the cliffs would never go away.

She picked up a photograph of our society members taken outside the Bennett Road Parochial Hall, our meeting place. 'I'm glad you're not showing our family to that funny old bunch. I don't know how you put up with them.'

'They're not a bad lot, and we're all doing the same thing, we snappers.'

'What's that same thing, Auntie?'

'We make time stand still. If we're lucky, we capture a fleeting moment.'

'Some of that lot capture too many moments and they're all the same. The only person there I really like is Carine.'

'Everybody likes Carine.'

'Except her husband.'

'What on earth makes you say that?' Harriet can be very acute in her observations. 'Was it something he said or did?'

'Oh nothing!' She fastened her coat. 'Do you think it's going to rain?'

'Probably.'

'My umbrella went missing.'

'Don't tell me you lost another brolly?'

'It wasn't my fault. I was in the queue to see *Rin Tin Tin* at the Scala. I was taking money from my purse for the ticket and it was such a crush that when everyone moved forward, the brolly must have slipped from my hand.'

'Did you look for it?'

'Yes, and I asked the manager afterwards.'

'Take the one with the broken spoke. Have it mended in the market.' I walked her to the door. 'Why do you say Mr Murchison doesn't like Carine?'

'It's not me who's saying it.'

'Who then?'

'Derek.'

Derek Blondell is eighteen years old, and works as a clerk in the newspaper library. I am beginning to think that Harriet likes him more than she will admit. 'What does Derek imagine he knows?'

'You know he helps Carine on a Saturday afternoon, when Mr Murchison goes to photograph weddings?'

'No, I didn't know that.'

'Well he does, and he suspects Mr Murchison of something.'

'What sort of something?'

'Mental torture and slow poisoning.'

'Nothing really serious then.'

'Auntie! Mr Murchison wants to get his hands on the business for himself and some floozy. It's Carine's studio, you know, not his, otherwise why would it be called Carine's Studio?'

'It's called Carine's Studio because her grandmother was also named Carine, and the name was passed on. And, Harriet, you mustn't spread gossip, or believe everything you hear.'

'I thought you would want to know, since Carine is your friend. Which reminds me . . . ' She fished in her pocket. 'Nearly forgot. One of the customers in the café gave me this newspaper cutting. I just couldn't believe it. It's all about us.'

I took the cutting, which was from one of our more scurrilous papers.

Saturday, 31 March 1928

The Mole of the World

The newspaper that shines a bright light in dark corners

Dispatch from Your Northern Mole

Ayes to the right!

Yesterday your reporter travelled by crowded train to the capital. Ladies and lassies filled the carriages. Mere males now fight for breathing space on trains that they designed, constructed, maintain, drive and conduct.

On this mole's train travelled a titled lady, her daughter who practises the art of detection, a successful photographer whose camera steals the soul of all those who come into her focus, and a lively gel there for the fun of it.

Determined females congregated outside the Houses of Parliament. Elderly Dame Millicent Fawcett had to be smuggled in by a side door or she would have been mobbed and crushed by enthusiastic supporters. The good dame was there to witness the triumphant conclusion of a victorious revolution that she helped unleash.

Those females with influence and sharp elbows found their way into the lower chamber to listen to the debate on the Equal Franchise bill. Should females at the age of twenty-one, regardless of sense or sensibility, have the vote?

It is historically impossible to stop, said the Ayes. We are doing what we believe to be right, said the Ayes.

In vain did an honourable gentleman of the Noes party mildly point out that the passage of this bill would give women absolute supremacy in the polls, outnumbering their opposites by 3,000,000. 'Vox Populi, Vox Dei – no longer the voice of the gods but of the goddesses.'

To which Viscountess Astor called, 'Hear, hear!'

Is there no stopping the March of the Women? It used to be said that 'Man has his will but woman has her way.' Now woman will have both the will and the way.

Your Little Mole, an admirer and supporter of the fair sex, asks this question, not presuming to address the goddesses in person: Ladies, now that you hold the upper hand, where will you strike next?

Answer came from the lady detective as she attempted to induct her protégée into the art of world domination. 'My dear, will you stand for Parliament soon?'

'Oh no,' said the protégée. 'I like my job as an usherette.'

Little Mole breathes a sigh of relief.

Ayes to the right 387. Noes to the left 10. History marches on, or does it?

I handed the paper back to Harriet. 'Who on earth could have written this?'

'That's what I'd like to know. At first I was really annoyed by it, but now I just think it's silly.'

'You're absolutely right that it's us – my mother, the titled lady, the daughter who practises detection . . . '

'That's so obviously you, Auntie.'

'Carine is the successful photographer.'

'And if I ever find out who called me a lively gel, I'll give them a lively slap in the chops.'

'I have never called you "my dear", and after seeing what those women Members of Parliament have to contend with, I would be unlikely to suggest you attempt to join them.'

'You'd be good at that though, being in Parliament.'

'Whoever wrote this had at least a little information about the debate, even if they made up the rest.'

'If you were a Member of Parliament, you'd discover everyone's secret crimes and blackmail them into voting the way you wanted.'

'I'll bear that in mind.'

'You could live in London. I'll stay here and look after the house while Parliament is in session.'

'Go to work! You'll be late.'

'I'm going, I'm going. But how did whoever wrote this know that I'm an usherette?'

I looked at the piece again. 'It sounds as if it's been written by a chap, but it could have been one of the other women in our railway carriage who listened to us talking. The *Mole* is such a scurrilous rag, but some people will do anything to earn a few extra shillings.' I walked her to the front door.

'I'm going to solve this puzzle, as to who knows all about us and our trip to Parliament.'

She picked up the old umbrella. 'Oh and I meant what I said, Auntie, about Carine. What if she really is in danger from that horrible husband of hers?'

'Don't pay attention to gossip.'

'Think of it this way, though. You look into crimes after they happen. Wouldn't it be much better to investigate before something bad happens, especially if Carine is in danger?'

She waved to me from the gate. I watched her go. Harriet had set me thinking. I must try and find out whether there were grounds for her and Derek to be worried about Carine.

Two

The Darkroom

It is 1901. Carine has been to Betty Cleverdon's birthday party, with five candles on the cake.

Now Carine is with her mammy, on Woodhouse Moor, sitting on a bench. Being with Mammy is better than watching the magician at Betty Cleverdon's birthday party because Mammy makes her laugh, and never holds a rabbit by its ears.

Betty is not to keep the rabbit. The rabbit belongs to the magician. But Betty has a pretty guinea pig with a fine cage.

Carine's mammy is clever with the camera. Everyone says so. As they sit side by side on that bench, Mammy takes a picture by pressing a rubber handle on the end of a tube. An old man with a Yorkshire terrier stops to stare. The terrier sniffs at the tripod.

When it comes to the next go, Mammy gives Carine the rubber handle to press. The terrier yaps. The man walks away.

Later, there are two photographs. They are nearly the

13

same. Carine has to pick one. She picks the one that she likes best, the one where her eyes are wide open.

'These are ours,' her mammy says, 'just for you and me.'

'Shall we have one with Daddy?'

'Another day.'

That night when she has tucked Carine in bed and told her a story, Mammy whispers that she will go away for just a little while. She will come back for Carine.

This will be their secret. She certainly will come back. At playtime and at home time, Carine must look at the school gates. That is where she will come.

Carine knows not to tell Daddy that Mammy is coming back. It will be a surprise. She pictures Mammy at the school gates, as promised. They would walk home together.

Carine always looked at the school gates.

Carine was allowed to leave school on her thirteenth birthday, not wait until the end of term. She did not have to wait until the end of the day either because her dad had called to say he needed her at home. Where he needed her was the darkroom, but he did not tell the teacher that, and nor did she.

When she was leaving school for the last time, she turned back to look. The sun behind the gates created a shadow, like bars on a window. The thought came to her: Mammy would not have taken her from school at playtime. She would have missed the next lesson. Carine wondered whether she had somehow become mixed up about what her mammy had said.

She was standing near the gates, thinking this, when someone called her name.

14

She turned.

It was Betty, hurrying to catch up with her. 'I slipped out when Miss went you-know-where.'

Carine had not felt lonely until that moment. There would be the walk home. It wasn't far, but usually there would be others walking, or running, glad to have been let out of prison.

Now that Betty was here, Carine saw that she did not know what to say. And then it came out in a rush, so she must have planned the words. 'We an't always been friends, Carine, but we will be if you want.'

'We can if you like, then.'

'When you came to stay for a bit, after your mammy left, and there was that thing with my guinea pig . . . '

Carine looked at her shoes. Black. One of the laces undone.

' . . . I blamed you, but I see now it wasn't your fault. We were little. You were sad. You were holding him too tight.'

Carine smiled. It was the smile everyone liked. She used to practise it in the mirror. Now it came naturally, when she wanted it to.

'So we'll be friends?' Betty persisted.

'Yes, Betty. We'll be friends.'

'Did your mammy ever write to you?'

Carine shook her head. She smiled again, sadly this time. She hated Betty. Betty would go back into the class-room. She would whisper, 'Carine has gone. Her mammy left her when we were five. She never came back and she never wrote.'

Betty would be important. 'Ta-ra then, Carine.'

'Ta-ra, Betty.'

Carine was glad to have left school. She would be in the darkroom. That was her job now. She would take the negatives that showed nothing, and turn them, as if by magic, into pictures.

She walked home slowly, careful not to step on a crack. The sun was behind her making her shadow stretch. Her shadow would be home before her. Unsure what might happen if she took a misstep, she kept her fingers crossed.

It was as she thought. Dad was waiting for her as she opened the door and stepped into the studio. 'Good lass. See how quick you can be.'

Carine switched on the light and went down the stone steps into the cellar. Perhaps it was the strangeness of being a worker, not a schoolgirl, but she took a misstep as she crossed the stone floor to the darkroom. She stood not on a crack but on that stain, and then could not move. She froze.

A moment later, her father was behind her. 'Where's the mouse?'

'There is no mouse.'

'You screamed.'

'No.'

'You screamed.'

'I stepped on the stain.'

He looked at the floor. 'There is no stain. It's gone.'

'I can see it.'

'Then it's only the damp rising.'

He manoeuvred her from her frozen place on the spot.

She shivered as she went into the darkroom and had to blow on her hands. As she mixed chemicals, the thought came to her: once before she had asked her father about that stain.

16

The answer then was, 'Your mother once spilled fixative.'

My mother never spilled anything. She was so careful.

In the autumn of 1913, Carine was in the studio alone, adjusting the saddle on the rocking horse. She had photographed a little boy. The only way to make him still was to promise that, after the photograph, he could ride the white horse to Banbury Cross. He did rather a lot of kicking. She was glad when his mother gathered him up. Carine gave her a ticket and told her that the photographs would be ready next week.

Moments later, the clapper sounded. She turned to see two young men, about her own age. Students. One was tall, thin and sandy-haired. He carried a gown over his arm, and held a cap in his hand, obviously here for a portrait, yet he hung back shyly. His friend nudged him towards the counter. The friend was not entirely handsome, being of middle height, with broad shoulders, black hair, rather heavy brows, brown eyes and a cast of skin that made her think he might be descended from one of those Spaniards said to have been shipwrecked off the coast of Ireland.

Yet he was the one whose photograph Carine would like to have taken. He had what she called character, something you did not always see in young students. Had this dark-haired young man been a little lad, she would have dressed him as a pirate. That was her thought. He couldn't take his eyes off her. She was used to that. This time, she stared back, until he looked away. She turned her attention to the shy boy.

'I want a portrait of myself, for my mother please,' the shy one said.

Carine invited him to put on the cap and gown. She showed him the mirror where he could look, to have his cap at the right angle.

He looked surprised. People often did. They expected her to call someone, the owner, her father.

She met the boys again, when she and Betty Cleverdon were leaving the Headingley Picture House on Cottage Road.

They said hello.

Carine told the shy boy, whose name was Frank Nettleton, that his portrait was ready for collection. 'I developed it straight away because I thought your mother might be anxious to have it.'

The truth was that she had developed it straight away because the roll of film was at its end, but a reputation for being obliging was important in business.

Frank thanked her.

'You know Frank's name, but you don't know mine,' the dark-haired one said. 'I'm Edward Chester.'

'And I'm Carine, and this is Betty.'

Betty fell into step with Frank Nettleton.

Edward smartly switched positions and walked on the outside of the pavement next to Carine, all of them going in the same direction. 'Is that your name above the studio?' Edward asked.

'It is, and it was my grandmother's name.'

Edward smiled. 'She was a thrifty gran, then. "There'll be no call to change that sign if we call the young 'un Carine."'

'I never knew my grandmother,' Carine said simply. 'She died when I was a baby.' She did not tell him that her mother left when she was five years old. Once, she could not speak those words at all. She went dumb if the question arose. Now, she could not speak those words without fear of tears, and so she kept silent.

Perhaps Betty told Frank and Frank told him. Edward knew not to ask.

They agreed that all four would go to the pictures again, the night after next.

She told her father she was going to Ilkley with Betty Cleverdon. This would have been true, but by then Edward's friend Frank had gone to see his mother, who had taken a turn for the worse. Only Edward was waiting at the station. Betty decided not to go.

Edward had brought a book. He asked what Carine liked to read.

'I don't have a lot of time for reading, and when I do I can't settle to it.'

'Then I'll read to you. I'll find a teaching post that has accommodation. You'll come with me. I will read to you every night. Every morning, I will bring you a cup of tea.'

She laughed. 'You're mad!'

She did not tell him her true thought: I belong in the studio where my name is on the window.

They walked from Ilkley station to the moor, and the Cow and Calf rocks. Carine had never climbed so high, but it presented no difficulty. Soon they were looking out across the moor, master and mistress of the world.

Something sprang up between them, a closeness Carine had never known before. He felt it, too, and reached for her hand. A new light created the world afresh. All became wondrous, and special, the day, the moor, the world. It was because they were together.

She did not notice the other people roundabout. Their voices and laughter were a babble of nothing. There were just two of them, Carine and Edward. Edward and Carine.

They left the Cow and Calf rocks far behind, striding across the moor as if floating. When they came to a rock that was all alone by a stunted tree, Edward took a chisel and a little hammer from his haversack.

'What are you doing?' she asked.

'You'll see.' He chipped at the rock. 'This is because you and I will be together always.'

He carved EC loves CW.

When he hit his thumb and finger with the little hammer, she took his hand and kissed it better. 'Have you ever carved anyone else's initials?'

'No, and I never will.'

They had found each other so unexpectedly, but knew without doubt that this was meant to be.

It was several months before they returned to the moors. They found a secluded spot where they could be alone. By then, there was a dark cloud on the horizon, but they turned their backs to it. And the talk was of war, but they did not listen. They held each other close. She liked that he recited to her. He did it in a way that made words new. She never could tell whether the lines were his alone, or borrowed from another voice.

'Only our love hath no decay; This, no tomorrow hath, nor yesterday, Running it never runs from us away, But truly keeps his first, last, everlasting day.'

The 'hath' gave it away. It wasn't his own poem.

On the day they were to be married, her father got wind of it and locked her in the cellar. He said that she would be grateful to him one day. A poet would be neither use nor ornament.

He went to the register office and told Edward that she had changed her mind.

Later, her father put on a great performance, which at the time she did not know was a performance. His heart would break. Her mother had gone, she could not go too. It was for the best, she must believe that.

When Edward came thumping on the shop door, and on the back door, and her father called the police, something inside Carine gave way. She came out in blotches, red blotches all over her body. Something happened under her skin. Something happened in her head. The doctor could not explain it. She was taken to Otley to stay with an aunt. By the time she was better, Edward had gone to war.

She went to drive trams when the call for women workers came. Edward would come back. He would have leave. He would not give up on her. She was right. He wrote to her. Luckily she got to the letter first, and wrote back.

The studio could not remain closed. Men in uniform came to have a photograph taken. Dad could manage that. Otherwise, he had become useless. He was drinking. Each night he staggered in. Sometimes he brought a woman.

She could not turn her back on the studio. Any photographs he managed to take, she made the best of, working late into the night when the trams had stopped running.

One night he stumbled in when she was just coming up from the darkroom in the cellar. She heard him fall on the stairs, and curse. Before she went to bed, Carine looked in on him, sleeping on the bed in his clothes. She unlaced his shoes and took them off. She pulled the eiderdown from under him and placed it over him.

When she looked at him, she knew something. What was it that she knew?

In a voice not her own she asked the question. He might think that, while he slept, an angel spoke. 'What did you do to my mammy?'

'She would have left us.'

'Did you do something to her?'

She did not want the answer, and no answer came.

Three

Magic Lantern Show

Headingley is named in the Domesday Book. This long ago 'Out-Township' to the north of the city, grew and grew. So did the city of Leeds, until it and Headingley could almost reach out and touch each other. Walking south, to the heart of the city, is no great distance from my house. On that spring evening, I walked north, up Headingley Lane, for the meeting of our photographic society. This takes me close to Carine's Photographic Studio. I was undecided about calling for her because I was early. She may be still working, or settling her invalid father for the night. Oh just do it, I told myself. If it's too early for her, she will say so.

People always stop to look at her studio window because she changes the displays frequently. That evening, daffodils in a painted earthenware vase provided a welcome splash of colour. On either side of the window was a three-tiered arrangement of cube-shaped boxes on which stood silver-framed photographs. On the left of the window was a wedding party from the last century; a couple in the first motor car to grace the streets of Headingley, and a 1902 charabanc outing. On the right of the window were modern photographs: a family portrait including six children and a fox terrier; a graduating student in mortar board and gown; an almost-smiling bride and a serious groom. Several old-fashioned cameras provided decoration in the centre of the window. On a stand, a simple white display card, lettered in gold, showed the price of studio portraits and ended with the lines:

HOME VISITS AND WEDDINGS
ENQUIRE WITHIN

The clapper sounded as I opened the door. Carine erupted from the back room, parting the beaded curtain, a smiling vision in a bronze dress draped with gold chains. A halo of red-gold wavy hair gives her the look of an angel in a Renaissance painting. But no painted angel was ever so full of life. This might sound fanciful but it is almost as if her nervous energy gives off an electric current that draws people to her.

'Hello, Kate. You're early for the big night.'

'I didn't know if you'd be ready to go yet.'

'Well I am, but there's plenty of time. We ought to have a glass of sherry.' She held the curtain open and we went into the back room.

There was a bottle, and two small glasses. 'I knew you'd call for me.' She poured. 'Here's to your picture show. Everyone will love it.' We sat down at the kitchen table. 'I'll be your assistant tonight and move the slides as you give me the nod.'

'That would be a great help.'

Never having put on a photographic display before, it was a relief that Carine had taken me through the process step by step. I am a latecomer to the gentle art of photography. Carine has been taking photographs since her fingers were strong enough to click a shutter.

I took out the cutting Harriet had given me, about our trip to Parliament.

'Did you see this? One of the café customers gave it to Harriet.'

She glanced at it. 'Tobias showed it to me. It's someone who knows us but I can't think who would write such rubbish. Could it be someone who goes in the café and hears Harriet talking?'

'By all accounts, she's too busy to talk.'

'Someone has pieced the nonsense together. We'll just ignore it.'

Carine looked remarkably well, yet there was something different about her, a slight air of distraction. I thought back to Harriet's remark, that her husband Tobias was persecuting her in some way. He would not be such a fool, would he? 'Is everything all right with you, Carine?'

She looked surprised. 'Does it show?'

'What is it?'

Carine let out a sigh. 'Do you ever think that you see a person on the street that you know? You want to catch up with that person, tap them on the shoulder. On a closer look you see that you are wrong.'

'Oh yes, that happens to me.'

'Then you won't think I'm mad if I tell you that I saw someone I had never expected to see again.'

'Who?'

'Edward. My first love. Like your Gerald, he didn't come back. Life's lucky dip gave me Tobias instead. But I've never forgotten Edward. I know I don't look as if I mourn anyone, but I have mourned him all these years.'

I felt a shiver when she told me this. I know so well that feeling of being utterly sure, for an instant, that you have seen the person you want to see. 'But it wasn't him?'

'Here's the thing. It was, I'd swear. It was his walk, his movement of the head. If only I could have heard his voice.'

'Did you see his face?'

'No.'

'That sounds so familiar, Carine. We see the person from behind and just for that instant they are back.'

'He was wearing a hat. I didn't even see the colour of his hair. He had black hair, dark brown eyes, brows that were a little too heavy, and the most gentle voice. He was a poet.'

'But he died. You told me that he died.'

We all knew the story. Edward and Tobias were in the same regiment. Tobias came back. Edward did not.

'Tobias was with him when he was wounded, and he said that he died, but what if . . . ' She made a dismissive gesture. 'I know. I should shut up about this.'

'No, of course you shouldn't. What regiment were they in? It will be straightforward to check.'

'Of course it will. I didn't think of that. East Lancashire.'

'So stop worrying about it now. We can enquire. The records are comprehensive and people are helpful. If you have any doubts at all, you ought to know, to put your mind at rest. I'll help you.'

'Thanks, Kate. If anyone can find out, it will be you. I wanted to ask you before but I held back.'

I took out my notebook. 'What was his last name?'

'Chester, Edward Chester. He was a poet and training to be a teacher.'

There was a sudden thumping on the ceiling from the room above.

Carine stood. 'I won't be a minute. I've settled Dad once, but he must be wanting something.' She walked to the door that led to the upstairs rooms.

I admired the patience Carine showed towards her father. She paid for a nurse to come in each day for an hour, but most of the caring was left to Carine, which she somehow managed, in between taking portraits and working in the darkroom, as well as designing greetings cards. No one knew how she managed everything.

When she came back down, I asked about her father.

Her look gave nothing away, neither affection nor exasperation. 'We just had a joke. He says that it's his ambition to be Dr Green's most interesting patient. If it's not the gout, it's his chest. If it's not his chest, it's the rheumatism and the dropsy.'

Surprisingly for us, we did not talk much as we walked up the lane. I was thinking about the presentation, and hoping it would go well. Carine was also preoccupied. She had a lot on her mind, with a sick father, a husband who drank too much and now the possible reappearance of her one true love.

The church bells chimed seven as we passed St Michael's Church. Once, the church's Yorkshire stone must have gleamed proudly. Fogs, brimstone and smoke from factory chimneys had slowly but surely turned the building soot-black.

We crossed the road and walked on, passing the Skyrack pub.

'Are you doing anything afterwards, Kate?'

'Only going home to read a book, so . . .'

'Then come back with me. Tobias will be going to the pub. We can have a bit of a chat.'

'Yes, I'd like that.'

Our society meets monthly in the Parochial Hall on Bennett Road. As I opened the door, we heard the ethereal sound of a Monteverdi song from the local madrigal group. They rehearse in the room on the left. Their voices added to a feeling of serenity, an atmosphere at odds with the occasional fractiousness of the groups that meet here.

The caretaker appeared and greeted us. 'Hello. You ladies are soon here.'

He has a way of turning a greeting into an accusation.

'I'm giving a presentation, Mr Tanner.'

Carine took the magic lantern. 'I'll set us up.'

The caretaker followed us into the meeting room. Giving the impression of having been born old and frown-marked, he carries himself with a stoop. His fading light brown hair blends with the colour of his smock.

He rubbed the bristles on his chin, sighed and began to set out the slatted chairs. 'How many tonight do you reckon?'

'Thirty or forty.'

'And a treat in store then, eh?' His special leer involves a twist of the lips and a narrowing of his eyes, as if to hide the light of interest. 'I recall that Mr Murchison had some seaside pictures not so long since, lassies in bathing suits, almost what you might call saucy.'

Carine set up the equipment on the table.

'Pop in and take a look if you like,' I said to the caretaker.

'I might just do that.' He nodded towards the open door, and the singers' rehearsal room. 'It'd shut me off from yon screeching for ten minutes.' He set out a few more chairs. 'Do you want this door shutting against the caterwauling?'

Carine gave him a smile that took the sharp edge off her words. 'No thank you, Mr Tanner. My friend Rita is one of the madrigal singers. Both Mrs Shackleton and I love their caterwauling.'

'No accounting for taste.'

I was glad to have Carine's support. My hobby has slid down life's list recently and I was a little apprehensive about giving my presentation. We now have members who are more adventurous than I, creating collages, silhouettes and *avant garde* images from unusual angles. Knowing how some of my fellow snappers are apt to be highly critical, I had chosen more conventional work from an earlier time, when I entered competitions and was twice commended. We checked the slides and tested the images on the screen that had been set up earlier by the caretaker.

A few members had begun to arrive. The caretaker had finished setting out the chairs but he reappeared, carrying an envelope. 'I forgot to tell you. One of your group called by earlier. She says sorry that she can't come, and left this for you.'

I thanked him and took the envelope. It was from our membership secretary. She had scribbled her apologies on the outside, along with the words, 'Applications for membership'.

I showed it to Carine, our treasurer, as it would no doubt

29

contain postal orders. 'Oh, I'll give it to Tobias to read out the names and welcome anyone new who turns up.'

Tobias is our chairman. A noisy belch announced his arrival. 'Hello ladies, and what is it you'll give me, my dear?' He tapped Carine's bottom.

How she puts up with him, I do not know. She handed him the envelope. 'New members.'

I caught Carine's eye as Tobias made his way to the table. She simply shook her head and gave a shrug. 'He is a lost cause.'

Tobias sat down at the trestle table and set out his papers.

Derek Blondell came in shortly after. Harriet has made a friend of him since he started going to the Hyde Park Picture House. She always tells me when he was at the pictures, and that she tore his ticket. He raised his hand, more salute than a wave. He is pale, and thin as a broom, with a neat haircut and an old but good tweed suit, with leather elbow patches and narrow strips sewn around the jacket cuffs. My friend the newspaper librarian tells me that Derek lives with his paternal grandmother, who brought him up when his mother died after giving birth to him.

Derek exchanged a greeting with Carine and then turned to talk to me. 'Did you notice I have an item on the agenda, Mrs Shackleton?'

'Yes, something about an outing.'

He nodded. 'I hope I'll win support.'

I drew him to one side. 'I'm sure you will, Derek. And you'll need the support of Tobias Murchison, so be careful. Slander might lead you into serious bother.'

He blushes easily. 'What do you mean?'

'What you told Harriet. Slow poison? Mental torture?'

He was about to protest, when someone came to sit on my row.

My presentation went well, with no tricky questions afterwards. Carine and I returned to our seats. Tobias waited for the applause to subside. He is a big man, perhaps fifteen years older than Carine, with a florid complexion and bloated appearance. He usually races through the agenda, unless it is something he has to speak of himself, and then he becomes quite long-winded. He began by welcoming everyone to the meeting. When he opened the envelope, containing membership applications, he made a humorous moment of it. 'Two applications! Our venerable society is becoming known. At this rate, we'll need to hire the Town Hall.' He read the first name. The person was not present, no doubt waiting until her membership had been formally confirmed.

He looked at the second form, and he looked again, and he adjusted his spectacles. 'We have an application from Edward Chester.'

Carine gasped. She reached for my arm.

'It's not an unusual name,' I whispered, but the moment I looked at Tobias, I knew that he thought exactly the same as Carine. A man has returned from the dead.

Tobias rocked slightly on his chair. 'Is Edward Chester in the room?' he asked, his voice sounding like that of a medium trying to conjure a spirit.

There was no reply.

With what seemed like relief, Tobias returned to the business on the agenda. Yet he seemed uneasy. Finally, he came to an item that sparked his displeasure. Immediately, he became his rather pompous self. 'I have here a proposal that under the auspices of the society there should be a group photographic excursion in August. I did have notice of this proposal and I will not pre-judge . . . '

Naturally, he immediately pre-judged. He looked about the room. 'I believe our members are sufficiently grown up and able to organise their own excursions, but in line with the rules, we will hear from the proposer.' He pretended to search for the name. 'D. Blondell.' He looked about, making a show of deliberately not noticing Derek. 'Is the proposer in the hall?'

This struck me as extremely odd, given that Harriet says Derek works in the photographic studio on his Saturday afternoons off.

Derek cleared his throat. He took out a handkerchief and wiped his palms. He blew his nose. He blushed at the sound of his own nose-blowing. Before he had time to take a breath, Tobias barked, 'Apparently the proposer is not present.' He made as if to move on.

Derek came to his feet. Very steadily, he held his arms by his sides, and then put one hand in a pocket. He raised the other hand, like a schoolboy in class.

'Oh it's you, young Derek.' Tobias feigned surprise, though he must have known Derek's surname.

At that moment, I became aware of the door opening and closing, and footsteps at the back of the room.

Derek glanced at the piece of paper in his shaking hand. 'It's as our chairman said. I propose that some members might go on a weekend photographic excursion together, under the auspices of the society.'

'Do you now?' said Tobias. 'That means dipping into the society's coffers, eh?' Pleased with his turn of phrase, he gave a tight smile.

'I thought there might be a contribution, Mr Murchison, I mean, Mr Chairman.'

'Then let us have your formal proposal.'

Derek took a deep breath, executing a half turn so that he spoke to those at the back of the room as well as to the chairman. 'The idea came when I was looking at old copies of the *Photographic Journal* and saw that Mr Arthur Conan Doyle made photographic expeditions with a group of friends and wrote amusing accounts for the magazine.'

Tobias interrupted him. 'Sir Arthur to you I think, and we have still not heard you give the proposal.'

'Mr Murchison, this was in the last century, when Mr Conan Doyle was a medical student, long before his knighthood for services in the African wars.'

'I believe we all know that the true reason for that gentleman's knighthood was because he brought Sherlock Holmes back from the dead.' Tobias waited for the amused titter. No one laughed. He tapped his pencil. 'I don't suppose for one moment that, as a young man, Sir Arthur looked to some society to do his organising, and cough up to subsidise his wanderings.'

The room grew quiet. There was a sigh of disapproval from the man in front of me, impatient with Tobias's bullying ways.

Derek held his ground. 'As a young man, Mr Conan Doyle was very hard up.' Derek jutted his jaw slightly, as if daring anyone present to accuse him of the sin of pennilessness. Derek continued. 'Arthur Conan Doyle supplemented his income by writing those pieces. Having found them most entertaining, I suggest that we consider doing something similar.'

Some wag in the audience thought Derek's proposal a capital idea. 'We might take snapshots to illustrate a Sherlock Holmes story.'

Derek maintained his dignity. He was trying his best. He could not afford to go anywhere, and this was a great wheeze. I admired his initiative.

He cleared his throat. He held the piece of paper in his right hand, and now grasped his right wrist with his left hand to keep the paper from shaking. 'I, Derek Blondell, propose that members of the Headingley Photographic Society organise a weekend trip for the purpose of taking photographs.'

Tobias looked down at his agenda. 'According to the rules I must ask for a seconder, preferably one who has grown a few whiskers on his chin.'

This snide reference to Derek's immaturity drew a whispered response from Carine who sat beside me. 'He doesn't mean to be cruel.'

It was just like Carine to see the best in people, even in her own boorish husband.

A gentle yet clear voice came from two rows behind us. 'Edward Chester, new member. If it is in order for me to do so, I heartily second the proposal.'

Carine gulped. She was pale, as always, but a sudden red rash appeared on her throat and neck. She began to shake. She reached out and squeezed my arm so tightly that her nails dug into my flesh.

The pencil slipped from Tobias's fingers. His booming voice became a hoarse whisper. 'Do you wish to speak to the motion, Mr Chester?'

I turned to look at the speaker, three rows behind us.

He was dark-haired, of middle height, broad-shouldered, smartly dressed in dark suit and red tie. It was obvious from the way he held himself that he was a former soldier. But there was another sign, too. He was disfigured and had benefited from the skill of a surgeon. He must have been badly burned. From the cast of his left eye, I guessed that it was blind. Yet he held himself proudly, no shuffling of feet, or lowering of his head as if wanting to hide. His voice was sweet and mellow.

I turned back, not wishing to stare at him longer than you might look at anyone who has begun to speak. Carine stared at the floor, without turning her head. 'It's him. Kate, it's him.' She gripped my arm.

'Do you need to go outside?'

'I can't move.'

In such a meeting, there are always sticklers for protocol. Our resident procedural expert cleared his throat. 'Colonel Richard Thomas. As a member in full standing, I thank our newcomer for his intervention, but point out that it is not in order for him to second the proposal since he has not yet formally been admitted to the society by the treasurer, nor served his probationary period.' Colonel Thomas allowed time for the weight of his wisdom to be appreciated. 'To ensure proper procedure, I second the proposal. If there is money in the kitty, let us encourage the young.'

This was a surprisingly encouraging intervention from the curmudgeonly colonel. I assumed that he wished to disoblige Tobias.

Mrs Howe on the front row – her special interest is photographs of her grandchildren – did not pause in the clicking of her knitting needles as she offered a 'Hear, hear!' Several more voices of support came from across the room.

'Will anyone speak against the proposal?' Tobias asked hopefully.

Answer came there none. I guessed that Derek had done his homework, and gained support for his plan.

Tobias pressed on. 'What does the treasurer say?'

At first, I thought Carine would not manage to speak. Her voice came out in a croak. I wished I had a glass of water to offer. 'We have sufficient money in the Society bank account, Tobias. Sorry, I mean "Mr Chairman".'

Tobias frowned at the subdued titter, and then put the proposal to the vote. The motion was carried, with four abstentions and no vote against.

For the first time, members of the Headingley Photographic Society would undertake a trip.

Tobias asked for volunteers to organise the outing. Derek and I raised our hands. Carine, who was still clasping my wrist, involuntarily raised hers.

In the time-honoured tradition of special interest societies that take themselves rather seriously, Carine, Derek and I became the 'Headingley Photographic Society Outings (1928) Sub-Committee'.

Derek had thought of everything. Winning approval for his scheme had boosted his confidence. He spoke to the room, without asking permission of the chairman. 'Please put suggestions as to where you would like to go in the little box on the table at the back.'

Derek came over to our side of the room. 'How about next Tuesday at half twelve, in the Kardomah for our sub-committee meeting?'

Carine gave her brightest smile but did not utter a word.

I admired her more than ever. She had just seen and heard a ghost, and yet she kept control. I turned to look once more at the man who had come back from the dead. There was no sign of him.

'Is he there?' Carine asked.

'No.'

'Did you see him? I daren't turn round.'

'Yes. Dark-haired, broad-shouldered. He was good-looking once, I'm sure.'

'Once?'

'I would say that he suffered burns.'

'Get me home, Kate. I'll go to pieces if I have to be talking to people. And get that envelope with the membership forms back from Tobias. He'd take it to the pub and set fire to it. He recognised Edward.'

I went up to the table and picked up the committee papers. 'I'll carry these back, Tobias. I'm walking home with Carine.'

Tobias was deaf to me. The colonel was lecturing him about committee procedures. For once, he was silent.

The caretaker is always quick to start putting away the chairs in a noisy manner that drowns out conversation.

As Carine and I left, Tobias was following.

A few stalwarts always go across to the Oak after the meetings. Perhaps it was the fresh air that brought Tobias back to something like his usual self, or perhaps he thought that the appearance of his old comrade was a mirage.

Tobias slapped Derek on the back rather too heartily. 'I don't suppose you're coming for a pint, young fellow?'

If Derek had been a cat his fur would have bristled and

his tail pointed at the moon. 'You suppose correctly, old chap.' He stressed the word 'old'.

'That's the ticket.' Tobias adopted his jovial tone. 'You see the ladies home! It's the closest you'll come to them.'

On the walk back to the studio, Derek seemed unaware of any strain or tension. He chatted about how well the evening had gone. My presentation had buttered them up to be partial to an outing, he thought. And he very much liked that new member who spoke up for him.

Carine fiddled for her keys. Derek shifted his hold on the magic lantern.

Finally, Carine found her keys and unlocked the door.

Derek carried in the magic lantern and suggestion box. She thanked him. 'I expect you'll want to be getting home, to your gran and your cocoa.' She turned to me. 'Kate, you'll bide awhile?'

'Yes.'

'Go through!'

As I stepped through the beaded curtain to the back room, I heard Derek say, 'Where do you want the magic lantern?'

'Just leave it on the counter for now. I'll see to it.'

Derek hesitated. 'I'll see you on Saturday afternoon?'

'Yes.'

'Usual time?'

'Yes.'

'Carine . . .'

'Goodnight, Derek.'

I turned round, intending to say goodnight to him. Through the curtain, I saw the two of them outlined against the glow of the street lamp. He had thrown his arms around her and she was not resisting. It was so very brief, that in a blink I could almost think I had imagined the scene. She disentangled herself, and pushed him away with a shake of her head.

He called goodnight. From behind the curtain, I replied.

He has just turned eighteen. She is thirty-two. He is motherless. She is childless. Perhaps there is something of that in it, I told myself, but was not convinced.

Moments later, we were once again at her kitchen table. 'I'd have known Edward's voice anywhere.' She reached for the society's papers. 'Let me see where he lives.'

She took the envelope with the members' names, but it was empty. 'If Tobias has . . . '

I sifted through the papers. 'It's here.'

'Let me see the writing.'

I passed her the form. The writing was cramped but painstakingly neat.

'He's left-handed. I recognise his writing.' She stared at the form. 'It's a care-of address, the newsagent's on Hyde Park Road.' She put her head in her hands. 'I have been so stupid.'

'No you haven't.'

'He isn't dead.'

'You could be right, but people have doubles.'

'I know that's supposed to be true and of course he's not the same, but I'd recognise his voice anywhere.'

'Do you still want me to check with his regiment? It all seems so odd.'

'Yes you must.' She looked again at Edward Chester's application form. 'The newsagent's might not just be a convenience address for his letters. Perhaps he has a room above the shop. I could wait there. He may have gone for a drink.'

'You mustn't start searching for him at this time of night, or chasing after him. Let him find you.'

'I should have gone to him before he left. I should have spoken. He was close enough to have recognised me. I turned my head slightly. And did you see Toby's reaction? He tried to hide it. They were like brothers.' She made a fist of her hand and rubbed it back and forth across her mouth as if sealing and unsealing her lips. 'I'm going mad. And to complicate matters, that chump Derek has fallen for me, and I let him. He comes here on a Saturday to help. I've become the highlight of his week.'

'He'll get over it.'

'He's just a boy. I don't know what I was thinking of, except I wasn't thinking. If I'd known that Edward would come back . . . '

'Where does Tobias fit in all this?'

'Good question.' She pointed to one of the many photographs on the kitchen wall. It was Tobias, and Carine's father, taken in the back yard. 'Tobias must have known Edward wasn't dead. They connived. Dad wanted me to have someone who would stay by me in the studio. He could have done no better for himself than encourage a man who would be his drinking buddy.'

Having in mind what Harriet had gleaned from young Derek, I came right out with my question. 'Is Tobias mistreating you?'

She shook her head. 'He's too conscious of who provides the bread and butter to do that. He does nothing worse than spend the profits and come up with grand schemes when he is in his cups.'

'I'm sorry.'

'It's a bit of a mess. Do you ever think that some of us, by accident or design, miss by inches the life we ought to have had?'

'Probably almost everybody!'

We laughed. She pointed out another photograph on the wall. This one was of a woman and a little girl. The woman looked just like Carine, and the little girl was Carine.

'I think my father must have driven my mother mad. I finally understand why she had to leave. Tobias and my father are very alike. If it wasn't for my dad's insistence and non-stop promoting of Tobias's merits, I would never have married him.'

I looked at the photograph again.

'You both look so happy.'

'Perhaps history will repeat itself. I'll run off with Edward. We'll live wild in some wonderful place.'

'What happened to your mother?'

She was silent for a moment. 'I'm not sure. People whispered that she had run off with someone. I listened in one night when a neighbour was talking to Dad. Dad said that her fancy man didn't want to be saddled with a child.'

'That's terrible, Carine.'

'I never gave up hoping that I would see her again.'

'Does your father ever speak of her?'

'For a time, he did. He used to say that she was the beating heart of our family, and of our business.'

'Just as you are now.'

'Except that we're not a family. And I'm kidding myself. I'll never leave this place. Because, you know, she may come back. Now that Edward has risen from the dead, I wouldn't be at all surprised to see Mammy at the door tomorrow.'

Yet the way she spoke told me that she believed her mother was dead.

She gave a sad smile. 'But if Edward . . . '

She did not finish her thought. At that moment, there was a thump, thump on the ceiling from the floor above.

We stood.

Carine said, 'I had better see what Father wants.'

'Goodnight then. Tomorrow, I'll put in a call to East Lancs Regiment.'

She was opening the door to the stairs as I crossed the studio. At the same time, the clapper sounded and the outside door opened. Tobias and I almost collided.

'Kate! You must let me walk you home.'

'No need.'

'Oh, but there is. The pubs are chucking out.'

'It's a fine night and no distance.'

'There'll be drunken rowdies. '

As I let myself out, I heard him walk across to the studio counter and open the cash drawer.

I had walked several yards, and walked quickly, before Tobias caught up with me.

'I know, I know. You don't want an escort, but I'm walking in your direction.'

'Why are you walking in my direction?'

He cleared his throat. 'I know you have a reputation for looking into things, Kate, but where I'm going is my business.'

'Then let me guess. Hyde Park Road.'

That stopped him in his tracks. 'How do you know?'

I kept walking as I called back to him. 'Because that's the address Edward Chester gave on his membership application and I saw your reaction.'

He hurried to catch up. 'Carine's been talking to you.'

'And you should be talking to Carine.'

'I'm going to Hyde Park Road, but nothing to do with him. I play a game of cards with a few pals.'

He was wrong about drunken rowdies. Headingley Lane was quiet. A few students hopped off the late tram. Someone revved a motorbike. A lone workman whistled as he strode towards the town.

Once more, Tobias fell into step beside me. 'Teddy Chester always had his head in the clouds. He was never a man to stand too much reality. Carine's father took to me right from the off. He told me straight, he said to me, "Carine has one part blood to two parts developing fluid in her veins, but no head for business." The old man entrusts me with keeping the business going for the next generation.'

I refrained from saying that after ten years the 'next generation' was a long time putting in an appearance.

'My father-in-law is determined Carine should stay put in the place she loves and not find herself out of her depth through failing to grasp the money side of things.'

'And you're very good at grasping the money.' I would not normally be so direct as to pick an argument with a friend's husband. The image of Carine, wearily going to see what her father wanted, while her husband had his hand in the cash drawer, infuriated me.

'A business is a business and needs a business brain. When Carine's grandmother started the game, hardly anyone had a camera. Now, it's snap, snap, snap all over the show. We have to keep up. I'm in high demand for weddings. You need to be convivial for weddings.'

I crossed the road. He followed. 'See, I did have a bit of experience with a camera before I met Carine. I took a few half decent shots myself at one time. Of course, the top brass soon put a stop to that. After some fellows took pictures of a Christmas game of football between us and the enemy, we had to hand over our cameras. A camera became *verboten*, a court martial offence.'

He was doing that very familiar thing of reminding me. We made such a sacrifice, for you.

'And did Edward Chester take photographs?'

'Scribbled. He did nothing but scribble.'

'So the man who turned up tonight is not some ghastly doppelganger? Your reports of his death were exaggerated?'

'It's him all right, and when I find him he'll wish he had stayed dead.'

'Go home. You're drunk.'

'I've never been more sober. And since we're on the subject, what do you think to young Derek Blondell?'

This was not an easy question to answer, given that the first words that came to mind were 'He is in love with your wife, and I wonder if they have done anything about it.' Carine had once said of Derek that he was a hardworking, ambitious young man. I repeated her words, not wanting to make trouble for Carine.

'Ambitious is right. We didn't fight a war so that young whippersnappers like him could sponge off their elders and betters. Nobody ever organised outings for me. Except the powers that be and that wasn't a jaunt I would have chosen.'

We had reached my street corner. 'Go home, Tobias. It's late. You're drunk. You'll end up brawling in the road.'

Whether he heeded my words I did not know. I walked up the street and turned at the gate. He was still standing on the corner, watching me safely in, playing the gallant gentleman.

There was a message on the hall stand.

'Your mother wants you there early on Sunday, before dinnertime.'

$\bigcirc$our

The Scourge of Gout

Carine listened for a moment behind the door that led to the bedrooms. She heard Toby offer to walk Kate home. She also heard him go to the cash drawer, which she should have emptied.

Slowly, Carine climbed the stairs.

Tobias had offered to walk Kate home because he would then call on one of his cronies, for a game of cards and a few drinks. Or perhaps he would go in search of Edward. Wherever he went, he would not be home before midnight.

Carine could not put her dissatisfactions into words. It was as if a heavy mantle lay on her shoulders. On top of that she felt the weight of something like a basket, the kind that hawkers carry. She dragged her feet up the fifteen steps, the heaviness of her mood turning her shoes into hobnail boots. She would no more let people know how she felt than she would sit naked in the studio window.

Everyone said how charming she was, how cheerful, how kind.

The back bedroom had been hers as a child. Magnanimously, her father swapped – a year after she and Toby married.

He must have guessed by then that they both wanted a bolster's space between them.

The back bedroom walls were distempered with a yellow wash. The little cast-iron fireplace barely glowed as the fire was almost past mending. She heard ashes fall through the gate to the metal plate beneath. The smell told her that he had used the commode.

'What is it?' she asked.

Her father's name was Percy. His bed was by the window, so that he could look at the sky. There was not much else to see, except the houses beyond.

'You were a long time at your meeting.'

'There was a lot to discuss.'

'I'm mithered with these corns. That nurse doesn't get at them like you do.'

Percy had been born gouty, due to an excess of uric acid in his blood, the doctor had explained. Spa baths had helped when he was able to indulge in such. He did not escape the classic condition of troubles in his joints, and degrees of ill health over the years. Now, he was mostly bedbound, though he sometimes had good days when he was able to come downstairs.

'The nurse only did your corns today, Father.'

'You used to call me Daddy.'

'I was a child.'

'Beyond that you called me Daddy. You've changed.'

She handed him the glass of water from the bedside table. 'You need to drink.'

'I want to get up.'

'Then get up.'

'Who were you talking to?'

'Kate Shackleton.'

'Why are you being like this?'

'Like what?'

'I don't know. Distant.'

'I'm tired.'

'You're too young to be tired. I need you to pare my corns.'

'You could wait for the nurse.'

'I want you to do it. What's a daughter for if she can't help her old dad? You've life enough in you for that lad that comes on a Saturday afternoon. I know what goes on when Toby is out photographing weddings.'

'I'll fetch a basin. You can put your feet in to soften the corns.'

'And sterilise the razor.'

'I always do. Can you manage to get to the chair?'

'Aye, since you claim I'm too heavy for you to help me.'

She left the room, to fill the basin with warm water.

As she walked downstairs, he called. 'It's both feet you'll have to do.'

While her father sat with his feet in the warm water, Carine went to the cupboard where she kept her scrapbooks and newspaper cuttings. She had taken Edward's advice and read newspapers. Some of the stories were very interesting. She had carried on buying a newspaper each day, not always the same one. Sometimes she would go in the library and read a paper there. The staff would save them for her. She liked to read about murders.

'You want to throw that lot out,' her father said. 'You hoard too much rubbish.'

She straightened the papers. 'I've an interest. I like to know what is going on in the world.'

'This is my bedroom. You've no right to keep your stuff in another person's room.'

She was looking for some of the poems she had copied out of library books. These poems sometimes gave her ideas for the greeting card verses. What she came across was some loose cuttings she had forgotten. They were about an interesting case from a few years ago, 1922.

A woman and her lover had been hanged on the same day. The lover had stabbed the woman's husband. Although Edith Thompson had taken no part in killing her husband, and knew nothing of Freddie's intentions, she was condemned. She was condemned because she had written him love letters that were presented in court.

It was all very well a poet saying a person should read novels, a person should write poetry. Words could be dangerous. Her words were never dangerous. She loved to create little verses for her flower greetings cards. She knew how to touch hearts.

'This water's gone cold,' her father said, taking his feet from the bowl.

She dried his feet with the thin towel. If I were Mary Magdalene I would dry his feet with my hair. The thought made her smile. Perhaps everything would have been different if she had married the poet, the love of her life. She sometimes thought of him as The Poet. It was less painful than saying his name.

'Which corn do you want me to see to?'

'Bottom of my right foot, and the left little toe.'

She sat on the stool in front of him, safety razor in her hand. 'Let me have your foot then.'

She scraped. He winced when she scraped the big corn a little too hard. She did not tell him that she drew blood.

'Go careful!'

Something had always been there at the back of her mind. It never took shape. She never let it. Now that Edward had come back, she knew that somehow she had been duped, first by her father, preventing her marriage, and then by him and Tobias together, because they were two of a kind.

And when she thought of herself, she thought of her mother whose image she was. That was what older people told her. She saw it herself, from photographs, and from her own mirror.

An intriguing thought came to her. I replaced Mammy. I took on her work when I was still a child. Did Dad treat Mammy as badly as he has treated me?

Of course when Carine worked and worked, he always said, 'Remember this studio will be yours one day. It has your name on it.'

Another thought came, which turned itself inside out. Toby and Dad had said that Edward died.

That was a lie. Dad said Mammy went away. Was that a lie?

'Do you remember, Dad, what you used to say to me?'

'I've said all manner of things.'

'You used to say, "Three things happened in 1901. The old queen died, the new king was crowned and your mammy left us." Why did you say such a strange thing?'

He winced. 'Be careful with that razor!'

'I'm nearly done.'

'You were always asking questions.'

'Why those facts about 1901?'

'If you have facts, you stop asking questions.'

'You wanted me to stop asking questions?'

'You never stopped. "When is she coming back? When is she coming back?"'

Carine felt that sudden pang that was always there, that pang of not knowing.

'Is that why you added something else, another fact?'

'What fact?'

'You said that the treadmill was abolished, in 1901. It wasn't. I saw it in Old Moore's Almanac. It was 1902.'

'What kind of conversation is this?'

'Did you think you and Mammy were on a treadmill?'

'That's a ridiculous thing to say.'

But suddenly, her mammy was in the room, this room. Carine could feel her presence, bending over to kiss her goodnight. Perhaps she had been the one on the treadmill.

'Where did Mammy go?'

'She ran off.'

'She would have come back for me.'

'She was too busy having a good time. Now let me back in bed.'

She pulled back the bedcovers, and helped him from the chair to his bed.

'My foot's sore.'

'It's bound to be. I'll fetch you something to soothe it.'

She picked up the basin and then put it down again. 'Edward is back.'

'Edward who?'

'My Edward. Edward Chester. You stopped me marrying him.'

'No I didn't.'

'Oh, so locking me in the cellar on the day of my wedding was something every father would do?'

All those years ago, she had eventually made herself swallow his story about accidentally locking her in. He had repeated it so many times, somehow making her take the blame.

'You shouldn't have gone down the cellar that day. I didn't know you were there.'

'Did you go straight to the register office to tell Edward that I had changed my mind? And then you came back and told me that he had joined his regiment.'

'We've been over this. I went for a bottle of whisky. When I came back you were gone. I thought you would go down to the register office with Betty.'

'You'd had a drink.'

'That wasn't a crime. It's not every day a man gives his daughter away.' He took a sip of water. 'Your poet was relieved. It gave him something to be tragic about, and he was joining his regiment the next day. You married a better man, a man I could get on with and who'll stay with you, and stay here and no nonsense about poetry.'

She built up the fire. He approved of that. He liked to be warm. Soon he would begin to sweat. The fire would be too hot. Hot as hell.

'Then you said that Edward was dead.'

'Toby came with that tale. He was in a position to know.'

'Will you ever tell me the truth?'

'About what?'

'About Mammy, and about why you and Toby lied about Edward.'

'You have the right husband for the business and for you. Now will you see to my sore foot?'

The water in the basin had grown cold. She took it and the towel downstairs.

It was a simple matter to mix a little something to soothe the cut on the sole of his foot and on his toe. She squeezed the ointment. She stirred in a little of this and that.

She spoke to the photograph of the woman and the little girl on the bench on Woodhouse Moor. 'Are you watching, Mammy? This is what you'd call disgusting.' She stirred the mixture. 'I'm doing this for both of us. Once I thought it was my fault you didn't come back. But I see him now, mopping the stain. It has never gone away. I remember a nightmare when I heard you scream, or perhaps the scream was mine.'

Back upstairs, she applied the potion so very gently.

'That's soothing,' he said with a sigh.

She bandaged his feet. Goodness me, she thought, Mary Magdalene must have been a saint.

The next morning, Carine was up early. She washed her father's feet and sponged him down. The fire had gone out, but even so he had a temperature. 'I'm burning up.'

'Sweating is a good thing for someone with gout.'

'How is he today, Mrs Murchison?' Tilly, the daily help, had a jolly and efficient manner.

'He's sleeping.'

Tilly cleared the bedroom fire grate and took up a shovelful of burning coals.

When the nurse came, Carine went upstairs with her.

'Father had a bad night. He is rather hot, and sweating.'

The nurse took the patient's temperature. 'I'll sponge him down.'

The patient stirred and opened his eyes. 'It's you, nurse. I thought . . . '

'Yes it's I, Mr Whitaker. You're a little on the warm side today, but we'll get that temperature down.'

The patient closed his eyes.

'Will you look at his corns, nurse?' Carine whispered. 'He has had a go at them himself, again.'

The nurse looked and tutted. 'Try not to let him do this. Hide the razor.'

'He finds it.'

'At least he's clean. I'll bandage his feet, just to be on the safe side.'

It was Tobias who went for the doctor. He went in person because he was not far off, and this was too important for a telephone conversation.

The doctor came straight back with him.

He examined the sweating, delirious patient and gave instructions to sit by him, let him drink water, make him comfortable, wipe his brow.

To Carine's plaintive whisper that surely it was a good thing for a gouty man to sweat, the doctor explained gently that this was different. He had noted a slight shaving cut on Mr Whitaker's cheek. When he removed the bandages, he saw a cut where the patient or his nurse had trimmed a troublesome corn. The doctor explained that an infection had entered Mr Whitaker's bloodstream through one of these cuts. It was only a matter of time.

Tobias wanted to talk, he wanted to know everything

and he wanted to tell everything. He wanted the doctor to know how the old gentleman was well cared for. Both he and his wife doted on her father. Percy wanted for nothing. They were up and down all day. All he had to do was tap his walking stick on the floor and there one of them was, like the genie from the lamp.

The doctor understood. He knew that Mr Whitaker would get himself out of bed, shuffle about in his bare feet, pick his nose and rub his cheek, take out his dentures and drop them down anywhere that suited him. There were plenty of opportunities for infection, no matter how careful the nursing.

Carine listened as the doctor whispered to Tobias as they stood on the landing. 'Women die this way, after childbirth. Nasty little bacteria find their way in. Infection spreads like . . . ' He struggled to find a simile that would not sound too harsh. Being a gardener, he found one. 'The infection spreads like bindweed. I can give Mr Whitaker something that will muffle his senses and ease his way, but there is nothing to be done to save him.'

In the early hours of the next morning, Tobias once more went for the doctor. The doctor was present at the death.

Carine sat by her father's bed while Toby and the doctor went downstairs, to have a drink, and for the doctor to write the death certificate.

She spoke to her father. 'You once asked me if I remembered anything about the time Mammy went away. I said no. I said no because I daren't say yes. I didn't know how to say yes. I couldn't have put something into words. And you expected me to say no. You willed me to say that. But there was something, and I've dreamed it since and will dream it again. So I'm glad you're gone. You can do me no more harm.'

But the damage was done, and harm will spread like bindweed.

After that day, certain people noticed a change in Carine. Some put it down to bereavement, or the shock of a returned fiancé.

Five

A Quiet Sunday

By Sunday morning, I had heard from my contact in the East Lancashire Regiment about Lieutenant Edward Chester. As a result of wounds, he underwent operations and spells of rehabilitation on and off for over four years. If his friends were told of his death in action, then their informant was wrong.

I decided to call on Carine before going on to my parents in Wakefield, for Sunday dinner.

It was a quiet morning. I stopped the car outside the studio. Knowing how much time Carine spends in there, I looked through the window. There was no one there.

I went round to the back and through the yard.

She answered my knock almost straight away. The sight of her, drained of colour, her lips white, dark shadows under her eyes, gave me goose bumps. For the first time, she looked her age, and more.

'Carine, what's wrong?'

'Oh, come in, Kate.'

There was a strange atmosphere in the kitchen, as if no one lived here, a sense of absence. She looked as if she hadn't slept. 'What's the matter?'

She pointed to a piece of white card on the table, and a paint box and brushes. On the bottom right corner of the card, she had painted three lilies. In the centre of the card, she had pencilled faint lines and the words CLOSED DUE TO BEREAVEMENT, which she had begun to fill in with black. She had blacked in the first three words.

'Carine, what's happened? Who has died?'

'Dad died.' She nodded, as if agreeing with herself, and then she grimaced. 'It was time for him to go.'

'Oh I'm sorry. When did he die?'

'In the early hours. Come up and see him.'

Naturally, I was obliged to pay my respects. I followed Carine up the stairs.

She showed me into the small bedroom. The curtains were closed. They moved slightly, in the draught from the open window. The fireplace had been cleaned, and a vase of tulips set in the grate. Mr Whitaker lay on his bed, very nicely set out, wearing a white nightshirt. A starched linen sheet trapped him to the bed, though his arms had been placed outside the sheet. A square of linen with knotted corners covered his head, the sort a man might wear on holiday to keep the sun off his bald patch. A white bandage had been tied around his head and under his chin.

We stood for a few moments in silence. I did not know him well and so would not kiss his forehead, as people sometimes did. I managed to say that he looked peaceful. In truth, he simply looked grey.

When we left the room, I asked, 'Did someone come?' Meaning, to lay him out.

'The nurse came. She brought the tulips from her husband's allotment. While she laid him out, I ran up his shroud from a sheet, on mother's sewing machine.'

'You must be exhausted.'

'Not really.'

We went downstairs. 'Where is Tobias?'

'At the pub.'

'Shall I stay with you?'

'You have somewhere to go, I can tell.'

'Sunday dinner with my parents. I can put them off, or you can come if you want to get out. I suppose Tobias will be back soon.'

'I suppose so. But you didn't come because someone had told you about Dad?'

'I came because of news about Edward Chester, from my contact in the East Lancashire Regiment.'

'What did he say?'

We sat down at the table. She picked up her paint brush, dipped the tip in an egg cup of water, dabbed it on the black paint and began to fill in the word Bereavement.

I told her what I had learned, and added, 'Perhaps Tobias made a mistake, and he thought that Edward had been killed.'

'No.'

'It does seem unlikely.'

'Tobias saw a place where he might get his feet under the table. I was the fool, not to enquire myself, not to try and find out more.'

'Do you think that Edward was unwilling to come back to you because of the seriousness of his injuries?'

'I can't think about that now.' She worked quickly, completing the word, Bereavement. 'Are you in a desperate rush?'

'No.'

'I want you to give me a lift. Will you wait while I wash my face and change my dress?'

'Yes of course. Where will you go?'

She reached for a scrap of paper and wrote a note. 'Gone out with Kate – put sign on door for tomorrow.'

'I'm not telling him but I need fresh air, peace and quiet. I'll catch a train to Ben Rhydding and walk on Ilkley Moor.'

With some misgivings, I dropped Carine at the railway station. She insisted that she would be all right.

Mother waved to me from the window seat. She had a book in her hand. By the time I opened the door she – usually the most languorous of souls who would not have moved from the spot or put down her novel – was by the front door.

She was wearing a Liberty print silk dress, smudges of spring colours, with the bodice in a contrasting design to the skirt and sleeves. 'Your Aunt Berta sent it,' she said when I admired her dress. 'Turns me into the peacock I used to be.'

The creamy turban may have been less a flag of fashion than a sign that her hair would not do as she intended. She was without stockings, wore sandals, and made me feel suddenly frumpy in the olive linen dress and jacket that she would dismiss as wartime khaki uniform.

Normally, I would have told her that a friend's father had just died, but she seemed in such an odd mood that I thought it better to say nothing about that.

She waved me in. 'Look around you.'

'At what?'

'This house. Look at everything. Start in the drawing room.'

No one else in the street calls this room a drawing room. For the old-fashioned, it is a parlour, for the moderns it is the front room.

'Look at it as if you have never seen it before . . . '

'Mother, how can I when I've seen it ten thousand times?'

' . . . and then the rest of the house.'

I looked about. Surely I would have noticed if she had changed something.

Dutifully, I did a visual inventory. The drawing room has English oak floorboards, highly polished enough for a person to break a leg if they step the wrong way onto one of the Indian rugs. The wallpaper is William Morris Acanthus. Cream linen throws cover the sofa and chairs. On one side of the fireplace is a rosewood writing desk, and on the other side a glass-fronted bookcase. Gracing the mantelshelf are silver-framed photographs of my parents' wedding and of me with my twin brothers when I was about nine years old and they were two. On the wall opposite the fireplace hangs an oil painting of Wakefield Cathedral by a local artist. Once there had been a large piano that my mother brought with her when she married. That disappeared before I began lessons. A smaller piano appeared in the dining room.

I turned to her. She had grown up with the expectation of marrying into the aristocracy and living in a stately home. Yet she followed her heart and married a policeman.

'This is far more comfortable and less draughty than

some of the piles you might have ended up rattling about in. And no one else would have moved into a police house and made it so very beautiful.'

She gave a satisfied snort, a substitute for tears. 'And with my own money.'

'I didn't know.'

'Neither did your father. He has no idea of quality or costs.' She patted my arm. 'You have understood.'

We walked through the hall into the kitchen and out into the back garden that sloped towards the apple tree. There was the swing, rusting at the hinges.

Mother gave it a push. 'So many arguments about that swing – whose turn it was to be pushed, and who pushed too hard.'

There was the spot where our failed police bloodhound was buried. We had named him Constable as his consolation for being dismissed from the force. Mother had said calling him Constable was a mistake. She claimed that being a bloodhound of little brain, he would forget his connection with law and order and imagine his destiny was to paint pictures. We saw how Constable's paws twitched when he slept, a sign that he dreamed of holding a brush. We would say, 'Look, he is painting in his sleep.' We discussed his specialism: gentle landscapes.

My young twin brothers, Simon and Matthew, loved drawing with crayons which they wore down to the stubs. They would sit with Constable, asking the dog's opinion of their pictures, invariably reported as favourable.

We walked back up the garden and sat on the bench under the window. I waited. She would come to it, whatever it was.

A blackbird lighted on the apple tree. Next door's cat, sitting on the wall, watched the bird. That cat so much wanted the gift of flight.

Mother took a deep breath. 'I curse that war. You and Gerald should have been here today with children. You would have had three. I dreamed of them, a girl and two boys.'

I thought perhaps she was dreaming of us, me and the twins. 'How old were they in your dream, these children?'

'Young, all young.' She took my hand. 'Are you going to find someone else?'

'It doesn't look like it. Not to marry anyway.'

'Your friend from Scotland Yard called.'

'Marcus?'

'It was a flying visit to Wakefield on some case. He brought flowers.'

'That was thoughtful of him.'

'I believe he hoped you might be here.'

'He knows where I am.'

'There has to be some iota of encouragement.'

'It wouldn't work.'

'Berta always says how plucky you are, making your own way. She's right.'

This was not a conversation I wanted to have. I attempted a diversion. 'You miss the twins. Perhaps one of them will marry.'

'They'd be here if not for that war.'

'You don't know that.'

'Yes I do. They met those Canadian soldiers, over to fight for the mother country but full of the joys and promise of a new world. Don't tell me Canada would have popped into my sons' heads if not for those charming young men.'

'I suppose you're right.'

'Of course I am. And I am right about what must come next.'

'And what is that?'

'Your father must retire.' She said this with such certainty that it brought us to a halt. Next door's cat walked along the wall, sat and stared at us for a moment and then leaped down and took up a position by the apple tree.

I could not imagine my father willingly retiring and said so.

'Well it's time he did, willing or not.'

Mother does not cook. She tried once but suffered a burn, so that was that. The accident left a small red scar just under her wrist, a scar now visible only to herself.

Mother's maid, Pamela, comes in for an hour on Saturday to leave everything ready, including the Yorkshire pudding mix. When Mother was a girl, staff did all the cooking at the kitchen range. Pamela refuses point blank to come in on Sundays, and also insisted on having a gas stove. Like my own housekeeper, Mrs Sugden, Pamela has very definite opinions about almost everything.

Some Sundays, I am Chief Cook. This Sunday, Mother persuaded Dad that he was carrying out some highly technical and semi-industrial activity when lighting the gas, taking out the joint of meat at the right moment, and putting the Yorkshire pudding in the oven. He also made gravy. Mother long ago explained to him that dealing with hot dripping is a dangerous task, suited to his rank as police superintendent.

I have vast admiration for my mother. She will meet her maker with the credential of never having boiled an egg.

We do not need to be sworn to secrecy regarding Dad's domestic tasks. He would be mortified beyond measure if such shameful activities became known outside the family circle.

After dinner, I washed the dishes and pots and Dad dried. This was our time for a chat. He couldn't help watching when I picked up the gravy boat that belonged to his mother and grandmother, back into infinity. It is covered in a thousand tiny surface cracks that obscure the willow pattern.

He took it from me, dried it carefully and placed it on the top shelf of the cupboard.

'Mother wants you to retire.'

I lowered the clothes airer from the ceiling and spread the damp tea cloth across. 'I'm staying here tonight. I'm not going home until you've talked to Mother.'

'Your mother has friends whose husbands have retired. I can't. We are missing a generation who would have come into the force to be senior police officers. I will probably die in harness, like some faithful old carthorse. I won't see my sons unless they come home. Some of us have to stay where we are and keep the wheels turning.'

After dinner, Dad went upstairs for his nap. Mother went up with him, to tuck him in, and left me to read *Wuthering Heights* for rather a long time.

When she came down, she looked pleased with herself. 'He has accepted that sixty-six is old enough to hand over his truncheon, metaphorically speaking.' She sat opposite me, placing a cushion behind her neck. 'He has agreed that we must do things together while we still can, and that will include a voyage to Canada, to see the boys.'

'He is not going to retire, Mother. He is saying that for a quiet life.'

She made a dismissive gesture. 'You must come with us to Canada. Leave Sykes and the admirable Mrs Sugden to hold the fort.' She did not give me time to reply. 'Not that the voyage is imminent.'

'What then?'

'We are to have a weekend away, near Haworth. He'll like the moors. We may move to the country when he retires. It would be somewhere I could invite my London friends.'

I picked up my old copy of *Wuthering Heights* that she had left on the sofa arm. 'Is that why this is here?'

'Haworth and the moors will be the coming place. Have you heard of the industrialist James Roberts? He was awarded a baronetcy.'

'The name rings a bell. But James Roberts is that kind of name. It sounds as if it belongs to someone solid and reliable.'

'He is a rags-to-riches Yorkshireman who owns Salt's mill. He has bought Haworth Parsonage for the nation.'

'How very generous.'

'In August, Lady Roberts will perform the opening ceremony. She will give the building into the keeping of the Brontë Society, for use as a museum.'

'That's excellent news. It will be much better than the little old museum above the bank.'

'You must come.'

'I will. I'd love to be there!'

'You should have joined the Brontë Society. Those of us who are already members in good standing have been allocated a special viewing spot.'

'I suppose one can just turn up on the day.'

'I hope you will. There are people I should like you to meet, and a house I want you to see.'

'Is this connected with Dad's "retirement"?'

We heard Dad's footsteps on the stairs. She put a finger to her lips. 'The parsonage will become a home for a valuable collection of Brontë memorabilia bequeathed by Mr Henry Houston Bonnell, a Philadelphia gentleman. He stipulated that the relics should be kept in a fireproof room.'

Dad came in.

'Are you bending Kate's ear about Haworth?'

Mother continued. 'I am just telling Kate about all the work that is going on. It's costing a fortune to lay down . . . What are those floors called, darling?'

'Ferro-concrete.'

'That's the word, and all camouflaged. There are to be fireproof steel doors made to look like the originals. Such a costly business but it would not do for the parsonage to resemble a bank vault.'

As she spoke, I thought about our photographic society's plans for a weekend away. We could do worse than go to Haworth. 'I think that would be a perfect place to go.'

'At a constabulary dinner dance, we sat with your father's old colleague Peter Porter and his wife. Mrs Porter inherited Laverall Hall at Stanbury, just a little way from Haworth. It is a seventeenth-century gentry house that she does not appreciate. She would like to move nearer to her daughter who is in some seaside resort.' Mother shuddered at the thought of moving to the coast. 'She has invited us to stay for that weekend at the beginning of August. The parsonage opening is on the first Saturday of August.'

Dad put in his two-pennyworth. 'Ginny, you won't like Stanbury. There'll be a butcher, a baker and a candlestick maker.'

'Then I shall admire the landscape, the moorland.'

'Just because you like the Brontë sisters' books, it doesn't mean you'll like the area where they once lived.'

'Credit me with a little intelligence, darling.' Mother shook her head at his persistence in being dense. 'I was thrilled by *King Solomon's Mines* as a gel but had no desire to visit Kukuanaland.'

Dad's driver called for him on Monday morning. Mother and I stood by the window and watched the car move away.

She turned to me. 'I'm glad you stayed the night, Kate.'

'So am I.'

'I hope we can move to the country. It would do him the world of good.'

Pamela approached the front gate and stopped to talk to a neighbour.

'Before Pamela comes in, let me just tell you something.' She smiled. 'Do you remember when you all used to walk Constable?'

'Yes.'

'I must remember to tell whoever comes to live here after us, not to dig where he is buried. Oh, and just so that you know, I put down our names for another dog. The next constabulary bloodhound that fails to come up to scratch will be ours.'

'Constable the second?'

She shook her head. 'Oh no. The next dog should have a position of rank.'

'Who will walk this dog?'

'I will, and when your father retires, we will walk the dear creature together. He will like being by the moors.'

'The dog?'

'Your father. Our weekend with the Porters will sway him. Mrs Porter is amiable, and it will be a change of routine. A dry run for when we visit the twins in Canada.' She sat back in her chair and played a trump card that must have taken a great deal of thought. 'The moorland is rugged. Canada is rugged.'

Six

A Brush with Death

The Headingley Photographic Society Outings (1928) Sub-Committee had arranged to meet on Tuesday, in the Kardomah Café on Briggate. We would now, without Carine, be a committee of two.

The café was busy and so I ordered two sandwiches and a pot of tea, knowing that Derek would be on his lunch break, and perhaps short of time.

He came in, looking pale and shaken. There was a scratch on his cheek and his coat was dusty.

'Whatever happened?' I thought he must have tripped and fallen.

'Someone tried to kill me.' He spoke rather loudly. Heads turned.

'What?'

'In a car, a lunatic driving down Albion Street. I swear he went straight for me, knocked me flying and drove on.'

'You must go to the dispensary.'

He shook his head. 'Luckily I'm not badly hurt, except

my ankle. No bones broken. Chap on the pavement saw what was about to happen, threw his arms around me and pulled me back. If he hadn't I might have been a goner.'

The waitress, who had just brought our order, overheard. She put our sandwiches, teapot and milk jug on the table. 'You poor lad! You need extra sugar in your tea.'

'That's what my gran would say.' Derek picked up the tongs and dropped four cubes in his cup. 'The maniac must have braked at the last minute before skidding off. He sent me and my rescuer into the gutter.'

The waitress tutted. 'They want locking up, these motorists. They've no notion of letting people go about their lawful business.' She glanced about and then silently mouthed, 'I'm going to bring you an iced bun, on the house.'

Derek perked up. 'Thank you.'

I poured tea. 'Did you see the driver, or note any details?'

'No. It all happened too quickly, but I'll tell you whose car it put me in mind of, same shape, same colour.'

'Whose?'

'Tobias Murchison's, and it's just the kind of driving you'd expect of him. I caught a glimpse of the driver's hat, like that homburg Murchison wears. But it couldn't have been because he'll be in the studio – what with Carine coming here.'

'Ah of course, you haven't heard. Carine can't come. Sadly, her father died on Sunday morning.'

'Oh? Was that sudden? I know he was bedridden.'

'It was rather sudden.'

'Should I go see her? Is there anything I can do?'

'Not for now, Derek.'

'The death isn't in today's paper. I could go in person and see what insertion they would like.'

'Tobias is dealing with everything.' It suddenly occurred to me that Tobias may have come into town to register the death and notify the bank and the solicitor. If he was distracted, he might well not have noticed Derek. On the other hand, he may have driven slowly down Albion Street, waiting for Derek to leave the premises at noon, and made a beeline for him. Bereavement might be a good defence against manslaughter of his wife's young lover. 'He practically threw himself under my wheels, your honour.'

I brought us round to the subject of our outing. 'We must decide, between the two of us, Derek. I've looked at the suggestions and my preference is for Haworth over that first weekend of August. On the Saturday, the deeds of the Haworth parsonage will be given to the Brontë Society by Sir James Roberts, for the benefit of the nation.'

'That will be newsworthy. I could be official photographer for the paper. I'm for Haworth then.'

'Yes.'

Derek seemed to have forgotten his brush with death. He leaned forward, asking anxiously, 'Do you think that will suit Carine and that she'll be able to come?'

'We shall have to see, nearer the time. I'll do my best to persuade her.'

It would suit me to be in Haworth on that day, especially since my parents were going to be there. Mother particularly wanted me to see the house they would stay at. She felt sure that I would be welcomed at the Porters', but I could hardly ask to bring along a gaggle of amateur photographers to occupy their attic.

Having demolished his sandwich and made a start on the iced bun, Derek seemed a little recovered.

'Derek, although I'm in favour of Haworth, we must look at other suggestions members have put in the box, and consider them.' I took the scraps of paper from the used envelope and placed them on the table.

Derek set them in neat lines. I had not looked at them until now. The fact that there were only six did not indicate wild enthusiasm for an outing.

'I thought we would have to put it to the vote at a meeting.'

'It's the kind of discussion that could go on for hours. I prefer to present a *fait accompli*.'

I was looking at one particular suggestion, block printed. 'Ponden, Stanbury.'

'Where's Stanbury?' Derek asked.

'It's two miles from Haworth. My parents will be staying there with friends. Oddly enough, I was going to suggest that we try and book accommodation at Ponden Hall in Stanbury.'

Although I could not be sure, I thought the writing was Carine's. I tried to remember whether I had mentioned my idea to her, but no. It had only come into my head after seeing Mother on Sunday. Today was Tuesday. I hadn't seen or spoken to Carine since Sunday morning, when I dropped her off at the railway station.

'And what's Ponden?' Derek asked. 'Is it an hotel or an area?'

'There's a Ponden Mill and a Ponden Hall, which is a working farm that does afternoon teas.'

'Have you stayed there?'

'Not stayed. Mother and Dad took me and the twins there, years ago. We had tea in the garden. Ponden Hall was said to be Emily Brontë's inspiration for Thrushcross Grange in *Wuthering Heights*. It's walking distance from Haworth.'

We looked at each of the other suggestions. Some were for the seaside – Scarborough, Whitby and Filey. 'We need to think about the travelling and accommodation. Over an August weekend, the resorts are going to be booked up. It might be difficult to find accommodation for a group.'

Derek pushed aside suggestions of York and Ilkley. 'We could go there and back in a day on the train.' He had eaten his iced bun and gulped down his tea. 'Do you mind hanging on, Kate? I'll dash up to the General Post Office telephone, and see if we're right, and if she agrees that we should choose Stanbury. I'll ask how she is, and if there's anything I can do.'

'Sit down, Derek. You don't telephone someone about an outing two days after their father has died. We could be wrong about the handwriting. I can't think how she would have come up with this. She's not a great reader.'

'Everybody knows about the Brontës. Perhaps Carine heard about the parsonage handover, as you did.'

'I think we've settled where we're going.'

Derek dabbed up the remains of the icing from his bun. 'Will it look odd that three supposedly impartial members all want to go to the same place?'

'You mean the three impartial committee members who are doing the work?' I put the suggestions back in the envelope, writing a slip of my own: Ponden Hall, Stanbury. This made two votes for Stanbury.

'I'm sure you'll find a way of making everyone see the sense of such a good choice.'

'You can rely on that, Derek.'

'That's decided then!' He wiped a speck of icing from his lip. 'My boss said I can use the office spirit duplicator to do a letter to our members. I'll add a tear-off slip to return if they want to go. I'll stay late and do it, and then I can deliver them tomorrow.'

'Wait until I've contacted Ponden Hall to see if they do bed, breakfast and an evening meal. Oh, and ask members for a five shilling deposit and give them a week to reply.'

'Five shillings!'

'What's wrong with five shillings?'

'I thought the society would pay.'

'Not the whole amount. We would have fifty applicants and an empty bank account. Save a shilling a week between now and August, and give what you can for the deposit.'

At that stage, my only misgiving was uncertainty about numbers and whether we might all be accommodated.

Derek's enthusiasm was aroused, his cuts and bruises from the run-in with a car forgotten. He beamed. 'I feel like packing my bags already. We have Sir Arthur Conan Doyle to thank for this. If it had not been for his early pieces in the *Photographic Journal*, we would not be going on a weekend outing.'

'Do you take the photographic magazines?'

'We have them at work, but it was Carine who showed me that piece.'

'Well it is such a good idea. And you know, Derek, it's not too soon to let members know about the plan to visit Haworth that August weekend. We can give details of where we'll be staying nearer the time, after I've contacted Ponden Hall.'

So it was that over sandwiches and an iced bun, we helped fate take its cruel twist. And there would be no Arthur Conan Doyle in Haworth to solve the dastardly crime.

The newspaper building where Derek works is on Albion Street. I walked back with him in that direction, intending to call at my library. Afterwards I would go to the newspaper offices and collect the mimeographed notices about the trip. We agreed that Derek would deliver half the notices to our society members. I would take the other half to Harriet, who had volunteered to do some legwork in return for being enrolled in the society. On hearing that it was Derek's idea, she had decided that society members were not such a bunch of old fuddy-duddies after all.

As we walked along Briggate, Derek had just one subject of conversation.

'I expect Carine will be feeling wretched.'

'Yes.'

'And wearing black.'

'Yes.'

'Do you think she is as beautiful as any star from the pictures? I offered to take a photograph of her to put in the studio window. She would be able to colour it.'

'Carine would not put her own photograph in the window.'

'I don't see why not. She does everything, you know. My gran said that she ran that place all on her own once.'

'When was that?'

'From a very young age.'

'I didn't know her then.'

'When her father was incapacitated.' He looked about and lowered his voice. 'Permanently drunk.'

'Poor Carine.'

'She is so gracious and lovely and, well, this may be presumptuous of me . . .'

'Oh go on, be presumptuous, Derek.'

'She still does all the work. Tobias takes the glory.'

'Well, we don't know that, do we?' From what I gathered, there was very little glory to be had in the Murchison studio.

'Don't you think Carine could be the subject of a painting?'

'I'm sure she could. Do you paint?'

'I enjoyed art at school, but I'm just a dauber. She would deserve one of the old masters.'

I changed the subject before he said something he might regret and made a complete idiot of himself. For a while we talked about his work.

As we chatted, I realised what an ambitious young man he is, just as Carine had said. Although he works as a clerical assistant in the newspaper library, or perhaps because he works in the newspaper library, he teems with ideas.

'Every week, I put a photograph on the editor's desk, and every other week, I write some little article about a topic of interest.'

'And has the editor used your material?'

'Oh yes, twice. And when I saw him in the corridor last week, he stopped me and gave me some advice.'

'Well done to have been noticed, Derek. What was the advice?'

'We are living in most uncertain times. People are hard up, uneasy, worried about the future and their children's future. In such times, reassurance is called for. People must be made to feel that there are possibilities and other ways of being. When that happens, they look back. They hope for better days – as in the days of yore.'

'Goodness, all that in a corridor.'

'When he spoke, a white light switched itself on in my brain.'

'Yes, I can see that might just happen. Did he say anything about your articles or photographs?'

'What he said was enough, more than enough. He threw a rubber tyre to a man floundering in a lake of possibilities.'

'And where might this lifeline lead you?'

'You'll see.' He smiled. 'Just wait and see what I will produce during our big adventure.'

'Our trip away?'

'Yes. I may need your help, Mrs Shackleton, if that is agreeable.'

'Of course, Derek.' He once more seemed so terribly young, and so hopeful, that I felt a pain in my heart. I was also rather wary of having his affections transferred to me when Carine rebuffed him, or when Tobias Murchison bopped him on the nose, or drove over him and broke his legs. 'What is it you may need my help with?'

'I'm not sure, only I don't believe people in the society fully accept me.'

'They would not have voted for your proposal for the outing if you were unpopular.'

'Do you think not?'

'I'm sure not.'

'Only I feel a little bit of a fraud.'

'In what way?'

'I've never won a single prize for a photograph, and I don't live in Headingley. My gran's house is in Little London.'

'That's near enough, and it doesn't matter in the least. No one else in the society has had articles in the paper.'

'Tobias Murchison doesn't like me.'

'Derek, here's a tip. Do not worry about whether people like you or not, just be yourself and do your best. That is all any of us can do.'

'That is good advice. Thank you.'

'Here's another piece of advice.'

'Oh?'

'Look both ways when you cross the road. I don't want you knocked down before you produce our circular to members.'

'You've just given me an idea!'

'What's that?'

'Ah, there are some ideas a fellow keeps to himself.'

We parted. He walked on, a young man of mystery in a cut-down suit, a medieval page devoted to his beautiful mistress, a spring in his step with the power to take him to the moon.

What on earth did he plan to do over our few short days away? More importantly, I wondered what he expected of Carine, and she of him.

And then I wondered, had I given good advice to Derek in telling him to be himself. It might have been better to tell him to stop drooling over Carine and give a wide berth to Tobias Murchison.

Afterwards, I drove up to see Carine again.

Her sign was on the door: CLOSED DUE TO BEREAVEMENT, with her watercolour of lilies on the bottom right corner.

Dominating the window was a photograph of her parents' wedding. The couple in the photograph looked so like Carine and Tobias that it gave me the shivers.

Wednesday, 11 April 1928

The Mole of the World

The newspaper that shines a bright light in dark corners

Dispatch from Your Northern Mole

Brush with Death

A dapper young man about town, not yet in his twentieth year, was the intended victim of a vicious driver in the centre of one of our great cities.

Your humble correspondent does not spare his blushes in admitting to being an unsung hero. While the young man's preoccupation with life and love did not allow him to see the motor car hurtling towards its intended victim, this correspondent did. He is rewarded by the knowledge that he saved a young man's life. The would-be lethal weapon on this particular spring day was a maroon Armstrong Siddeley motor.

Driver – you were seen. Your dark glasses and pulled down homburg did not fool this observer.

The car hurtled down a main thoroughfare, scattering horrified pedestrians. Our young fellow, full of the joys of spring and with a singing heart, stepped onto the road oblivious of the threat to life and limb. Had not this reporter grasped him and pulled him to safety, there would have been blood, much blood and the crushed bones of a fine young Englishman.

There is a dark heart at the centre of this story. That

beating organ belongs to the driver of the killer car. The whisper among those who know is that the bloated sot behind the wheel suspects his fair wife of harbouring tender feelings towards the handsome young fellow whose undoubted attraction for the opposite sex almost cost him his life.

$\mathcal{S}$even

$\mathcal{A}$ Fine Funeral

The funeral service for Carine's father, Percival Whitaker, was held at St Michael's Church. He was buried at Lawnswood Cemetery. Naturally, my sympathy was for Carine, and for Tobias, who had been close to his father-in-law. Yet I also felt sorry for the nurse who had attended Mr Whitaker. She looked about her with an air of defiance, as if half expecting to be accused of neglect, or worse. She dabbed her eyes with a lace hanky, and seemed more upset than Carine.

Afterwards there was a funeral tea in the Skyrack. The nurse did not attend.

The shopkeepers of Headingley turned out. Carine's many friends came to offer their condolences and support. Tobias's drinking cronies from the Oak greatly enjoyed the proceedings. Some of those who were in employment managed to take a day off, knowing there would be plenty to drink. A couple of well-dressed men, whispered to be from the Leeds Club, put in an appearance.

There was hardly a moment when Carine was alone.

Finally, she managed to extricate herself from the mourners and the ham sandwiches. She drew me into the yard, seeking a breath of air.

Carine's friend, Rita, followed. Rita is an engaging young woman who holds a steady job at the local pharmacy, and is known to be well travelled. She frequently dresses in silks, brought back from India. On her travels, she picked up the habit of smoking a rather exotic leaf with a sweet scent, which she now grew in the pharmacist's greenhouse.

When the three of us were out of earshot of the other mourners, Carine confided, 'Father made Toby the executor of his will. Everything goes to Toby, on the grounds that he will take care of me.'

Rita exploded. 'That's outrageous, Carine. It's your studio. It was your mother's, your grandmother's, that can't be right.'

Carine smiled at us. 'I'm sure Daddy knew what he was doing. He and Tobias were very close, and very alike. I have no head for business. Tobias will take care of everything.'

She seemed so remarkably calm and detached, almost as if none of this had anything to do with her. I wondered had she taken some sedative.

Rita persisted. 'Something must be done. You need a legal opinion. You must speak to Andrew.' She turned to me. 'My friend is a solicitor.'

I wished Rita would be quiet, at least for now. Carine seemed determined to remain serene. I felt a chill at what seemed her extreme quiescence. 'Carine, you, me and Rita will talk about this again, when you are over the shock.' This was a day to be survived.

It would be terrible for her if life changed for the worse. Without the knocking of the walking stick on the bedroom floor, the plaster on the downstairs ceiling would remain secure. But Tobias would have his hands on the purse strings.

Carine smiled. 'Ours was almost an arranged marriage, you might say, arranged by Daddy. But we are a good pair. Toby will take care of me.' She gave the slight grimace that today passed as her smile. 'And I will take care of him.'

Rita embraced her friend. 'You are a saint.'

I spotted Tobias, making his way unsteadily into the yard, heading for the lavatory. He had been drinking heavily.

Smiling, he executed a low, mocking bow to the three of us. 'When shall we three meet again, in thunder, lightning or in rain?'

Carine lowered her head. Rita stared at him, open-mouthed, but nothing came out.

One of us had to answer. 'When the hurlyburly's done, when the battle's lost and won.'

Carine had begun to tremble. 'The truth is, I'm beginning to be afraid of him. He has everything now. I fear he'll take my life as well.'

Rita caught her breath. 'Oh, Carine, what has he done?'

'Nothing. It sounds ridiculous.'

'Has he threatened you, been violent?' I asked. She shook her head. 'Then what makes you afraid?'

'I was at the top of the cellar steps. He came behind me. I knew he was going to push me down. I couldn't move, I couldn't breathe, my heart was racing.'

'Did he touch you?'

'I knew he wanted to push me down the stairs. I knew what he was thinking, one good shove.'

'Carine, that's terrible.' I was glad that she had told us and tried to think what to say or do.

Rita's reaction was quicker than mine. 'It is a premonition. You must leave him at once. And what you have just told us, you must say again in the presence of a witness, a man of the law.' She turned to where her friend Andrew and the pharmacist, Mr Norton, were talking to each other. 'Andrew, a moment, please. Mr Norton, too.' The two men came across. It was a surprise to me that Andrew Barrington and Rita were friends. He dresses soberly, every inch the neat and reticent family solicitor. Rita's employer, the pharmacist, is in his sixties, with sparse hair and rimless spectacles. He wore a well-brushed black suit that must have attended many funerals.

Rita urged Carine to repeat what she had told us. Carine did so, adding, 'It keeps coming back, that I know he will do it. I dream that I am falling. I hit the cold hard flags and I know that if a dream ends like that it is because you have died. And I hear myself scream. I'm so afraid.'

Mr Norton said, 'Mrs Murchison, you have been under a terrible strain. Do please see your doctor. What you have described sounds like a classic symptom of anxiety.'

Carine had stopped trembling. She glanced at Mr Norton as if he had said the very words she wanted to hear. 'So you believe I'm imagining this?'

'Your anxiety is as real as you feel it to be, but the sort of dread you describe could attach itself to anything, even a worry about crossing the road. That seems to me the most likely explanation.'

'Then perhaps you are right. He never touches me.'

Mr Norton smiled. 'There you are then. You need a rest, Mrs Murchison.'

Andrew Barrington said softly, 'Come and see me at any time, Carine. As a friend.'

I looked about, just in case Carine's long-lost fiancé, Edward Chester, had found his way here. I had seen a slim volume of his poetry in the bookshop and had bought a copy. He was good, very good.

It may be that when the hurlyburly was done, neither Rita, I, nor any other of Carine's friends would see her again. She might run off with her poet. If she did, good luck to her.

But the poet was not at the funeral. Nor did he come to the society's meetings in May, or June. Between them, Harriet and Derek had posted flyers through the letterboxes of every member, about the August outing.

Harriet had been surprised to deliver the one for Edward Chester to the newsagent's shop on Hyde Park Road. The owner had said she would send it on.

The response to the proposed outing was disappointing. The only good point about the low level of interest was that we would be an intimate group, and more easily accommodated at Ponden Hall.

After a decent lapse of time, I persuaded Carine that she ought to come. If she was worried about the studio, I felt sure that my housekeeper would keep an eye on the premises during our weekend away.

I spoke to Mrs Sugden. She took up the idea with enthusiasm. Yes, she would certainly be willing to help out.

When I reported this to Carine, for the first time in ages, she looked happy. The thought of going away cheered her. 'Oh good. Kate, I'm asking people not to tell Tobias we're staying at Ponden Hall. I told him it would be a surprise, but I did so in such a way that he thinks we'll be in the Black Bull for the weekend.'

Eight

The Failed Bloodhound

Mrs Sugden made herself a late breakfast. She loved the idea of being sole occupant of Batswing Cottage for the whole weekend, just her and the cat.

She had seen them off this morning. Mrs Shackleton left at the crack of dawn for Wakefield. She would drive with her parents to Stanbury. Young Harriet set off to catch the train, with that look she had when feeling important and full of herself.

There was also the added prospect of doing something a bit different and earning extra money. That never went amiss. Life had taken a good turn for her since she came to work for Mrs Shackleton. You never knew what might happen next.

She was charged with the responsibility of sitting behind the counter in the photographic studio. She had friends who worked in shops. Like as not, they had to stand all the time. The Murchisons were civilised. There was a chair behind the counter. It gave her a shiver of excitement to think of herself as minding the shop.

She had made notes of everything that Mr Murchison told her. Customers would come to collect the photographs that they had left for developing and printing. If they forgot their ticket, she must check the name and ask when they brought in the film. If any person wanted to book a wedding photograph, or a studio portrait, she should enter details in the diary, and make a note. Passing trade might be customers bringing in a film to be developed. She should take the film, give them a ticket and tell them to come back in a week.

Mr Murchison, a proper gentleman, had also said there would be an extra job, and he would leave a note. It would be sorting out the cellar, a surprise for his wife. He's the new broom, Mrs Sugden thought when Mr Murchison asked for her help. He's the new proprietor who intends to sweep clean.

She let in the cat and fed her. Sookie then went upstairs to sleep on Mrs Shackleton's bed.

At twenty past eight, Mrs Sugden was just about to put on her coat and set off walking to open up the studio, when there was a knock on the door, one of those big thumping knocks that send the heart racing.

She went to answer. On the doorstep was a young police constable with a bloodhound on a leash.

'Mrs Shackleton?'

'Mrs Shackleton's gone for the weekend. I'm her housekeeper, Mrs Sugden. What's the matter?'

'I've brought the dog.'

'So I see.' She looked down at the morose creature. The animal looked back, wagging its tail in a half-hearted fashion, unsure of its welcome. 'Why have you brought a dog?'

'It was on order, the first failed dog was to come to Superintendent Hood. If it was a Leeds dog, it could be brought here and he would fetch it.'

'Superintendent Hood and Mrs Hood are away, and so is their daughter, Mrs Shackleton. You'll have to hold onto it until they come back.'

'When will that be?'

'Mrs Shackleton is off for the weekend, I can't speak for her parents.'

'That's a shame.'

'Give me a telephone number. I'll ask Mrs Shackleton to speak to you about it when she returns.' She opened the door wide so that he could step inside, and went to the hall table for the notepad. 'You're safe. The cat's upstairs.' All the same, she kept an eye out, in case Sookie came down.

The constable pulled a face. 'It's a shame.'

Mrs Sugden felt impatient with people who repeated themselves. 'What's a shame?'

'I'm told if it can't be off our hands within the next hour, I've to have him put down. Apparently, he's too friendly by half and a bad influence on the other dogs.'

'Oh.' Mrs Sugden did not ask in what way such a gentle-looking creature could be a bad influence. It looked intelligent. She thought it might understand if its failings were corrected in a kindly manner.

The constable looked down at the dog. 'And I know that Superintendent Hood has been on the list a long time, only there haven't been any failures up until now. Not in Wakefield and none here. This fellow is the first write-off.'

The dog lowered its head.

Mrs Sugden wondered if she imagined it, but the creature appeared somewhat apologetic. That subdued demeanour might conceal a vicious streak.

'How has it failed?'

'It's good at the sniffing out, only it doesn't know when to stop.'

The dog sat down on its haunches and looked up at Mrs Sugden, waiting for her to speak.

'I don't know what to say. I haven't the authority. Can't you take it home?'

'I'm in the constables' residence. It's not allowed.'

He was very young, and had clearly been given this job because no one else wanted it.

'It seems a quiet enough creature.'

'Oh it is. I had to walk him up from town. He was no trouble.' With a stroke of inspiration, he added, 'He saw a cat and didn't make to chase it.'

'Has he been taught to lie down and stay put?'

'Oh yes.' The young man looked at the seated dog. 'Down!' The dog lay down. 'Stay!' he dropped the leash and walked towards the gate, calling back to her, 'You see, he'll be no trouble.'

'Not so fast, constable!'

He stopped.

The dog looked up at her. She did not want to have to say to the nice Mr and Mrs Hood that a dog came to be given a home but had to be done in because of the inconvenience. It was the face that did it. Whenever she saw a creature with a sad face and a touch of longing in its eyes, she knew they were just like us, but different.

'Go round the back. You'll see a gate into the wood.

Walk him round there in case he wants to do something, and then take him to the back door.'

Mrs Sugden unlocked the door of the photographic studio. She stepped inside and turned the sign to Open. The dog padded in and began to sniff about. 'Do you have a name?'

The dog gave her a look of infinite sadness, or perhaps that was just the cast of its features.

'Well I can't name you. I don't want to cause confusion.'

She had brought a dish and went through a door into the back room where there was a sink in the corner. The dog followed her. She filled the dish with water and set it down. She decided that it could stay in there, out of the way, so as not to frighten timid customers. 'Stay!'

She went back into the front of the shop and sat down behind the counter, opening a drawer. Mr Murchison had left a float. The dog followed her. She counted the money and made her own note. Eight half crowns, ten florins, twenty shilling pieces, thirty tanners, eight threepenny bits and two shillings in coppers, making three pounds and nineteen shillings.

With the change was a piece of notepaper, folded in two, with her name on it. She unfolded the paper.

Mrs Sugden, if you see your way to clearing up the cellar, there'll be two guineas for you. T. Murchison

That was not to be sneezed at.

At ten minutes past nine, the first customer came. He brought a ticket and collected a packet of photographs.

Mrs Sugden was satisfied. Doing this would make a nice change. It also kept her from having to introduce the cat to the dog.

By eleven o'clock there had been just one other customer, coming to make an appointment for a wedding photograph.

The dog whimpered.

She went through and took it into the yard. When it came in from the yard, it expressed a strong preference not to stay on its own but pushed its way into the shop. The day was warm. The dog was panting. 'I'll open the door to the cellar steps and you can lie down on the cold stone.'

This seemed agreeable to the bloodhound. For several minutes it lay still.

When she looked, it was gone. She switched on the electric light and walked down into the cellar. The dog was sniffing at a pile of old film that had been thrown in the corner, dribbling over it too. Someone had tipped tea leaves on the top so she knew it wasn't wanted. Nearby was a sack. Once upon a time somebody must have decided to clear this lot.

A door on the opposite side opened onto a darkroom. She saw at a glance that this area was speckless, and closed the door.

Not being one for a mess, Mrs Sugden decided she would make a start. The shop clapper was loud enough, and even if she didn't hear it, this canine ought to bark. She began to clear the pile of old film. It was not pleasant to the touch, being brittle and somewhat smelly with a pong not easily identifiable.

The bloodhound agreed. It walked round and round and would most certainly have helped her if it could.

Mrs Sugden changed her mind. It would not do to sit behind the counter looking mucky and smelling stale.

She cluck-clucked to the dog and told it to come on.

It took no notice but turned its attention to the wall along from the darkroom. It began to sniff, and paw as if trying to dig. As it did so, it whined in a low plaintive manner so that at first she thought it had hurt a paw.

'No wonder you failed your test. There's nowt there of interest.' She took the dog by its collar and dragged it away. 'Don't you know a distempered wall when you see one?'

Perhaps not. If this creature had been brought up in kennels or a stable with others of its kind, and a police handler barking orders, it wouldn't know about houses and cellars and how walls were of no great interest except for standing the dresser against or hanging pictures.

She hauled the dog back upstairs.

The creature was quiet enough after that. It went to sleep, sprawling against the cellar door which Mrs Sugden had shut firmly.

In the early afternoon, Jim Sykes called in to see how she fared.

She explained about the bloodhound and its failure to meet required standards.

He made a fuss of the dog, scratching its ears. 'No one can spoil you, you've spoiled yourself.'

She told him about the cellar, and about the dog's antics, and the extra two guineas for clearing and cleaning the cellar, which was a generous amount that she'd be willing to split.

'I wonder what he sniffed that caught his attention?' Being Jim Sykes, he had to go down and take a look.

When he came back up, he said, 'Let me know when you want to start on that cellar. I'll give you a hand.'

She opened her purse and gave him a bob. 'Fetch me

a pork pie and an egg custard. We'll make a start when I shut up shop.'

'You're on. Does this animal have a leash?'

'He does.'

'I'll take him off your hands for a while, and fetch you that pie.'

'And egg custard.'

'I won't forget your egg custard.' He clipped on the leash. 'And what's its name?'

'That'll be up to Mr and Mrs Hood to decide.' An idea struck Mrs Sugden. 'I don't suppose you'd fancy looking after that animal until Mrs Shackleton arrives back from Stanbury?'

Surprisingly, he agreed. 'The kids will love it. We'll walk it on the moor.'

'I didn't know you liked dogs.'

'When I was in the force, I applied to be a dog handler but it wasn't to be.'

$\mathcal{N}$ine

Such a Journey

Early on Friday, 3 August Mother, Dad and I set off for Stanbury by car from Wakefield. The others would be going by train from Leeds.

That morning's drive stretched into infinity. Mother and I share private knowledge. My father, although superb at his job, passably good at golf, a thoughtful husband and a kind parent, is an abominable driver. Like many people who are bad at something, he has great confidence in his abilities. When he gets behind a wheel, something in his brain must switch off. Given a globe, he would be able to point to the most obscure places on earth. Given an open road, he somehow wants to keep going. He never sees a signpost until he has passed it, and so there is a great deal of turning back because he does not trust that anyone else in the car may have seen it first, and read it properly. Our neighbour next door takes care of the mechanics and the petrol. Dad assumes that will be satisfactory until the next time.

Mother puts these foibles down to the fact that he never

drove a car until long after he was driven by a constable. Following on from that, he somehow assumes that a car has a mind. This belief is reinforced because his car does indeed know the way to the golf course.

Naturally, he would not let me take the wheel. It would be extremely embarrassing for him to be seen, even by total strangers, being driven by a female.

Not wishing to hurt my feelings, he made the excuse that his Crossley Coupe was a big car and I was unused to it. Mother reminded him that I have a Rolls-Royce in my garage – a gift in lieu of cash from a grateful client. Dad advised me to sell it before I had an accident.

Only once did I break my unspoken vow not to upset him, and that was because he upset me. When he sees two women in a car together, he exclaims, 'Budgies, Ginny! Budgies!' This is his way of saying that they are doing nothing but chatter, without a thought for where they are going, for other road users, or unfortunate pedestrians who step into their path.

'Dad,' I said in as controlled a fashion as possible, 'just remember they are budgies who now have the vote. They won't look across at you and call you a jackdaw.'

Mother wanted me to be with them on the journey in case Dad got hopelessly lost. Dad wanted me to be there to ensure that Mother would be suitably accommodated.

Mr Porter, my parents' intended host at Stanbury had sent hand-written direction cards, supplied by the Automobile Association. The cards had been well used and were somewhat dog-eared. I called out directions as I juggled the unwieldy map and kept the cards in order. We stopped on the outskirts of Shipley, at tea rooms where water went off the boil in 1913.

Plan A was that Mother and Dad would spend a week with the Porters. Plan B was that if, by Sunday, they and the Porters were sick of the sight of each other, I would find some urgent reason why I must be driven home.

It was a relief when we finally arrived at Laverall Hall, at the west end of Stanbury village. A long drive led to the Tudor-arched doorway. Dad brought the motor to a stop outside a handsome two-storey house in dressed stone with a slate roof and double-chamfered mullion windows with attractive round-headed lights. The house had three gables and the centre of the building was set back a little from the sections on either side, like the roast beef in a sandwich that does not come all the way to the crust.

I climbed out first and went to help Mother who appeared to have become fixed to her seat.

Over the door was an oval panel containing illegible letters and the date 1641.

Mother stared. 'Goodness. Is this it?'

Father and I agreed that it was.

This house was grander than she expected.

Mr and Mrs Porter had heard the sound of the motor. They came out to greet us. He walked to the car, looking very pleased, as if we were the first visitors they had ever welcomed. Mrs Porter followed close on his heels.

'It will be all right,' I said to Mother in answer to her whispered question, through lips that did not lose their smile, as to did I think they would have indoor plumbing.

After an exchange of warm greetings and assurances from Dad to Mr Porter that our journey had been splendid, we stepped directly into a room with low ceiling beams, a flagstone floor and four stone doorways. An elderly spaniel with rheumy eyes rose clumsily from a rug in front of the range and made its slow way across the room for mutual inspection.

We all sat down. A pleasant-looking woman, her grey hair pleated into a narrow roll, brought in a tray with tea and hot water and put it on the table in front of the fireplace, near to a second table that was set with china cups and home-made biscuits.

When the dog, introduced as Max, trotted over and sat beside me, I felt oddly flattered.

Mrs Porter said, 'He has an instinct for who might pat his head and give him a biscuit.'

We females listened politely while Dad and Mr Porter exchanged news about old comrades, where they were now, and which men had left this earth for the great police parade ground in the sky.

Mrs Porter led Mother upstairs to the bathroom. Mother's sense of relief at the naming of such a room was palpable.

Later, Mrs Porter, Mother and I went outdoors to admire the garden.

'I hear you are staying at Ponden Hall, Kate?' Mrs Porter frowned.

'Yes.'

'Well I expect you will be all right. As long as it doesn't rain.'

'What happens when it rains?'

'The roof could do with a little attention. I do know that there's a great scramble for sufficient buckets to catch the leaks. I've seen people from the Hall at jumble sales, buying up any cheap and useful containers. We all know what they're for. Our own roof isn't perfect, but . . . ' She did not bring herself to finish the sentence.

'It will be characterful,' Mother said, looking about the garden like a person suddenly satisfied, her worst fears allayed. Not only was Mrs Porter amiable, she had a bathroom. What's more, she knew how to create a garden.

'Is there anything else I should know about Ponden Hall, Mrs Porter?' I asked.

She thought for a moment. 'I wouldn't want to put you off. I'm sure Mrs Varey will have gone to a lot of trouble to ensure your comfort. She really does need the income. Of course, it will be her daughter Elisa that you will have dealings with. Don't let her rather brusque manner put you off. They are a family living in the shadow of personal grief and lost expectations.'

Ten

The Keighley Train

Harriet looked at the clock on the station concourse. She was in good time. Auntie Kate had given her the choice of going to Wakefield first and travelling in the car, or catching the train to Keighley and changing for Haworth.

Derek would be taking the train. Harriet had taken a liking to him.

Time off meant swapping shifts at the Hyde Park Picture House. It also meant losing pay by missing her hours at the café, but it would be worth it.

She saw Derek. Seeing him set her at ease. She had come to the right station. He was standing close to the barrier, waiting. He always looked the same, that same suit, but today he carried a haversack on his back and held one of those tripods like a walking stick. Someone must have lent it him.

He did not see her at first, though he was looking out for people. Harriet stared at him. I see you, you don't see me. Thank you very much. Feel my stare.

He did feel her stare. He looked and waved.

She joined him. 'We're to go onto the platform.'

'Yes I know. Don't think the others are here yet.'

'Well I'm going through. You might have missed them.' Not adding, 'You nearly missed me.' She took the ticket from her pocket, joined the short queue and went through the barrier, taking a deep breath of smoky air. He did not follow her.

I am a seasoned traveller. No flies on me. I have travelled on a milk train.

Auntie Kate had described Rita Rufus and said that she was one of a kind and could not be missed. True. That must be her.

She wore purple silk trousers so wide they could be a skirt, a big-sleeved white blouse with embroidered bodice, a turban the colour of her trousers and peep toe sandals of a kind Harriet had never seen in any shoe shop. Rita wore a woven stole, draped over one shoulder. On the opposite arm she carried a carpet bag, patterned with dragons.

Rita raised her hand and took a few steps towards Harriet who went to meet her, a little uncertainly. Harriet wondered how Auntie Kate had described her to Rita. She probably would have said, shiny dark hair cut short, big hazel eyes, probably wearing a blue dress with white polka dots and navy bar shoes.

'You're Harriet.' Rita took Harriet's hand rather firmly and shook it.

'Hello.'

'I'm Rita Rufus. You don't see me at meetings because they clash with madrigal rehearsals. I'd rather sing than listen to self-important men drone on about developing techniques and "My Best Seaside Snap".'

'I don't go either. I'm usually at the Hyde Park Picture House.'

'Very sensible.' She looked about. 'Where's Kate?'

'Gone by car with her parents. Mr and Mrs Hood will be staying with friends in Stanbury.'

Just then, Rita waved. 'Here they are.'

Harriet turned to see Tobias and Carine Murchison, and Derek. So that's who he had been waiting for. Derek was gazing at Carine.

Harriet had never been struck by lightning, but it must feel a little bit like this. Like the realisation that Derek was not only carrying Carine's canvas bag, but a torch for her. Carine was old enough to be Derek's mother. Harriet felt herself blushing for him, blushing for his ridiculousness. She never swore aloud, only in her head.

I hope he drops her bloody canvas bag. I hope his bloody tripod rolls under the bloody train.

He is a sappy article.

The smoking train curled chokingly into view.

I hope he gets grit in his eye the size of a bloody lump of bloody coal.

Yet she could understand why he would fall for Carine, with her perfect face and her curling hair. Carine came up to Harriet, smiling, touching her arm. She wore a pale green dress with a dipped hem that made Harriet realise her own dress was too short. 'I'm so glad you are here, Harriet. You are such a good photographer, and it's a delight to have a young person with us old fogies. I'm sure we'll all have the most marvellous time.'

Harriet found herself smiling back. She offered Carine a wine gum.

It took several minutes to settle into the carriage. The five of them were in a carriage for six. Harriet sat by the window, Derek seated beside her. Opposite Harriet sat Tobias Murchison, Carine beside him, and Rita Rufus next to Carine.

The Murchisons had a large portmanteau which Tobias did not allow into the luggage van. It was too big for the rack and had to be stood on end.

The stationmaster blew his whistle. The train pulled out of the station.

Mr Murchison lit a cigarette.

Rita arranged the woven stole across her knees, gazed briefly and admiringly at her own toes, and produced a newspaper. Before turning her attention to the newsprint, she made an announcement.

'We are a mixed bunch. An usherette, a young newspaperman, a superb studio photographer, watercolourist and versifier and . . . ' she hesitated, 'and her husband.'

Tobias Murchison glared, but Rita Rufus was unaware of this because Carine sat between them. Harriet smiled. Since he had given her a tour of Carine's darkroom, Harriet had developed a confused and uncomfortable feeling about Mr Tobias Murchison.

Derek leaned across and said something to Carine, about her canvas bag.

He lifted it onto the luggage rack. 'Safely stowed, Mrs Murchison.'

She smiled. 'Derek, first name terms! It's Carine, as you well know. All friends in the eye of the camera.'

Harriet had noticed before that Carine had a perfect face and smiled a great deal. A person could not help but

103

like her. She would have to be the most patient and kind woman to put up with that husband. Harriet shuddered. How would a person know, when she married, what a man might turn out to be like? They might start off young and handsome and turn into a horrible boorish pig, though that would be unkind to pigs. Carine was a saint to be so nice to Tobias.

When Harriet had asked her auntie about the funeral for Carine's father, Auntie Kate had hesitated before she answered, 'It was well attended.'

'Was Carine very upset?'

'She seemed so. Carine has unexpected inner strength and reserves. She is a remarkable woman.'

Auntie Kate changed the subject then, and Harriet wondered if that was because of something she did not want to say. On the other hand, perhaps Auntie Kate thought Harriet might remember back to when her father died, as if she could ever forget. Auntie Kate had come to see them. She came to find things out, so at least they knew. Or, Harriet did. Austin had been too young to understand.

There was an odd, unsettling atmosphere in the railway carriage. Perhaps because they were, as Rita said, a mixed bunch.

Carine tried to put everyone at their ease, saying that they must all be thrilled for her because her contract with the greetings card company had been renewed. This weekend, she would photograph wildflowers, moss and heather, and from these she would create her images for the greetings cards.

She insisted that everyone divulge their plans, teasing her

husband and saying she knew he wanted to be secretive, so he would be excused. She kissed Tobias's cheek and said his secret was safe with her.

What a knack Carine has for making us comfortable with ourselves, Harriet thought. They all shared their plans. Rita's was to take no photographs at all, except in her mind's eye. She instead offered to be the model for anyone who wanted a figure in their picture.

Harriet wiped her hand across the steam on the carriage window and looked out. There was not much to see. Factories, mills, smoke.

Carine leaned back and closed her eyes. She had long lashes like those on an expensive doll in the County Arcade toyshop.

Harriet decided she must be mistaken about Derek. He and she always chatted when she tore his cinema ticket. They liked to talk. Twice he waited for her and walked her home, because they had more to say about the picture. He couldn't fall for an elderly doll.

She would give him another chance.

'There's a picture house in Haworth and one in Keighley.'

'I suppose there would be.'

'We could find out what's showing.'

He nodded. 'We could.'

She had thought he was like her, wanting to go to the pictures all the time.

She asked him what he hoped to photograph over the weekend.

Derek's replies were so brief that she gave up. After that, he did not so much as glance at her. His gaze was permanently fixed on the supposedly sleeping Carine.

Harriet knew Carine was not asleep. Her head would loll or her mouth open. She was pretending.

Tobias Murchison brought a silver flask from his inside pocket and took a sip.

Suddenly, from out of nowhere, there was what people call 'an atmosphere'.

Harriet looked out of the window again. She could see the reflection of the three people opposite: Carine feigning sleep; Rita's and Carine's hands touching; Tobias staring across at Derek with a look of pure hatred.

They arrived at Keighley, where they were to change trains. Derek jumped up and opened the carriage door. He climbed out first, so as to give a hand to Rita, and then Carine. Harriet expected he would not give her a hand, but he did. So did Tobias Murchison, from behind, and not the kind of hand she welcomed.

Tobias looked for a porter to bring the big portmanteau.

'What about your luggage?' Carine asked Harriet.

'Auntie Kate arranged for it to be delivered to Ponden Hall.'

'Oh, good!' Rita had stepped back from reading the timetable. 'There's time for me to buy wellington boots before the Haworth train leaves. A walker friend advised me to bring stout footwear. Don't go without me!'

Carine hurried after her. 'If you're having wellington boots, so am I.'

Harriet knew that wellington boots did not count as stout footwear. Her own boots were safely packed. She did not intend to hang about with Derek and Tobias Murchison. Let them keep each other company. They looked ridiculous, side by side. Murchison was big, broad and bloated. Derek was so skinny that the gust of a passing train might knock him off his feet.

They were ignoring her anyway. Derek was looking up at Mr Murchison, telling him a story about a car sending him flying on Albion Street. 'It was a car very much like yours, Mr Murchison.'

Harriet went to wait for the Haworth train. She sat on a bench next to a sad-looking old man who nursed a Cairn terrier. The little dog dribbled onto his master's sleeve. He spoke to it in a consoling voice.

'Is your dog poorly?' Harriet asked.

'Bless you, no, lass. He's as well as you or I, but he likes to know that all is well and all manner of things are well, especially when he is travelling.'

As they left the train at Haworth station, a brass band played. For a mad moment, Harriet thought that this must have been laid on by Auntie Kate. It turned out that there were important people arriving. Two motor cars waited for them. The important people climbed into the cars which drove off at a funeral pace behind the town band.

Harriet, Rita and Derek all stood on the kerb, watching the band and the cars wind their way out of sight.

What now, Harriet thought. She had copied her auntie and carried a satchel. It held comb, purse, diary, pencil and a copy of *Jane Eyre*. She had reached the point where Jane Eyre knew that her only course was to leave Thornfield Hall and seek a new kind of servitude. Harriet was very glad that times had changed, and that she could work at the café and be an usherette. Life would have been so much brighter for Jane had she been able to go to the pictures.

Rita was wearing her wellington boots and held onto

her carpet bag into which she had squeezed the brown paper parcel containing her fancy sandals. Derek paused to slide his arms through his rucksack and adjust it on his back.

Rita said cheerfully, 'I looked it up. Stanbury is not much more than a mile off. We can walk.'

Derek cleared his throat. 'We don't know the way.'

Harriet felt a sudden surge of pity for him. He had never lived anywhere but with his gran and only been once to the seaside, on a day trip. He strode about like a man of the world, but his world was small and now he was out of it.

'I'd soon find the way,' Rita said confidently. 'I can read a map upside down and inside out. I look at the sun and I know which way to go. Every decent photographer knows what the sun is doing.'

'You don't take photographs,' Derek said, sounding a little peevish.

'I don't need to. If you know where the sun is, you can find your way from one end of the country to the other.'

Harriet had no intention of spoiling her shoes by marching about the countryside. 'Auntie Kate has the map.'

The porter brought up the rear with the Murchisons' portmanteau on a squeaking trolley. Tobias clutched Carine's arm.

'Call you a cab, ladies and gents?' The porter waited for his tip.

Tobias handed him a penny. 'We'll want a cab to the Black Bull, porter.'

The porter swung the trunk to the ground, pretending not to hear. He retreated with his trolley.

Carine touched Tobias's arm. 'No, dear, the Black Bull was fully booked.'

'Are we staying at the Fleece?'

'You'll see.'

Five of us and a massive suitcase, Harriet thought. We'll never all fit. She waited for Carine to tell Tobias where they would be staying. Carine said nothing.

Tobias turned to Derek. 'We'll catch the bus. Derek, take an end of this portmanteau.' Harriet saw that Tobias was taking revenge because Derek was an idiot who adored Carine. Tobias thought that Derek would not be able to keep up his end of the heavy case.

Derek made a move as if to do as Tobias bid. No one said, 'We are not staying in Haworth, we are going to Stanbury.'

Harriet, having withdrawn five shillings from her savings account, grabbed Derek's arm. 'Auntie Kate told me that you and Rita must come with me in a cab. It's provided for. Be so kind as to catch that porter.'

She felt pleased with this speech, which worked.

Derek was a sappy article, but a nice sappy article. She did not want to see him bullied.

The porter called them a cab, and made it clear this was for them – the sixpenny tippers. The 'cab' was a horse and cart.

'Come with us!' Rita called to Carine. 'Let Tobias follow on with the luggage.' Carine stayed by her husband. 'You three go ahead. We'll follow.'

As she scrambled onto the cart, Harriet gave a quizzical look at Rita and Derek. Did they know why Carine had kept their destination secret?

Rita said, 'He's in for a shock.'

Harriet smoothed her dress. 'A good shock or a bad shock?'

Derek sometimes liked to show off because he had stayed at school longer than anybody needed to. 'Is a shock ever good, or must a shock by its nature always be bad?'

Harriet ignored him. She knew, that for some mysterious reason, Mr Murchison was in for a bad shock.

Eleven

Ponden Hall

Harriet guessed from the name Ponden Hall, and Auntie Kate's account of it, that this would be a fine-looking place. It was reassuring that the man she saw, as the cart rattled and shook along the winding and bumpy lane, was on the scruffy side, with a sheepdog at his heels. No toffs. Not yet.

The views on either side delighted her – a huge reservoir on one side, fields and hills on the other.

The driver stopped outside a long two-storey house built of stone. Harriet paid the fare, having the money ready in her hand. She wondered now if she had been rash in offering, and pretending that it was on Auntie Kate's instructions. She knew you were supposed to give a tip. Feeling important, feeling nervous, not sure how much to give for a tip, she guessed at sixpence. That had been appreciated by the porter. A driver would expect no less.

Harriet was surprised at the sight of the house, which was solid-looking and might once have been grand. Though this was not an Auntie Kate sort of place. The entranceway was rough ground. There were no pots of flowers nearby. Smoke rose from the chimney. They must keep a good fire, even in August. Stone pillars stood on either side of the wide entrance.

She, Rita and Derek walked up the broad paved drive. An elderly couple sat on a bench, drinking tea and pretending to be lords of the manor.

Rita was busy looking around her, breathing in deeply as if needing to taste the air. Derek had stayed a few paces behind.

The door was firmly shut. Rita rapped the knocker. Moments later, a youngish woman appeared. Tall, square-jawed, plaits wound around her head, she wore a black dress and kept her hands in the pockets of a white crosso-ver pinafore.

'We're the party from Leeds,' Harriet announced, 'come to stay.'

The young woman nodded. 'Right then. You're the first of them. Which ones are you?'

'I'm Harriet Armstrong. This is Miss Rufus and Derek Blondell.'

The woman took her hands from her pockets. 'Follow me then.'

'What's your name?' Harriet asked.

'I'm Elisa Varey,' the young woman said, as if this was stating the obvious and no one need ever ask. 'You'll want to see where you're stopping.'

She led them along the passageway, passing a stand for hats, coats and sticks and a rack for boots. Doors to the rooms on the left were closed. The passageway walls were done in a dark green wash. At the end of the first passageway, they turned. Harriet heard the low murmur of voices from an immense room on her right. People were gathered at tables, eating, and drinking tea. 'Walkers,' Elisa paused. 'We do teas and cake.'

A massive chandelier hung from a beamed ceiling. The ceiling sagged so deeply that Harriet imagined it to be a series of hammocks. A massive sideboard held stuffed birds and animals. There were reindeer heads on the wall.

'This is where you'll have your breakfast,' Elisa announced. 'We call it the hall. You'll be on your own here for breakfast and supper. These are ramblers and day trippers, calling in midday until teatime.'

The kitchen on the opposite side of the corridor gave off a sweet smell of baking.

Elisa led them to a staircase, and up into another corridor. This was the kind of house where a person could get lost in the maze of stairs, landings and rooms off. You might go through a wrong door and never find your way back into the real world. Elisa flung open a door. 'This is for the lady who booked . . .'

'My auntie, Mrs Shackleton.'

' . . . and for you, Harriet, and for Miss Rufus here.'

They were in the biggest bedroom Harriet had ever seen. What's more, it gave off a sensation of opulence. The floor was almost entirely carpeted in scarlet, though the carpeting was in strips and squares, neatly joined like a jigsaw puzzle.

There was a clothes-press, an old sideboard and two crimson-covered chairs. A great chandelier hung from the ceiling, its glass drops on silver chains sparkling in the light from the window. As well as two narrow beds, there was an uncomfortable-looking couch that Harriet thought must be called a chaise-longue. She had seen one illustrated in a book.

'Does one of us sleep on that?' she asked.

Elisa waved at a large oak case with squares cut out at the top like little windows. 'There's the box bed. Slide that door back.'

Harriet went to look, and took a fancy to it straight away. It was almost like a little room, with the bed inside taking up all the space. There was a candlestick on the window ledge. A person could spend the day in there. She climbed in. 'I fancy sleeping here.'

'Then you shall,' Rita said. 'I'm used to sleeping on a straw mat under the stars and this carpet would suit me well enough, if there were no beds.'

Elisa glared at her. 'What's wrong wi't beds?'

'The beds are grand. I'm just saying. I crossed Africa, you see.'

'That's you settled then,' Elisa said somewhat abruptly. 'Where's the feller gone?'

'I'm here,' Derek said from just beyond the doorway. 'Follow me.'

Harriet noticed the little casement window covered with ivy. 'I do like it in here.' She glanced over at Rita who was rubbing her foot. 'Hadn't we better toss for it or something? You or Auntie Kate might want this bed.'

'You nab it, girl. I should think a person might have interesting dreams in a bed like that.'

'I don't dream much.'

'Of course you do.' Rita padded across the room and sat down on Auntie Kate's trunk which had been placed by the wall. 'Do you record your dreams?'

'No.'

'You should write them down. You'll have brought a diary or a notebook?'

'Yes.'

'Take it from one who knows, write down your dreams and you will be in for a revelation. Listen to any words that are spoken while you sleep.'

'Who will speak to me?'

'That I am not sure. Some say it must be your inner voice, others more spiritually inclined say that it is an angel or spirit guide who watches over us. Some say it is God. Personally I do not imagine that God would trouble the ears of the world's light sleepers.'

'I suppose not.' Harriet was intrigued. 'Do you hear voices in your sleep?'

'I do, and sometimes they are nonsense which is why I am quite sure it is not God who speaks. Other times, the words come as a warning. I am very relieved there are just six of us on this outing.'

'Why?'

'On the night that I paid my deposit for this trip, I clearly heard the words "Seven will come and only six return."'

'How strange.'

'Indeed! But we are six! You and your aunt, Carine and Tobias, young Derek and moi.' She sighed. 'Would you not think that with an active membership approaching thirty-five we would have had a better take-up? Mind you, it's just as well or this room may have turned into a dormitory.'

'I suppose so. Six is a good number.'

'And I heard something else, just before I woke this morning.'

'What?'

'The voice distinctly said, "Someone you love is in jeopardy".'

'Where is Jeopardy?'

'It's not a place, dear girl. Jeopardy means to be in a state of peril or hazard.'

'And is it true?'

'Possibly. But to be forewarned is to be forearmed.' She rubbed her other foot. 'I must wear socks with my wellingtons. Do you have spare socks in this trunk?'

'Auntie Kate does.' Harriet sat up and looked out of the window. The pane had not been washed. Ivy almost blocked out the view, except for a large tree whose branches moved so slightly in the wind that they might be doing it just to please. 'Who is in jeopardy?'

'No details emerged. Of course, the voice may be speaking through corridors of time and space. You won't have anything to worry about.'

'If that's the kind of thing the voice says, I don't want to hear it.'

'Yes, but if you are given a sign, be forewarned. You will never again dither about the direction of your life.'

'I don't dither.'

'Good. I like a girl who doesn't dither. I like your aunt and I like you. We shall be good roommates.' She wound the woven stole around her shoulders. 'I don't suppose those spare socks are near the top of your trunk?'

'I'll look.' Harriet swung down from her special bed. She took the key from her satchel. 'Shift then!'

Rita moved so that Harriet could open the trunk.

She found a pair of socks and tossed them to Rita.

Rita put them on. She pulled on her wellingtons and tucked in the silk trousers. 'I had these pants run up in Jaipur. People think silk impractical but it is warm enough and dries easily.' She knotted the stole. 'Now, I'm off across the moors. Will you join me?'

'No, I'll unpack our trunk and wait for my auntie.'

Rita tilted her head to one side and looked at the trunk. It was Auntie Kate's smallest trunk but when Rita looked at it, the item took on massive proportions. 'People take too much with them. I crossed Africa with a small haversack and India with a cloth bag on a rope.'

'You should've brought it today, and put a pair of socks in.'

'My travels were charmed. If you give off the right aura, people leave you alone, or are helpful. Which reminds me to say, did Tobias Murchison pinch your bottom as you stepped from the train?'

Harriet blushed. 'Yes he did, and not for the first time.'

'It's because you are young and he thinks you dare not say anything. I'll tell you what you must do.'

Harriet, who hoped for adventure at some point in the future, listened carefully.

When Rita had gone, and Harriet was looking about the room for somewhere to put their clothes, she made a mental note to ask Rita how a person might set about crossing continents. She had also meant to ask Rita if she knew why Tobias Murchison had the impression they would stay in Haworth.

Auntie Kate had packed suitable clothes for being invited to the Porters' on Sunday. These, Harriet laid in the clothes-press. There was the sideboard, with two cupboards and two drawers.

When Harriet planned how she would furnish a place of her own, a sideboard came near the top, along with a gramophone and cat's whiskers. She must ask Rita if she had these desirable items, and a room of her own to put them in. She wondered what Rita did, or who she came from, that allowed her to dress so well, cross Africa and India, and have silk trousers run up in Jaipur.

The sideboard's top drawer held someone's underclothes and a nightdress.

She opened the bottom drawer.

In it was a baby's outfit, finely knitted, the colour of fresh dairy cream and soft to touch. She could see straight away that it had never been worn: leggings, jacket, bonnet and bootees. Who is going to have a baby, she wondered. Beside it was a broad-brimmed hat decorated with a cabbage rose. The hat might once have been pink but was now well past its best. Harriet did not hear the footsteps.

'What do you think you're doing?'

It was Elisa Varey. Harriet saw now that her lived-in face wore a deep frown mark. Her eyes turned hard and angry.

Harriet dropped the outfit back into the drawer and closed it. 'I'm looking for somewhere to put my clothes, what's wrong with that?'

'Keep your stuff in your own trunk,' Elisa Varey snapped. She pushed her way to the sideboard, opened each drawer and took out the nightdress, the baby's outfit and the hat. 'You've got our room and now you want all else on top.'

'You showed us into this room.'

'The room yes, the sideboard no.'

'Do you mean to say we've taken your bed?'

'Aye.'

'Well, good.'

Elisa had turned to go and now turned back. 'What did you say?'

'I said good, because anyone less rude would pretend to make us welcome.'

'Well then, hear this from the rude piece of work. Mam says you're to come down. There's tea and sandwiches.'

'My aunt isn't here yet.'

'You better not eat it all then, but I expect you will.'

A sudden thought came into Harriet's head, and it was about the knitted outfit, just the size for a new-born baby.

She spoke softly this time. 'Was that outfit for your own bairn?'

'Do you always push your nose into other people's business?'

'Often I do.'

'No. It wasn't my bairn.' She strode to the door. 'The bairn never wore it, so shut your cake hole and leave that drawer alone.'

With that, Elisa was gone.

Harriet felt an anger rising up in her. It was not anger for Elisa Varey because she saw that she was close to tears. It was that old anger particular to Harriet herself, that helplessness and hopelessness that would hit her suddenly out of nowhere.

She wondered about the baby that died.

Harriet gave herself a little shake. She placed her night-gown on the box bed, to claim it, and wondered what sort of dreams she would have.

Elisa Varey popped her head around the door.

Harriet looked at her.

Elisa said, 'I might ask you summat, since you're a know-it-all.'

'What?'

'I said might. I might and I might not.'

'Well I can see you intend to ask, so do it.'

'This Mr and Mrs T Murchison that are coming, what is his Christian name?'

'Tobias.'

Elisa's mouth opened. She stared at Harriet. 'He's big, he has a red face, he's rude.'

'That's him.'

'How dare, how dare he come here?'

Twelve

Nothing Bad Ever Happens Here

Relieved to see Mother and Dad comfortably settled with Mr and Mrs Porter, I decided it was time for me to set off for Ponden Hall. I couldn't wait to see the place.

Mr Porter offered to show me the way. After my exhausting journey with Dad at the wheel, I was glad to be walking, and to have an escort through unfamiliar territory.

The village of Stanbury seemed to me to be a single long street with a mixture of houses and shops on either side, with the added bonus of a tea room. It was the kind of place where people knew each other. Every twenty paces, or so it seemed, Mr Porter exchanged a greeting with fellow villagers. Outside the Co-operative Store, by the butcher's and the baker's, there were pauses for thoughtful observations about the weather: presently fine and breezy, but – and this was not unanimous – likely to rain.

Mr Porter pointed out the Manor House, the Co-op, the church, the school, and the house where a police constable lived. He came to a halt at the bus stop. 'You'll catch the bus to Haworth here. Or if you prefer, go back the way we've come, pass our place and at the end of the road turn left. It's no distance.'

'What if I take the bus in the other direction?'

'I shouldn't bother about that if I were you. You'll have enough on in the short time you're here.'

The village of Stanbury came to an abrupt stop, as if the place grew tired of putting on a busy face. Now fields and moors stretched for as far as I could see. The sky was a deep blue, dotted with a gliding parade of picture-book fluffy clouds.

We crossed the road. The ground rose towards sloping hills.

Determined to give me topographical instructions, Mr Porter stopped again. 'Now the way to Ponden Hall by the road is to continue along in the direction we've come. The road twists and turns so watch out for mad motorists and lunatic cyclists. You'll pass a public house on your left. When you come to a mill, turn left and keep walking.'

'But we're not going that way?'

'We're going the scenic route from Hob Hill, and cutting off the corner.'

We turned onto a track, passing a house on our right.

After a few yards, I stopped to admire the fall and rise of the moors. Ancient patterns of fields were clearly marked by drystone walls. In the distance, heather bloomed a deep purple. Sheep looked up from their grazing to watch us, and then ambled closer for a better look.

'I admire the chaps who come struggling up here with

a ton of equipment in the hope of photographing a curlew mid-flight. Oh, and don't be deceived by the clear sky. A mist can descend very quickly, even in August. Taking a wrong path is easily done.'

Mr Porter gave me an account of the farms in the area, the names of the families who remained and those who had gone.

'It must have been a hard life,' I commented.

'It was what folks knew, along with the quarrying. Women found work in the mill, when the handlooms went out.'

'And now the tenant farmers at Ponden Hall increase their income by providing teas and taking in guests.'

'They'll be glad to have you. Now tell me all about this photography hobby of yours. I've only ever taken snaps of the kids at the seaside.'

I did not say very much before he told me where I would find good views on a fine day. 'So many ways of looking at the world, eh? It is not what we see but what we make of it.' He named the farms on either side of our path, Cold Knoll, and Cold Knoll End. 'Where will you go today?'

'The waterfall and Top Withins, and perhaps into Haworth.'

'There's talk of fencing off Top Withins to stop the vandals.'

'So there is crime in this idyllic spot?'

'It's a free country, Kate. We can't keep you townies away.'

For a while, we walked in perfect silence, with the only sounds coming from the cry of a bird and the crunch of our footsteps. The air was clear and fresh. Even in my tucked away part of Leeds there is always the sound of the tramcar, children playing, horses' hooves on cobbles. The smoke from factories rises and though it is blown south and east there is always a pall hanging over the city, blackening its buildings and bringing the gift of coughs, catarrh and bad chests.

Where the ways forked, we paused near a row of cottages. 'We're at Buckley Green.' He pointed to one of the cottages. 'Timothy Feather, the last handloom weaver lived there.'

'When did he die?'

'Eighteen years ago, and a way of life went with him.' He took out a map. 'Now your best way to Top Withins is to pass Timothy Feather's cottage and stick to the farm track.' Expertly, he folded the map and held it for me, tracing the routes with his finger. 'There's Top Withins. From there, you'll go across and downhill for the waterfall. It's a poor specimen of a waterfall but tuneful enough. Lydia tells me Emily Brontë loved its song. And from there a path takes you into Haworth.'

I thanked him and would have been willing to continue the rest of the way alone but he insisted on walking with me, back onto the right fork of the path. 'That's Buckley Farm.' He opened a gate that led us onto a rough track where wildflowers grew on the bank at either side. 'This takes us to Ponden Lane.'

We startled a rabbit that made a dash for its burrow. As we walked, he told me stories that I might hear about goblins and the Gytrash in the form of a barrel of fire rolling down the hill. 'There's a lot of superstition around these parts.'

'The barrel of fire sounds scary.'

'It can all be explained. There are marsh gases across these moors, and sometimes small explosions.'

At the end of the track, by a farm gate, hens, geese and ducks pecked at the ground. We reached the lane. I had glimpsed the reservoir from above. Now the stretch of bright water came into view, sparkling in the sunlight. It was an impressive and yet somehow eerie sight. When I see man-made stretches of water, I always wonder what was there before, some lost village, or a stretch of meadow.

A broad road crossed the reservoir.

Mr Porter followed my gaze. 'A lass from Ponden Hall lost her life there some years ago.'

'How tragic.' The thought made me shiver. It seemed to me that there was not a stretch of water or an acre of land that did not nurse a history of human grief. Even this peaceful scene held concealed dangers, and lurking threats. 'How did it happen?'

'She was crossing the reservoir road on her way to Scar Top chapel on a Sunday morning. This was about fifteen years ago. Her hat blew off. The daft lass, she had a reputation as a daredevil, climbed the wall because she could see her hat lying on the overflow. A young fellow saw her. He was at the other end of the reservoir and too far away to help. She toppled in, and couldn't swim.'

His words stunned me into silence.

He continued. 'You can't go wrong from here. Follow this lane round the bend and you'll see Ponden Hall. And you know where we are if you need anything.'

'Thank you, Mr Porter. You've been very helpful.'

He cleared his throat. 'Your father told me about the

unlucky incidents you have been wrapped up with in recent years.'

'Ah, yes. My investigating.'

'After forty years in this area, I can vouch for the law-abiding nature of this place. Oh there's poaching, there are Saturday night incidents of drunk and disorderly. We have trespass difficulties, usually with people from the towns, but never anything more serious than that.'

'That's reassuring.'

'You are in a safe place here. I've made something of a study of local history and I can tell you that there has been no murder in these parts for a thousand years.'

Did he believe that, or was it for my benefit? Did he really imagine he knew of all the jealousies and rivalries of the past millennium, the moments of madness, blind and drunken rages? But then neither did I know about them and so I said, quite mildly, 'What about William the Conqueror's harrying of the North?'

'Oh that,' he said. 'When it comes to murder, I leave aside war and politics.'

He was determined to reassure this little woman that she would be safe from harm. It was kindly meant. Even with the most reasonable and intelligent men, there is so often that revealing moment when one experiences the unbridgeable gulf.

We parted.

Only the low murmur of the wind disturbed the afternoon's stillness. Mr Porter must be right. Nothing bad could happen here.

The first frisson of excitement came as I approached Ponden Hall. This was where Branwell and the sisters were made welcome when they visited the Heatons. They would have entered the door that I now approached, made themselves at home, chatted with the family, gone up to the library to see what they might read.

Did they all troop here together, or come in twos? Had Emily and Branwell visited on a winter's day, looking for a change of scene, a warm fire and fresh conversation, or on a day such as this when they might sit in the garden?

I had exchanged letters with the present mistress of the house, Mrs Varey. Now I would meet her. I tapped on the knocker, and waited, half expecting a latter-day Nelly Dean.

No one came. The door was ajar. I stepped inside and walked along the corridor, calling hello. It would be too much to hope that Mrs Varey, like Mrs Dean, would be sitting with a fist on either knee, and a cloud of meditation over her ruddy countenance, ready to regale me with some fascinating tale.

The smell of baking drew me to an open door. It was a large kitchen with an open fire and a gleaming black-leaded range.

A youngish woman did not pause in the spreading of mashed potatoes on the top of a large pie. One pie tin had already been prepared. She looked up.

I said hello, and asked, 'Is Mrs Varey here?'

'She's doing summat. I'm her daughter Elisa. Are you Mrs Shackleton?'

'Yes, how do you do.'

'Do you want me to show you your room, only your lot are waiting for you in't field, to go on a walk.' She gave me an odd look, as if there might be some secret and nefarious purpose behind the proposed walk.

I looked at my watch, remembering that we had agreed to meet half an hour ago. 'Oh, then I'll speak to Mrs Varey later.'

'I'll tell her.'

I heard a grunt and a sneeze, and glanced to the corner of the room where the sound came from. There was a box bed, the kind that one sometimes sees in old farmhouses. Its door was firmly shut. Tactfully, I ignored the occupant.

'Where is the field?'

'You'll see a gate opposite our entrance. That's it.'

Her directions led me to a wild space, dotted with trees. It was a pretty place, as much a wood as a field. Canopies of leaves created dramatic contrasts of light and shade. On either side of an overgrown path there were purple orchids, red campion, dog roses, honeysuckle and wild garlic – a dizzying combination of scents.

In a sheltered spot between the trees stood a small tent. What an idyllic place to camp, if a person liked camping.

I called Harriet's name, hoping that she and the others would be somewhere nearby, but no one answered. Perhaps they had given up on me and set off. I walked a little farther turning right onto another path. Someone was walking towards me. I did not want to bump into a stranger in the wood, yet as he came closer, I saw that the figure was familiar, a man of middling height, with broad shoulders. Closer still, I saw the scarred face that was not in the least ugly. There was a kind of beauty about him, and a grace of movement.

So many men wear suits, or parts of suits. He wore a check shirt, open at the neck, and flannel trousers with turn-ups. His head was bare.

What was he doing here? He had not signed up for our outing. Perhaps it was pure chance that Edward Chester had chosen the same place and the same weekend. I dismissed that thought straight away. The information would have been forwarded to him.

I felt suddenly ill-at-ease, with a sense of foreboding. Carine's first love, who moved so gracefully towards me, appeared to me to be everything Tobias was not. He was an acclaimed poet whose work I had read and admired. Little wonder the memory of him turned Carine's world upside down. This weekend would be about more than photographs and a new museum.

'Hello, Mr Chester. It is Mr Chester?'

'Edward. And you are Mrs Kate Shackleton.'

'Yes.'

'I enjoyed your photo display that evening. You and Carine made a good pair. I could see that you were friends.'

We were facing each other on the narrow path.

'Are you staying nearby, Edward?'

'I'm at Ponden Hall, like you. I have been here a couple of days. I thought I would join your party, if that is agreeable.' He did not wait for an answer. 'I spotted the others, striding along by the stream.' He lit a cigarette. 'I suppose some explanation is required, my turning up like this.'

'Was it a last-minute decision?'

He smiled. 'Not exactly. Being a new member of the society, it would have been presumptuous of me to jump on the bandwagon and accept the society's subsidy and organisation.'

'That is why you did not return your form?'

'I did not return my form because I thought that if I did,

Carine and Toby would not come. After all these years, it's time for me to speak with them.'

'Do the others know you are here?'

'No. They were just disappearing round the bend. I expect they'll be back shortly. Elisa, Miss Varey, said they would be meeting you here. I thought I would wait and say hello, so I hung about by the bee boles.'

'The bee boles?'

'Come and see.'

Curious, I walked alongside him. I had heard of bee boles but never went out of my way to look at any and would have passed these by had he not stopped and pointed them out.

'Usually, a bole is a recess in a wall. Each recess is big enough to hold a skep, the coiled-straw hive.'

These were set into an angle of the field, where the ground sloped. 'I haven't seen any like this before, even from a distance. Now that you mention it, I know I've spotted them in castle walls.'

'They've got the flat stone lintels and the sills. They're seventeenth century.'

I stepped closer, treading on small thistles, and heard, or imagined I heard, a sound from within. 'They face in two different directions.'

'Four boles are south facing and four west facing, to give protection from the worst of the weather.'

'Who is the beekeeper?'

'Mrs Varey. She and her daughter Elisa are the joint keepers of bees, so if there's honey for tea we'll know who to thank. Oh, and they sell beeswax candles.'

A crow alighted on the top of the bee boles, tilted its head and fixed us with its beady eye. It was all very well having a lecture on bees, but I wondered how the lecturer's presence would affect our weekend.

'That's all very interesting, Edward.'

'But?'

'Exactly.'

'Kate, I'm not here to cause trouble. It's ten years since I spoke to Toby. He and I were very close once. It's time for me to know him again, and to see how we three stand.'

'Is that wise?'

'Perhaps not. If they want me to leave, I will.'

From a little way off, I heard my name. I turned to see Harriet and Rita waving to me as they walked back along the stream. I presumed that the others were a little way behind them.

'Well, Edward, are you ready to join the party?'

'I am indeed.'

We walked down the slope together. I made the introductions. 'Rita, Harriet, this is Edward Chester – the last member of our party to arrive. Edward, Rita Rufus and my niece Harriet Armstrong.'

Rita looked at the newcomer as though he presented a puzzle that she must solve. They shook hands. 'So we are seven. You have broken my dream.'

She and Harriet exchanged a look.

'How do you do, Rita, Harriet. We've chosen a fine spot.'

I looked about. 'So where are the Murchisons, and Derek?'

Rita said, 'They're not far off.'

'I'll whistle.' Edward put his fingers to his lips and let out a short and a long whistle.

'They'll think you're a cuckoo,' Rita said.

'Wrong time of year.'

After a few moments Carine, Tobias and Derek appeared.

'Told you,' Edward said. 'Whistle and they'll come.'

I walked on a little way, prompting Rita and Harriet to come too. It would be better to let Carine and Tobias decide how to treat this reappearance of the resurrected poet.

Rita, oblivious of the potential drama of the situation called back to them. 'We're setting off for Top Withins now. Keep up!'

Derek must have caught a whiff of being unwelcome. He fell into step with me, Rita and Harriet.

'What's going on between those three?'

'Just keep walking, Derek.'

Thirteen

Top Withins

Under a hot sun, we strode towards Top Withins. Our newcomer, Edward, was determined to fall in with Carine, regardless of the fact that Tobias stuck doggedly to her other side.

Carine put one foot before the other like a woman in a trance.

Tobias soon got out of breath. Pretending he wanted to look at something in the distance, he would catch Carine's arm to make her pause.

Only Edward was in control of himself, a man biding his time. He chatted a little, behaving as if to turn up after a decade of being pronounced dead was the most natural thing in the world.

We were on a carters' track where there were some oddly shaped flat stones, and here and there paving stones on either side. To our left there was evidence of quarrying, and a distant crane. Beyond that, the hills rose. I imagined how green this beautiful valley would have been before quarrying began. Even now there was an astonishing variety of textures. The land dipped and rose, as though waiting to come to life like a turbulent sea.

Tobias grew irritable. As we passed Lower Heights Farm, he began to complain about the heat. The air was still and the day glorious. Heather turned the hills purple.

Harriet had been walking alongside Derek. She hung back and joined me. We kept to the rear.

'There's something funny going on, Auntie.'

'Do you mean the arrival of the poet?'

'No. I mean besides that. Back at the house, when Rita, Derek and I arrived, Elisa asked me about Mr Murchison, his first name and how he looked. She knows him. And Carine hadn't told him we were coming here. He was under the impression he'd be staying at one of the pubs in Haworth.'

'Wishful thinking on his part probably. What makes you think Elisa knows him?'

'I don't just think that, I'm certain. I listened in the hall when Elisa was telling her mother about us. I know you say don't eavesdrop but you've done it plenty of times.'

'Only in the line of duty.' I like to encourage Harriet in good habits when possible. 'So you saw Mrs Varey?'

'No, just heard their voices. Elisa said, "Mam, it's him." And she said, "Get him out of this house or I'll batter him." Elisa wouldn't. She said they had to have our money and if he went we'd all go. Then there was a slamming sound and I heard the mother say, "I'm not coming out till they're gone."'

'Not coming out of where?'

'I don't know. Her voice was muffled as if she was speaking from the pantry.'

'It must have been the box bed. I heard a noise from there when I went in to ask for Mrs Varey. If you're right—'

'I am.'

'It's not surprising I didn't see her.'

Our conversation was cut short, because we were almost at the house. Top Withins came into view. We caught up with the others, and gathered round. Tobias glared at the house. 'I'm glad we didn't have to come any farther to see this. There's nothing special here. It's a house like any other.'

Edward was beside him. 'Where's the romance in your soul, Toby? This is the farmhouse, said to be Emily Brontë's inspiration for the home of the Earnshaw family in *Wuthering Heights*. Just as importantly, it provides a livelihood for an old soldier.'

Tobias said nothing.

Derek and Harriet went into the garden.

I called to them that someone lived there, and not to make nuisances of themselves.

'I read about him in the paper,' Edward said. 'He came out of the army unfit for his previous work and took a course in keeping chickens. Ernest Roddie is his name. It's the main reason I wanted to come.'

Tobias grunted. 'If this is the best he can do, Teddy, I pity the fellow.'

'I thought I'd see how Roddie is getting on. I've brought him a packet of smokes.' Edward took cigarettes from his pocket and a bar of chocolate.

The chickens had left their mark, with droppings and scratched up soil on what might once have been a garden. Of the old soldier, there was no sign.

A window pane was broken. There was no peat, coal or logs in the storage place.

The door was unlocked. Edward pushed it open and looked in. 'No one here. No furniture, except for a battered chair.' His disappointment was great. 'He didn't make a go of it then.'

Derek went in, calling back to us, 'Someone could make this habitable again.'

Tobias followed him.

Tobias came out first. 'I don't recommend it, ladies, the inside is rather insalubrious.'

Harriet immediately decided to explore and went inside.

Carine was looking out towards the hills beyond. Tobias touched her arm. 'Are you warm enough?'

When Harriet came from the deserted house, Edward gave her the chocolate. She offered it round but sharing melting chocolate proved difficult. She and Derek ate it.

Edward spoke with such command that the wind may have carried his voice to Haworth. 'Attention all! I know this is a photographic outing and not a literary pilgrimage but I have brought my copy of *Wuthering Heights*. Judge for yourselves whether this is truly Miss Emily's model, or whether she transposed some other house and kept the surrounding landscape.'

He read. Harriet, Derek and I listened. Carine was trying to, but Tobias took her arm and drew her away. Rita had taken off her wellington boots and socks and was wiggling her toes.

I walked up the slope at the side of the house and sat down on a large flat stone.

As we had walked, the wind seemed still. Now, sitting

low on my perching place, I could hear and feel the wind. Imitating the sound of the sea, it blew against the back of my neck, tickling my hair. Even had the wind not stirred today, I would have known its direction from the leaning of the stunted tree.

Perhaps Edward was one of those men who need an audience, or perhaps he was regretting his intrusion and hiding the awkwardness by resorting to what he knew best: words. Holding his copy of *Wuthering Heights*, he came to sit by me and Rita, and cleared his throat. 'The narrator is Mr Lockwood. You'll know that Wuthering Heights is the name of Mr Heathcliff's dwelling.'

'Yes, it's a favourite of mine, Edward,' I said. This did not prevent his continuing.

'"Wuthering" describes the wildness, "the atmospheric tumult to which its station is exposed in stormy weather. Pure, bracing ventilation they must have up there at all times, indeed."'

'It's certainly bracing,' I agreed.

Rita yawned.

I watched Carine and Tobias's faces as Edward read. After a moment, I had the feeling that although Rita and I were nearer to him, it was Carine and Tobias, pretending not to hear, who now listened most intently.

They stood side by side. In the same instant they turned to each other and a look I could not fathom came over them both.

Edward put away his book.

Rita whispered to me, 'We know nothing about Edward. He is either a resting actor or a defrocked clergyman.'

'He is a poet—'

'Ah, that explains it. I have decided to like him.'

'—and a teacher.'

Before me lay the still landscape all greens and browns. Below was a considerably larger house. No smoke came from the chimney. Perhaps it had been built for some younger son whose bones now rested in the churchyard.

Criss-crossing the moorland were dry stone walls, some beginning to fall into disrepair as men and women, defeated by time and progress, left the land.

A red kite flew low across the roof of the house, as if on some urgent mission. I felt sympathy with the visiting photographers Mr Porter described, who had come hoping to capture a bird in flight. Looking across the dip of the valley, I was tempted to bring out my camera but I knew the result would be disappointing.

Rita said quietly, 'Is he *the* poet? Carine's poet?'

'Yes.'

Now that we were here, no one quite knew what to do next. Everyone seemed dissatisfied with everyone else.

What I could do was take a photograph of someone in the house doorway. If this house stayed untenanted much longer, that door might soon be carried off, by vandals or ruined by the weather.

Tobias was taking a picture of the house. He had begun, confidentially, to explain to me a plan that he considered an invention. He would provide a projected backdrop for his and Carine's portraiture. That partly explained why he had decided to come. Of course there was also the small matter of keeping an eye on his wife and Derek. No one had anticipated the complication of the poet.

Derek, in a state of indecision, took out his camera and

put it away again. Probably he had a limited amount of film and was being cautious.

Edward passed round a bag of toffees.

Carine drew me aside. 'I'm sucking a toffee to keep from crying.'

'What's wrong?' I caught myself holding my breath.

'Edward hasn't said it, but he wants me to choose. He wants me to choose by Sunday. He is challenging Tobias, daring him to try and stop us.'

'How do you know?'

'I just do. My father came between us once. That can never happen again.'

There was something in her tone that struck me as odd. Discordant. It could never happen again because her father was dead. Perhaps she was connecting the thought that her father had died so soon after Edward had put in an appearance at our meeting in April. The person to stand in her way now was Tobias.

'Tobias has everything that is mine. If I leave him, winner takes all.'

What followed felt like a dream, as though nothing was quite real and there might be some sudden switch to another time and another place. Rita came over and listened, and caught the drift of our conversation. 'Carine, where has Edward been all this time?'

Carine said quietly, 'He teaches in a boys' school, less than thirty miles from here.'

As Edward took out his pocket Ensign, he pretended to be oblivious to the effect he had on everyone. Edward was photographing Tobias, as Tobias photographed the house. I had the mad thought that we could all copy him. There would be seven photographs of six photographers, photographing each other. If we stood in a circle, then would we all be included? No, there would always be six.

We might create a new collective noun: a shutter of photographers, a shudder of photographers, a blur of photographers.

What did each one of us look for as we held a camera lens between ourselves and the world?

I turned to Carine. 'Do you want to go home?'

After a long time, Carine said, 'Who was it told me that if in doubt about what to say and do, say nothing and do nothing?'

Rita said, 'The poet has a lovely voice. Does he sing tenor?'

I took out my camera. I would photograph Harriet, standing in the doorway of Top Withins. At the very least, I would be able to send it to my sister, and to Harriet's granny.

Tobias set up his tripod a little way from the house, and summoned us. 'This will be a group photograph for the society's records.'

Dutifully, we gathered.

He had a long cord attached to the camera so that he could include himself in the shot.

The seven of us formed a group, blinking against the sun.

Edward objected. 'If you're going to make us all look into the sun, we might as well be having the photograph taken in 1836 when no one was ever photographed with their eyes open.'

Tobias grumbled that no one else was offering to do this, but then he changed the angle. We shunted ourselves to face the camera.

The shutter clicked.

It was time to move on, downhill on the rough track that led to the waterfall. The space, the openness and the moorland breeze created a sense of solitude as we walked in single file, each wrapped in our own thoughts.

Tobias led the way. At Top Withins, he had played the part of a stranger to the area. I watched him. You have been this way before, Tobias. Carine knew. That was why she let him think they would stay in Haworth. The Vareys had not forgotten him.

From our spot above, the waterfall looked barely worth the walk, but we descended all the same, and I was glad we did.

We stepped into a bubble of tranquillity. The gentle melody of water urged us to listen as it flowed through and over pebbles. A perfect peace descended as we each found a spot to stand and stare, or sit and listen to the water music. For several serene moments, no one produced a camera.

Tobias had crossed the bridge to the other side of the stream. He broke the spell by opening his walking stick tripod, digging its feet into the ground to make it steady and fixing his *Noiram*. He looked into the view finder, across at Carine who had stayed on the other bank. For a moment it appeared that he intended to take her picture. He raised his head and waved at her with a dismissive motion. 'Sorry, darling, just move along a bit, I'm after the backdrop you know.'

That seemed to me deliberate, a deliberate slight.

Carine made no attempt to move. She looked at him in confusion but did not ask why he had set up his camera opposite her if he wanted a view of the scene. Derek came to her rescue, offering a hand onto the bank.

Guffawed is not a word I use lightly but that was what Tobias did. He guffawed and said, 'There's a shot! Gallant newspaper boy comes to his lady's aid.'

It must be a trial to Derek that he blushes so easily. He and Carine moved away.

Tobias clicked the shutter.

Rita whispered, 'I hope he drops his camera down a deep ravine. If there's any justice, he'll topple down after it.'

Edward was staring at Tobias. Because of the tightness of the skin on Edward's face, it was difficult to read an expression, yet watching him gave me a cold shiver. I felt as if I had looked into his soul. He loved Tobias because they had a shared history, had been comrades. He also loathed him.

Derek, reasserting himself, insisted the waterfall was tuneful but lacked visual interest. He can be a silly boy, never knowing when to say nothing.

Harriet had taken off her shoes and socks and splashed her way between the rocks until the water reached her calves. 'Anyone who doesn't paddle is a sissy!'

Derek and Rita accepted the challenge.

Rita squealed at the freezing temperature. 'If the Brontë kids went in for this, I'm not surprised they all died young.'

And then Edward chimed in, with a quote that he half whispered to Carine. '"Why am I so changed? Why does my blood rush into a hell of tumult at a few words? I'm sure I should be myself were I once among the heather on those hills".' He took her hand.

For a mad moment, the pair of them looked ready to run. Go on, I willed them. Just run, just go, be together.

They released each other's hands.

Harriet and Derek went on paddling, moving away downstream.

Carine clasped her arms around her chest. She stared at Edward. 'Don't!' She swayed slightly. 'I can't.'

Rita clambered from the stream and would have put her arm around Carine, but Carine moved away.

All this while, Tobias had been taking photographs.

Carine turned her back to us and picked up her camera bag. 'I'll go back now. I don't feel well.'

'Nonsense, darling.' Tobias folded his tripod back into a walking stick. He slid the *Noiram* into the canvas bag. 'We must press on. We three old friends have things to discuss.' He turned his head to look at Derek. He and Harriet were making their way back towards us and the bridge. 'Your water nymph and his friend won't lose their way. It's a well-trodden path to Haworth. I don't suppose you've told Teddy that you have a young swain ready to do your bidding.'

The three of them stood close to each other, Tobias and Edward on either side of Carine.

It was Carine who spoke first. 'Come on then. Let's hear what you have to say to each other.'

They set off walking uphill, on the path to Haworth.

Rita sat on the ground, drying between her toes with her woven stole.

Harriet and Derek put on their socks and shoes. The four of us set off along the path, walking briskly, shortening the distance between ourselves and Carine, Tobias and Edward who moved like sleepwalkers.

The path towards Haworth became steep, yet it was not that sending me dizzy. Suddenly I was in a story, not real life. Perhaps two stories, or a thousand. Carine's. Mine. Everything and everyone who had never really gone away, and yet came back.

People do come back, like ghosts. People come back from the dead. They are always hovering, waiting. Some return in flesh and blood. Others tantalise.

Rita walked beside me. As she walked, her bag bounced against her back. She pretends never to be cold but I saw the goose bumps on her arm in spite of the sun's warmth. We were keeping a reasonable pace, although it felt as if I dragged my feet through a swamp.

The altitude, or the bracken or heather, caused Rita to snuffle. She took out a hanky. 'Kate, are you thinking what I'm thinking?'

'Probably not.'

'I'm thinking that round the next bend there'll be a rather steep drop, there'll be a big shove and then instead of three people walking ahead of us, there will be two.'

'In that case I'd better take out my binoculars, in case I'm required to give evidence.'

'Do you have binoculars?'

'Yes.'

'I'm short-sighted. It would be up to you.'

'Thank you for the responsibility.'

We were overtaken by Harriet and Derek, unaware of the recent drama.

Harriet turned back and grinned. 'Not that it's a competition but we'll be there first.'

'If we don't see you, be by the Co-op at five o'clock.'

'Why the Co-op?' Harriet called back.

'There might be a need for chocolate.'

The two of them strode out, as if intending to win a bet. They soon overtook the Murchisons and Edward.

'It's Carine I'm worried about,' Rita said as we reached Haworth. 'Those two were pals, comrades. They might find some way of turning this situation into her fault.'

'You mean Edward will blame her for marrying someone else. Tobias will blame her for still holding the candle for Edward.'

'Something like that. Tobias fell on his feet, meeting Carine. Her father welcomed him with open arms, another man about the place. Knowing his beloved daughter would not be left alone in his precious studio. He was always afraid she would give it up.'

Only the pair of them, Tobias and Edward, knew what had really happened. Perhaps they were each telling their own version of the story to Carine as they walked.

It was a marvel to me that Carine could stay upright, putting one foot before the other.

The three of them went into the Black Bull.

Rita read my mind. 'At least they are in a public place. If they cause an affray, the landlord will call the police.'

'Not if he is serving out of hours.'

It's often the case that one doesn't like one's friend's friends, but I liked Rita.

'Rita, has there been new advice from your solicitor friend regarding Carine's father leaving everything to Tobias?'

'He has been very discreet, pretending he's seeking information for a case study. It's hopeless, Kate. The will was properly drawn up and there are no grounds for contesting. All he could suggest – in a vulgar fashion that

I won't repeat – was that Carine ensured her husband undertook strenuous physical acts sufficient to give himself a heart attack.'

After the warmth and the absurdities of the day, escaping the afternoon sunshine into the cool, hallowed atmosphere of the Church of St Michael and all Angels felt like a step back in time. Rita took a deep breath. 'Can't you just hear the echo of the Reverend Brontë preaching here, his children sitting in a row?'

'It's not the same church, Rita. The old church was demolished and this one rebuilt on the same site.'

'No matter. There's a trace in the air, a memory of prayer and hope and longing. I felt it on the banks of the Ganges and I feel it here. I must see the sisters' tombs.'

'There are no tombs. They weren't royalty, simply geniuses.'

Their resting place in the vault below was marked by a brass plate at the foot of a pillar. I had the odd thought that Anne Brontë would not mind being apart, in her grave in Scarborough. It's strange the way we think of the dead. I imagined Anne Brontë resigned herself to dying far from the moors, and finding herself by the sea. 'A change is as good as a rest. I'll have both for all eternity.'

Rita came to join me, speaking softly. 'I wonder what the family would make of the fact that the parsonage has been bought for the nation?'

'I imagine the sisters might laugh. Branwell would be thinking of the Black Bull, and should he have had that last pint, or gone home sooner and created a masterpiece.'

'Do you know I have a patron saint?' she asked.

'No I didn't.'

'Saint Rita is the patron of women in an unhappy marriage, women cruelly treated by their husbands. I wanted to light a candle for Carine, but it's not that kind of church.'

'Say a prayer instead.'

'I shall. It's interesting that there are bee boles at Ponden, because when my saint was an infant in her cradle, a swarm of bees flew into her mouth. They did her no harm, and that was how everyone knew that she was special.'

'How extraordinary.'

'Bees are regarded as messengers between our world and the world of the spirits, between the living and the dead.'

'Now that you mention it, I do remember something about that.'

'Kate, this may not be the place to tell you this, but I consulted my solicitor friend about divorce. Not for me, obviously, for Carine.'

'Oh?'

She interlaced her fingers and stretched her hands until her bones made a cracking sound. 'Carine could obtain a separation on the grounds of adultery, and not forgo her rights to support from her husband. It might be the only way she will have a small income from what should rightfully be hers.'

'Has Tobias been unfaithful?'

'Yes, regularly, once a week with a cook called Molly. She's buxom and fair, works at the Leeds Club and serves him pancakes.'

An elderly woman came into the church and hobbled towards the front.

'Rita, I think we should go outside.'

'I'll just say my prayer.'

Moments later, we walked out, turning our back on the churchyard, making our way to the parsonage garden. A gardener was clipping several untidy leaves from a shrub. We asked his permission to sit on the garden bench.

'Make most of it,' he said. 'It'll be trampled to billio tomorrow when hordes descend.'

The day had stayed warm. In the late afternoon sun, the flowers seemed to shimmer. There were hollyhocks, wall-flowers, geraniums, nasturtiums and a lavender bush that gave off the most perfect scent.

Rita reached out and touched the lavender. 'I love Carine, you know.'

'We all do.'

'No, I mean I really love her.'

'Ah.'

'Yes, "ah". What else is to be said?'

'Does she know?'

'How could she not? I've told her. It's not the same for her, and now that Edward has turned up I expect she'll go away with him.'

'I'm not so sure. We might have something looming that we dread, and it turns out not to be so terrible. Perhaps the reverse is true. We build up something romantic and astonishing, and it turns out to be commonplace.'

'Oh no, not for Carine. That bloomin' poet, he's the love of her life, I'm sure. Just as she is the love of mine.'

'Will she leave her studio?'

She made a dismissive sound. 'Tobias's studio now, with Carine's name on the place. He'll fall apart in no time.'

'This solicitor friend of yours—'

'Andrew.'

'Is he in love with you?'

'Oh no. He and I are kindred spirits. He is what they call a confirmed bachelor, disinclined towards ladies except as friends. He would invite me to legal functions, but I don't dress properly for that sort of thing.'

'Has he met Carine?'

'Of course, and he finds her fascinating but—'

'What?'

'He says she will do me no good, and something else I probably shouldn't repeat.'

'Well you must, now you've said that.'

'It's not something Andrew knows about directly, but from the senior partner in his practice. At the time Mrs Whitaker – Carine's mother – disappeared, it was suspected that Mr Whitaker had murdered her, but there was no proof. I have never said this to Carine, it would be too cruel and especially now. As if her life wasn't bad enough with Tobias, and then that ghost from the past turns up. I could kill those two.'

'Goodness, both of them?'

'Don't joke, Kate. I'm deadly serious.'

'Then you shouldn't have told me.'

'I wish I could be a fly on the wall in the Black Bull.'

Fourteen

The Black Bull

All this will pass, Carine told herself as she gazed into her glass of stout. I'm the filling in the sandwich, the fob on a watch chain, the glue on the envelope that cuts the tongue when you lick. And I'm not feeling well. She tried to remember a time when she did feel well but it was so long ago. Apart from the Sundays, apart from the Sundays when she began to meet Edward again.

After he came to the photographic society meeting, they both knew when and where to meet again, without needing to make arrangements. He was waiting for her, on Ilkley Moor, by the rock where he had carved their initials on that long ago day, when they were young.

They did not talk about the past, or the future, they simply loved one another. Enchantment took away words. Now that was changing.

She sat in the Black Bull, with her back to the wall. Tobias and Edward sat opposite her. Edward had lacked the courage to come back and claim her, but she forgave him. To sit opposite him was to be in the field of a magnet. He was disfigured. One eye was blind, but he was still her Edward. How could she go on thinking this, while knowing it was over? Perhaps it was not over. She was mistaken. She could have him for her own.

Tobias, flabby, awkward, a man with little talent, a man on the make, treacherous to his friend, had taken advantage of her when she was too tired to resist the blandishments of both him and her father. If Edward had lacked courage, so had she.

Tobias had fetched up at the door ten years ago, when she was out. Her father, recognising a fellow spirit, invited him in. By the time she came home, the story was off pat. 'I am sorry to tell you that your fiancé did not make it through.' She had asked Tobias what happened. He spun some yarn. If she remembered correctly, the story included Edward's 'last words'.

I'm a perfectly nice woman, she told herself. A perfectly reasonable woman. How did this happen to me, and today it is happening in such a public way.

'You are both to blame. Edward, you should have come to me.'

Edward scratched his neck. 'I was at low ebb. The way I looked, you wouldn't have wanted to see me.' He turned and glared at Tobias. 'He knew that. He should have told me to wait, to write to you, to explain.'

Tobias held his pint with both hands. 'It was kinder to tell her you were dead than say you needed to break the engagement because you looked a monster.'

'And I suppose you thought it kinder to tell me Carine had married, than to tell me that you jumped in yourself.

151

I've watched. I've seen. I've asked questions. Carine does all the work, you drink. You parade. You come up with schemes. I came back because I wanted to make sure Carine was all right. She's not.'

'Stop talking about me as if I'm not here.' Carine watched the landlord polish a glass. He was pretending not to look at them.

'She is all right. We have a life that suits us, isn't that right, Carine? We have an arrangement.'

It was not an arrangement. An arrangement was something that people entered into, agreed, came to a conclusion. Her life was simply something that happened. She wanted to go on believing that she and Edward had a love that would last forever. A growing feeling warned her against that hope. It was no longer enough to imagine herself as his poetic inspiration.

She stared at the two men opposite her, picturing them on a field thirty yards apart, holding pistols, prepared to fight a duel. It would be dawn, the sun just rising. They would each have a friend acting as their 'second'. That was how it was done. Tobias's second would be someone from the darts team at the Oak. Edward's second would be an old pal from the teacher training college, if any were still alive. When they both simultaneously shot each other through the heart, the seconds would cart them off. Or the seconds might run away. There would be some criminal charge for being a second in a duel, aiding and abetting, something of that sort. Yes, they would run away. 'Nothing to do with me, sergeant. I was just walking by and saw these dodgy geezers pointing revolvers at one another.' That would be Tobias's second. Edward's would be more eloquent. If the two men lay dead, it was Edward she would cradle in her arms, and stride across Tobias's body to get to him.

Edward swivelled on the bar stool. 'You're vainglorious and selfish, Toby. I should have known what you would do. You should have told her the truth, or my stupid lie that was meant to be kind, and you should have stepped away, like a friend and a gentleman. Instead, you looked at Carine, and that studio, and you wormed your way in. You saw a woman with a business coming to her, and you stepped in, began drinking the profits, and waited for her father to die.' He raised his eyes from his glass and gazed at Carine, his eyes as dark and lustrous as always, but only one that could see. 'I'm right aren't I, that's what he does?'

Carine couldn't help the small sound that came from her throat, the sound of a cornered animal. He should not be firing arrows at Tobias. He should take her in his arms, sweep her off, leave this place and never turn back. She was wrong to think it was over. They would always be together.

That was what he had pleaded for in Ilkley, for her simply never to go back. Leave everything. But how could she? Her name was on the window, her name that was also her grandmother's. The photograph of her mammy was on the wall. She was locked to that place, locked into it, yet she wanted to be free, to soar. She couldn't leave it for Tobias to spoil, to trample over.

Carine finished her drink. She looked at the sign on the wall that said Pork Pies and at the jar of Scotch eggs on the counter. If she did not eat something, she would not have the strength to go from this place. It wouldn't be acceptable to begin eating Mrs Varey's sandwiches in here. 'Would one of you get me a Scotch egg?'

Edward jumped to his feet. 'Another stout, Carine?'

She shook her head. Adoration was what she wanted.

Tobias raised his empty glass in a meaningful fashion.

Edward walked to the bar and called, 'Landlord!'

While he was out of earshot, Carine asked Tobias, 'Will you give me grounds for divorce?'

'Carine, we rub along. Don't listen to him. He is down on his luck. Why else would he turn up after all these years? He knows he made the wrong choice when he didn't come back to you. Once he knows the studio is mine now, he'll be off like a shot.' As an afterthought, he reached his hand across the table to grab for hers. 'I love you, Carine.'

'Most people love me. I'm a very nice woman, and competent too which is not always a winning combination.' She pulled her hand free. She wondered where it came from, this ice in her heart, this numbness of feeling. All this might be happening to a stranger.

Tobias stared at his empty glass. 'I don't understand you.'

'No. I don't suppose you do.'

Edward returned with the Scotch egg on a plate.

The barman followed him, bringing two pints. He took away Tobias's and Edward's empty glasses.

Carine considered the egg, thinking she should have ordered a pork pie. A pie would be easier to take out without a wrapping. She wouldn't stay here. If she ate that egg, she would be sick.

'Are you sure a Scotch egg is wise?' Tobias adopted his most solicitous tone. 'With your upset tummy?'

'It's too late,' she told them. 'It's too late for any of this.' She rose, trying to breathe evenly so as to stand without losing her balance. 'I'll leave you two to talk about old times. Don't come to blows. Ask the landlord to supply you with salt and pepper pots if you need to play out battles.' She pulled on her cream lace gloves.

It was Edward's turn now. He reached across and took her hand. 'Don't go yet.'

She waited.

He looked at her gloved fingers, as if for inspiration, and then at her. 'A master has left. There's a house vacant. I couldn't keep us on a poet's pence, but I have a good job. You'll be able to draw, paint and write your greetings card verses. The other wives will envy you.'

'Other wives? She's my wife.'

Carine stared at the ashtray, which for some reason allowed Edward to think he could go on talking, or perhaps he thought he did not need a reason to spill his words into the air. He was spoiling everything. By being here with Tobias, he was breaking their spell. How could a poet not understand that? She willed him to stop. He did not. It was as if he was asking Tobias's permission to claim her.

'I've saved every penny I've earned. You would want for nothing. Leave him. We'd need to say we are married, that's all. You're not happy. I see it in your eyes. If I'd come back and seen you happy, I would have gone away, I swear.'

Tobias bit his lip. 'Charming I'm sure. You told me to tell her you were dead.'

'I didn't mean it. It was one desperate day when I wanted to be dead. You should have known better.'

She held the edge of the table. 'You were a Bobby Dazzler, Edward. You should have had faith in me. I would always have seen the dazzler in you.'

'It was myself I lost faith in.'

Carine turned away, leaving the Scotch egg on the table. Let them fight over that. This was not how it was supposed to be. She and Edward should be on the moors, resting in the heather while he declared his undying love.

The brass handles on the pub door gleamed. She opened it. The door closed heavily behind her.

Fifteen

Haworth Churchyard

Harriet liked to look at gravestones, reading the names. What was sad about Haworth Churchyard was the number of tiny children named on huge stones, stones big enough to kill them had they been alive and unfortunate enough to have one fall on them. Some graves were marked with stone slabs, flat to the ground, that she stepped round. Other slabs were raised, like a table. Yet there was life, too. A crow perched on the branch of a tree whose leaves made a dappled pattern. A thoughtful tabby cat sat on the wall, watching two cockerels peck at the grass.

Derek wasn't looking properly. He was walking about, glancing at headstones, moving on. Harriet suspected he was bored. 'Are you fed up? Clear off if you want, don't mind me.'

'I'm not fed up. I'm wondering if there's anyone famous. I can't see the Brontës.'

'Go look in the church.'

'I won't be able to take a photograph in there.' He reached in his haversack and brought out a woollen cloak with hood. It was reversible, plain green and purple on one side and the same colours repeated in a tartan pattern on the other side. 'Will you pretend to be a Brontë? Stand by the gateway, sideways on, so that you could be a person from the last century.'

'Why?'

'I want to enter a competition. The theme is "waiting". Imagine you are waiting for someone.'

'If I do that, will you do something for me?'

'What?'

'Lie down on a tombstone and pretend to be dead.'

'Why would I do that?'

'I want a photograph that will make people look twice, something startling that will shock them. Instead of "oh, here we are again, one more picture of someone in their best hat standing by another person's motor car, someone in a bathing suit".'

He grinned, a little maliciously she thought. 'Or standing in a doorway.'

'Leave my Auntie Kate out of this. I like her doorway photos more than Carine's stupid flowers.'

'What do you have against Carine?'

She took the cloak from him. 'You haven't answered my question.'

'What question?'

'Will you pretend to be dead for me if I wear this for you?'

'As long as no one sees me lying there. It's probably against the rules. It's probably sacrilege.'

She put on the cloak. 'The dead won't mind. If they see

anything, if they know anything, it will break the monotony of being dead.'

They walked together to the church gate. She pulled up the hood. 'Where did you get this?'

'It's my gran's.'

He walked through the gate onto the street, took a few steps, judging the correct distance for the best photograph. He took out his Thornton-Pickard Reflex. 'Take the hood back, just a little. I don't mind your hair showing, but they wouldn't have had short hair.'

Harriet would have disliked posing on her own account but she was pleased to wear the cloak and be someone else, even if it did make her look more like a gran than a Brontë.

He took the picture. 'I'm good at getting it right first time.'

'You won't know that until it's developed.'

'Right, now if you go to the door of the parsonage, and stand as if you're about to go in.'

'Doorways, eh? Copycat.'

Harriet walked up to the parsonage gate. She liked those grey Georgian houses, the kind of house a child might draw. She glanced through the window. There was not much to see. Someone had been cleaning. There was a brush, mop and bucket.

'A Brontë wouldn't look through her own window. Act as if you're just about to open the door.'

'Which Brontë am I?'

'Branwell.'

'Ha ha, very funny I don't think.'

He took the picture. 'Just one more, in the garden, looking as if you're going to do something to a shrub or a flower.'

159

'Such as?'

'Anything you like, snip, sniff, dig with a pretend trowel.'

She took up what felt like an awkward pose. 'I bet you wish you were taking pictures of Carine.'

He took the picture. 'You make a better model for this setting.'

That was not the answer he was supposed to give. She took off the cloak and handed it back to him. 'Come on then. Be dead for me.'

He looked at his suit. 'Have you brought a clothes brush?'

'I've chosen the spot and I dusted it with a big hanky.' It was a lie but rain washed the slabs clean enough. She led the way, and pointed. 'You can fold your own cloak and lie on that if you like.'

He hesitated.

She took out her Kodak. 'Three photographs of me for one of you. Just do it, Derek.'

He set his haversack on the path and lay face down, nose flat against the slab.

'Turn round! Lie on your back and cross your hands on your chest like a proper corpse.'

'No! And I'm not turning my head. I don't want anyone to see me as a dead person.'

Harriet clicked the shutter the instant he stopped pro-testing. 'Now turn over. We made an agreement.'

'I don't know why you'd go in for shockers. It's bad taste.'

She snapped him again. 'Bad taste is being in love with someone old enough to be your mother.' She hadn't meant to say it. It just came out.

'What?' He got up. He stared at her. 'Who says that?'

'I do.'

'I'm not in love. I just think a lot about Carine.'

'That's obvious.'

'I wouldn't, if she were with someone half reasonable. Tobias is the most hateful person I have ever met. I do believe he tried to kill me, run me down. And anyway, what if I am in love?'

'That's more stupid than playing dead.'

'Better to play dead than to be dead.' As soon as he said that and saw her face, he knew it was the wrong thing, but she was a very annoying girl.

She was looking beyond him, into the little lane between the churchyard and the Sunday school.

He turned to see what or who she was looking at.

There was Carine, alone. Even from this distance, he saw that she was crying.

'You've forgotten your gran's cloak,' Harriet called, when Derek started to run. He did not hear her.

AMATEUR PHOTOGRAPHER MONTHLY

In his new series of amusing articles, Mr Sanity, Amateur Photographer, entertains readers of Amateur Photographer Monthly with tales about his photographic adventures.

A keen band of amateur photographers gathered at the railway station in the City of L. Destination: the wilds of Yorkshire and the queer little hill town of Haworth. For a long weekend these snap-happy individuals would give themselves over to the gentle art of photography with the aim of coming out on top in the picture stakes.

Intention: to capture for posterity some intensely dramatic view in the style of the old masters; to turn a wrinkled peasant into a work of art; to shake off the cares of life and find, for the briefest time, another way of seeing and to remember that life can be a bit of a lark. Far be it from your informant to claim that every single snapper on this outing wanted to win life's prize; that is simply the impression created.

Let me introduce you to our band. Beauty comes with a Beast, her sot of a husband. Our single lady is the Mystic. The Mystic, it transpires, does not deign to carry a camera. She vows to keep all images in her mind's eye. You will hear little of her for that reason. The young gel we will call the Undertaker. She likes nothing better than to take her box Brownie for an outing to the churchyard. An expired rabbit will be her delight.

Making their own way to our destination – separately your informant hastens to add – are the Poet and the Observer. The Poet searches for the perfect image that he will reduce to words. His heart holds secret yearnings, perhaps connected with the Beauty, the Mystic or the Observer. Certainly he loads his new Noiram so clumsily that he has the unique ability to ruin pictures before they are taken.

For the Observer, doors hold a particular fascination. She pretends that it is the subjects who stand in the doorway that gain her attention. Mr Sanity mistrusts this claim. Undertaker, the Observer's protégée, is almost left behind as the mists descend because she has found the skull of a ram, which discovery is her very heaven.

Beast has brought his tripod and portable darkroom. He has ambitious plans for pictures on a grand scale, taking in fifty miles of hills and dales. He will square these down to the size of a postcard and sell them for sixpence a time. Beauty has yet to take a picture. She is no doubt waiting to capture that magnificent moment when Beast tumbles over the rocks into the quarry below.

In such a setting, Mr Sanity turns to the historical. He had the good fortune to point his Vesta into the tunnel of time and capture a Miss Brontë waiting by the gate for her future, and turning into the door of the parsonage when that future evaded her.

[Editor's Note: Mr Sanity's Photographs on page 7]

Sixteen

A Last Supper

We gathered for supper, acting as if nothing unusual had happened that afternoon. Edward came in last and sat as far away from Tobias as possible, which given our small number was not very far. I sat with Tobias on my right, Rita on my left and Carine on her left. Derek sat opposite Tobias, with Harriet to his right and Edward beside Harriet.

The nearest Carine had come to confiding about the events of the day was to say to me that she did not want to sit next to Edward or Tobias.

Elisa brought dishes of rabbit soup to the table, two at a time. She made a point of pulling a funny rabbit face at Harriet.

Elisa seemed an odd young woman. I had tried to locate Mrs Varey and had begun to wonder whether Elisa had given her frequent doses of knock-out drops. Twice I had gone into the kitchen and Elisa had pointed to the box bed in the corner, made a shushing motion and indicated that her mother was asleep.

The sight of food put everyone in a state of muted cheerfulness, which was the best we might expect.

In a confidential voice, Tobias paused from slurping his soup. 'Kate, that idea I was telling you about earlier, you'll keep it to yourself?'

'It's flown out of my head already.'

Tobias's schemes grow in proportion to how much time he has on his hands, and how much alcohol he has drunk. I had no wish to be his confidante.

He leaned towards me. 'Your slide show gave me the notion. You'll have seen the way we set up the studio for portraits.'

'I've seen the way Carine arranges it.'

'It's a bit formal, you know, and artificial, not designed to put folk at their ease. While we're here, I'll take country scenes. I'll project them onto a solid screen using magnified glass. My subjects will look as if they are standing in an attractive landscape, a wood or by a stream. It would especially suit foreigners who want to send home a portrait against a backdrop that fits the idea of what is forever England.'

Elisa placed a large pie on the table, and a platter of boiled beetroot and green beans. She glared at Tobias with such a look of dislike that I wondered whether he had made a nuisance of himself with her. He does have something of a reputation.

Edward Chester, having arrived a couple of days before us, seemed to have made a good impression on Elisa. She cut the pie and dished it out, giving Edward the largest slice and an extra portion of beets and greens.

It had been an exhausting first day. At about ten o'clock,

the three of us who were sharing a room went up together. The stairs were dark and we had but one candle. Harriet climbed into her box bed for the purpose of changing into her nightie. 'I've a window in here but it's overgrown with ivy so I can't see out. The ivy across the pane looks like fingers.'

'Do you want to swap?'

She came out and hung her clothes over a chair. 'No. I like it in there.'

Rita had brought a large bottle of gin and a small bottle of Indian tonic. She came round with mugs, one for me and one for Harriet. 'With just a drop of gin for you, Harriet, to help you sleep.'

After the long day, and the gin, I expected to sleep well but lay on my back looking up at the ceiling. Something twinkled above. I could not at first tell what it was, and then I realised. It was a star.

As my eyes became accustomed to the darkness I tried to see whether any other parts of the roof were open to the sky, but I could not tell.

Harriet had gone quiet, which meant she was asleep.

Rita was murmuring, saying her prayers, and so I did not interrupt. They were odd prayers. Not that I was listening, but I could not help but hear her say, 'Oh Lord, seven of us came, let seven go home.'

I had not expected to hear mystic Rita talking to God, but perhaps she regarded this as an emergency. Did she have stars above her head, too, and expect the roof to fall in on us?

Now giving up on sleep, I got out of bed and walked about the room, looking at the ceiling. The roof was so full of holes it might as well have been open to the sky. Through every gap I could see stars, so many worlds above us and so far away.

Now I understood why Mrs Porter said she hoped it would not rain. Mrs Varey should have instructed us to bring large umbrellas, or tents.

In the corner of the room, I noticed an odd shape and went to look. It was a collection of buckets and bowls.

I climbed back into bed, now knowing what must be done in the event of a deluge.

No sooner had I closed my eyes than I heard the floorboards creak.

In a sleepy voice, Rita said, 'Carine!'

There was a shuffling and more creaking.

'Is Tobias snoring?'

Carine said, 'No, but I'll tell him he was.'

I stared at my own private star and tried to remember who it was said that stars were worlds. The answer came to me as I fell asleep.

My last thought as I tumbled into dreamland was that tomorrow would be Saturday, 4 August, a day of celebration. From tomorrow, the parsonage would be known as the Brontë Parsonage Museum.

But we visitors would remember the day for a very different reason.

When I rolled out of bed the next morning, Rita was already up and dressed. She bobbed down, looking at herself in the single blemished mirror, running a comb through her hair.

'There are no proper looking glasses in this place. Do you think they are expecting Count Dracula?'

Harriet took the comb from Rita. 'Your hair's sticking up at the back.'

We all managed to shuffle into place in time for a breakfast of bacon and eggs, bread and butter and dishes of blackberry and strawberry jam.

Derek was last to the table, his hair wet and slicked down, a cut on his chin from shaving. He wished us all good morning.

Everyone answered, except Tobias. I wondered had Tobias wakened and discovered Carine was not beside him. He may have made a false assumption about whose bed she shared last night.

Carine smiled. 'Derek! I thought I was going to have to come and wake you.'

Edward's Kodak was on the table. 'I don't know if it'll come out but I took a photo of Elisa Varey in the milking parlour earlier. She's from an old family. As we talked, I had this queer sensation that I'd stepped into the pages of *Tess of the D'Urbervilles*. It was that same story of a fine family toppling down the social scale, and a father convinced that something is due to them.'

Harriet stirred her tea somewhat aggressively. 'I like Elisa.'

'Oh, so do I,' Edward said quickly. 'She does not hold a grievance about the past, or carry a sense of entitlement. It is more a kind of obligation to let it be known that there is a history to her name. The sensation of being in *Tess of the D'Urbervilles* fled as soon as she started to tell me about a *Rin Tin Tin* showing at the Hippodrome.'

'Which *Rin Tin Tin*?' Harriet asked.

Edward could not remember.

When there are seven of you around a table, people offer up their own little titbits that don't always lead to a conversation.

I took charge of the teapot. Cups were handed along for a refill.

Harriet passed the milk. 'Did anyone see *The Ring* when it came out? I missed it and that's on in Keighley.'

Derek spread his jam very thickly. 'I liked it. But why do people who work in picture houses always go to the pictures on their evenings off?'

Rita took a sip of tea. 'I saw *The Ring* but I didn't like it. Too much boxing. There's a Charlie Chaplin on.'

'Which Charlie Chaplin?' Harriet asked. She dislikes vagueness when it comes to the discussion of pictures.

Rita shook her head.

Elisa brought in our packed lunches, wrapped in snowy white napkins. The invisible Mrs Varey was going to a lot of trouble. We represented a serious addition to her income and she was determined there would be no cause for complaint. Elisa whispered something to Harriet. Harriet laughed, and Elisa looked pleased with herself.

'What did she say?' I asked Harriet when Elisa had gone.

The others were now busy chatting. Harriet whispered her answer. 'She hasn't spat on my sandwich because she didn't know which was mine.'

'What a cheek!'

'No. She's saying she likes me. She's let me off for being nosey.'

I do not usually roll my eyes, but in Harriet's company they occasionally seem to roll of their own accord. 'What were you nosing about this time?'

She did not lower her voice. 'I just happened to look in the sideboard drawer, at a battered hat. And I was curious about some baby clothes. They'd never been worn.'

Tobias dropped his knife. It clattered to the stone floor making far too much noise for a knife.

Only later did that clattering sound echo in my thoughts, taking on a new and sinister significance.

I pushed back my chair. 'Come on everyone. We need to be early if we want a good viewing place.'

But first I decided to have a word with Elisa, or her mother. I did not know how I would approach this, but the story of the unworn baby clothes and Mr Porter's tale of the drowning of a young woman troubled me. It was late in the day, but if there was a connection to Tobias Murchison and his presence upset Elisa and Mrs Varey, he should leave. The Black Bull would suit him better.

I tapped on the kitchen door, and opened it. No Elisa. No Mrs Varey. A woman in a turban stood at the sink, washing dishes. 'Sorry to intrude, do you know where I might find Elisa or Mrs Varey?'

The woman hesitated just a little too long. She glanced, probably without meaning to, at the box bed. 'Elisa's off to see the do at the parsonage. Mrs Varey's not here.'

I remembered Harriet's account of the conversation between Elisa and her mother. Mrs Varey was almost certainly there, in her box bed – listening.

Seventeen

A Deadly Outing

We walked into Haworth along the road. Harriet wore her new navy blue sailor dress that she and Mrs Sugden had made, with V neck, squared collar and white linen bow tie. She wore navy Cuban heels and a neat little navy hat trimmed with white. Derek glanced at her several times. She ignored him and chatted to Rita who was decked out in her silks and bejewelled slippers.

The Haworth band had taken up a position outside the Yorkshire Penny Bank. They were playing 'Sweet Lass of Richmond Hill', with great gusto. Villagers turned out, dressed in their best. If some curmudgeonly persons decided to stay indoors, they were not missed. The place teemed with visitors, all attempting to come as close as possible to the parsonage.

Our small group stuck close because we planned to have a meal at the Fleece afterwards and had booked a table.

Walking the pavement became a difficult business. Visitors were arriving from all directions, on foot from the railway station, and on bicycles that wobbled as riders swerved to avoid pedestrians. More motor cars than had ever been seen in that place coughed their way up Main Street whose cobbles were not designed for motor transport.

Members of the Brontë Society, including my mother and father, with Mr and Mrs Porter, took up their allotted place in the garden at the front of the parsonage. The well-tended garden borders were so close on the churchyard that if a fierce wind demolished the wall, garden and graveyard would happily merge.

That morning, Tobias's knee had troubled him after yesterday's long walk. He had brought his silver-topped cane and leaned on it, giving him a slightly slanted stance that matched his view of life. 'What a palaver!'

Having achieved a good place on the path that led from the lane, we stayed put, apart from Harriet and Derek who manged to slither in and out of the crowd and return carrying bottles of ginger beer and bringing exciting news of increasing multitudes.

We would have a reasonable view of proceedings. It was astonishing to experience the sheer numbers and be part of such a crush. I felt this odd sensation of being in two different eras. There we were in the here and now, waiting, ready to witness the important event, a milestone for Haworth and all of us who loved the Brontës. Yet at the same time, I half expected Charlotte to come bustling through, asking who were all these people and why was there such a fuss.

The front door opened. There was a whisper and then a subdued round of applause as Sir James and Lady Roberts emerged, ushered by the President of the Brontë Society. Someone had placed a cordon a yard or so from the entrance, one of those obligatory plaited red silk cords that even the most modest villages keep tucked away for use on grand occasions.

The President introduced Sir James Roberts. We strained to hear his speech. A Haworth-born lad, young James Roberts had risen in the world but never forgot his roots or his days at the Haworth Sunday School. Sir James spoke of his boyhood. As a youngster he had listened to the sermons of the old and frail Reverend Patrick Brontë.

I missed a few words as Tobias, murmured – too loudly – 'Here it comes. This is where the self-made man tells us he pulled himself up by the cheeks of his own bum.'

I was not the only one to shush him.

It was left to Carine to tell her husband to behave himself and not show us up.

Sir James's words were few. He was honoured to play a small part in keeping alive the memory of that humble parson and his industrious and talented children.

As the crowd applauded, Carine whispered to Tobias and then to me, 'Kate, I'm going to sit in the Sunday school. I'll be sick if I stay in this crush.'

'I'll come with you.'

'No! Don't worry about me.'

The moment she moved, those ranked behind her shoved up, and so I could hardly have pushed my way through had I wanted to.

It was Lady Roberts's turn. She said a few words that I did not catch and then in a loud clear voice declared the Brontë Parsonage Museum open. She handed the deeds to Sir Edward Brotherton, President of the Brontë Society. A little girl gave Lady Roberts a sprig of heather. A murmur of excitement followed as Lady Roberts unlocked the door to the parsonage with what was whispered to be a golden key. The hurrahs and clapping began anew.

Tobias bumped against me. I thought his knee must have given way. The crowd was too dense for me to move. A woman nearby clutched her child close, wary of the push and crush. 'Come on, love, there's jam tarts in the Sunday school.' Excusing herself, she began to move away.

As the woman moved away, Tobias staggered and slumped against me. I turned. His mouth was open, his eyes wide. He would have slid to the ground except that the solid mass of the crowd held him steady.

I thought at first the cane had slipped from his grasp and that his gammy leg had given way. I moved to help him. He seemed to stare at me with eyes full of fear, but they were clouded by death. His lips were parted but he made no sound. He was no longer holding his stick. The silver top of the cane gleamed by his foot. I called to people to give way, let us have some air, though it was too late for air.

Still the crowd pinned us into intimacy. It was not until I managed to persuade those around to push back and give room that Tobias slumped.

I saw what had happened. Tobias's silver-topped cane was no normal aid to walking. It was a swordstick. The pressing of a catch had transformed it into a deadly weapon, letting loose a long sharp blade.

A trickle of blood stained his tweed jacket, making its way through a slit in the fabric, at the level of his heart.

Bending down beside him, I called out that we must have a doctor.

Edward took up the cry so loudly that it might have

echoed all around the little hill town. The cry was carried across the crowd and at some point the call changed from simply 'A doctor!' to 'Where's Dr McCracken?!'

As he lay on the ground, I put pressure on Tobias's wound, even while I knew that action must be in vain. 'Help's coming, Tobias.'

The blood from his wound was on my gloves and on the cuffs of my coat. I looked up at a blur of faces. A small group of strangers intermingled with our party. Someone, Edward I think, told people to stand back. Edward fell to his knees and was feeling for a pulse. Like me, he must have known it was too late.

Rita said, 'Where's Carine?'

Bizarrely, Derek was taking photographs. He stopped and pushed the camera in his pocket, turning to me and Edward. 'Your camera! I'm out of film.' No one responded. He took Harriet's camera from her hand but she did not notice. Harriet stood still as a statue, her face white. She was shaking. In that split-second way we have of knowing what must be done, I knew that it was Harriet who mattered now. She was sixteen. Only three years ago she had found her father's lifeless body. With childhood logic, she had blamed herself for his murder.

I stood and took off my coat. Derek was clicking Harriet's camera again. 'Derek, stop it!' I put my coat around Harriet's shoulders. She had refused to wear a coat that morning, saying it was August, saying it was summer, wanting to show off her new dress.

Derek paused in his snapping. In a sulky voice, he said, 'I'm photographing the scene of the crime and the witnesses.'

Someone in the crowd yelled at him to show respect or he would fetch him a clout around the ear 'ole.

Subdued, Derek took a cloak from his haversack. He and Edward laid it carefully over Tobias, covering his face.

At that moment, our earlier cries for a doctor were answered. A murmur went up that the doctor was here. There were calls of, 'Here's the doctor,' and 'Make way for Dr McCracken!'

I spoke to Derek. 'Don't let anyone touch the swordstick.'

In a state of disbelief, I glanced at Harriet. White and shaken, she shivered as I pushed my way through the crowd, my arm around her, leading her towards the garden.

Had she seen what happened? We were pushing against the tide as people were leaving the garden. I only hoped that Mother and Mrs Porter would still be there. Most people ignored us but several gave us an odd look. They had heard the commotion and the call for a doctor. It is likely that both Harriet and I looked as if we needed medical attention.

Someone was calling through a megaphone. His hollow voice floated around our heads like fog. It might as well have been a foreign tongue.

Through a gap in the crowd, I caught a glimpse of Mother's cherry-coloured hat. At the same time, she must have seen us. She rose from the bench and hurried towards me. 'Darling, what's wrong?'

'Something happened.'

'We saw the commotion and thought we should wait as you'd know where to find us.'

I did not answer straight away. Words would not come, and when they did it was not an answer to her question. 'Where's Dad? I have to take Harriet home.'

Mother put her arms around Harriet and drew her to the bench. 'He and Mr Porter have gone to help. They heard the call for a doctor.'

Mrs Porter fumbled in her bag, as she made room for me to sit down. 'I have smelling salts.'

Mother opened her bag. 'The girl needs brandy.'

Though Harriet tried to resist, Mother made her take a sip from a small flask. Mrs Porter waved smelling salts under Harriet's nose, and then put them on the bench beside me.

Mother said quietly, 'Let me take your gloves.'

I glanced at my gloves and saw that they were soaked in Tobias's blood. I peeled them off. She whipped them into a handkerchief and then passed me the brandy. I took a sip, and another, but handed back the smelling salts, preferring not to start a sneezing fit.

Only a dozen or so people were now in the garden. Heads turned as the police officer with the megaphone strode towards our bench. He greeted Mrs Porter politely, nodded to Mother in the same manner and then turned to me. 'Mrs Shackleton?'

'Yes.'

'I believe you are responsible for the party of visitors that is staying at Ponden Hall.'

Now that our chairman was dead, I suppose I was the person responsible for our party, though 'party' seemed an odd word under the circumstances. 'I arranged the visit, officer.'

'Then I should like a word with you, please.'

He walked a little closer to the wall that separated garden and churchyard. I followed him. He placed the megaphone wide side down on the grass and took a notebook from his pocket.

'Your full name and address, please, madam.'

I answered, wondering whether he would have been so polite if I had not been in Mrs Porter's company.

'Now I must ask you to hand over your camera, Mrs Shackleton.'

For the moment I had forgotten I ever had a camera and must have looked at him blankly.

'I will give you a receipt and it will be returned to you in due course.'

I handed him the camera.

'And you are staying at Ponden Hall?'

'That is correct.'

'Until?'

'I want to take my niece home today, as soon as possible.'

'Please do not leave the area until you have police permission.' He glanced at Mrs Porter, as if including her in his remark would ensure that we did not run off.

'Is that necessary, officer? I can give you my address in Leeds.'

'We will try to detain you no longer than necessary. You were the first person to give aid to the unfortunate gentleman. Would you please tell me what you saw?'

Of course I had seen nothing that could possibly be of use. I was aware of something having happened to Tobias only when it was too late. 'I didn't see what happened to Mr Murchison. He collapsed onto me, nearly took me down. I saw straight away that there was nothing to be done. He was wounded. It was afterwards that I took in the sight of his swordstick, lying on the ground.'

He made a brief note. 'And the young lady on the bench?'

'She is my niece, Harriet Armstrong, staying at my address.' I gave him Harriet's full name, and her family address. He hesitated, and then went to Harriet. 'Miss Armstrong?' She looked up at him, without answering. 'Harriet?'

She nodded. 'Just for the record, Harriet, can you confirm your address?'

Harriet did not speak, and then she began to give the address she had before she and her mother and brother moved away from Great Applewick.

'Harriet,' I said gently, 'you moved from there. And then you came to stay with me.'

'Oh yes.' It took her a moment to think of her mother's address, and mine.

Mrs Porter intervened. 'Constable Briggs, the child has had a shock. Please take Mrs Shackleton's word, and give her and the girl time to recover.'

Constable Briggs nodded. 'Very well, Mrs Porter.' He glanced at Harriet. 'Do you have a camera with you, Miss Armstrong?'

This she understood and seemed relieved to be able to answer a question. 'Yes.' She looked in her bag. 'It's not there.'

'Derek took it,' I said. 'Derek Blondell.'

The constable consulted his notebook, where perhaps he had a note that Derek had handed over two cameras. He snapped his notebook closed. 'Miss Armstrong, why did Mr Blondell take your camera?'

Harriet seemed not to be taking in the conversation. When the constable repeated the question, she said, 'I don't know.'

Speaking quietly and out of Harriet's earshot, I said, 'I believe he thought it a good idea to take photographs at the scene, and must have run out of film.'

The policeman looked momentarily pleased at this initiative and then puzzled. His eyebrows rose of their own accord. 'Why would he do that?'

'Derek works for a newspaper.' Realising this made Derek sound like a fiendish and insensitive opportunist, I added, 'Perhaps it was an instinctive reaction.'

Before I had time to clarify, the constable asked, 'Is he a reporter, or a photographer for the paper?'

'Neither. He works in the library.' It was my turn to ask a question. 'Constable, where are my friends?'

'Mrs Murchison is being taken care of by my sergeant's wife, Mrs Hudson. At Dr McCracken's suggestion, she will rest and be helped with her state of shock until the doctor can examine her. Miss Rufus and the gentlemen are in the Sunday school tea room.'

'And our husbands?' Mrs Porter asked. 'Mrs Hood and I should like to return to my home.'

'Mr Porter and Mr Hood have offered their services to Sergeant Hudson.'

Mrs Porter rose. 'I suppose I ought to have known they would be needed.'

The constable once more turned to me. 'Sergeant Hudson is arranging for a room to be reserved above the Co-operative Society store. Statements will be taken from those in the vicinity of the accident. Would you please make yourself available there, along with your friends?'

That made the decision for me, about where I must go next. He had not asked the most important question, and so

I volunteered the information. 'When I saw Mr Murchison's wound, I applied pressure, to try and stop the bleeding.' Mother gave me a nudge to shut up. 'Mother has my gloves. They are covered in his blood.'

'My daughter spent five years nursing,' Mother explained. 'You have an evidence bag, Constable?' He looked at her blankly. 'Then I shall give the gloves to your inspector.'

'We have no inspector in Haworth. It's a sergeant's posting.'

'Sergeant then,' Mrs Porter said. 'Thank you, Constable Briggs.'

He acknowledged his dismissal.

Mother spoke to Mrs Porter in a low voice and they came to some agreement.

Mother put her arm around Harriet. 'Come on, Harriet. We're going to take you back to Laverall Hall. You need a lie down in a warm bed with a hot water bottle.' She looked at me. 'Do what you need to do, Kate. Harriet will be safe with us.' Then in a low voice she added, 'I'm surprised at you. Never answer a question that has not been asked.'

'I could hardly withhold evidence.'

She smiled. 'Don't worry about Harriet. Think of yourself now.'

I knew Harriet would be well looked after, but I also felt responsible towards those in my party, as the constable had put it. Carine was in the company of strangers and might be in no fit state to deal with what was to come. My three other companions, Edward, Rita and Derek, who must all at some point have wished Tobias dead, would be feeling wretched now that he had died in such a dreadful manner.

Why had he chosen to use a swordstick as an aid, and how could he possibly have mortally wounded himself with the wretched thing?

I wanted to escape to Laverall Hall with my mother and Harriet, but the constable had left me no choice. Now I must find out more about what had happened, and give comfort to my friends. After all, I was the one who had decided we should forgo all other suggestions and plump for Ponden Hall and this momentous event in Haworth.

Mrs Porter gave me a tight smile. 'It's all right, Kate, I can drive our car and take your mother and Harriet back to the hall.'

Mother and I exchanged a glance. She drew Harriet close to her. Harriet did not resist. I knew that she would be better off staying at Laverall Hall. 'Go with your Auntie Ginny, Harriet. She'll take good care of you. I'll come for you just as soon as I can.'

Eighteen

View Finder

The Haworth Co-operative Society took up a long stretch of the main street, with its separate shops: butcher's, bakery and general store. Alongside the shops, a separate door stood open, with stone steps leading to the floor above. This must be where the police were taking statements. Now that Harriet was safely with my mother and Mrs Porter, I could think more clearly about the horror of what had just happened, and how and why.

As I entered the building, Derek was on his way down. He looked pale and gaunt. His eyes were unusually bright. Something dreadful, and yet exciting, had happened.

'Kate, you'll make that constable listen. He won't say what will happen to my film, or when I'll get my camera back.'

'Be patient. He'll follow procedures. Your photographs of the scene could be useful.'

'I suppose.'

'Did you see anything, Derek? Did you see what happened?'

He ran his hands through his hair. 'No! I wish I had. I wasn't taking notice of any of us. I was watching the presentation and listening to the speeches.'

'We all were.'

'I saw Carine go, looking a bit queasy, and I didn't even offer to go with her. I wanted to be able to write an eye-witness account of the parsonage event.' He slapped his forehead. 'I'll be a laughing stock at the newspaper.'

'You were standing behind me. When you get back to Ponden, would you do a diagram of who was on either side of you, and who was roundabout?'

'You're investigating, aren't you?'

'I'm simply anticipating what will be needed when the detectives step in.'

'I was just asked that very question. I couldn't remember who was where. It was so crowded. There was a bit of pushing and shoving, people trying to see what was going on. I saw Elisa, and a chap with her. They were near us.'

'Give yourself time. It's a shock for all of us. When you're alone, and feeling calm, you might remember.'

Something else popped into my head. It was the thought that Tobias Murchison ought not to have come to Stanbury. He should certainly not have stayed at Ponden Hall and risked a hostile reception. It would be just like him to imagine that he had changed over the years and would not be recognised. Or perhaps he thought that Elisa's sister had kept their affair a secret.

'Derek, in the Kardomah, when we were deciding on a destination—'

'You were deciding.'

'Did you ever find out who else suggested Ponden Hall?'

'No, I forgot all about it. Why?'

'No particular reason.'

Of course, I did have a particular reason for asking. Harriet had said that Tobias expected to be staying at the Black Bull, yet he had fallen in with going to Ponden Hall. There had been one other suggestion, 'Ponden, Stanbury'. I had thought it might be Carine's handwriting. Yet the person most likely to know of Tobias's past sins was his comrade and former pal, Edward Chester.

At that moment a woman in a blue hat came down the stairs. Derek waited until she had gone.

'The police officer wanted to know what kind of man he was. I told him the truth.'

'And did you tell the officer that you are in love with Carine?'

He blushed. 'Well, no.'

'You probably didn't need to. It must have been written all over your face.' For a moment it looked as if he might stamp his foot and walk away. I remembered that he is still so young, and felt a kind of pity for him. 'Be careful, Derek.'

'I have nothing to be careful about. In fact, I'm going to be very objective and telephone in a report to my newspaper. I don't suppose you can give me change for the telephone?'

'No I can't. If you telephone in – and you must seek police permission first – give the briefest details and leave it to someone with more experience.'

He frowned. 'Why, when I'm on the spot?'

'Go back to Ponden Hall, lie down in a dark room and try and come up with your diagram of the scene.'

The room above the Co-operative Store looked as if it might be used as a dance hall or a meeting room. Three trestle tables had been set in a row; two were manned.

To my surprise, I saw that my father sat behind one of the tables, speaking to a young man in baggy trousers and tweed jacket.

Dad caught my eye and gave the slightest of nods towards the nearby table. Naturally, it would not be quite the thing for me to give a witness statement to my own father.

Behind the other table was the constable I had talked to in the parsonage garden. He was interviewing Elisa Varey.

I waited my turn.

As she left, Elisa gave me a nod and indicated that she would wait for me.

After a polite enquiry after Harriet's welfare, and a thank you for my co-operation, the constable began his questions.

'Mrs Shackleton, it has been suggested that Mr Murchison fell on his sword. As someone close to him, would you regard that as a possibility?'

It was not a good question. Close might mean personally close, as in well-acquainted, and having an insight into Tobias's mental state. It might also mean physically close, as in near enough to stab him.

'I suppose that is a possibility, officer, but he would have had to stoop to lean onto the blade. Unless his stick retracts, it would have struck the people in front. We were in such a crush. My only thought, when I realised what had happened, was to stop the bleeding. But he was beyond help.'

'Why was that?'

'The blade had pierced his heart.'

Now that I gathered these images and put these experiences into words, I knew that if Tobias had turned his swordstick upside down and fallen onto it, the chances of the blade piercing his heart would have been slim. I tried to picture how a person might aim for his own heart, especially in such a crowd, but the image would not come. If Tobias had fallen, or been stabbed by his own secret sword, it would probably have caught him under the chin.

I waited until Constable Briggs had finished writing.

'There's something else.'

'Go on.'

'When I saw the swordstick on the ground, the blade was shining and unmarked. No one could have stabbed himself in his own heart, withdrawn the blade, and wiped it clean.'

'You are very observant, Mrs Shackleton.'

He made this sound more like an accusation than a compliment. I indicated my dad, seated at the nearby table. 'Then I'm my father's daughter.'

Elisa Varey was waiting for me in the street.

'Will I show you the way back along the road, Mrs Shackleton?'

'You mean to walk?'

'Yes.'

'I'm going to take the bus. If we walk along the road, we'd risk being run down by departing motorists.' The truth was that I could not face a two-mile walk. I also needed to talk to Edward and Rita. I felt sure they must be back at Ponden Hall by now.

'I'll show you to the bus stop. I suppose you're feeling the loss of your friend.'

Was she testing me? I thought of the conversation

between Mrs Varey and Elisa that Harriet had reported to me. Mrs Varey had retreated to her box bed, unable to bring herself to look upon the man she blamed for her elder daughter's death. If I were to find out anything from the Vareys, they would need to know that I was not enquiring out of compassion for Tobias.

'It's a dreadful thing to have happened, and I'm sorry for his death, but Tobias Murchison wasn't my friend.'

By the time we reached the stop, the bus was about to leave. I took Elisa's arm. 'Come on, take the bus with me.' I had change in my pocket and paid our fares.

Elisa knew the driver. They talked together, in low voices, while I went to sit down. When the bus set off, she joined me. We were silent for the first part of the journey. Yet there is something about sitting side by side on a bus that eventually may lead to chatting. If I began by asking questions, she would clam up.

Eventually, Elisa said, 'I came into Haworth on a cart with Timmy Preston. Timmy works for us on the farm. He was supposed to be taking me back.'

'Did you miss each other?'

'No. He came to find me, to tell me. He has been enrolled as a special constable, him and a few others.'

'I wonder what they will be doing as special constables?' I said.

She shook her head. 'Search me. When a child was lost, everyone searched. We had no need for specials. They're full of self-importance when they take that on, swear an oath and think themselves sheriffs of Nottingham.'

I smiled. 'You don't have such a great opinion of them.'

'Oh, they'll do what's expected.'

'The local sergeant and constable sprang into action quickly enough.'

'That's true. And I suppose you know about these things. I heard your parents are staying with the Porters and that your father is in the force.'

'Yes.' Now I understood. She knew a special constable, I knew the top brass. Was it too strange to imagine that she was trying to enrol me as her informant? We verged on dangerous ground, and for the rest of the journey said little.

I looked out of the window. The sun had retreated. Buildings took on a dark and brooding appearance. The stretches of land between seemed barren and empty. After our long silence, Elisa asked me, 'How did he die? I was too far away to see.'

'Even though I was so close that he fell on me, I can't say for certain.' She would already know, or soon find out from Timmy Preston, that Tobias was stabbed. It would be better to tell her what would become common knowledge. 'He was wounded through the heart.'

But perhaps you already know that, I thought. You were close enough to kill.

She might well have been speaking to herself, her voice was so low. 'His heart?'

The bus driver, who took little notice of official stops, dropped us at the end of Ponden Lane. Elisa had fallen into silence. We walked together, passing the mill, keeping pace along the side of the reservoir.

A change swept through her. It was not simply that she grew quiet, but as if the core of her being had shut down. I do not know how to describe the feeling of walking beside her. Some impulse made me take her arm. The thought came to me that if she was a candle, she would have been snuffed out.

The feeling lasted until we had passed the reservoir. She ought not to live here, if this was the effect that the stretch of water had. 'Is it always like this for you?' I asked.

'Not always. You have heard the story, I suppose?'

'Mr Porter told me about a young woman who died here. Am I right in thinking she was your sister?'

'Yes, my big sister. Picotee.'

'What a beautiful name.'

'She was a beautiful sister. And it would never have happened if he hadn't got her in the family way and then left her. She shouldn't have been hoisting herself over that damn wall.' The anger felt raw, as if all this happened only yesterday.

'And the man?'

'She never told us his last name, only that he was called Toby. I teased her. I said his surname must be Jug.'

'It was Tobias Murchison?'

'Yes.'

'How can you be sure?'

'He was a cyclist in those days. I found out his name a long while ago. One of the old Keighley Cycling Club members came here for tea. He told me his name.'

'Is that why your mother has not put in an appearance? She and I exchanged letters. I expected to meet her.'

'I wrote the letters.'

'If you don't mind my saying, you seem to do everything.'

She shrugged. 'I have help from women in the village. Mam sometimes needs to keep to her bed. My brother takes care of the sheep, and we have Timmy, when he is not commandeered by the police.'

We were almost back at the Hall when I released her arm. She squeezed my hand in a brief acknowledgement.

'Elisa, perhaps someday you will be able to move away from here.'

She shook her head. 'Not now. It's fate, though once the Vareys had a fine name. We held land, farms, woods and a grand house.'

'Where was that?'

'Across the border, not so far off. I went to look once.' We had reached the courtyard. Elisa said quietly, 'And before you think it – or if you do think it – I didn't kill that man.' She stretched out her hands. 'Do you see blood?' She wore no gloves, and nor did I. Mine had been covered with Tobias's blood when I tried to stem the flow.

Nineteen

The Camper

Edward and Derek were seated on the stone bench in the courtyard. Derek was nursing a colourful woollen cloak. He raised it towards Elisa, who ignored him.

Edward stood. 'Kate, I'm sorry I didn't wait for you.' He turned to Elisa. 'Elisa, is there anything I can do to help you?'

Elisa paused and looked at him. 'A certain account has been settled.' She strode to the door.

Derek jumped up and followed her. 'Elisa, excuse me, Elisa, the thing is my gran's cloak needs washing. There is a stain.'

Elisa looked at the cloak. 'You can't easily wash that.'

'The stain is only in one place.'

'What's the stain?'

'Blood. We covered Mr Murchison with it.'

'His blood?'

'Yes.'

'Wash it yerself.'

'But you'll have to tell me what to do. Is it salt you put on it? Gran will go mad with me.'

His words were lost to us as he followed Elisa into the house.

Edward sat down again.

The afternoon stillness was broken only by the sound of the bees in the kitchen garden behind us.

Edward lit a cigarette. 'I can't believe this has happened. I don't understand how Toby and I could come through what we did, those four years of death and injury and mayhem, only for him to die on a sunny Saturday near a parsonage garden.'

'It's shocking. And poor Carine, I can't imagine how she's feeling.'

He lowered his head. 'She was in the refreshment room in the Sunday school when we carried in Toby's body. I'll never forget the look on her face, the pain, and it was as if I wasn't there.'

'What happened?'

'The police sergeant's wife, Mrs Hudson, she's a very motherly sort of woman, took Carine under her wing. The doctor said she should be taken somewhere to rest. He would visit her later. She's at the police house on Mill Hey.'

'Did anyone else go with her?'

'I wanted to and so did Rita, but we were kept there to answer a few questions. Afterwards, Rita went to see if she could stay with Carine.' He blew a smoke ring. 'What about Harriet? Where is she?'

'With my mother, at the Porters' house in Stanbury.'

Like Carine, she was in the house of a police officer, albeit a retired one – if police officers can ever truly be said to have retired.

Each of us must be under suspicion.

A man in plus fours came into the courtyard with two children, asking, 'Are they serving teas?'

I advised him to knock on the door.

'Edward, where do you teach?'

'Giggleswick School.'

'I was there last year, to witness the eclipse. I don't remember seeing you.'

'I started in September.'

The question came from my lips without a plan, seeming like a guess. 'September? That was when you began to see Carine again.'

'She told you?'

She had not told me that they began to see each other. She told me only that she had spotted him, and watched him catch the tram. I know what I would have done in that situation. I would have run after the tram and jumped on. She must have done the same, and decided to say nothing to any of us.

'Ilkley must have been a convenient place for you to meet, a halfway point?'

'Yes. We meant to keep it secret, but I suppose all women talk to their friends.'

He was right. Carine and I did talk, but she had not told me the truth.

'You and I should talk, Edward.' I stood. 'If we stay here, Derek will come to ask for help with the bloodstain on his gran's cloak, or Rita will come back, with blisters on her feet.'

'I could do with stretching my legs.'

We crossed the path.

He held the gate for me. 'Carine said you have a knack for investigation. And now I know who you are. The science master told me about you, but not your name. His star pupil met you last year.'

'A brilliant young man.'

In the field, sturdy saplings grew alongside the sparse trees. It felt blissfully peaceful after the turmoil of the day.

Edward spoke first. 'You think Toby was murdered.'

'Don't you? And whether he was or not, you may not see another September in Giggleswick. I should think masters are meant to avoid scandal.'

We walked down to the stream. 'You are right. A scandal may be imminent. I have been asked by the police not to leave the area until my address has been verified.'

'We all have to stay here for the present.'

There is something calming about the sound of water lapping over rocks and pebbles. Humans must have listened to that sound since time immemorial and would go on doing so until the end of time. I bobbed down and scooped a drink. It was the purest water I had ever tasted.

Edward copied me. 'Elisa says the spring supplies the house. It would almost be worth moving here for this.'

'Perhaps there'll be a vacancy at Stanbury School.'

He smiled. 'A Miss Greenwood was appointed head in 1920. I doubt that she is ready to retire in favour of a scandal-drenched poet with scarred countenance and a motive for murder.'

'And are you guilty?'

'I'm guilty of a great deal, and as a soldier I know how to kill.'

'Most of us know where the heart is.'

'Not everyone. People do miss.' He threw a pebble into the stream. 'Toby was my mate, my comrade. We stuck by each other all through that nasty show. He dragged me to safety. I would have died if not for him. There was a time when I wished he had let me die.'

'And yet?'

'He came to see me in hospital. I was covered in bandages. I had no idea why I was still alive. I thought my face had been entirely blown away. Those doctors, one in particular, he was a marvel. But that didn't stop me reeling when I saw myself in a mirror with my one good eye.'

At least you came back, I wanted to say. But one does not say that.

'My clothes had been burned off me. I'm not going to tell you, we don't, do we?'

He already had, but perhaps he thought he was talking to himself.

'It wasn't me in that mirror. It was some freak, some monster. The surgeon operated again, and again. I couldn't have gone back to Carine.'

'Why not?'

'She is exquisite now, but you should have seen her then, the bloom on her. I couldn't have presented myself and kept her to her promise. We would have been beauty and the beast.'

'No, no beast, Edward. You were still yourself.'

'I gave Tobias my poems, to give to Carine, and said to tell her that I died.'

'Is that what he did?'

'He refused at first, but I said that if he did not, I would die. I would turn my face to the wall and die.'

'And did Tobias deliver your poems, and your message?'

'He did. For a while I wondered had I done the right thing. One of the nurses was very friendly, and kind to me. She said of course I would recover and of course I must teach. She made me laugh. She said no artist would want me for the subject of a romantic oil painting, but what man with a vocation to follow would waste precious time sitting for an artist?' Edward smiled at the memory. 'I've often thought of that nurse. Now I see her differently. Her words were a declaration of kindness, even of love. Then, I thought only of Carine. Part of me hoped that Tobias would tell her the truth, or that if he did tell her my lie she would not believe him.'

'You shouldn't have done it. You shouldn't have lied to her.'

'I know. I was a coward.' He sighed. 'I waited to hear, from her, or from Tobias. I still have the letter Tobias wrote to me. Do you want to hear it?'

'No.'

He took out the letter. 'How's this then for treachery?'

He cleared his throat and read in an impeccable tone that so mimicked Tobias's pitch that, in a different life, Edward might have become an actor.

'"*Dear old chap, I did as you asked and called to see Carine. The news of your passing hit her hard. She will treasure your poems. Her father urged her to be brave, as you had been brave. I am sorry not to report sooner as you must have been wandering.*"'

Here he paused and lowered the letter as if he had tired of reading. 'He meant wondering, not wandering.'

When I did not comment, he continued. 'Here's the best bit. "*I have heard now that she is making a new life. The best of wishes, old fellow, from your old comrade, Toby.*"'

'He didn't say that the new life was with him. When I found out they'd married, I asked myself, How could she marry a man who says you must have been wandering, when he means wondering?'

'I suppose that might be a common mistake.'

'And do you know what she said yesterday? That I was her Bobby Dazzler and I always would have been her Bobby Dazzler.'

He cupped his hands and took another drink from the stream.

'Did you kill Tobias?'

'That's what the policeman asked me.'

'That's what they asked, or will ask, all of us, one way or another.'

'Do you think I would tell them if I did?'

'Did you know that Tobias had a swordstick?'

'I've seen one like it before.' Placing the palms of his hands on his cheeks, he rubbed his fingertips across his cheekbones.

'Does your face hurt?'

'Yes. It helps when I splash it with water, or put on ointment at night. I like this stream here. I had a notion earlier that if I lived here and washed my face in the stream for a year and a day, I'd be my old self again.'

'That's an attractive notion.'

'I've read too many stories.' He stood. 'Fancy a walk?'

'Yes, but before we do—'

'What?'

'I'll be doing this, and asking the others. Will you draw a diagram of where we were all standing when Tobias died? You were behind us.'

'I was.'

'And anyone else who was within your sight.'

'For you?'

'Why not? As you say, I have a knack for investigation.'

He reached out a hand. For once I was glad to be helped to my feet.

Ahead of us, between the trees, the young camper, whose tent I'd seen earlier, was packing up his gear. He poured water from a billycan onto the embers of the fire. He wiped a knife on the grass. So busy was he in his preparations to leave, that he did not notice us until we were almost beside him.

'Where next?' Edward called.

The camper, surprised to see us, mumbled a few words about setting off for the coast.

I could see why Edward might be a good teacher. He switched into schoolmaster mode, wishing the student good luck for his coming term. 'You'll be able to tell your teachers and fellow students that you were in Haworth when the Brontë Museum came into being.'

'I didn't go,' the lad said. 'I'm more interested in the geology than in museums and books.'

'Odd,' Edward said. 'I thought I saw you there.'

The lad shook his head. He lifted his great pack onto his back.

I also thought I had seen him in Haworth. 'Something happened today in Haworth. The police may want to speak to you about it.'

'I told you, I wasn't there.'

'They are speaking to everyone, you better tell us your name and where you are going.'

He shrugged. 'My name's John, but I've nothing to say to the police, and I've a long way to go before nightfall.'

He spoke with an accent from the other side of the Pennines, though I could not place it. He was from 'over the border', where the Vareys, according to Elisa, had their ancestral home. Perhaps he had been engaged as an avenging angel. Short of making a citizen's arrest – for which there would be no grounds – or asking Edward to tie him to a tree, there was nothing I could do, except watch which direction he went and memorise his thin face, slightly crooked nose and light brown hair.

'It's an odd time of day to be setting off for the coast,' Edward said as we watched him go.

'And he seemed anxious. I'm going to ask Elisa about him.'

When we returned to the house, Elisa was preparing the evening meal.

'Your camper has gone.'

She shrugged. 'They come and go.'

'Isn't it an odd time to be setting off?'

'I suppose so.'

'He said his name was John. Do you know his last name, or where he's from?'

'We don't ask for a life story. People know we allow campers in the wood. They turn up, pay for their pitch, and that's an end of it.'

Twenty

Perspective

The evening was still light with a gentle breeze as I set off to retrace the path to Stanbury and call at Laverall Hall. I wanted to see how Harriet was. I hoped that by tomorrow I should be allowed to take her home. Under the circumstances, Dad might trust me with his precious motor car.

I had walked only a few yards when Constable Briggs, who had taken my statement earlier, came into view, strenuously pedalling his bicycle up the bumpy track. He wobbled to a stop as we drew closer.

'Mrs Shackleton, just the person. I have a message for you from Mr Porter and Mr Hood.'

'I was just on my way to the Porters.'

'Well they say to tell you that Harriet is sleeping, and to leave her be for tonight.'

'Thanks for telling me but I'll still just walk along there and speak to my mother.'

'Ah, there's the thing, madam. Your mother sends her good wishes and she will see you tomorrow. My sergeant asks if you will ensure that all of your party remain at Ponden Hall tonight.'

'Three of us are here, Derek Blondell, Mr Chester and I. Mrs Murchison and Miss Rufus haven't returned from Haworth.'

'Mrs Murchison is under the doctor's care for the present. Miss Rufus is on her way back. I saw her to the bus stop myself. We would all be much obliged if you would ensure that your party remain in residence here. Certain enquiries need to be made, you see.'

'Yes, I see.' So we were all under suspicion, and one of us might make a run for it. It would be awkward for my dad and Mr Porter if I kicked up a fuss. If I were in the shoes of the police, I would be of the same mind. Keep the outsiders in one place.

'Very well, Mr Briggs.'

After all, if Harriet were sleeping and Dad and Mr Porter providing assistance to the local police, it would be best to keep away from Laverall Hall tonight. There would be nothing I could do. 'Do you intend to come up to Ponden Hall, or shall I pass on your request?'

'I'll walk up with you, madam. I'm to stay at the hall for the present.'

'You are guarding us?'

'Oh no, nothing like that, just a presence you know, a police presence, for reassurance.'

He began to wheel his bike. We walked back up together.

'Constable, this may be nothing, but there was a camper in the wood who was in Haworth this afternoon, I'm sure of it, and yet he said he was not. He packed up and left about twenty minutes ago.'

'And did he say where he was going?'

'He was a little vague, but said he was on his way to the coast.'

'Funny time to set off.'

'That's what I thought.'

Mr Briggs took out his notebook and pencil. I gave him a description of the camper. 'He said his name is John and that he is a student of geology.'

'I'll pass that on. Thank you.'

We continued our walk to the house. As we drew closer, Mr Briggs asked, 'Anything else about this camper?'

'He was putting out his fire . . . '

'Very commendable.'

' . . . and wiping a knife on the grass.'

The constable perked up, either at the mention of a mystery camper wiping a knife on the grass, or Elisa banging the gong and calling, 'Supper's ready.'

We stepped inside.

Constable Briggs wished Elisa good evening. He explained that he had been asked to come along, and just make sure everyone was safe and well, and would remain safe and well overnight.

Elisa eyed him suspiciously. 'We're well enough, Mr Briggs.'

'That's good. Then I'll pay my respects to your mother.'

'Mam's not up to seeing you. She's having one of her poorly days.'

'I need a word with her about stopping with you all until morning.'

'Bed and breakfast, when you've a home to go to?'

'I won't be in the way and you can all rest easy in your beds.'

It was very tactful of him to say so, since we were the

ones who might be thought to pose a danger to the good people of Haworth and Stanbury. I could just imagine what certain people might say. Everything was all right, until that lot came along.

'Elisa, since Constable Briggs is going to stay with us for a while, might he join us for supper?'

'We cooked for seven and we're down to three — four if Miss Rufus comes back — so I don't see why not.'

Mr Briggs looked pleased at this. 'Thank you. I'll just see who's about.' He walked along the hall, his boots clattering on the tiles.

When he was out of hearing, Elisa thrashed the gong again, and then turned to me. 'Mam's in a bit of a knot with herself. She thinks you won't want to settle up, what with the weekend turning out as it has.'

'Of course we'll settle up. Give me your account now if you like.' I followed her along the corridor and into the kitchen. 'Smells good.'

Elisa pointed to the box bed by the fireplace. Indicating that we must not disturb the occupant, she put a finger to her lips and whispered. 'Pork and beans.'

The door to the box bed was tightly shut. If Mrs Varey truly was in the box, she must be running out of air by now.

I whispered back. 'Give us ten more minutes for the food, Elisa. Rita is on her way back.'

Derek appeared. 'Elisa, did you see that I put my gran's cloak in your washing place?'

Elisa forgot we were supposed to be whispering. 'I'm not touching anything that's touched that man.'

'Can anyone else do it? I'll pay.'

'Go find someone else. I've a meal to serve.' Elisa handed me our account. A voice from the box bed said, 'And we don't want nowt of that man in this house and no mention of his name.'

Derek and I escaped into the corridor. 'Don't worry about the cloak. Your gran won't need it in August.'

'That's why I knew I could borrow it, but she'll spot a stain straight away..'

'My housekeeper is a genius at removing blood stains.' I had no idea whether this was true but strongly suspected that such a task would be well within Mrs Sugden's capabilities.

'Oh thank you. That's a weight off my mind.'

'Now there's something you can do for me.'

'Just say the word.'

'First, go meet Rita. She should be coming up the lane from the bus. She will be feeling miserable and worn out.'

His worried look fled, now that he had something to do.

'Right-o, and what else?'

'I want to talk to you later. Did you do that diagram for me?'

'I did.' He took out his notebook and tore out the page.

'You and I will see whether we can shed some light on this whole dreadful business.'

'I'm off then.' He marched along the corridor, like a man with a mission of national importance.

As it turned out, Constable Briggs was the only one of us with anything like an appetite. I sat beside Rita urging her to at least taste the leek and potato soup, and to have another spoonful, and another. She had come back looking pale and exhausted. One of her bejewelled shoes was torn and she had lost her shawl.

'The sergeant's wife wouldn't let me see Carine, said she was sleeping. I don't know what they must have given her because I know she's a light sleeper. They wouldn't let me in.'

Edward glanced at Rita. He put down his spoon. 'A sleep and a forgetting.'

Rita glared at him. 'What's that supposed to mean? Where were you?' She turned to Derek. 'And where were you? If we had all gone and demanded to be let in, we might have taken her home.'

Mr Briggs said gently, 'No one will be going home yet, Miss Rufus. You will be asked to stay only for as long as the enquiry into this tragic incident continues. Mrs Murchison will be well looked after.'

'She needs her friends. Kate stayed with Harriet and we should have stayed with Carine.'

There was a crocheted blanket on a rocking chair by the fireplace. I went to fetch it, and put it around Rita's shoulders. 'It wouldn't have done Carine any good to come back here, Rita. We'll wait for her. She'll know that we're waiting.'

This seemed to calm her a little.

When the pork and beans came, we made an effort.

After a couple of mouthfuls, Rita began to cry onto her plate.

Edward, stony-faced, put down his knife and fork.

There was a long pause, and then we all tried again.

Rita left the table first. Edward took the tray of dishes and carried it into the kitchen. Constable Briggs followed.

Derek and I were left alone.

'We might not have long, Derek. Thanks for your sketch of where we all were.'

'Does it tell you anything?'

'Not yet, but at least we've done this while our memories are fresh. There's something I want to ask you. Why did Tobias agree to come here?'

'I don't know. He seemed to think he was going to the Black Bull. To be honest, I don't think he was all that keen on going anywhere but he doesn't trust Carine, doesn't want her out of his sight. I've no idea why.'

That seemed a bit rich, coming from him. I pressed on. 'Did you have any other thoughts about who else may have suggested Stanbury for our outing? When we were in the Kardomah, making plans, one of the slips of paper was for Ponden.'

He hesitated just a little too long. 'I really don't remember. Is it important?'

'Probably not. I'm just trying to understand.'

'What is there to understand? Tobias stabbed himself with his own swordstick.' He gulped, and struggled to control his emotions. 'It could only be because Edward came back, and he knew. He knew Carine loved Edward.'

Constable Briggs came back, just in time to catch these words.

'Mrs Shackleton, Mr Blondell, I have spoken to the others and I'll say this to you. I'd be obliged if everyone remains in the house for the rest of the night.'

When I went upstairs, Rita was lying on her bed, shivering. 'I'm freezing, Kate. I haven't been warm all day.'

I went across to her. She was worryingly cold. 'Why

didn't you say?' I took a cardigan and a pair of socks from my trunk. 'Sit up and put these on. I'll find a bed warmer.' I helped her into the cardigan. She was shivering so much that she could not pull on the socks. I put them on for her. 'Here.' I took the hip flask from my satchel.

'It's my own fault,' she said, taking a sip of brandy. 'August, I thought. My holiday, I thought, silk will be perfect.'

'Yes, well it might be, in Jaipur.'

'It's the monsoon season.' She looked as if she might burst into tears. 'I lost my shawl somewhere along the way. My lovely shoes are ruined. They were a gift from the woman who made my shalwar kameez.'

'I'll go down and find bed warmers. When I've warmed up the box bed, move across there. Harriet's not coming back tonight.'

Elisa was sitting at the kitchen table with Edward, deep in conversation. I got the impression she was trying to divert him from his misery, and perhaps his guilt.

'I don't know how many generations ago,' she was saying, 'but we were landowners, and had a coat of arms.'

'Elisa, Miss Rufus is very cold. Will you find bed warmers for her, please?'

Edward pushed back his chair. 'Let me help. Is she ill?'

'I believe she's caught a chill. It can't have helped that she was chasing about, worrying over Carine while in a shocked state herself.'

Elisa lifted a copper bed warmer from a hook on the wall and took it to the fire. Edward scooped a shovel of hot coals into it. 'There's another,' Elisa said, taking an earthenware pot from a shelf. 'Kettle's boiled. I'll fill this one.'

Moments later, the three of us went upstairs, Elisa leading the way with the earthenware pot, me following, and Edward behind me with the long-handled bed warmer.

He waited by the door while Elisa and I went to the box bed. I drew back the covers. Elisa wrapped the copper warmer in a little blanket she had brought, while speaking reassuringly to Rita. 'Come across. You'll be cosy in here. It's a good little spot.' Encouraged, Rita crossed the room. Elisa plumped the pillow. 'Nobody ever died in this bed. Well, not for a long time. I always think it's best if dying people take to a bed with two sides. It's very awkward otherwise.' She turned to me. 'There's a nice big eiderdown in the Murchisons' room.'

'I'll get it.'

Edward was still by the door, now writing in a notebook. He must have felt a poem coming on. 'Where is the Murchisons' room?' I asked.

Edward wrote one more word. He put the notebook in his pocket. 'I'll show you. It's just beyond the library.'

I had meant to look at the library. The day's events had put that thought from my mind.

Edward went into his own room and lit a candle, because there was no natural light in the corridor. I followed him.

He flung open the door to the Murchisons' room. 'This is it. There's another room beyond, the peat loft Elisa says.'

It was strange to go into the bedroom where Tobias had spent the last night of his life. 'It's enormous, Edward. I've been in stately homes where the main bedroom is smaller than this.'

'It was the room where the weaving was done. That's why there are so many windows.'

Perhaps it was the literary shadows cast by previous

visitors to the house but as I approached the double bed, I felt like a thief. *A Christmas Carol* came to mind, and the scene where Scrooge watches what passes after his death, seeing the cleaning woman steal his belongings. Somehow it felt wrong to be here, taking the eiderdown from the bed where Tobias and Carine had slept.

'Let me.' Edward handed me the candle and took the unwieldy eiderdown, folding it into a manageable size.

We walked back along the corridor. 'Anything else I can do, Kate?'

'I should think Rita will start to warm up now. You might ask Elisa to bring her a hot drink in about half an hour, and a piece of that cake none of us ate.'

There was a movement somewhere nearby, perhaps at the bottom of the stairs. In a house this old and this size, it was difficult to know where the sounds came from.

'That'll be our resident policeman,' Edward said quietly. 'He has taken off his boots and found himself a comfortable chair in the parlour. From there he'll be slip-sliding on patrol, expecting to hear something incriminating.'

'Will you keep him talking for ten minutes? I want to talk to Rita, and I'd rather he wasn't earwigging.'

'I'm sure he'll be pleased to speak to me. I must be suspect number one.'

'It was sitting on that wall outside the police house that made me so cold.' Rita was propped up on pillows in the box bed. 'I've made such a mess of everything.'

I climbed in at the other end and we faced each other. 'You haven't made a mess of anything. You tried to help Carine.'

'I wanted to go in there, and I told the sergeant's wife that I killed Tobias.'

'And did you?'

'No, but they weren't to know that. She could have made a citizen's arrest and let me in.'

'What did she do?'

'Kept me waiting there and she must have sent for that blooming constable because he turned up on his bike and asked me questions. How did I kill him, what was the weapon, did anyone see me do it.'

'Did you say you used the swordstick?'

'What swordstick?'

'Tobias had a swordstick.'

'Someone might have told me that. I said scissors, a pair of scissors that I threw away. Of course that wasn't good enough. He wanted to know where I'd thrown them. Well I didn't know, did I? "Take me to the place," he said. Next thing I know we're at the bus stop. "You have a choice," he said. "You can get the next bus to Ponden or I'll have one of the specials take you to the lock-up in Keighley. You'll be charged with wasting police time."' She crossed her arms around her chest and hugged herself. 'That's gratitude for you.'

'Where were you standing in relation to Tobias?'

'Behind him.'

'Can you remember who was nearby? If I give you a sheet of paper, could you draw who was standing where?'

'No. I'm hopeless at drawing and my brain is numb.'

'But you might try, just matchstick figures, to see who—'

'Who might have done it?'

'Yes.'

'If you like.'

'I know it was a bit of a crush.'

'Well it was and so many strangers near us. It wasn't like a queue for the tram where everyone knows their own and everyone else's places. There was shuffling about and taller people letting a little one stand in front and some child being lifted up onto a dad's shoulders.'

I left Rita with a page from my notebook and a pencil and went downstairs to chase up the hot drink.

Edward was in the kitchen. He and Elisa stopped talking as I went in.

Elisa looked up. 'I'll make Miss Rufus a cup of cocoa.'

'Thank you.' This felt a little awkward, knowing the angel of vengeance in the form of Mrs Varey might still be in the box bed, but I said it anyway. 'I know our statements were taken in a hurried fashion today, but I believe it would be useful if we each did a sketch of where we were standing when Tobias died.'

The voice came from the box bed. 'Keep your pencils behind your ears until whoever did for that man is safely out of reach.'

Twenty-one

Telling the Bees

Our bedroom was at the end of a corridor. Next door was what I thought was Edward and Derek's room, to share. The door was ajar and I saw that it opened onto yet another short corridor, with a room on either side. So they each had a small room that afforded privacy.

I went into our bedroom, where Rita slept soundlessly in the box bed. All was still and quiet. As I lay in my narrow bed, looking at the stars through the holes in the ceiling, I found something new to worry about. Edward had spoken of himself as a possible suspect. Derek was also an obvious choice. Devoted to Carine and convinced of her mistreatment, had he taken it upon himself to find a way to stab Tobias?

Derek could be annoying and self-centred, but he was very young. I had heard him clatter his boots to the floor as he made ready for bed. Earlier, he had hidden himself away in the library.

It must have been three o'clock in the morning when

I heard a creaking floorboard, and then silence. Shortly after, a door opened. I heard a low whispering. One voice was Edward's. I got out of bed, thinking Carine might have come back, and yet how could she at this hour of the night, or early morning?

A door closed. The low murmur of voices came from the landing, sufficiently close to distinguish who was speaking.

It was Edward and Elisa. This was no romantic tryst. From Elisa, I caught the words, 'dead' and 'someone must tell them'.

Edward spoke again, and then there was silence.

A new and extraordinary thought occurred to me. Edward, as he admitted himself, had good cause to take revenge against Tobias. Elisa still ached for the loss of her sister, and blamed Tobias. When we arrived, Edward had already been here two days, or that was as much as he admitted. Perhaps these two had concocted some devilish plan, and may have drawn in others to help. Timmy Preston, the farm labourer, was now acting as a special constable. He would be in a position to tamper with evidence. And what of the mysterious Mrs Varey, who was supposedly hidden in the box bed? What vengeance might she have taken for her dead daughter and unborn grandchild?

I clearly heard Edward say, 'I'm ready.'

He must have gone back into his room, to put on coat and shoes. Once more, the floorboards creaked.

I lit a candle.

If I saw anyone else, at the pictures, or in a scene from a book, about to do what I was going to do, I would say to them, 'No! Don't do it. You are alone and it's the middle of the night.'

I put on my coat. I had left my boots by the front door. By the time I stepped onto the landing, all was silent. Much as I tried to be quiet, I disturbed Rita. She spoke to me from the box bed, and I thought this must be how a voice would sound if a corpse spoke from its coffin.

'Kate, is that you?'

'Yes.'

'Has something happened? Have they brought Carine back?'

'Nothing has happened. I just want a glass of water. Try and sleep.'

'It was my premonition, you know, that seven of us would come here and only six of us would return, and now I'm glad.'

'Why?'

'If six of us return, that will mean we are not under suspicion. Tobias did away with himself.'

'Perhaps you are right. Are you warm enough now?'

'Yes, but I won't sleep easily until I know that Carine is all right.'

'I'm sure we will see her tomorrow.'

Shielding the flame of the candle against the draught as I opened the door, I walked into the corridor. I paused on the landing and listened. Whoever it was had gone downstairs. In this labyrinthine place I might never catch up with them.

Slowly, I made my way down the staircase, tiptoed through the main hall. I glanced into the parlour. Constable Briggs was comfortably ensconced in the rocking chair by the fire, snoring in a tuneful rhythm of snort and blow. He had left the door ajar, presumably to hear any comings and goings. There was no one in the short part of the L shaped hall, but I heard a sound as I reached the turning. Someone was opening the front door.

Fortunately for me, the pair at the door did not look round. I was right. It was Edward and Elisa. They went outside.

I put on my boots, and tried the door. It was unlocked. I snuffed my candle and set it on the ledge by the side of the door. It would be a waste of a candle to keep it burning, and would alert anyone else who found sleep difficult and wandered through the house. I would have to find my way back upstairs in the dark. I opened the door, just a crack.

I saw the two of them cross the track that led into the field.

I followed, half expecting to find myself witnessing the meeting of a coven of villagers who had conspired in murder, and now needed to agree their stories.

It was lighter outside than indoors. The moon was on the wane but still bright, lighting the path. It was a mild night, too, though as I watched and thought what I must do, a dark cloud crossed the moon. Surely this was the moment when an owl would hoot.

Silence.

I was hoping for something other than a dastardly conspiracy. Perhaps that lone camper had changed his mind about moving on from this site, and Elisa had seen him. If so, the constable could question him in the morning.

They had dutifully closed the gate. As I opened it, something flitted close to my head. I immediately raised my hands to protect myself from what must be a bat. I had a sudden vision of claws sinking into my scalp and never letting go. The thing disappeared. This was madness. What if someone, the constable, had deliberately left the door unlocked to see who might come and go, someone who might behave in a suspicious manner?

Anyone could feign snoring.

The night was not silent. Something moved through the undergrowth, perhaps a hedgehog or a fox. With that acute hearing that night brings, I listened to the stream below. There was another sound, a little way ahead. Someone spoke.

I followed the sound, keeping to the edge of the path. Trees provided cover for me. I moved from the path and instantly realised the disadvantage of doing so. Twigs cracked beneath my feet.

I edged closer. I should have guessed that there was something between Edward and Elisa. He had sung her praises, thinking her some heroine from a Thomas Hardy novel. She held a lantern. She handed him strips of what appeared to be dark cloth.

Elisa spoke in a clear voice, I suppose to ensure that the bees would hear and understand. Without drawing closer, I caught every word.

'He is dead. He brought us nothing but shame and sorrow that man, that Tobias Murchison. He will trouble us no more. When you go into the next world, tell my sister and her little one that the man who brought her trouble is busy picking his way to hell through thorns and burning coals. We are free of him. All is well and so do not leave us, dear bees. We need your honey.'

Edward began what must have been an ad hoc recitation. The words bees, and honey, and how welcome bees and honey were, formed part of the verse.

Now was the time for me to step back smartly, the way I had come, and to gain entry to the house before they did. Elisa would surely lock the door once they had completed their mission.

The door creaked open as I re-entered the house. I took off my boots, which had been clean. If anyone looked now, they would see that the soles were covered in soil and bits of grass. I remembered to pick up my candle, though unlit it was not much use. I felt my way back along the corridor, the only light coming from the fire in the hall.

The constable was still snoring. I wondered whether Elisa had put something in his drink, or whether he simply felt secure in the knowledge that all his suspects were safely tucked away for the night.

By keeping a hand on the wall, I reached the stairs, stubbing my toe on the first step. The stairs creaked. What an idiot! I remembered there was a flashlight in my trunk and I had not unpacked it. I managed to find my way back into the room where Rita slept soundly.

I sat on the edge of my bed, considering what to do. I could confront Edward and Elisa with suspicions of some collusion. They would, of course, deny it.

As Rita had reminded me when we spoke in the church, bees were regarded as messengers between the living and the dead. The Ponden hives were an important part of day-to-day survival for those whose living came from the land, and from nature. It was natural that a countrywoman like Elisa would follow the tradition of placating the hive.

I heard Edward on the landing. He must be carrying his shoes, but creaking floorboards betrayed him.

For now, I would hold tonight's experience in my

thoughts and wait to see how it might fit the bigger picture, if ever I could see that bigger picture.

No sooner had I climbed exhausted into bed than a drop of rain blessed my forehead, and another, and another. I was almost too tired to move. From my knowledge of the many holes in the ceiling, I knew it would be a long task to place buckets and basins everywhere.

One more drop of rain, and I left my bed. I clambered into the box bed, at the bottom end, carefully fitting my legs to one side of Rita's. Sleep was a long time coming.

Twenty-two

What the Bloodhound Found

Mrs Sugden would never dream of working on the Sabbath Day. A person needed some private time in the week: a spell in chapel with someone else doing the talking; a walk along the lane without carrying a shopping basket; a window-shopping tour of the town, without rush, push, clatter.

On the other hand, she had no intention of losing the generous payment promised by Tobias Murchison for the simple task of cleaning a cellar. She and Jim Sykes had made a start. Jim had shoved that pile of film into sacks. He had been ready to do the same with the old newspapers, but she had set them aside for firelighters. She had swept the floor. How good he would be with a mop and bucket was an open question but he had brushed away the cobwebs on the ceiling.

The chapel would have to manage without her today. God would understand that a woman had obligations. She had thought to do the cleaning at the crack of dawn on Monday, but the Murchisons might take it into their heads to come back early and she would miss the opportunity to bottom that cellar. Also, Jim might find himself otherwise occupied, if one of those insurance companies required his services.

She let herself into the studio. The mop and bucket stood in the back room, where she had left them. Mrs Sugden put several handfuls of borax in the bucket and set a kettle to boil.

Jim arrived, bringing that dog, which she thought he would leave with Rosie.

'Rosie's going to see her sister,' Sykes explained.

The dog came up, slobbering, wagging its tail. Mrs Sugden patted its head. 'I've seen you. Now go lie down and try not to get in the way.'

'And the kids have gone to the park with their friends.' Jim unclipped the animal's leash. 'They wanted to take the dog but I daren't risk it. Now that they're grown, they go in a café. They'd fasten him outside for someone to steal and then where would we be?'

The dog followed them down the stairs into the cellar. Sykes set to, filling another sack with rubbish.

Mrs Sugden went round the ledges with a dustpan and brush. The dog joined in, scratching at the flags by the wall, making a nuisance of itself.

'It's not doing any harm,' Sykes said, as he took a couple of bags of rubbish upstairs. 'Let it be.'

The cellar floor took two lots of mopping to have it anything like approaching clean. 'Right, Jim, that's done. I'll go up and make a pot of tea. I brought us a bite to eat.'

'I'll be up in a minute then.'

Jim didn't come when she called. She drank her tea

and ate a sandwich. The dog appeared. 'Mr Sykes fed up of you, is he?' The dog jumped up on its hind legs and ate a sandwich. 'Is that what they teach you at the police dog school?' She shut it outside with a bowl of water, hoping it wouldn't try and jump the fence. She had no idea how you teach a dog to stay put. At least with a cat you can smear butter on its paws.

When she had eaten a slice of cake, she went back down to the cellar to see what Sykes was up to.

'What on earth are you doing, Jim?' The room was full of dust. 'You've made a bigger mess than when we started.' The loose plaster set her coughing.

'Look at this! Come over here!' he said. He had scraped the plaster off the wall along from the darkroom.

'Are you mad? We're doing this for two guineas. We'll have to pay him a fiver for ruining his wall.'

'I've a friend who's a plasterer. He'll skim it back to how it was, only better. They won't know the difference. It wasn't even distempered, just plain plaster. Only I wanted to see what was attracting the dog. He's been at this wall on and off since we arrived.'

She saw that there was a door in the wall. It had been plastered over and plaster still clung to it. Sykes was trying to open it, but there was no handle.

'Leave it alone, Jim. You'll be letting yourself into next door's property.'

He was edging a big screwdriver all the way down the side of the door, and then he put his shoulder to it and shoved. More plaster came falling down. He shoved again and the door opened. He took a torch and shone it.

'You meant to do this, you monkey, or you wouldn't have

brought that torch. You've made a right mess now. There'll be no putting this right by morning.'

He closed the door. 'I think you're right, Mrs Sugden. There'll be no way of turning the clock back on this.'

'What is it?'

His voice was hoarse. The dust had got to him. 'Go upstairs. I need to telephone the police.' His face was pale, and not just from the plaster dust.

She went back up the stairs. Sykes followed. Mrs Sugden had put a saucer on his tea to keep it warm. She brought it through. 'Have a drink or your voice will fail you.'

He took a drink and picked up the telephone receiver.

It was less than ten minutes before there was a rap on the shop door. Mrs Sugden recognised the young constable who had brought the dog on Friday.

Sykes let him in. 'Are you on your own, constable?'

'I am. I didn't expect anyone to be here. I'm told that the owners are away.'

'Well, who do you think rang?' Sykes asked.

'No one rang. My sergeant sent me, to gain entry. I thought I might have to come to the back door but I saw you through the window.'

'I rang,' Sykes said. 'And this is a CID job.'

'Well it might be, but not yet. Now I need to know your names.'

Mrs Sugden intervened. 'Just a minute! Are you telling us that you're not here because Mr Sykes just rang to report something?'

'No.' He took out his notebook. 'Your names, please.'

'You know who I am. You left the dog with me.'

'Just your names, please, and your business here.'

'Well, what do you want? I'm Mrs Sugden, same as I was yesterday. I've been left to look after this studio for the weekend, so will you please tell me what brings you here if it wasn't in answer to Mr Sykes's telephone call.'

'So you're Mr Sykes?'

'James Sykes. What's this about?'

'I'm not supposed to say.'

Sykes took charge. 'Mrs Sugden, I think we need to explain to the constable.'

'Can't you see we're upset, constable? We've had a shock. I've had a shock. Your dog and Mr Sykes might take this kind of thing in their stride but I don't. Now what's this about if it's not about what's in the cellar? Have you come for the dog back?'

'No.'

'Then what are you here for? Because as Mr Sykes says, he thinks this is a matter for CID, not the constabulary, and if Mr Sykes says that, then it's true.'

'What are you talking about?' the young constable asked. 'I think we're at cross purposes.'

'There's a body in the cellar,' Sykes said. 'I just reported it.'

'Oh.'

'But that's not why you're here?'

'No. I'm here in connection with a Scotland Yard enquiry over an incident in Haworth. We've been asked to co-operate.'

A sergeant appeared behind him. 'Why don't you walk down Headingley Lane with a rattle and a loudhailer, telling the world police business?'

'Sorry, sir. This is Mrs Sugden and Mr Sykes, they're looking after the premises.'

'Are they now?'

'And it seems there's a body in the cellar.'

'Well I'm here to secure the premises prior to the issuance of a search warrant, so I'll just take a look in the cellar first.'

'I'd rather you didn't, sergeant.' A third police officer entered, this one in plain clothes.

The dog barked.

Mrs Sugden recognised the man who spoke. It was Detective Inspector Wallis. You would know him by the one good worsted suit.

He straightened his maroon tie. 'Mr Sykes?'

'That's me,' Jim said.

'You telephoned.'

'Inspector, a word please,' the sergeant pleaded, 'only we have had a communication from Scotland Yard asking us to secure the premises in connection with an investigation of an incident in Haworth.'

Twenty-three

A Rain-Sodden Room

Rain continued steadily during the night. I woke intermittently. Pitter-pattering raindrops made a variety of sounds, depending on which piece of furniture or floor they landed. Sharp, almost bell-like chimes must be raindrops hitting the galvanised bucket in the corner. Rain slapping into the enamel basin beside it struck a softer note. I listened until rain music lulled me into a fitful sleep.

By morning, the rain had stopped.

Exiting the box bed when Rita was sprawled at the other end, still sleeping, required a careful manoeuvre.

I managed to sit up, and found a way of moving my legs so that I was ready to climb out. Without looking down, I placed one foot on the floor.

Water and muck oozed from under the strip of once-scarlet carpet that was now a muddy brown. The squelch felt toe-curlingly horrible.

There was a tap on the door. Derek said, 'Breakfast is ready.'

'Derek, be a dear and fetch my cream boots from by the front door, and Rita's wellingtons if they're there.'

'Right-o.'

Rita stirred. 'What's the matter? I was dreaming!'

With what I thought was remarkable restraint, I said, 'It rained in the night. The carpet is soaking.'

'Is that all? I've been having such dreams. Do you think the visions of past dreamers have been trapped in this bed? Only one of them was about cats and I never dream of cats.' She sat up. 'No, wait! I tell a lie, I once dreamed of a leopard. I still see its eyes.'

'I've asked Derek to bring up our boots. The floor has turned into a marsh.'

'Oh, I've trodden barefoot through marshes. At least we don't have mosquitoes.' She took a hanky from the pocket of her nightie and gently blew her nose. 'Only in this dream I see cats curled up in a chair, and four of them are dead and two alive. Another dream swiftly followed, or it may have been the second act of the first dream. I dream in three acts. Well then, some time had passed, a night, and it was morning. All the cats were alive. Some had just been tired and the others needed food. I felt so pleased. I think it was because my brain couldn't bear the thought of seeing them dead. I'm not sure what that signifies.'

'I feel sick, Rita. This floor is the last straw.'

'I haven't finished telling you. There was a third act. In this third act there were dead rabbits in the chair. Now here's the interesting thing, why should my dream response be different? To see a dead cat upsets me. I can look at the bodies of rabbits with sadness but without repulsion.'

The floor was more than soaking. Here and there strips

of carpet had somehow managed to float. Whoever created the carpet jigsaw had not thought to nail it down. Below the carpet pieces was a layer of something dark and a little lumpy. It could have been flocks from a mattress, or blackcurrant jam. In a dream by Rita, it might have been caviar.

Rita paid no attention. 'I have it! I see the connection. Perhaps in my dream – before they came back to life – my subconscious thought the cats had been poisoned.'

'Rita, why would anyone go to the trouble of laying carpets rather than mending the roof?'

'The connection is poison.'

'What connection?'

'The connection between my subconscious and the dream. You know I work in Norton's pharmacy?'

'Yes.'

'Do you think I should admit to the police that I had it in mind to poison Tobias?'

'That's probably not a good idea.'

'Only he was poisoning Carine. I'm sure of it, from Carine's symptoms.'

'What symptoms?'

'Upset stomach. Sickness. He was always dosing her with something. So much so that I took samples of the dandelion tea and the tonic wine. He never touched that you see, it was always for her.'

She had my attention. 'And what were the results of your tests?'

'There was nothing. He was too crafty. He obviously added something afterwards.'

'Rita, did you murder Tobias?'

'No.'

'Then don't say anything that will put a noose around your neck.'

Derek did not come back with our boots.

It was Elisa who brought them. 'Ah,' she said when she saw the floor. 'I did wonder, only I slept through.'

I supposed she would have slept through, given that she was out late telling the bees about Tobias's death.

Perching on the side of the bed, I put on my boots, glad that my clothing was in the trunk, and dry. I crossed to the trunk, and wiped water from the lid with the sleeve of my nightgown.

There was a squelching sound as Rita stepped from the bed. 'I see what that stuff is now. It's the kind of thing to expect in the country.'

'What do you see?' I scooped up my clothes, intending to dress elsewhere.

'We had to do summat when there was to be seven people staying the weekend,' Elisa said somewhat defensively.

Rita wiped the soles of her feet with the edge of the blanket. 'It's chicken shit. I'd know it anywhere, worldwide. Everyone in Africa and India who could afford chickens would keep them. And do you know what? It's the same in the poorest parts of Leeds. Pigs as well, though they're not supposed to.'

Elisa shrugged. 'We hoped it wouldn't rain. We kept the chickens up here last year, just to be cracking on you know.'

I didn't know, but nor did I know what to say. The words came to me. 'Elisa, would you please send up tea and toast to the library? I'll change in there.'

Along the landing was the little washroom. Someone had placed a jug of hot water there, and a clean, well-worn towel. There was a bucket to empty the water, and a tablet of carbolic soap.

Feeling a little revived after my ablutions, I went into the library, which I had so longed to see. There was a book on the table, *Agricultural Implements and their Best Usages*.

Rita came in shortly after me, wearing her silks and a familiar long cardigan. 'Is it all right to borrow this cardigan?'

'It's Harriet's. She won't mind.'

'Thanks. I stupidly left your other one on the chair and it's soaked. Shall I tell you something else?'

'I'm just going to take a first and last look at the books.'

I hoped we would be leaving soon, and that I would never come here again as long as I lived. The ghosts of the former owners and their Brontë visitors were welcome to the place.

'You know I told you that Tobias was unfaithful to Carine.'

'Yes, weekly at the Leeds Club, with a buxom cook called Molly who makes pancakes.'

'Carine was past caring about it. Tobias talked in his sleep. That's how she got wind of certain things.'

'What kind of things?'

'Well, Molly the cook, and that he got a girl in the family way. It must have preyed on his mind. Even the worst people might have a guilty conscience and troubled dreams.'

'Did Carine find out any more about this girl, who she was or where she lived?'

'He said her name sometimes. It was the name of a flower, or something like a flower. Now what was it? Not pansy, but something beginning with p.'

'Perhaps it will come to you.'

'I suppose it will.'

I did not want to name 'Picotee', Elisa's drowned sister, the daughter that Mrs Varey mourned. It began to seem as if Carine may have deliberately manoeuvred us into coming to a place where Tobias might at the very least be uncomfortable and unwelcome and, at worst, in danger from people who bore him a mighty grudge. If that was the case, it would be better if Rita remembered the name, so that any account she might give would not be prompted by me.

Of course, Carine could not have been sure that we would follow her suggestion. The terrible thing was, I made the final choice on our destination.

As a girl I used to play whip and top around Whitsuntide. We would chalk colourful patterns onto our tops. As the top spun, the pattern became a blur of colour. I felt at the centre of such a blur and needed to be outside, to walk, to clear my head. If I could still my brain, I might make some sense of a senseless situation.

The door to the kitchen was open. Collusion. Someone must have colluded.

I went in and tapped on the door of the box bed. No one answered, but I knew Mrs Varey was there. 'Why are you avoiding us, Mrs Varey? The deed is done. Why are you lying low?'

I waited. 'I know you're in there.'

'And what if I am? You're in and out of this kitchen like a new broom. The public isn't allowed in here.'

'Answer me this if you've nothing to hide. Had you ever met Carine Murchison before we arrived on Friday?'

'I never met her before and I never met her now or since.'

'But the knife that killed Mr Murchison came from this kitchen, didn't it?'

It was a wild guess, an attempt at provocation.

She did not reply.

So much for my interviewing techniques.

The air was fresh after the rain. I left Ponden Hall and set off on the path to Stanbury. I hoped to take Harriet home. Even if I had to return and answer more questions, it would give me peace of mind to know that she was safely with Mrs Sugden and able to return to her work at the cinema. That would divert her, if nothing else did. If Dad or Mr Porter put a word in, I would be able to set off right away.

I had reckoned without Mrs Porter. Mother was glad to see me. She and her hostess were enjoying a late breakfast. Mrs Porter was quick to intervene when I said I wanted to see Harriet.

'Don't trouble yourself, Ginny,' Mrs Porter said. 'I'll take Kate up.'

She led me upstairs to a room where the curtains were tightly drawn. Harriet was curled under the eiderdown. The Porters' dog lay beside her. Harriet had her hand on the dog's head. Something about her told me she was not sleeping.

'I'll sit with her awhile, Mrs Porter.'

'Of course.' There was already a chair by the bed. I sat down. Mrs Porter went quietly from the room.

'Harriet, are you awake?'

She turned and opened her eyes. 'Yes.'

'We should be able to go home soon.'

'Is Mr Murchison dead?'

'Yes.'

'Ah, only I thought I might have dreamed it. Mrs Porter gave me something to drink, she called it Nighter. It sent me to sleep.'

'Well that's good that you've had some rest.'

'Was it my fault?'

'What?'

'That he died.'

'No, of course not! How could it possibly be your fault?'

'I was going to tell you.'

'What?'

'It seems so silly now.'

'Harriet, just tell me.'

'When we were getting off the train in Keighley, to change for Haworth, he pinched my bottom.'

'Go on.'

'Rita saw him and I told her it wasn't the first time. She said there was a way to deal with a man like that.'

I suppressed the urge to ask why she had not told me, and I braced myself to hear Rita's method of dealing with the business. 'What did she say?'

'She said you must on the instant grab the man's hand, pass it back to him forcefully and say, "If you do that again I will call a policeman".'

'And he did it again?'

'On the landing. I did what Rita said.'

'What did Tobias say?'

'Nothing. I think he was flabbergasted, and of course there was no policeman to call.'

'No.'

'But he must have been so ashamed and embarrassed by what happened that he fell on his sword. He must have thought I would tell Carine that he had been cheeky and rude.'

'Harriet, we don't know exactly what happened, but it wasn't your fault. His death had no connection with you and what he did.'

'Oh. Are you sure?'

'Entirely sure.'

'What time is it?'

'Ten o'clock, Sunday morning. Are you hungry?'

She shook her head. 'Auntie Ginny sat by me while I ate a boiled egg. She said I should rest a bit more.'

I put my hand on her forehead. She had a temperature.

I poured water into a glass. 'Sit up then, eh?' The dog adjusted its position and she was able to move. 'Here, take a drink. I have a little bottle of aspirins. Hold out your hand.' I tipped a couple of aspirins onto her palm. 'Take those.'

There was a creaking sound on the landing by the door.

I crossed the room as quietly as I could but in an old house there are always creaking floorboards. By the time I opened the door, Mrs Porter was at the other end of the landing. She had been listening.

'Mrs Porter!' She turned, not looking in the least guilty, but then why should she? This was her house. She might eavesdrop if that was her pleasure. 'Do you have a flannel I might dampen for Harriet's brow?'

She did. I heard her open a cupboard on the landing, and then walk to the bathroom. She came back with a wet flannel and handed it to me, not having squeezed it well enough. Water dripped onto the floor between us.

'Thank you.'

When she left, I squeezed excess water into the chamber pot and placed the folded flannel on Harriet's brow.

Rest and sleep would be the best cure for her now. 'Are your feet warm?'

'Yes. Auntie Ginny found a pair of Uncle's socks for me.'

'Good.'

'Is she still here?'

'She is downstairs and will come and say hello. And Max is staying by you.' I stroked the dog's head. 'Is there anything else you want?'

She shook her head. 'I like this bed, and it's so quiet here, but I want to go home soon.'

'We will. Rest a little longer.'

It would be wrong to move her until she got over the immediate shock. Strange as it seemed, less than twenty-four hours had passed since Tobias's death. The time since then had both stretched to infinity, and flown like a startled bird.

'How is she?' Mother asked when I went downstairs.

'I've given her a couple of aspirins. Sleep will be the best remedy.'

'Did she know the deceased gentleman well?' Mrs Porter asked. 'She seems to be taking it very hard.'

Mother looked surprised. 'Lydia, she's just a child. What happened yesterday would be a terrible shock for anyone.'

'Mother, I told Harriet you would go up. She was asking for you.'

'Bless the child. Of course I will.'

Mother went upstairs, leaving me with Mrs Porter.

'I couldn't help overhearing,' Mrs Porter said.

Obviously not, since she had stood by the door listening.

Unblushingly, she continued. 'Had Mr Murchison made a nuisance of himself with your niece?'

'You will have heard her say that he has – had – wandering hands.'

'Do you think he did anything worse?'

'I have no reason to think so.' It was difficult to know whether Mrs Porter had appointed herself special constable, was being nosey, or was genuinely concerned about Harriet.

'I ask because of his reputation hereabouts. People have long memories. I suppose he thought no one would recognise or remember him. My aunt told me the story years ago, and my maid brought it up when your party arrived at Ponden Hall.'

'What is his reputation?'

'It was Tobias Murchison who got a mill girl pregnant and never showed his face again. She drowned. It wasn't thought to be suicide but no one with her wits about her and in her Sunday best would climb a reservoir wall to chase a hat.'

Oh but they would, I thought. That is exactly what a person might do if she loved the hat. Mrs Porter continued. 'It's said that she was distracted by her predicament. And how that man had the nerve and was foolish enough to show his face here again I do not know.'

'Are you suggesting Mr Murchison's death may have been some sort of revenge?'

'That sort of thing has been known. The blood boils in certain circumstances. I had a friend . . . '

It was going to be one of those stories, I thought. Whenever one hears the words 'I had a friend', in a certain tone of voice, that is usually a substitute for saying, 'something happened to me', and it is a good idea to listen carefully.

'I had a friend who when she was nineteen and visiting relatives in Dublin, in a household where supervision was rather lax, was courted by a man who led her something of a merry dance. One day, out walking with him by the Liffey, he confessed that he had become engaged to someone else. She felt an urge to push him into the river, and knew he could not swim.'

'And did she push him?'

'No, and I believe she regrets it to this day, because she could have made good her escape. He would not have dared – had he lived – reveal her name.'

'Goodness.'

'So, what I am wondering, Kate, is whether anyone took similar revenge yesterday afternoon. The Varey girl was there, I think, the sister. Elisa.'

She had come up with two suspects in as many minutes. 'Are you suggesting that Tobias was murdered for his past sins, or his recently wandering hands?'

'Either is a possibility.'

In that moment, I wanted to rush up the stairs, throw Harriet over my shoulders in a fireman's lift, take my father's car and drive away from this dreadful place.

I remained calm. 'Mrs Porter, you ought to be writing novels.'

She gave a superior smile. 'It's funny you should say that. It did once cross my mind to write something more profound and grammatically correct than the books one sees on the shelves these days, but I have so many more important calls upon my time.'

I waited until Mother came down, reporting that Harriet slept again. When Mrs Porter's attention was turned to the maid's removal of the breakfast things, Mother caught my eye and indicated that she wanted to talk to me.

'Well, I'd best be off,' I said. 'Mother, as soon as Harriet is feeling better, I want to take her home.'

'Of course,' Mother said. 'Kate, I could do with a walk myself, I'll come with you part of the way.'

Before self-appointed special constable and would-be novelist Mrs Porter had time to intervene, we were at the door.

'See you shortly,' Mother called.

As we left the grounds of the Hall, Mother said, 'Do you think Harriet is so deeply affected not just because of what happened this morning, but because it brings back the memory of finding her father's body?'

'That's exactly what I think.'

I was undecided whether I should tell Mother about Mrs Porter's wild suspicions regarding Harriet. After all, Mother would be staying there at least a week and I did not want to do or say anything that would make her feel uncomfortable.

We were in the main street. Bells were ringing. People were making their way to the church. Those who weren't, or had been to church or chapel earlier, found a reason to be visible. Because of the fine day, and the increased likelihood of good gossip, there were several people seated on chairs in cottage doorways. Since the doors opened directly onto the street, we had to be circumspect.

Mother spoke quietly without moving her lips. 'There'll be a lot of speculation going on round here. I swear that old woman in the doorway was trying to read your lips.'

We proceeded cautiously, returning greetings and appreciation of a blue and almost cloudless sky, along with the absence of rain. It is sometimes difficult to come up with a variation on that theme, but no one seems to mind. It is not the words about the weather that matter, but the fact that they are said.

When it was safe to speak, I told Mother about the camper, and also about Constable Briggs spending the night at Ponden Hall.

Mother waited until we were at the turning, the parting of our ways. 'Mr Briggs would have sent a special constable with your message about the camper. I know there was a search for him. They also have special constables out searching for a knife. The doctor says the swordstick wasn't the murder weapon.'

'I knew that it would have been far too unwieldy.'

'It is horrible to think that someone came up really close to him and stabbed him in the heart. Who could have hated him that much?'

I decided I ought to tell her of Mrs Porter's thinly veiled hints that Harriet might have had something to do with the death.

'That woman is preposterous. She was so charming at the functions. It is never a good idea to base one's judgement on a person one has only met while wearing an evening dress.'

'Are the police making any progress at all?'

'They are bringing in Scotland Yard.'

'Thank goodness for that.'

'Whoever it is might be here by now. He was booked on the overnight sleeper from King's Cross. Wouldn't it be nice if it were Marcus Charles?'

'No, it would not!'

Twenty-four

The Man from Scotland Yard

I saw Marcus before he saw me. I had just reached the track that led to Ponden Hall when I heard the car's motor. I held back, and looked to see who was coming. The car was being driven by a uniformed officer. Marcus sat on the back seat. He was looking in the direction of the reservoir and so did not notice me. When it comes to investigating cases in Yorkshire, he seems to be Scotland Yard's first choice. He and I have become close over the years. As my mother has pointed out to me, any woman of sense would have married him. He did propose. I turned him down. He now says that next time, I must propose to him. I do wish Scotland Yard had sent someone else.

I took my time walking the rest of the way, thinking about what might lie ahead, for all of us. Once the car had gone from view, it was as if it had never been. The morning was as peaceful and quiet as one might have wished. Only a slight breeze caused a rustle in the air. A red grouse stopped pecking at the grass, and turned to stare.

As I came in sight of Ponden Hall, Rita appeared, carrying a posy of wildflowers. She looked a little upset. 'All I was doing was gathering a few flowers as a welcome back for Carine.'

'Is she back?'

'Not yet, but the constable thinks it likely. Only the field is teeming with special constables tripping over each other as they search for something. One of them said I was impeding his investigations. I ask you! How can picking buttercups and daisies impede anything? I might have helped if they'd told me what to look for.'

'They should put someone on the gate if they want to keep people out.'

'Exactly! Anyhow, I'm glad that Carine will be back. I'll put these on the table in the dining hall. I'm thinking, Kate, that she won't want to go back to the studio. She might want to stay with me.'

I didn't want to dash her hopes. 'That's a possibility. She'll be relying on her friends.' Rita needed to feel she was doing something useful. The courtyard was deserted. 'Let's sit down. Did you do that sketch I mentioned, of where we were all standing?'

'I had a go. I'm hopeless at drawing and I don't know whether I've remembered properly.' She dipped into the pocket of her silk trousers. 'I made a mess of my first effort. Edward gave me a sheet of paper from his notebook.'

The diagram was neatly drawn, the figures numbered. 'You have such a good memory, Rita.'

'You learn to be precise if you work in a pharmacy. It's just a snapshot and it might not be exact. I've put Carine in but I don't know who took her space when she moved away.'

'Did you see her go?'

'If I had, I would have gone with her.'

'I offered but she said no.'

Derek came to meet us. 'A detective has arrived from Scotland Yard. All the photographs from our cameras have been developed and printed. They are spread on the big table for us to look at. He sent me to find everyone. A constable from Keighley is searching our rooms.'

I thought of the squelching carpet. 'I hope he's wearing good boots.'

The three of us trooped inside. Rita popped into the kitchen to beg a vase for her flowers.

Marcus, of course, looked immaculate and fresh as the morning. He is good at sleeping on trains. He was wearing a grey suit, a spotless white shirt and a blue tie, with the tie pin I gave him for Christmas. Looking up from the photographs that were grouped on the table, he tilted his head and raised an eyebrow. Briefly, I held his glance.

'Good morning, ladies and gentlemen.' He spoke with cold courtesy. 'I am Chief Inspector Charles of Scotland Yard. I extend my condolences for the loss of your friend, Mr Murchison. I have some questions for you, with the intention of gaining a picture of what happened yesterday.' He cleared his throat. 'An officer is upstairs, taking a look around. We are in possession of search warrants.'

'I don't understand,' Rita said. 'Wasn't it just a terrible accident? I thought such matters were for the coroner.'

'That is something you will be able to help me with. I'm sorry to keep you standing but it may be the easiest way for you all to take a look at these photographs.'

Marcus has become a little more impressive over time.

When I first knew him, he was rather abrupt and made no attempt to hide that he suspected everyone he met of some hideous crime, if not recently, then in their dim and distant past. I looked at my friends. Rita and Derek were certainly taking him at face value. It was not so easy to read Edward. His scarred and reconstructed face did not allow for a change of expression.

Marcus began with Derek, first ascertaining his name. 'Mr Blondell?'

'Yes.' A surprised shiver of importance made Derek stand taller. No one ever called him mister.

'You handed two cameras to the constable on duty yesterday, your own and Harriet Armstrong's.'

'Yes.'

'Would you tell me which of these photographs are yours and which are Harriet's?'

Before Derek said, 'These are Harriet's,' I knew straight away which photographs were my niece's. There was a dead hare, just on the point of decay; a ram's skull; a ring of daisies encircled by sheep droppings, giving the impression of a wreath. In a picture that made me blink with astonishment, Derek lay on a gravestone, his hands clasped in prayer on his chest. The *avant garde* set would love these.

'Whose idea was it to have a photograph of you lying on a grave?'

'Harriet's, sir. I took these of her wearing my gran's cloak, so that she would look like someone from the last century. In return, she asked me to pose for her.'

Everyone stared. No one said a word.

Marcus continued, moving on to the next group of photographs. He had separated the images of the moments after

Tobias's collapse. 'Mr Blondell, you took Harriet's camera from her . . . '

'Yes, my camera was out of film.'

I wanted not to look but could not turn away. In the first photograph, Tobias was lying face down. In the second, I had somehow managed to turn him over, which I had no recollection of doing. I was kneeling over Tobias, a look of horror on my face. In the next, there was Edward, his mouth open in the moment that he called for people to stand back.

'You began to take pictures with your own camera, when Mr Murchison had collapsed.'

'I did.'

'Why was that?'

'For the record, I suppose. I thought it might be evidence.'

'Was that thought uppermost in your mind when you decided to take the photographs?'

'I can't say it was. I work for a newspaper. There is sometimes a photograph that only one person could take, and on that day it was me. I took pictures of who was there, who was nearby.'

'So you did,' Marcus said calmly. He asked us all to identify ourselves in the photographs. We were all there, except Carine, or partially there. Rita's head had been cut off. There were other people in the photographs whom we did not know, but Marcus had their names. 'Does anyone have any other film that was taken since you arrived, any waiting to be developed?'

No one did.

'Miss Rufus.' Marcus turned to Rita, not quite managing

to hide his surprise at her appearance. Her silk was now looking rather crumpled. She wore the cardigan that Marcus had bought for me in Selfridges, and that I had passed on to Harriet. 'Miss Rufus, you did not hand in a camera.'

'Well no, I didn't bother to bring one.'

'But you came on a photographic outing.'

'Yes, well it's a weekend away isn't it, with friends. I am a member. I'm entitled.'

'Of course.' Marcus moved on to the photographs I had taken. The landscapes were a disappointment. Whoever had developed the photographs had done a good job. I could not help but be pleased to see Harriet standing in the doorway at Top Withins, sharply focused and with the shadow of the wall adding a sense of atmosphere. The circle of photographers would have been more interesting, except that in the foreground of my picture I had Rita, who was pretending to hold a camera.

Carine's photographs were all of flowers in close detail, except for one. She had taken a picture of the camper in the wood.

Derek said, 'There's the camper again! He's in my photo too, taken after the . . . after Mr Murchison collapsed.'

'He packed up his tent and left,' Edward added. 'Said his name was John and he had a long way to go. We thought it odd that he should leave in the evening. Most people would set off in the morning, if they had a long walk ahead.'

'Did he give a last name?' Marcus asked.

Edward shook his head. 'And you asked, didn't you, Kate? Elisa says that they don't keep a note of who stays, that there's no reason to do so.'

We all perked up. A stranger had slipped away.

Marcus moved the photograph of the camper to one side.

We were now looking at Edward's photographs. There were not many. Edward's gaze fixed on one. It was Elisa Varey, seated on a stool, milking a cow. He had taken it from the doorway of the milking parlour, with the sun behind him, and so the image included Edward's own shadow. Apart from that, it was a beautiful shot. Edward had turned Elisa into Tess of the D'Urbervilles.

'They have just one cow,' Edward explained, ever the schoolmaster. 'Because of the reservoir, farmers are discouraged from keeping any cows at all — otherwise the water might become contaminated.'

Edward's few remaining photographs were less successful. In the group shot, all heads were chopped off.

'Have you been a member of the photographic society for long, Mr Chester?' Marcus asked him.

'Not long.'

'But you wanted to come on the outing.'

Edward became defensive. 'No one told me that a person had to pass a proficiency test.' Edward glanced at Derek. 'About my clumsiness putting film in the camera, which somebody noticed . . . ' Edward rubbed at the palm of his hand. 'I'm not as dextrous as I once was.'

Marcus moved on to the final group of photographs.

It was unsettling to look at the pictures Tobias had taken. His landscapes were well-framed. He caught an unusual cloud effect.

He had lied about wanting to take a picture of the scene at the Brontë waterfall. One picture showed Carine close to Derek. Another caught her in an intimate moment with Edward.

Rita said bitterly, 'I expect he would have been pleased with these.'

Constable Briggs hovered by the door. Marcus motioned him to come in. He did so, bringing pencils and several sheets of drawing paper which he set down on the table. He then proceeded to gather up the photographs.

'I apologise if what I am going to ask of you sounds like a school exercise.' Marcus gave a nod to the constable who placed four sheets of paper and four pencils around the long refectory table. 'Mrs Shackleton, Miss Rufus, Mr Chester and Mr Blondell, I want each of you to provide me with a sketch of where you were standing yesterday afternoon when Mr Murchison died. Please include, to the best of your memory, where everyone else was too. If you remember any particular person who is not part of your group but was nearby, please include that person. If you cannot name them, give a number, and write a description. If you remember anything that was said in the moments before, please include that too.'

The others looked at me.

Rita said, 'We've done this for Kate.'

I took the sketches from my satchel, including the one I had done myself, and handed them to Marcus. 'I thought it might be a good idea to do these while recollections were still fresh, Chief Inspector.'

'Thank you.' Marcus glanced at the sketches. 'And they're named and dated. Excellent. But I would still like you to do the drawing again now, along with a note of anything significant that you remember.'

Rita sighed. She picked up a pencil. 'I'm sure Kate would have given me ten out of ten for the last one.'

The library at Ponden Hall became the interview room. Marcus had decided that he would speak to me first.

He and I are fond of each other, in spite of our differences, and this was not the kind of meeting either of us would have wished for.

'I'm sorry your outing ended so tragically, Kate.'

'So am I.'

'Whose idea was it to come here?'

'Mine.'

'Ah, because . . . ?'

'Because of the importance of yesterday's event, and because I wanted to see this place. Its connection with the Brontës made it seem perfect.'

'Did anyone object or have other preferences?'

'There were a number of different preferences but I was not the only person to be attracted to the area. Someone else had named Ponden in the suggestion box.'

'Do you know who?'

'It may have been Carine Murchison, but I can't be sure.'

'Have you kept those suggestions?'

'I believe I have, at home. It occurred to me that there might be some dissension at a future meeting and then I could justify the choice.'

'Was anyone against this decision?'

'According to Harriet, Tobias had it in mind to stay at the Black Bull.'

'I have been briefed about why he would have been reluctant to come here, though it was fifteen years ago, and at the time no one knew his surname.'

'He would have hoped people would not connect him with the man who abandoned the elder Miss Varey.'

Marcus looked at the sketches we had done for him. 'Carine is not in any of the sketches.'

'She felt unwell. It was a terrible crush. She wanted air.'

'No one thought to go with her?'

'I offered but she said no. It all happened so quickly.'

'You took Harriet away from the scene immediately.'

'She was upset.'

'Your gloves had Tobias's blood on them.'

'I tried to help him.'

'Yes. We have someone who was by the wall who saw that. Did it occur to you that you should go to Carine?'

'I knew that Edward, Derek and Rita would take care of Carine. Harriet is my responsibility.'

'Harriet disliked Murchison, his familiarity was unwelcome. She tried to keep her distance from him.'

'When did you speak to her?'

'I was briefed by the local sergeant. I know you are protective of Harriet, but I must ask.' He scratched his neck. 'Harriet practises ju-jitsu.'

'She has been to half a dozen classes. You have been listening to Mrs Porter, who does not know Harriet at all. She suspects her on the grounds that Harriet, unusually for a girl her age, had the gumption to object when Tobias pinched her bottom. If every girl who had her bottom pinched committed murder, there would be a string of corpses from John o' Groats to Land's End.'

'She is obsessed with death. She is strong enough to wield a knife.'

'Are you doing this deliberately, so that I will come up with some suspect that you haven't thought of?'

'Of course not.'

'As for her being obsessed with death, I don't need to remind you that Harriet found her father's body.'

'That was a long time ago. Children forget.'

'It was no time at all and children do not forget. I think you may have forgotten that you chased your own phantoms and arrested Harriet's mother.'

'I am not accusing anyone. Sometimes one has to choose a roundabout way to arrive at the truth.'

In that moment, I remembered why I had turned him down. 'Marcus, Mrs Porter has a vivid imagination but that is not true of her husband or my parents. Do you imagine they wouldn't know the difference between a girl who is in shock and a girl who is guilty of murder?'

'You won't mind my saying this Kate—'

'Oh, I probably will.'

'You sometimes overreact.'

'Do you have any more questions for me?'

'Did you know that Tobias carried a swordstick?'

'No.'

He was playing games now, checking whether I knew that there was a search going on for the real murder weapon.

'Who might have known?'

'You'll have to ask.' It occurred to me that the one person most likely to have known was Tobias's wife. Carine was also the only person who did not feature in our sketches of who was there when Tobias died.

He picked up Derek's sketch. 'Derek is friends with Harriet?'

'They are close in age and both love being at the picture house.'

'Harriet holds a grudge against Tobias Murchison.'

250

'Hardly anything as strong as a grudge.'

' . . . and Derek – contradict me if you think I am wrong – is deeply attached to Mrs Murchison. That is the impression he has given investigating officers.'

When I did not comment, he said, 'Sometimes, people act together to commit a crime that neither would contemplate if left to their own devices.'

Knowing his techniques, and that he can be rather provoking, I remained calm. 'As a general observation there is probably truth in what you say. But suggesting that Harriet and Derek colluded in murder is pure poppycock, and you know it.'

There was a tap on the door. Marcus rose and went to open it.

It was Rita. 'I've just thought of something and it might be important, about the blonde woman.'

'One moment.' Marcus closed the door.

'I think we're done for now, Kate, unless there's anything else?'

'Am I free to return home, and take Harriet?'

'Not yet if you don't mind.'

'I do mind, very much.'

'Then I'm sorry, but I have a job to do. Until I have questioned everyone, and made some progress, I want no one to leave the house.'

Twenty-five

Jim Sykes's Mystery Tour

When Jim Sykes suggested to Rosie that they take the dog out to the country, he thought it best to keep the destination a surprise, at least until they were well underway. This was not unusual. They would often take a jaunt on a Sunday. Rosie thought of these as Jim's Mystery Tours. She soon realised that today they were going a much greater distance than a run out to Roundhay Park, or to Ilkley Moor.

The dog, seated upright in the dickey seat, seemed curious about their destination. It breathed on the back of Rosie's neck, sniffed her hair and slobbered on her collar. After several miles of this, Rosie began to ask questions.

'The thing is, Rosie, you know Mrs Sugden was keeping an eye on the photographic studio over the weekend.'

'Yes, she told me.'

'I went up to see how she was getting on, and I found something of interest.'

'What?'

'I'll tell you later, but Mrs Shackleton needs to know about it.'

'Mrs Shackleton? What about the owners?'

On the grounds that he had persuaded her to come out under false pretences, she winkled it out of him long before they went through Shipley. He tried to soften the news. 'This body, it might have been in the cellar a very long time. It might have been there since the houses were built.'

'Why disturb everybody?' she asked. 'Mrs Shackleton and Harriet are having a nice weekend away. Can you not leave them and the Murchisons in peace until tomorrow?'

'Well, no, because I had to report it.'

Rosie clammed up until Keighley, when she said, 'You could have left it to the police.'

But he saw that she was looking about her with interest. He took advantage of the lapse in her interrogations to volunteer a crumb of information. 'You see, I have a feeling Mrs Shackleton needs to know today. Wouldn't you want to know if you were off for the weekend and two lots of police turned up at your friends' house and those friends were in your company?'

Rosie turned her attention back to her husband. 'First off, we don't go away for weekends, second, it's not Mrs Shackleton's cellar, and third – no, I would not be in a hurry to know about a body in a cellar.'

'I always like to have you with me, Rosie. You know I wouldn't go anywhere on a Sunday without you, love.'

She groaned. 'Butter up your bread, not me.'

But Sykes knew that she was pacified.

He was glad he had brought an extra can of petrol

because the road was long and winding. He had to stop and ask the way to Ponden Hall.

It was a left turn onto a bumpy lane. At the bottom of the lane was a young police constable. He waved them down.

'What's your business, sir?'

Aye, aye, Sykes thought. It can't be every Sunday that there's a police post at the end of a country lane. Having come all this way, he was determined to see Mrs Shackleton and did not relish parking the motor in the road and finding some roundabout way up to Ponden Hall. Rosie was at the limits of her tolerance.

'It's in connection with a matter that I'm assisting with. The officer in charge is Inspector Wallis of Leeds CID. I need to see a party who is staying at Ponden Hall.'

The constable hesitated.

Sykes sometimes felt at a disadvantage when people thought he looked like a police officer. Today that would work in his favour. There was the added advantage of a police dog overseeing proceedings from its vantage point of the dickey seat. Sykes climbed from the car, taking the cloth and the bottle of water that he kept handy, and began washing dead insects from the windscreen.

While he washed and wiped, he kept up a chat with the young constable. 'You never know where you'll be in this line of work, eh? I expect you didn't think you'd find yourself on duty here on a Sunday morning.'

That was quite true, the constable agreed. He had expected to be playing cricket in Keighley. 'Sorry to stop you, sir, but we're being asked to tell anyone who is calling at Ponden Hall for cups of tea and cake to turn round and go to the tea rooms in Stanbury.'

So something was seriously wrong up at Ponden Hall, Sykes surmised. It must be if the serving of refreshments was banned.

Sykes thanked him and drove on, negotiating a deep pothole in the lane.

Rosie stared straight ahead. 'You are going to find yourself in big trouble one of these days, Jim. And don't come crying to me if this lane shreds your tyres.'

'I didn't say a word that was not perfectly true.'

He had intended to stop the car a little short of Ponden Hall and walk up, just in case there was a more experienced constable on duty. The hall appeared sooner than expected. In spite of the supposed ban on tea and cakes, there were tables in the garden. A group of ramblers sat taking refreshment. There was already a car parked opposite the hall. He drove a little farther on, towards farm buildings.

'Come on then, Rosie. If ramblers can have a cup of tea, so can we day trippers. Come on, Failure. You better come as well.'

'Jim, don't call the dog that.'

They got out of the car and walked back to the hall.

A tall fair young woman, her hair plaited and pinned up, was carrying a tray of empty cups back to the house. 'Are you here for refreshments?'

'Yes.'

'We're only serving outside today.'

The dog sniffed the ground. It sniffed the air. It sniffed the young woman's feet.

'Why's that then?' Sykes asked.

'I'm not allowed to tell you, and I don't have time. Find a seat and I'll be with you directly.'

'Oh, and miss?'

The young woman turned. 'I said I'll be with you.' She began to pick up empty cups and saucers and put them on the tray.

Rosie and Sykes helped, passing them along. 'Bit of a palaver for you, to and fro-ing from the house.'

'At least we're able to serve you. What'll you have?'

Rosie was quick off the mark ordering sandwiches, tea and cake.

'Let me help.' Sykes moved to take the tray from her, offering to carry it in. She was too quick for him and snatched the tray.

'I know you're busy, miss, but I'd like a word with Mrs Shackleton who's staying here.'

'Unless she's already left,' Rosie added.

Sykes knew that Rosie would crow if Mrs Shackleton had gone home.

'None of them have gone,' the young woman said. 'They're not allowed to.'

Twenty-six

Ways of Seeing

I left the library, where Marcus was questioning Rita, and went back into the bedroom. I put my nightwear in the trunk, along with the items that Harriet had placed in the press. I picked up my shoes, which had not escaped the deluge, and carried them downstairs.

Edward was seated at the table, unseeing, staring into space. I had entered the room quietly and caught him unawares. It was difficult to read emotion in his face, yet it was naked, in a way a face sometimes is when the person believes they are not observed. He sat upright, and yet gave the impression of being broken. His arms hung limply by his sides. A newspaper lay on the floor.

I had begun to blame him for not caring, for showing no regard for Carine and making no effort to enquire after her. He became aware of me, and looked up.

I did not want to make him self-conscious and so barged in with a request. 'Edward, if you've read that paper, I'd like a couple of pages to stuff my shoes.'

The change was instant, as if he had been ordered to stand to attention. 'Elisa mentioned you were rained on. Give them here and I'll see to them.' He seemed glad of something to do, regarding seeing to shoes as a man's job, especially when that man was a former soldier.

'Thanks.' I handed him my shoes.

He set them down, tore a sheet of newspaper and began to make neat little balls of it. 'As the paper gets damp, replace it. Don't put them too close to the fire or the leather will crack.' He spoke as if he did not expect to be here to complete the task.

'What's eating you, Edward? I thought you were too calm for words but you're not, are you?'

He began to make another newspaper ball for the second shoe. 'I feel such an idiot, Kate. I've made a mess of everything.'

'And now you're stepping back, for fear of making the situation worse.'

'You're very astute.'

'How have you been an idiot?'

'In every way. Why should a man, who teaches at a school near Settle, pretend to live in Headingley so that he can join a photographic society?'

'That's easily explained, surely? It's odd, but not a crime.'

'I'm the last to be interviewed because then I must be driven to Keighley police station and asked to give evidence of my identity and address.'

'Is that so terrible?'

'Some of our pupils hail from Keighley. My being a person of interest to the police could be all round the school within ten minutes of the new term. This could be the end of me, and do you know what? I don't care because that is the least of it.'

'What do you mean?'

'Let them just hang me. I'm the obvious suspect, and if it was someone else – if this is connected to the Vareys, well they've suffered enough.' He began to stuff the balls of newspaper into a shoe. 'By now, the landlord of the Black Bull will no doubt have come forward bearing witness to a blazing row between me and Tobias.'

'He might not.'

'It wasn't just a row, Kate. When Carine left us both sitting there, the landlord came between us to stop us from brawling like drunken sailors. You see where the finger will point.'

'May I ask you something, Edward?'

'Please do.'

'Why did you come back, after all this time?'

'I'm a solitary man. When it's school holidays, I'm at a loose end. Can you believe that I was so stupid that I wanted to see Carine and Tobias again? I'd found out you see, that he'd married her.' He began to stuff the second shoe, putting in too much newspaper, making the leather bulge. 'Carine was the woman I loved. Tobias saved my life, and I had saved his. I came back because in all these years no one has replaced them. It wasn't just idle curiosity, but I wanted to look at them. All right, not them – her. Only she saw me. I jumped on a tram. She ran and jumped on after me.' His lips moved in the memory of a smile. 'The conductor said, "Is this lady bothering you, sir?" I said that yes she was and he said, "This lady could bother me any time." That was last year. We rode all the way to the terminus without speaking.

Part of me knew then that there was not a tramline in the world long enough to take us anywhere. It was too late.'

I took the shoes and set them down on the edge of the hearth, to give myself time to think. 'And yet?'

'Some feelings don't change. She is the most astonishing and sensuous woman and she loved me, and I loved her. We were meant for each other and yet she had married an oaf, a eunuch. He could never be a proper husband.'

'Meaning?'

He raised his hands, holding them an inch from his scarred face. In a gesture of inclusion, he drew his hands down his chest and across his arms. 'We all had different injuries, some like mine that you can see. Many of us shared the same injuries, of heart and mind. Tobias also had a bodily injury that prevented him from ever consummating a marriage. I am guessing that he did not tell Carine that. Perhaps he thought she was ignorant and would know no better. If he thought that, he was wrong.'

'You could have gone away together.'

'She is imprisoned by that studio. Don't ask me to explain because I can't. There are things about Carine that I don't understand, that no one will ever understand. Sometimes, I'm afraid for her.'

'And afraid for yourself?'

He seemed relieved not to answer. At that moment, Derek put his head around the door. 'Edward, you're next to see the chief inspector.'

Edward once more looked nakedly miserable. 'Where do I start, Kate?'

'We all harbour secrets and surprises. It's part of being human. Tell him the truth. Answer his questions. He won't condemn you for who you are. He wants to find out who killed Tobias.'

A big dog lolloped into the room. For a mad moment, I imagined it to be our old dog, Constable, because this creature was also a bloodhound.

'Whose dog are you?'

It nuzzled my hand.

When Sykes appeared, he made me jump.

'What are you doing here, and why did you sneak up on me?'

'I see you've met Failure.'

'What?'

'Rosie said I shouldn't call him that. He's your parents' dog, delivered on Friday.' The dog wagged its tail. 'He's taken a liking to you.' Sykes sounded a touch grieved. 'I'm the one who's been looking after him.'

'So you came to bring the dog? Mother already chose his name. Sergeant.'

'There's something else. We're at the far side of the garden. Rosie asked for an extra cup and plate.'

'You've picked an odd day to come.'

'Yes I heard. The people at our table told us. We didn't know what to think when they said one of the people from Leeds had died, though I knew something was amiss.'

'It was Tobias Murchison, yesterday.'

'The poor man. But we're not here on a day out, or even to bring you the dog. I have some news too.'

Like a spectator at a tennis match, the dog was looking from Sykes to me and back again. I patted its head. 'Don't look so worried. We're not talking about you.'

The dog lay down, wagging its tail, thumping the ground.

At that moment, I did not think I could bear any more 'news'. 'Let's have that cup of tea and sandwich, Mr Sykes.'

'Right you are. I can't say what I need to say in the garden, but we won't leave the tea to go cold.'

I relented. 'Tell me now. I can't bear the suspense.'

He whispered about the discovery in the cellar.

I wished he hadn't. I should have been sitting down.

'Sorry,' he said, as we walked through the garden. 'Let's put it aside and exchange pleasantries over our refreshments. We'll find a quiet spot later.'

Over ham sandwiches and cups of tea, Sykes told me about Mrs Sugden taking possession of the bloodhound, and of the drive from Leeds by way of Keighley. Rosie praised the bloodhound as having an equable temper. It certainly sat quietly enough. Given everything that had happened, I felt that the ham sandwich ought to have stuck in my throat, but it was surprisingly good. There is something pleasant about eating in the open air during an English summer. For just the shortest time it was possible to pretend that the events of yesterday, in Haworth and in Leeds, had never happened.

Rosie decided to explore a little, and to see whether she might give a hand to the young woman who was run off her feet. 'I'll tell her I'm a friend of yours and used to work in a café.'

'Her name is Miss Varey. Elisa.'

Sykes and I also left the table, to find a quiet spot where we could talk. The dog placed itself between us and kept step.

The accounts of Tobias's death that Sykes had gleaned, from fellow day trippers in the garden, had been colourful but not entirely accurate.

I told him what had passed, and listened to his account of finding a body in the studio cellar.

'There can't possibly be a connection, can there?' Sykes asked.

'I don't see how. From what you say, that body could have been there for decades.'

'I said that to Rosie, but I've no way of knowing. And that was not my only reason for coming, Mrs Shackleton.'

'Oh?'

'Inspector Wallis came to the studio, in response to my telephone call about the body, but a constable in uniform arrived moments before him, acting to assist Scotland Yard. He and his sergeant wanted to make sure that the studio premises were secure and accessible, prior to a possible search. Now I understand why.'

'Yes. I can imagine Mr Charles would have made those contacts with Leeds police before he left London. He'll want to find out everything he can about society members, and their connection to Tobias.'

'There's something else.'

'Go on.'

'The young constable who brought the dog was the same chap who came to the studio. He made the connection that you and the Murchisons were all here, visiting Haworth. Unless Mr Charles is able to make an arrest soon, I expect he'll order fishing expeditions – requesting search warrants for all of your properties.'

'I really don't want Leeds police poking about in our office files. And it would be unfortunate for society members to have their privacy invaded unless there's a very good reason. Rita Rufus works for a fussy old pharmacist and lives above the shop. She already has a colourful reputation.'

'And Mrs Sugden says Derek Blondell lives with his gran.'

'Yes.'

'And I believe she is in poor health.'

'Something like this could finish her off.'

A call came over a loudhailer for someone to move the black Jowett. Sykes groaned. 'I've been rumbled.'

'I'll move the car. You go to the house. If anyone asks about the owner, I'll say that you're with the chief inspector. As soon as I've moved it, we'll speak to him.'

Sykes walked towards the house. I set off to find what had once been my Jowett. I could understand why Sykes had it painted black, but I wished he hadn't.

As I drew nearer, I saw why I had to move the vehicle. It was blocking the way of a constabulary motor. In the back of that motor was Edward Chester.

Elisa Varey was standing by the car, remonstrating with the driver.

Edward was speaking to her through the closed window, but she was not looking.

A swarm of bees went whirling by our heads towards the reservoir. I spoke aloud, 'Oh goodness. Bees, please don't leave. The Vareys need you.'

Fortunately, Elisa did not see them go.

Twenty-seven

Ambient Light

Marcus looked up from his notes. 'Kate! I've spoken to Edward Chester and I expected Elisa Varey. Have you seen her, and does Mrs Varey really exist?'

'I'm sure Elisa will be up shortly.' I decided not to mention the fact that she had been kept busy catering for ramblers and day trippers who had circumvented the police barrier at the bottom of the lane, and that she was objecting to police interest in Edward Chester.

'I saw Edward Chester being driven away.'

'Yes.'

'To Keighley police station?' He nodded. 'As a suspect?'

'Whatever else Chester has done, he didn't kill Murchison. He was standing a little way behind you. The statements of people who were nearby all mention him, a man with a scarred face, upright like a soldier. There was a couple with two little children. The father hoisted one onto his shoulders and Edward Chester hoisted the other. Even the most determined killer would be hard pressed to stab a man in precisely the right place while balancing a child that clutched at his hair.'

'Then why have you taken him into custody?'

'I felt a false confession coming on and sent him packing. His belongings have gone with him. He'll sit in a cell for a couple of hours before being escorted to the railway station and told not to come back unless sent for.'

'So we won't say goodbye, and he won't see Carine.'

'There's no time for sad farewells. The man was an unnecessary complication.' He straightened his notes. 'You came in with the air of having something to tell me.'

It took me a moment to answer, as I thought of Edward being ignominiously driven off and going back to an empty room. That seemed to me desperately harsh. 'Marcus, something has come up that you need to know about. Mr Sykes has driven over from Leeds.'

'If he has come to give you a lift back, I don't want you to go – not yet.'

'You will want to hear this.' Briefly, I told him about Mrs Sugden being asked to help out in the photographic studio on Friday and Saturday. 'I'll let Mr Sykes tell you the rest.' There was just one chair on my side of the desk. 'Do you want me to sit in?'

'Of course.'

'Then we need another chair. And don't worry, I will call you Mr Charles and you will call me Mrs Shackleton. And please put your animosity towards Mr Sykes on one side.'

'I have no animosity towards Sykes. I just don't know why he left the force.'

'And I don't suppose you ever shall.'

Marcus sighed. 'Show him in, Mrs Shackleton.' He brought another chair and set it opposite the desk.

As I opened the door, Marcus saw the bloodhound on the landing. 'Whose is that dog?'

'He seems to think he belongs to me. Mr Sykes brought him over.'

'Why?'

'I'll explain later.' I turned to Sykes. 'Mr Sykes, we can go in now.'

With his usual clarity, Sykes gave an account of discovering the body in the cellar of Carine's Studio. He set the scene, how he had helped Mrs Sugden clear the cellar, shoving old film and newspapers into sacks, stacking photographic plates in a cupboard. 'The work was interrupted whenever Failure here – sorry, he is not to be called Failure – whenever the nameless bloodhound galumphed into the cellar.' We all looked at the dog. Sykes continued. 'It kept pawing the wall along from the darkroom. I decided to investigate. When I tapped that wall, I discovered that there was a different sound, hollow. A cupboard had been boarded and plastered over. I thought we might surprise the Murchisons by finding an additional useful space – until I saw the body.'

When Sykes had finished his explanation, Marcus asked, 'Are you able to say anything about the body? Age? Sex?'

'From the clothing I'd say it was a woman and that she had been there a long time. I informed Leeds CID. Inspector Wallis arrived. There was a little confusion because a young constable arrived before him, to check the premises.'

'I made that contact before I left London. I thought there may be some link to the studio.'

Sykes reached into his inside jacket pocket. He turned to me. 'Mrs Shackleton, I asked Mrs Sugden for a list of society members. She gave me the list, and copies of your correspondence with Ponden Hall, regarding the reservation.'

I nodded, for him to give it to Marcus.

Marcus took the list of names and the correspondence. 'I need to speak to Carine Murchison before Leeds CID find her and start questioning her about the body in the cellar. I don't want the woman tipping over the edge. And I also need a telephone.'

When Sykes had said he thought the body might be that of a woman, the image came into my head of young Carine with her mother, the mother who went away and never came back. My mouth felt dry. I thought of the photograph, mother and daughter on the bench on Woodhouse Moor. The words would not come.

Marcus glanced at me. 'What is it, Mrs Shackleton? What's on your mind?'

'Something Carine told me, about her mother. I hope there's no connection.'

'But?'

'When Carine was about five years old, her mother went away. She said she would come back for Carine, but she never did.'

Marcus let out a noisy breath. 'It's Leeds CID that need to know this. We're going to get into some kind of tangle, I can see it coming.' He tapped his fingers on the table. 'Mr Sykes, would you mind leaving us for a short time?'

Sykes stood. 'I'll be downstairs.' The dog looked from

Sykes to me, and decided to stay put. Sykes got as far as the door, when Marcus spoke again.

'Mr Sykes, would you kindly enquire where Miss Varey has got to? I need her statement.'

When Sykes had left the room, Marcus said, 'Kate, I appreciate what you said earlier regarding not wanting to speculate about your fellow photographers. And I'm sorry if I hurt your feelings through not ruling out Harriet on the grounds that she is your niece.'

'That is not what I said.'

He held up his hand. 'I don't want to fight with you. When I took the call about this case, it seemed straightforward. A man surrounded by hundreds of people is stabbed in broad daylight. Around him is a tight knot of individuals who must have seen something, but they might as well be blind, deaf and dumb.'

'You have our statements. There's another connection, Marcus. Is someone trying to track down the camper?'

'Of course.' Marcus looked at his notes. 'There are politics involved. Sir James Roberts is well connected.'

'He is a wealthy industrialist. To say Sir James is well connected is like saying the King has a nice house.'

'I was briefed yesterday evening. We need a speedy resolution. The Brontë Society's influential members would go to war to prevent bad publicity for their religion – and it is a religion, don't argue with me over that, please.'

'Come to the point, Marcus.'

'Keighley police haven't the expertise. Leeds CID will now try and keep me off their patch as regards the photographic studio. I did not expect to say this, but I need your help.'

Silence descended for almost a minute. 'Marcus, I am an interested party. These people are my friends. Not to mention that you pointed a big fat finger at Harriet.'

'It is most unlikely that Harriet would have sufficient motive for wanting Tobias Murchison dead.'

'Well there's something we agree on.'

'I cannot yet rule out her friend, Derek Blondell. Harriet would be unlikely to help him eliminate the man he sees as an impediment to his one true love, Carine.'

'I am not sure why you need me.'

'False modesty doesn't become you, Kate. The local forces will co-operate with me, but only if I can specifically say what I want from them, and at present I can't.'

'You have the specials searching for the knife. I'm guessing that they haven't found it.'

'Correct.'

'It would be too obvious for it to be here.'

'I would hate to overlook the obvious. Now are you open to hearing my proposal?'

The word 'proposal' sat uneasily between us, but we pretended otherwise.

'Of course.'

'Kate, I am proposing that you enter into a formal arrangement with me, with a Scotland Yard contract, for giving assistance on this case only. You would need to sign the Official Secrets Act. We would agree a rate of pay.'

'What kind of arrangement?'

'A standard arrangement. We occasionally work with outsiders who have some expertise or who will be able to infiltrate groups or befriend individuals who might be resistant to the police. I would not be doing anything unusual in recruiting you.' He smiled. 'What do you say?'

'I say yes, if it includes Mr Sykes.'

'I thought you would say that. Sykes is proving himself an asset. He could be very helpful.'

'That is your yes then, regarding Mr Sykes?'

He nodded. 'Be sure about this, Kate, given your earlier reticence about revealing your friends' secrets. You would be acting the friend, and at the same time looking for evidence of guilt or innocence.'

'I want to know who killed Tobias Murchison. He was an annoying, bombastic man who should never have married Carine, but he served his country and paid a high price.'

Marcus stood. 'I'll gather up Mr Sykes.'

'Before you go . . . '

'Yes?'

'We haven't discussed terms.'

'Ah. There is a standard rate of pay.'

'And expenses?'

'Of course.'

'When you say there is a standard rate of pay, in my experience there is rarely any such thing. There is almost always a top rate and a bottom rate. I need your word that we would be paid the top rate. As you rightly pointed out, we have insiders' knowledge.'

'I will have the contract drawn up.'

'Let me fetch Mr Sykes. I want to ensure I have his agreement. He started out as my assistant but he has always been more than that. Over the years, he and I have become partners, purely in a professional sense.'

'Then since you are going downstairs, please send

up the elusive Elisa Varey before I charge her with obstruction.'

The dog followed me to the door. 'Marcus, you'll understand that I hope this crime was committed by an outsider.'

'Of course you do. But I hope you'll still keep an open mind.'

'I will. There is something that it would be difficult for me to enquire about.' I glanced along the corridor to make sure no one was within earshot.

'And that is?'

'I've heard it said that a war wound left Tobias Murchison impotent, and yet it is also said that on a weekly basis he was having intimate relations with a cook at the Leeds Club. Sykes can find out whether there is truth in the story concerning the cook, but you would have to look into the other aspect.'

'I'll speak to the pathologist.'

I walked downstairs to find Elisa, and to talk to Sykes. The bloodhound sniffed every stair in a businesslike fashion.

I spoke to Tobias, in my head. 'You must have had some good qualities. I never liked you, but I'll find out who did this. You shall have justice.'

And yet, it may have been that whoever killed Tobias, believed that *they* were achieving justice, or vengeance.

Twenty-eight

Dangerous Letters

Rosie Sykes never ceases to surprise me. She was carrying a tray along the corridor towards the front door. 'The dog's taken to you then?'

'Rosie, why are you wearing an apron?'

'I said I'd give the lass a hand. She only has one person in there helping.'

'Where is Elisa?'

'In the kitchen.'

I put my head round the kitchen door. A woman I had not seen before was filling a kettle. Elisa was standing at the table.

'Miss Varey!'

She held a knife in her hand, and was just about to slice a cake.

'You are wanted in the library straight away.'

She pulled a face.

'Mr Charles won't bite,' I added, stupidly thinking she might be in awe of the man from Scotland Yard.

'He might not bite but I will. Laying down laws, taking over our rooms for his interviews, trying to stop us earning a living.'

'You need to speak to him.'

She took off her apron. 'I'm going up there now. I hope he intends to pay rent for being here. It's not as if that man died on Ponden premises.'

It had become increasingly clear that Elisa was in charge here. I had seen men working on the farmland roundabout. Marcus would need to talk to them, as the people most likely to take vengeance against Tobias for wronging one of their own. Since all the special constables were local men, if they found a knife they would be just as likely to hide it in a better place than hand it to the police.

Sykes was in the main hall, looking out at the view.

I sat in the other chair by the window. My mother's new dog claimed the space between us.

'We have had a request from Mr Charles. He wants you and me to sign up to assist Scotland Yard in this enquiry. What do you say?'

'I'd say it's about time we had official recognition.'

'Then let us make a plan.'

About fifteen minutes later, Elisa came into the room. 'That Mr Charles was quite nice. He didn't say it in so many words, but I don't believe he suspects any of us, including Edward.'

'I'm glad you've talked to him.'

Sykes said nothing.

'When I told him about my sister and Murchison, he was very kind. So the thing is, I don't have the heart to tell him that his plan to keep ramblers and day trippers away didn't work. The lunchtime ones have mostly gone. I'll send the stragglers packing, tell them we're closing until teatime, and then he won't see them.'

Being not yet officially signed up to assist Scotland Yard, I said, 'We'll keep quiet, Elisa, unless specifically asked. And if you think of anything at all that will help discover Tobias Murchison's killer . . . '

'I'll keep it to myself. In fact, I'd give whoever did it every last penny from my Post Office savings to leave the country. I told that to Mr Charles as well.' She turned to go. 'Oh, and someone came from Leeds, a despatch rider, and gave him a package. I thought you'd want to know.'

A few moments later, Marcus came into the room. He was carrying a bundle of letters. 'Well?' he asked.

'Mr Sykes and I have discussed your offer, Mr Charles. We accept.'

Sykes stood. 'Glad to be working with you, sir.'

Marcus nodded and extended his hand. 'Good to have you with us, Sykes.'

Marcus put the bundle of letters on the table. 'Inspector Wallis has taken over the investigation into the body in the cellar at the photographic studio. He made a search of the studio and the flat above, and found these letters. I've read them.' He handed me the bundle. 'The inspector had them sent over to me, rightly believing they might be relevant to our enquiry into Tobias Murchison's death.'

I took the first letter from its envelope, and read it aloud so as to include Sykes.

Dearest darling Carine,

I cannot sleep for love of you. This will sound silly and I could only say it to you. When I climbed on the rocking horse with you behind me, I had this feeling that I was galloping into a new and better life. There is only one person in the way of that life and I wish he was the one who would gallop away and leave us free to be happy ever after.

Your devoted Derek

I glanced at the next letter, and the next, not reading aloud but passing each one to Sykes. They were all from Derek Blondell to Carine, expressing devotion.

'He hasn't dated them.' Sykes made a note of the post-mark dates.

Marcus asked, 'What's the business about a rocking horse?'

Sykes said, 'There's a rocking horse in the studio, sir. I suppose it's used when there is a child to photograph.'

'Is it big enough to hold two people?'

'Yes, if they squeeze tightly together.'

When Sykes had finished making a note of the post dates on the envelopes, Marcus took the letters back. 'I'll see what Blondell has to say for himself about these.'

It was as he reached the door that I thought of the question. 'Mr Charles, do we know whether the letters were reciprocated, or was it a one-sided correspondence?'

'No letters were found at the Blondell house. He works at the newspaper offices I believe. I'll have his desk and locker searched.'

'Would you please let me take care of that part of the search? I know his boss, the librarian. I would hate for Derek to lose his job if this is just the boy's foolishness.'

Marcus thought for a moment. 'Very well. Since it's a newspaper, I would rather be discreet than have this turn into a scurrilous story before we gather evidence.' He put a scrapbook on the table. 'There's this, too. Take a look, just in case there's anything of interest.' He put on his hat. 'You can contact me through the local station.'

Carine had written her name on the scrapbook. There were items from the local paper, an account of a fashion show, a piece about the renovation of a church, advertisements for the latest camera, and an article about photography. Carine had also pasted in samples of the greetings cards she had designed.

When Marcus had gone, Sykes asked, 'What is he like, Derek Blondell?'

'About eighteen, friendly manner, self-centred, aspires to rise in the world. He goes to the pictures a couple of times a week and sometimes walks Harriet home when she's working at the Hyde Park Picture House.'

'Do you know what those letters put me in mind of, Mrs Shackleton?'

'I believe I do.'

'I'm thinking of that case a few years back. Edith Thompson and Freddie Bywater. It ended with a double execution.'

'That came into my thoughts too. He stabbed the husband, and she tried to stop him.'

'That's right. She didn't know that he was going to kill her husband. Bywater said Mrs Thompson was innocent. He took the blame.'

'There were witnesses too, who said she tried to stop Freddie Bywater wielding the knife. Yet that did not stop her from being dragged to the gallows.'

'If your friend Carine has written compromising letters to young Blondell, heaven help the pair of them, whether they did it or not.'

'I think Carine realises she has been an idiot for not discouraging Derek. I find it difficult to believe why she would have bothered with him.'

Sykes said, 'Mrs Sugden knows the lad's grandmother. It could kill the old lady if her grandson turns out to be a murderer.'

'We have to keep an open mind, or we'll be as wrong as the jury who found Edith Thompson guilty, and the judge who sentenced her to hang. Writing love letters does not make Derek a killer, any more than receiving them makes Carine guilty.'

'All the same, it looks bad. Is this the strongest lead so far?'

'It could be. Poor Mrs Blondell. Will you go see her?'

He nodded. 'Of course, though it's too late to alert her, since her house has been searched.'

'And she'll be expecting Derek home, and worrying about him.'

Sykes opened his notebook. 'I have her address from the list of members who are here on the outing.'

'Mrs Murchison must have written back to Derek. That was too big a pile of letters for a young chap to pen if he receives no replies.'

We both had the idea at the same moment. Sykes got to the scrapbook first. He turned every page, looking for letters, looking for any articles that might give some clue to Carine's state of mind. There was nothing of that sort. It was simply a scrapbook relating to her interests, and her work.

Sykes reviewed his notes. 'So I'm going to call at the Leeds Club, and talk to the buxom cook. I'll break the news that her liaisons with Mr Murchison will be no more, and find out where she was on Saturday.' Sykes tapped his pencil. 'There's something else. At the time it didn't register as being of more than passing interest.'

'But now . . . ?'

'On Friday, Mrs Sugden sent a chap packing. He had come to take details of the premises. Mrs Sugden thought him a crook. She didn't like the cut of his jib. He gave her his card, which claimed that he was a property agent. His name is Hazelgrove. He has an office in the town centre.'

'Carine might shed some light on that. I'll mention it to Marcus and say that you are looking into it.'

'Do you know what else I'm thinking?'

'It will be easier if you tell me.'

'I'm thinking that I am not the person most suited to gaining the confidence of old ladies.'

It was unusual for Mr Sykes to admit to being less than perfectly suited to any and every task under the sun. He looked at me, to see if I followed his train of thought.

'You are thinking it might be better for Mrs Sugden to speak to Derek's grandmother.'

He nodded. 'She will be in her element. And if Mrs Blondell has had police tramping all over her house and making a show for the neighbours, she won't thank me for adding to her woes.'

'You'll call on Mrs Sugden?'

'I will. As soon as we get back.'

I sighed. 'At least there is one thing I can be sure of.'

'What's that?' Sykes asked.

'Carine did not murder her husband. She was nowhere near when it happened.'

Sykes picked up the scrapbook. 'Shall I take this, then there's no possibility that your friends will spot it and jump to the wrong conclusion?'

'Good idea – until we hand it over to Mr Charles.'

Sykes and Rosie were ready to set off. Elisa had supplied sandwiches and a bottle of tea for their journey. Sergeant bloodhound was now on his leash. We had walked to the stream and watched him paddle and drink.

Sykes moved to lift him into the dickey seat. 'Come on, Sergeant!'

Sergeant wriggled away, whined and stuck by me. Nothing Sykes or Rosie could say would persuade him to budge.

Rosie patted his head. 'You think you've come to find your mistress, don't you?'

I spoke firmly to the dog. 'You're not mine, Sergeant.'

Sykes said, 'Bloodhounds can be very stubborn.'

'Perhaps he can't face another car journey,' Rosie said. 'And he's definitely taken to you, Mrs Shackleton. He must have got it into his head that was why he came here.'

'I suppose I'd better hold onto him then.'

Just as we were saying our goodbyes, Harriet appeared. 'Auntie Kate!'

The resilience of youth! When I saw her that morning she had looked as if she might lie forever in that comfortable bed with the Porters' dog for company. Now she came dashing towards us and greeted Mr and Mrs Sykes. 'Are you all just going? I didn't even know you were here.'

She spotted the dog and made a fuss of it. Sergeant accepted her admiration.

Harriet turned to me. 'When are we going home?'

'I thought you were going to rest and recover.'

'I have, but I've to be at the café by eleven tomorrow.'

'The thing is, Harriet, I have to stay on here for a little while.'

'That's all right. Mrs Sugden will be there, and I've got my key.' She eyed the dickey seat at the back of the Jowett and then looked back at me. 'Is it all right if I go, or do you need me to stay?'

I knew that I ought to clear this with Marcus, but he had already left.

'No, that will be perfectly all right, if that's what you want to do.'

'Auntie Ginny is glad for me to be going back. She said do it quick before Mrs Porter returns from visiting an old invalid. She'll pass on my thanks and apologies.'

'Climb in,' Sykes said.

'Wrap that blanket round you,' Rosie ordered.

I hated to keep them waiting but had only just thought of what I needed to do. 'Give me five minutes to write a note to Derek's boss, Mr Duffield. You must deliver it in the morning, Harriet, by half past eight.'

Sykes had already started the engine when I handed Harriet the letter for Mr Duffield.

Elisa appeared, to wave them off. She and I walked as far as the bend in the lane, still waving.

'Do you suppose Edward will be coming back soon?' Elisa asked me.

'I hope so.'

'They can't think that he would kill anyone. Someone who has been as hurt as he was in the war knows the value of life.'

'I'm sure you're right, Elisa. But someone is guilty.'

'Do you know much about him, Edward I mean?'

'Not very much. He teaches English at a boys' school.'

'Is he married?'

'No.'

She did not ask me any other questions but gave me a useful titbit of information.

'This morning, I don't know where you were when he did it, but Mr Porter searched your rooms.'

'I thought somebody would. Did he tell you that we have to stay another night? Will that be all right?'

'Mr Porter didn't tell me, but Mr Charles, the Scotland Yard man, he told me. I asked him who would pay the bill. He said to talk to you about it.'

'Where will Rita and I sleep tonight? I don't want to go back in that room.'

'I'll have beds made up in the library.'

'Thank you. And now, I'm going to see whether I can speak to Mrs Murchison. It's dreadful to think what she must be going through. I suppose she is still at the police house.'

'Will you go see? Mr Porter would know.'

'I'll go to the station house. Where is it?'

'It's on Mill Hey. If Sergeant Hudson isn't there, Mrs Hudson will be.'

I took out my map. 'Show me.'

She looked at the map and pointed out Mill Hey, and the route. 'Do you want to borrow a bicycle?'

'Yes please.'

Ten minutes later, I was cycling down the lane. I had the dog on its leash, with an extension of a length of rope. So far that was working. Knowing bloodhounds, I feared that any interesting smell might catch its attention, and land me in a ditch. Just as I thought that, I saw someone extraordinarily like Harriet coming towards us.

It was Harriet.

Having shown no great interest in Harriet earlier, the dog now decided he must make a dash for her.

I stopped the bike. 'What happened?'

'I changed my mind. You're staying here to clear up the murder, and to take care of Carine.'

'No, Harriet, the inspector from Scotland Yard is here.'

'I know he's your friend. I'm not going to tell anyone, but I'll help you.'

'What about the message you were going to take to Mr Duffield tomorrow?'

'Mr Sykes said it will be just as well if he takes it. I think he wants to talk to Mr Duffield.'

'And what about your jobs?'

'Mrs Sykes will go to the café and offer to take my place.'

'You're not going to miss going to the pictures?'

'Monday is my night off, remember. I'm hoping we will have solved the murder by tomorrow.'

'I admire your optimism.'

'And I admire you for not toppling off the bike. Where are you going?'

'Into Haworth.' I untied Sergeant and spoke to him

firmly. 'This is Harriet. You can trust Harriet entirely, and I want her to be able to trust you. Go with her back to the hall and wait for me there.'

He listened carefully to my words. Meekly, he allowed Harriet to take the leash and set off back up the lane, only once making a small whimper as I watched them go.

Twenty-nine

The Blue Lamp

The station house on Mill Hey announced itself by the blue lamp above the door. I parked my bicycle by the wall and rang the bell. It was answered by a woman who was still shushing children as she opened the door. By the time I stepped inside, the children had disappeared, save for one little head peering round the door at the end of the hall. An older child must have pulled him back, because the door between police station and living quarters quickly closed.

I introduced myself, and asked if I might see Sergeant Hudson.

'My husband is out, but come through.' Mrs Hudson gave a friendly smile and we were soon in the office part of the house, just to the left of the front door.

I have a great deal of sympathy for police officers' wives, especially when they live above the shop, so to speak. Early in her career as police officer's wife, my mother failed miserably in that role. When asked to visit a female prisoner in the station lock-up, she took an extravagant picnic. When she learned that the woman had a child, Mother immediately appointed herself counsel for the defence. There was a good outcome for that particular station as they soon saw the advisability of recruiting a female constable.

Mrs Hudson went to the other side of the counter and opened a ledger. 'I'll just write your name and the time. As soon as the sergeant comes back, he'll see that you called.'

'It's Mrs Kate Shackleton.'

'Ah, it was mentioned to me that you might come.'

I waited until she had finished writing. 'I'm wondering how Carine Murchison is, and whether she is still here?'

'She was here. My husband asked me to bring her. With all the crush and hubbub yesterday, and the crowds, there was nothing else to do but walk her down the main street. I brought her by way of the park.'

'And now? I'd hate her to think that her friends have abandoned her.'

'The doctor found a bed for her in the local clinic, Lindisfarne on Bridgehouse Lane. She was taken there this morning.'

'Is she ill?'

'More shocked than ill. The doctor gave her a sedative and she had a good night's sleep.'

'And how was she this morning?'

'She was as well as might be expected, under all the circumstances.'

Mrs Hudson would quite rightly give nothing away. I admired her for it, but wished she was more forthcoming. As someone unofficially helping Scotland Yard, I had no entitlement to push her for more details.

'Do you think it likely I would be allowed to see her?'

'I doubt it, not without permission.' She gave me what might almost be described as a meaningful glance. Such glances only work if one can interpret the meaning. I should have asked Marcus to arrange some kind of special dispensation.

'I'll go there anyway.'

She reached for a scrap of paper and sketched directions. 'Will you find the way?'

'I'm sure I will. Thank you.' I hesitated. It was worth one more try. 'Mrs Hudson, if it is at all possible to contact your husband, or the investigating officer at Keighley, I believe they may grant permission for me to see Mrs Murchison.'

I had said the right thing. Occasionally there are magic words that allow something to happen. Mrs Hudson made a telephone call. She waited, she said her piece, she listened. Permission was granted. 'Someone will contact the hospital.'

Coming with me to the door, she spoke quickly, as if uncertain whether she should speak at all. 'Mrs Murchison is a nice lady. I hope all will be well for her.'

As I cycled through the hospital gates, I saw two familiar figures standing by the doorway, smoking. Rita Rufus and Derek raised a hand in greeting and seemed so pleased to see me that I might have been the relief cavalry coming over the hill.

'Kate!' I thought for a moment that Rita would throw her arms around me. 'I'm glad you're here. Not only do they forbid us from seeing Carine, they won't say a word about her.'

'How did you know she was here?'

'We called at the police house.'

Derek had his haversack on his back. He was ready to go home. Knowing that Marcus wanted to interview him at the station, I knew that he would not be going home just yet.

'I should have known they wouldn't let us in.' Derek's hunched shoulders dropped. 'We have no visiting permit. When Gran was in hospital, I had to wait until the following Sunday and show my pass.'

Rita was not to be pacified. 'Your gran was ill. She had you as her next of kin and named visitor. Carine is not ill and she is not going to be visited by Tobias, unless he comes as a ghost. She needs her friends.'

'You two wait here. Let me try.'

They both spoke at once. Derek told me that I would be banging my head against a brick wall. Rita pleaded that I must make the duty porter see sense. 'He's the most obstructive man imaginable.'

Taking a deep breath, I went inside.

The weary porter looked up from his desk, showing some relief that I was not Derek or Rita, and suspicion that here was yet another troublesome civilian come to interrupt his completion of the crossword puzzle.

Yet when I gave my name, and asked to see Carine Murchison, he showed a change of heart. Mrs Hudson's telephone call had done the trick.

He raised his eyebrows, glanced over my shoulder towards the door, as if expecting Rita and Derek to mount a charge. He then picked up the telephone receiver. After much winding and waiting, he spoke. 'Porter here, Matron. I have a lady to see Mrs Murchison. Her name is Shackleton and she has police permission to see the patient.'

Like a man who had heard all this before, he did much nodding of the head to himself, and shaking of the head to me. 'I'll tell her, Matron.' He hung up. 'Matron says that she does not wish the patient to be disturbed. You can come tomorrow at 10.30.'

'Very well.'

My gracious acceptance of the inevitable elicited some sympathy from him.

'It wouldn't matter if you were Lord Chief Justice, you'd have the same answer from Matron.'

'I was a nurse. I understand. There is something you could do for me, which Sergeant Hudson I know would appreciate.'

'What might that be, madam?'

'Call me a taxi, so that I might take my friends back to Ponden Hall.'

'Right away.' He made the call. 'Mr Taylor is setting off now.'

'Thank you.'

Not wanting to enter discussions with Derek and Rita, and so that they would not grow restless, I went to the door opened it, and waved. 'Give me five minutes!'

I shut the door before they had time to ask me what would happen after five minutes. It was then I remembered the bicycle. The porter had a nameplate on his desk.

'I'm sorry to trouble you over something else, Mr Jagger, but I came on a borrowed bicycle, from Ponden Hall. Is there somewhere safe I can leave it?'

'Leave it with me, madam. I live in Stanbury and I'll see to it. I'm off duty at eight and I'll ride it back myself.'

I thanked him. That was definitely worth a shilling.

As the taxi drew into the yard, I called goodnight to the porter and left.

'Aren't we going in to see Carine?' Rita wailed.

'Ponden Hall, driver,' I said. The driver opened the door and I bundled my friends inside. 'I've made an arrangement, Rita. I'll explain later.'

'I need to go to the railway station.' Derek had taken the haversack off his back and held it on his knees. 'I'm sorry you two, but I can't miss work tomorrow.'

'Derek, I've sent word to Mr Duffield. He doesn't expect you tomorrow morning. I'll explain when we get to Ponden.'

'But I have to be back at work.'

We had a journey of a couple of miles, during which time I could consider how to break the news to Derek. Thanks to his love letters, he was a prime suspect in the murder of Tobias Murchison.

As it turned out, I did not need to explain. As we drew up at Ponden Hall, two uniformed officers stepped out of a waiting constabulary car.

'Mr Blondell?'

'Yes.'

'We must ask you to accompany us to Keighley police station.'

Thirty

Looking Like a Policeman

On Monday morning, Jim Sykes set out for his ports of call. He sometimes felt a spark of annoyance when people said he looked like a policeman. These were the times when he was trying to pass as a regular person, with no connection whatsoever to the world of law and order. On this particular morning of Monday, 6 August, when he was setting out to investigate circumstances that might cast a light on the death of Tobias Murchison, Sykes intended to make good use of his ability to look like a plain-clothes man.

On his way into town on the tram, the tram conductor gave him what he had come to call 'that look'.

On the rarest of occasions, Jim Sykes saw himself living another life. This life might have been his if he had been born with a silver spoon in his mouth, or some mysterious benefactor had taken an interest in him at an early age, some windfall had come his way, or at a turning point he had compromised his principles and turned a blind eye to a dark deed.

In such a life, he would have belonged to a gentlemen's club. In that club, he would lounge in a smoking room, where deals were made on a handshake. He would help himself to whisky from a decanter and enjoy a long lunch in a dining room where the waiters wore penguin outfits. This place of his imagination would take a definite shape when he turned into Albion Place to call at the Leeds Club. But first, he would speak to Mr Duffield at the newspaper offices on Albion Street.

Mrs Shackleton had told him that Mr Duffield's advanced years did not deter early rising. He always arrived promptly at eight o'clock. When Sykes arrived at the newspaper premises, a van was just backing into the yard at the side of the building, having delivered the early edition.

He stepped inside, breathing in the smell of newsprint and cigarette smoke. The commissionaire looked up, showing interest in this visitor who gave off an air of importance. Sykes asked to see the librarian, Mr Duffield. After a short wait while the telephone upstairs was answered, Mr Sykes was invited to go up. Sykes hated lifts that rattled. He took the stairs.

Mr Duffield met him at the library door. They knew each other professionally, through Mrs Shackleton.

A clerk stood on a ladder at a high shelf. Sykes glanced at him, and back at Mr Duffield in a way that said, 'I need to speak to you alone'.

They withdrew into a back room where the only natural light came from a small window high in the wall. Sykes explained, as briefly as he could, the events that had taken place in Haworth, the police investigation and that Mr Duffield's clerk, Derek Blondell, along with every other member of the photographic society group, would remain in Haworth for a while longer. Mr Duffield looked concerned. 'We'll manage well enough. I hope the lad is all right.'

It took slightly more tact and discretion for Sykes to ask the awkward question of whether they might search Derek's desk and locker for any personal or private correspondence. Mr Duffield hesitated. He agreed only when Sykes explained that this would be preferable to involving the police, and that Mrs Shackleton had discussed the matter with Mr Charles of Scotland Yard.

'What precisely are you looking for?' Mr Duffield asked. 'I feel uneasy about a general search. For all I know, Derek may keep his diary here.'

'It is difficult to be precise.' Sykes had a brief image of a newspaper advertisement or a receipt for a knife that might have been purchased, or a diary with an incriminating entry. He hesitated to say love letters. 'As I say, I believe the interest is in correspondence. It is a murder enquiry. The sooner your clerk can be eliminated from enquiries, the sooner he can return home, and to work. Would you like to speak to Mr Charles?'

'I have met the gentleman.'

'He is working out of Keighley station. I can give you the telephone number. He will perfectly understand if you prefer to wait until the police acquire a search warrant.'

'That won't be necessary. We will take a look at Derek's desk, and his locker.'

They left the small room and stepped back into the library.

The clerk on the ladder had moved along to another part of the top shelf. Mr Duffield called up to him, 'Raymond, make us a cup of tea please, and see if there are any of those digestives left. One for yourself as well.'

'Right-o, Mr Duffield.' He was down the ladder in no time, and seemed glad of it.

When he had gone, Mr Duffield went to a tidy desk and opened the drawers. 'Raymond will be a few minutes. He is very quick at typing but slow at tea-making.'

The search of Derek's desk revealed an index book, a work diary listing his tasks, pencils and stationery.

'So, to the locker,' Mr Duffield said with a sigh. 'It's in the basement. Fortunately, I have duplicate keys for library staff lockers, so we'll go down there now.'

The lift creaked and groaned its way into the basement. Sykes opened the doors, stood aside for Mr Duffield and closed them again.

Mr Duffield switched on the light and led the way to a row of metal lockers. He fumbled with the keys, and opened locker number sixteen. By contrast with the scrupulously neat desk, this locker contained bundles of papers, manila folders, a manuscript tied with string, letters in brown envelopes and a tartan tie.

Mr Duffield took out the papers, handing them to Sykes.

Sykes glanced at the pile of material, typescripts and carbon copies.

'Mr Sykes, we can safely look at this in the library. Raymond will be up the ladder most of the day, sorting out material for the archive.'

Over tea and digestive biscuits, Sykes and Mr Duffield looked through Derek's papers.

'A piece for the *Amateur Photographer Monthly* – rejected,' Sykes said.

Mr Duffield's gulp of tea went down the wrong way when he glanced at the next piece. It took him a moment to recover. 'I thought he was a decent lad.'

Sykes looked with interest at what had changed Mr Duffield's opinion of his clerk. 'It's just an article.'

'It's scurrilous nonsense, for *The Mole of the World*, of all papers.' Mr Duffield took a sip of tea.

Sykes began to read the first page of a carbon copy manuscript whose plot was summarised on the title page, 'Reporter on the Moon'.

A mad scientist, with a strong resemblance to Mr Duffield, entices a young reporter to his mansion in the country on the promise of examining an unusually designed flying machine. The dastardly plan is for the young man to be sent into space on a night when the moon is full, and ready to receive him.

Mr Duffield poured himself another cup of tea. 'I shall have a word with that young man. I could sack him for this – using office stationery for personal use.' He gave a slight chuckle. 'He is very ambitious. I saw that from the first.'

'There's nothing here to interest the police,' Sykes said. As far as he could tell, these outpourings would be of interest only to knaves and fools. Sykes had no time for far-fetched fiction, whether it was written as a novel or an article purporting to be based on truth and facts.

'The young scoundrel!' Mr Duffield passed a carbon copy of a neatly written piece to Sykes.

It was the mysterious article about the trip to London by a titled lady, her daughter who practises the art of detection, a successful photographer and a lively gel.

'I'm not sure I want that young man on these premises any longer. Who knows which of us he will next misrepresent?'

'Don't be too hard on him. You said that he was ambitious.'

Mr Duffield rose, to see Mr Sykes out, and walked him to the lift. 'Ambitious, yes, but there is no call for deceit and lies. Pressmen have a responsibility for factual reporting and telling the truth as we see it.'

The commissionaire gave Sykes a respectful nod. He thinks I'm plain-clothes police, Sykes thought to himself.

He strode the few yards to the sandstone building that never advertised itself but was known to aficionados as the Leeds Club.

There was a time when Sykes would have gone to the tradesman's entrance because he knew the caretaker. This time, he climbed the steps and rang the bell. He had done a good turn for Jack Piggott, the commissionaire. Piggott had a good memory, but a big mouth. By dinnertime, anything you said to him would be broadcast verbatim across the city.

'Hello, Mr Sykes.'

'Nah then, Jack. Is Old Billy in?'

'Aye. You know where to find him.'

Billy, a champion player, had taught Sykes everything he knew about the game of billiards. Sykes made his way to the billiards room and put his head around the door. Billy was in there with a young chap. He introduced him. 'Mr Sykes, here's young Edwin Boocock, come to work here while he perfects his game. Edwin, Mr Jim Sykes, a man worth knowing.'

They shook hands. Boocock seemed a likely enough lad, but Sykes needed a word in confidence. Billy cottoned on straight away and sent the young chap on an errand.

'What can I do for you, Jim?'

'It's a delicate matter.'

'I'm good at delicacy, as you know.'

'Have you come across Tobias Murchison? I believe he had membership here.'

'Yes, I've come across him. Useless player. I hope he's better at taking photographs.'

'Unfortunately he'll be doing no more photography or billiards playing. He died on Saturday.'

'I'm sorry to hear that.'

'There'll be more news coming out about it, but here's what I want to know. It's been said that he was in regular contact with a woman by the name of Molly who cooks here. I'm told she is blonde and buxom.'

Billy raised his eyebrows. 'Is that so? Well I'd like to meet her myself but we've never had a woman working here, not ever. You've seen the chef, big fellow with greasy hair, in need of a barber. He wouldn't have a woman in his kitchen.'

'That's what I thought, but times move on. What with young females getting the vote, I wondered whether there'd been a change of heart.'

'It's in the rules. We'd have mass resignations if we let them in. A female cook would be seen as the thin end of the wedge.'

'What can you tell me about Mr Murchison?'

'Not a lot. He came in on Friday nights, had a game of billiards. Caused a right rip in the cloth last week with his clumsiness. He was most apologetic and offered to pay. Had a drink, had supper.'

'Was he pals with anyone in particular?'

Billy shook his head. 'Not that I noticed. He paid his dues and made use of the facilities. Oh, he'd discreetly mention his line of work. If any member had a daughter about to be married he'd raise the topic. I believe he got a bit of business that way.'

'Any enemies?'

'Not that I know of.'

'Thanks, Billy.'

'What happened to him?'

'It'll all come out.'

'This might not be the time to ask, but where would I send the bill for a damaged billiard cloth?'

Sykes left the Leeds Club by the front door, believing you should always go out the way you came in. He turned right, and then left, back onto Albion Street. He was heading for Park Row and the property agent.

It was a fine line between looking the part of a detective, and being accused of impersonating an officer of the law. Sykes glanced in the window of Beeker and Cartwright, estate agents. There were photographs of shops for sale and to rent.

When Sykes came through the door, the young man behind the counter looked up, hopefully, and wished him good morning.

Sykes returned the greeting, and produced his card. 'Is Mr Beeker available?'

'Mr Beeker is out of the office at present. Perhaps I can help?'

'Perhaps so. Mr Beeker called at Carine's Photographic Studio in Headingley on Friday afternoon.'

'Ah yes. It was not a convenient time for the proprietor, I understand. Are we able to arrange another time?'

'Sadly, no, not at present.'

'Is there a difficulty?'

'Would you consult the file for me, please? You see I am acting for the family after a sudden bereavement.'

The word bereavement often put a stop to obvious questions. The questions ought to be, who has died, when and what are your credentials? The clerk did not put the questions but gulped, went across to a gunmetal filing cabinet and brought out a manila folder.

'We were instructed by Mr Murchison ten days ago.'

'What were his precise instructions? The family is distraught at present and I do not want to pester them with business matters, at least not until they have buried their loved one.' Sykes was pleased to hear himself sounding like a man of business, rather than an enquiry agent. His words had the desired effect.

'Of course.' The young man perused the folder. 'The property in Headingley will be put up for sale as soon as practicable so that the purchase of the Boar Lane premises can proceed.'

'Ah yes, the Boar Lane premises. Are you also handling that part of the transaction?'

'No, that property is being dealt with directly by the seller himself, through his solicitor of course. I understand that Mr Nettleton and Mr Murchison entered a private agreement regarding Mr Murchison's purchase, including fixtures and fittings.'

'Thank you. You've been most helpful.' Sykes stood and picked up his hat.

'And thank you for letting us know, Mr Sykes.' He hesitated. 'I will keep the file open and await the family's further instructions.'

'We'll be in touch.'

Sykes rather liked the royal 'we'. It gave the impression of a substantial company of professionals, which is what we are, Sykes decided. Mrs Shackleton, Mr Sykes and Mrs Sugden.

Thirty-one

Mrs Sugden Investigates

No sooner had Mrs Sugden put on her coat than the dratted telephone rang. She wished it had never been invented. Most people got along perfectly well without it, although she had to admit that when you were running a business and had an employer who went haring off at a moment's notice, the contraption did come in useful.

Her first guess was that it would be Mrs Shackleton's mother, but as she went to pick up the receiver she placed a bet with herself that it was not.

Telephone operators had a certain way of making themselves known and a standard turn of phrase. 'I have a call for Mrs Sugden.'

'I'm Mrs Sugden.'

'Putting you through now.' There was a pause. 'Caller, you are connected.'

It was Mrs Shackleton. 'I'm glad I caught you, Mrs Sugden. Tell me you haven't been to see Mrs B yet.'

Mrs B was Mrs Blondell, young Derek's grandmother.

Mrs Shackleton was being her usual cautious self in not naming names on the telephone. 'That's right, I haven't. I'm just setting off now.'

'There has been a development.'

'Don't you want me to go?'

'Yes, but be prepared. Proceed as you planned but be warned, in case she has heard some news. A charge may be brought against her relative.'

'What charge?' Mrs Sugden asked, though the feeling in the pit of her stomach gave the answer before Mrs Shackleton spoke.

'The most serious charge possible.'

'Oh.' Mrs Sugden immediately thought of treason, but this was peacetime and Sykes had told her just the night before that Mr Murchison had been murdered. She had barely slept with the horror of it. Now the shivers came over her. That poor grandmother, such news could be a mortal blow.

'Will Mrs B have heard then?' Mrs Sugden asked.

'I don't know, but at least now you are aware. If there is anything at all that you need to tell me, go to the nearest post office and send a telegram. You have the address?'

'Yes.'

'Thank you, Mrs Sugden. Any questions?'

'No questions.'

No questions, Mrs Sugden thought, as she fastened her coat, except how will I keep the pity from my every look and word? How will I be able to face the woman knowing such a terrible blow will fall, or has already fallen?

She went into the dining room and opened the top drawer of the sideboard. This was where they kept the tobacco tin with petty cash. Mrs Sugden took a pound note – not so petty – and entered the amount in the book. There was no telling how long this telegram would need to be. There might even be the need to take a train out to Haworth if there was something to be delivered, some vital piece of evidence.

The awareness of the importance of her task grew. Mrs Sugden cut through the wood at the back of the house and turned into the street that led to Little London. She was heading for Camp Road. She had the house number, but it could be anywhere all along that road. There was a mixture of houses. She guessed it would not be one of the three-storey ones with an inside bathroom, but you never knew.

She wished she did not know the young man, and was unsure whether she did know him. There were two clerks and one of them had brought her a cup of tea when she visited the newspaper library offices. When he typed something for her, his fingers moved so fast across the typewriter keys that he made the Remington sing. It was hard to believe that this young man could commit a heinous act. Yet the most benign appearances might conceal evil hearts.

It was no distance to Camp Road for a person who could stride out, as Mrs Sugden did. Within the half hour, she located the house.

She knocked on the door, telling herself – don't look at her in pity. Perhaps she does not know.

The door opened. The old woman who opened it looked at her with something like hostility, and fear, frowning, her fists clenched.

'Mrs Blondell, I'm Mrs Sugden. We met at the chapel Christmas fair.'

'Oh aye?'

'I'm housekeeper to Mrs Shackleton who took the group of photographers to Haworth on Friday.'

The frown diminished. The fists unclenched. The door opened wider. Mrs Blondell gestured for her visitor to step inside.

'What have you come to tell me, Mrs Sugden? Had I best sit down?'

'I think we both better sit down.'

'I'm in the dark. What does it look like to the neighbours if you've plain-clothes men turning up in a car, and braying on your door? They came searching, chucking stuff about, lifting the rug, looking at the back of the oven, spoiling my rice pudding, burning their hands, refusing to say what they were after.'

'I'm sorry for your trouble. You don't deserve it, Mrs Blondell. You've done your best. Anyone can see that.'

'What's it all about? Do you know?'

'Now calm yourself and don't think the worst because the police will be checking on every person who went on the outing. Mrs Shackleton won't let anyone wrongly take blame for what happened.'

'Someone died, I know that much, but what's that to do with our Derek?'

'The person who died was Mr Murchison, from the photographic studio in Headingley. It seems that your Derek was very fond of the Murchisons like, but probably more fond of Mrs Murchison.'

'I knew that would bring him trouble. She had him

working for nowt on Saturday afternoons. I said they should pay him or he should leave them alone, but she had him under a spell, anyone could see that.'

'I'm going to be blunt, Mrs Blondell. Derek wrote letters to Mrs Murchison. I know nothing about them, but the police have them in their hands. Now Mrs Shackleton wonders if Mrs Murchison wrote back to Derek. Happen that's what the police were looking for – letters.'

'They said summat about letters but I didn't make the connection. She did write to him, I know that for a fact, egging him on, as I saw it. But it was no use telling him. I couldn't tell him that I'd read her letters or he'd have packed his bags.'

'Do you know where those letters are?'

'He burned them. You know how writing paper makes a certain delicate ash, that's how I know he burned them. She mun have told him to do it. She mun have known she was in the wrong. But why does it matter so much about letters?'

'Because Mr Murchison's death may not have been an accident.'

Mrs Blondell had little colour in her sallow face but now that colour fled, leaving her as white as her pinafore. She closed her eyes and placed her fingers on her temples, as if her head might burst.

'Is there anything I can get you, Mrs Blondell?'

'A glass of water.'

Mrs Sugden went to the tap and ran the water until the cloudiness disappeared. 'I have some aspirins in my bag.'

The older woman nodded.

'I brought a buttered scone and a bite of cheese, thinking you might not have eaten.'

'You're right.'

Mrs Sugden waved at the cupboard. 'Do you mind?' When the woman shook her head, Mrs Sugden took a plate from the cupboard, transferred the scone from the napkin to the plate, and doled out two aspirins.

'You're very kind.'

'Think nothing of it. You'd do the same I'm sure.'

'I would.'

When she had taken the aspirins and a drink of water, Mrs Blondell said, 'I've thought of summat.'

'What's that?'

'She stopped writing to him. I thought that meant he'd stopped writing to her. I'd seen him burn her letters. One last letter came from her. He was always first to pick up the post, and very secretive about it. That last letter went next door by mistake. My neighbour brought it round. And I thought, I'm not giving it him. He can whistle for it.'

Mrs Sugden held her breath. 'What did you do with it?'

'Kept it. Out of instinct.'

'How do you mean?'

'I knew Derek burned her letters. I thought if ever her husband comes braying on this door to punch my grandson, I'd throw the letter in his face and tell him. His own wife was no better than she ought to be. And she's the one who's old enough to know better.'

'And what did you do with it?'

'I put it somewhere, somewhere safe.'

Mrs Sugden had that sinking feeling. She was very good herself at putting something in a safe place. That 'something' might then evade her for a year, or fall into life's deep shadow and never be seen again.

'Did the police find it?'

'I don't think so. I sewed it into a lining.'

'That's a funny hiding place.'

'Not if you had a husband who was a drinker, ready to drink you out of house and home. Just disguise any coins in a bit of soft wrapping and sew them in.' She stood and went upstairs.

After a long time, she came down. 'My cloak has gone. They must have felt the lining, but I did it so careful. They must have taken it.'

'Well if they did, they will know that Mrs Murchison wrote to Derek, encouraging him. Don't distress yourself.'

'I've let him down. My poor son's boy, and I've let him down.'

Thirty-two

A Tender Shining

Rita was still sleeping when I woke on Monday morning. It was a glorious day. The sun shone brightly through the library windows. Harriet had once more slept in her box bed, the worst of the sodden carpet having been removed from that room. I went through to speak to her. The dog padded alongside me.

'Harriet, I'm going to the hospital early, to bring Carine back. It's probably better if I do this on my own. So will you take Sergeant for a walk?'

She sat up immediately. 'He'll like that. I'll take him to the stream.'

'Good. Don't let him pull you. Say "heel!" and have him walk properly.'

'We can't just call him Sergeant.'

'Why not?'

'Everybody has a name. Sergeant Somebody.'

'Sergeant Bloodhound?'

Harriet is very good at derisory noises. She made one now. 'Sergeant Dog?'

The creature in question wagged his tail.

'He seems happy enough with that.'

'Good.'

'Will you also keep Rita company, and keep her occupied?'

'How am I supposed to do that?'

'You'll think of something.'

'Has Derek come back?'

'Not yet.'

'This is horrible, Auntie. What if they think he killed Mr Murchison?'

'They wouldn't think that without evidence. We must be patient, and watchful.'

'Are we investigating, you and me?'

'In a way, yes. We want to make sure the truth comes out.'

'Tobias was a nasty person. What if someone killed him because they just lost their mind for a minute?'

'What kind of world would this be if every nasty person had a perfectly nice person waiting to kill them, with the excuse that they briefly lost their mind?'

'I know all that. And being nasty doesn't break the law. But I'm hoping that it was an accident. I don't see why it shouldn't have been. Or that it was someone else, for a reason we can't understand, or a maniac.'

I now regretted that Sykes and Rosie had let Harriet out of the car to come back here. But it was too late for that.

The same porter was behind the desk at the hospital. He looked like a man who enjoyed his work, and I expect they paid him overtime for Sunday nights.

He made no comment on the fact that I was early. 'Good

morning, Mrs Shackleton. I'll let Matron know you're here.' He picked up the telephone, and wound the handle.

The tapping of footsteps announced Matron's arrival in the lobby. From the porter's description of her steely will, I had expected an amazon of a woman with her watch pinned to her front like a campaign medal.

'Good morning, Mrs Shackleton. I'm Matron.' The woman with title in place of name was tiny, matchstick thin, jet black of hair, and a smile that came and went so quickly I wondered had I imagined it.

'Good morning, Matron.'

'Chief Inspector Charles left a message. You are to take Mrs Murchison back to Ponden Hall.'

'Very well. And how is she?'

'Still shocked and upset. She knows of her husband's death but seems not to have grasped what happened. It may be necessary for her to hear details from the police again.'

'I'll say as little as possible and leave it to Chief Inspector Charles.'

'Does Mrs Murchison have family to rely on?'

'No, but good friends. We will all do our best.'

'Then I will leave her in your capable hands. Please make sure she sees her own doctor when she returns home.'

'I will. Thank you. Should I arrange a taxi? Is she steady on her feet?'

'We have a driver who will take you back to Ponden Hall.' She waved towards the porter who acknowledged her signal. 'An easy walk would do her good. Take her on the moor, let the cobwebs blow away, but nothing too strenuous, given her condition.'

'Her condition?'

'Ah, she hasn't told you.'

'No.'

'Then perhaps you ought to know, since she has no one else. I suppose it would have been good news, had her husband been alive.'

Or it might not be such good news, if Edward's story of Tobias's impotence was correct.

Suddenly, I understood. This explained why Carine had complained of being sick. I felt stupid for not having realised, and not having noticed a change in her.

'How far gone is she?'

'Three months or so.'

'Thank you for telling me.'

'My staff nurse will bring Mrs Murchison downstairs. Good luck, Mrs Shackleton.'

With that, she was gone. Good luck. It seemed an odd thing to say.

'You're honoured,' the porter said. 'She wouldn't spare an ambulance driver for everyone. I do believe your friend has been a bit of a hit with the staff.'

I smiled. 'She has always been popular. People love her.'

Carine and I sat side by side in the back of the ambulance. She looked pale. Not surprisingly, her usual animation had fled. The ride towards Stanbury was generally smooth, until the vehicle bumped its way onto the turn-off, passing the mill.

The calm waters of the reservoir reflected the blue of a clear and almost cloudless sky, I thought of Elisa Varey's sister and her unborn child. It must be such a trial for Elisa to see this view every day. Perhaps that played a part in why Mrs Varey had taken to her bed.

Carine had not spoken. I must wait until she felt ready to speak, and not indulge in chit-chat that might seem insensitive, given all she had been through.

She glanced through the vehicle's back window. 'I do believe Tobias was happy here once. He spoke of the place in his sleep.'

'Is that why you suggested coming here?'

'I don't remember making any suggestion, Kate. Quite honestly I didn't know whether we would come at all.'

The ambulance stopped outside Ponden Hall. The driver came round to the back, to help us out.

Carine got out first. She said nothing to the driver, leaving the acknowledgement to me. Normally she would have thanked him and bestowed her smile. That she did not was a sign of her despondency, or distraction.

When I began to walk towards the entrance, Carine hung back.

'I'd rather sit outside. I don't want to go in there again. I want to go home.' She sat on the bench in the courtyard. The sun was now hot, the sky bright. A few small white clouds looked as if they were gliding towards a predestined harbour.

I sat down beside her. 'I should think we'll be going home very soon.' Of course I had no idea when we might be allowed to. There must by now be a sign on Carine's studio door saying CLOSED UNTIL FURTHER NOTICE. 'I know that an inspector from Scotland Yard wants a word with you.'

'Scotland Yard?'

'Mr Charles, investigating Tobias's death. There's no car so he isn't here yet.'

'But someone said, on Saturday, it was Toby's swordstick that opened.'

'Perhaps that is what he is here to confirm. We're all in the dark.'

She was quite dry-eyed, though she took out a hanky and sniffled.

'I just want to go home. I want it to be last week, and for none of this to have happened.'

'I know.'

'Where is everyone?'

'You wait here. I'll see if I can find out what's going on.'

When I saw that the hall was deserted, I popped my head around the kitchen door. Not a soul in sight. The only sound was a chesty cough from within the box bed by the side of the kitchen range. I beat a retreat from the kitchen, but as I reached the door, a voice croaked from within the recess.

'They're in the field.'

She must have recognised my footsteps. I backtracked and spoke to the bed's wooden frame. 'Who?'

'The young lass, the dog, and the woman who smokes funny-smelling cigarettes.'

'Harriet and Rita. Thank you.' How did she know everything? Was there some spyhole, or did she interrogate her daughter?

'The young feller hasn't been let free from the lock-up. The poet slung his hook.'

'Thank you, Mrs Varey.'

So Derek was still in custody, in a cell or an interview room. His love letters might be causing him a good deal of regret. They may even have led to his being charged with murder.

As I went upstairs for my boots and Carine's walking

313

shoes, I thought again of the Thompson and Bywater case. Bywater was dizzy with love. He had been drinking, was enraged, and his was a mad striking out. If Derek had stabbed Tobias, it was calculated, cold-blooded. Had Carine known that he intended to do it? Another thought occurred to me, that they had colluded, and he gave her a signal to leave. Was that the true reason for her being absent at the moment when the deed was done?

Sitting on the bench beside Carine, I set down her shoes and began to put on my boots.

There was no point in sitting and waiting. Marcus would arrive when he was ready. Harriet had taken my request to heart, that she divert Rita. But they might return at any moment. I did not want to deal with Rita's exuberance, and what would be her undoubted determination to whisk Carine away. Besides, I hoped that Carine would tell me of her pregnancy, without my having to ask.

'Carine, Matron advised a walk. If you're steady enough on your feet, let us do that. Otherwise we will be sitting here like two spare parts.'

I had expected her to object, but she seemed relieved to be under orders, and to have something to do.

'Yes I'd like that, Kate, but I don't want to pass any of the places we went on Friday.'

'We won't.'

'Perhaps Edward will be here when we come back.'

'Come on then. I looked up a walk to Ponden Kirk.'

'Kirk? That's Scottish for a church, isn't it? I don't want to visit a church.'

'It's not a church, it's a rock. It may have pagan or druidic connections.'

'Rita would like it then.'

'I suppose she would. It's said to be the inspiration for Penistone Crag in *Wuthering Heights*. There's a fairy cave and legends.'

'What sort of legends?'

'It's said that if a maiden climbs down underneath it and crawls through the fairy cave – the space in the rock – she'll be married within the twelve month, but I don't think we need take notice of that.'

We set off.

'It's such a beautiful day, Carine. A tender shining after the rain.'

'You should write poetry, like Edward.'

'That's not original. It's how Jane Eyre described a fine day.'

We walked along an upward sloping path, passing cottages and outbuildings. The earth was grooved, marked by the carts that had passed. The way then became enclosed by grey dry stone walls. The walls created the sensation of there being nowhere to turn.

Carine paused by a tree and looked across at the reservoir.

'It looks different from here. How the water sparkles today.' A few sheep ambled towards us, one bleating. 'It's telling us something,' Carine said, 'and we will never know what.'

A little farther on, men worked a quarry. There was a sudden blast, an explosion. A cloud of dust and small stones filled the air. We now climbed steadily towards the moor. It felt like a release when the path gave way to a wide stretch of grass and heather. It was not clear which way we should go. I tried to remember the map, and to look for where others might have walked before us. I must follow the track until reaching a stream.

'Another waterfall,' Carine said.

There was nothing dramatic or grand about the waterfall, as if water had taken on the gentle role in this landscape, leaving the drama to the wild moor, the rocks, and those of us who trod there, full of hopes and dreams, or despair. Someone had placed stepping stones across the stream.

We paused and looked across the valley.

'We're on the top of the world, Carine.'

The view was wide and open, and full of muted colours. In the distance a slight grey mist, perhaps a heat haze, merged with the sky. Even the sky could not keep to one colour, or still the clouds. It changed by the second. We walked on, and saw Ponden Kirk, its great slabs of stone reaching for heaven.

Knowing that the earth and rocks can be damp even in summer, I had brought a small blanket. I spread it on the ground.

Carine arranged her skirt. 'That rock, it would be just like Edward to be there, and to come clambering round. I have a feeling he might just appear and run to me and the horror of this weekend will slip away.'

'That would be a miracle.'

'A miracle?'

'What were you told, at the police house, and at the hospital?'

She sighed. 'It's all a bit of a blur. The sergeant's wife was very kind but as shocked and speechless as I was. In the hospital, they just wanted me to be quiet, and to rest. You must tell me something or I'll go mad.'

'What were you told about Tobias?'

'That he is dead, and something about a wound, and his swordstick. I warned him about that damn thing. I told him it was dangerous. What happened?'

'I hardly know myself, Carine. I took Harriet away, to be with my mother. She was so upset. We all were, and concerned for you.'

'I should have stayed with him. I should have stayed by him, but I felt a dizzy turn coming on, and that sickness. I didn't want to make a fool of myself and faint or vomit in public.'

'You did the right thing.'

'Did Edward know you were coming to fetch me this morning?'

'Edward has gone. He was interviewed by the officer I told you about and advised to return to his own place.'

'Why didn't he wait for me?' Big tears formed so quickly and rolled down her cheeks. She had powdered her face and the tears streaked away the powder. 'Oh, Kate, I had a fear something bad had happened. Tobias and Edward were at daggers drawn and Tobias thought Derek was in love with me. Do you think Derek . . . I can hardly say it.'

'The police are treating the death as suspicious.'

'Did someone kill Tobias?'

'Edward is in the clear. Derek is at Keighley police station.'

'Do you think he may have done it, and may have confessed?'

'If he did, the police will tell you.'

'That foolish boy. I tried to shake him off kindly, I really did.'

317

I thought of the embrace between them on the night that we agreed there would be an outing. Unless I was remembering it wrongly, she did not look like a person trying to shake off an admirer. She had pushed him away with a 'not now' shake of her head, or perhaps that was simply kindness.

'I can't stop thinking that the police must have evidence, if they are holding Derek. I would never forgive myself if he had harmed Tobias on account of me.'

'Had he ever said anything to make you suspect that he would hurt Tobias?'

'Yes. He got it into his head that Tobias mistreated me, and he did say . . . '

'Go on.'

'No. I can't. I won't say anything that would get him into trouble. Kate, I did not encourage him. You must believe me. On the day we were to meet at the Kardomah to plan this outing, after my father died, I had half a mind to have nothing to do with the outing because it gave Derek an excuse to see me.'

And yet, in spite of her denial, I felt sure that the suggestion of Ponden was hers. I should have asked her about this earlier. I hoped that I had kept the suggestions and could check the handwriting. If, as she had let slip, Tobias talked in his sleep about the place, he may have betrayed his guilty secret. Ponden Hall must have been the last place he wanted to come.

'It's as plain as day that Derek worships you.'

She began to sob, great wrenching sobs that shook her body. I put my arm around her, trying to calm her.

It was long minutes before she stopped sobbing, and still

318

the tears rolled down her cheeks. Her face was blotchy, her nose and cheeks red and shining. 'Edward has done it again. He's left me again.'

'He's gone back to his school.'

'No. I know him. He's gone again.' Finally, she became quiet, and stared across at Ponden Kirk. 'I hate that rock. It's sinister.' A note of panic entered her voice. 'A person could fall, top to bottom. The cold stone ground would come up to meet her.'

'We'll be all right, Carine. We haven't come far, and we'll easily find our way back.'

She gave a small scoffing sound. 'There is no way back.'

Carine stumbled as she rose. I made a sudden and anxious grab to steady her and my look gave too much away.

She said quietly, 'Matron told you then.'

'Yes.'

'Then apart from me, and everyone in that clinic, you are the first to know.'

'How are you feeling?'

'How do I look?'

'Wretched.'

'Then my look doesn't lie.'

We walked on, retracing our steps. The beck we had crossed seemed to flow more rapidly. Being overcautious now, I watched Carine take the stepping stones carefully, and kept close behind her. She reached the other side. I could relax because she was safely across. Perhaps that moment of self-forgetfulness made me lose my footing. I fell, full length into the water, hitting the hard rocks below, giving my right arm a terrible thump, soaking my clothes and myself.

I let out a yell, and then groaned – not from pain but annoyance.

'Oh, Kate!' Carine reached out a hand but I did not trust myself to take it.

'I don't want to drag you down.'

'I can't be dragged any lower.'

I found my feet and regained my balance.

I trod carefully across the remaining stepping stones to the opposite bank. This could have been worse. If Carine had taken my tumble, she might have lost the baby.

Perhaps my fall had helped her gain a sense of balance. She seemed calm, almost resigned to something. I could not ask her again how she was feeling now. All the same, she told me.

'I am feeling as if I shall have a little girl, and that her middle name will be Carine. Her first name will be Geraldine, for my mother. And no one will come between us.'

The last words were almost a whisper, and a plea.

Thirty-three

An Odd Place to Hide a Letter

Carine and I arrived back at Ponden Hall. Her eyes were puffy and her cheeks swollen from crying. After the unwanted dip in the stream, my clothes were soaked through and I was shivering.

There was a constabulary car on the track outside Ponden Hall. Marcus had arrived. He was seated on the bench in the courtyard.

He was, as usual, perfectly composed as he stood to greet this bedraggled pair.

He raised his hat. 'Can I get you a towel, Mrs Shackleton?' He kept a straight face and looked neither over-concerned nor, thankfully, amused.

'I'll be all right thanks. I'll just take off my boots in the hall and then sort myself out.' This was the first time I have undertaken a formal introduction while dripping wet. 'Carine, this is Mr Marcus Charles from Scotland Yard. Mr Charles, Mrs Murchison.'

I left them to fend for themselves, and escaped inside.

There is a convenient chair where people may sit to remove their boots. I sat down and unlaced mine.

Marcus and Carine came in, tactfully paying me little attention. He is actually quite good looking, in an overbearing way. Carine seemed pleasingly calm as they walked along the corridor.

I set my boots by the umbrella stand. It contained several walking sticks, and three umbrellas. One of them had a broken spoke, which reminded me that Harriet was supposed to have had our broken umbrella mended. I wondered if she had taken it to the stall in the market. As so often happens, it is the trivial things of life that catch my attention at odd moments. An image came into my head: Harriet in the cinema queue. She had dropped her umbrella, while taking money from her purse for the ticket.

Elisa suddenly appeared from the direction of the kitchen. 'Whatever happened?'

'I slipped in the stream.'

'You come with me where it's warm. I'll give you a towel.'

I followed her into the kitchen. There was a worn roller towel on the wall. Elisa released the towel and handed it to me.

'Get your wet things off and wrap yerself in this.' She handed me a blanket. 'I'll fetch you something from your trunk. Oh, and there's a telegram for you.' She pointed to the mantelpiece, and then went into the hall.

The familiar telegram envelope stood beside the clock.

I forgot about the towel and opened the envelope the minute she had closed the door. The telegram read:

MRS B SEWED MRS M'S LETTER TO D IN LINING OF HER CLOAK BUT CLOAK MISSING

As I dried my hair, and then myself, I read it again, inserting the names, and the missing words that would have added to the cost of the telegram.

I could not fathom why Derek's grandmother would sew Carine's letter into a cloak. A five pound note, for safety, yes. I had heard of people sewing money and valuables into their clothes. Still, mine was not to reason why. Mrs Blondell's cloak was missing. It was missing because Derek had brought it as a prop to take photographs of Harriet.

The cloak had covered Tobias, and was stained with blood.

Elisa came back, carrying my clothes. She brought underwear, the peach silk dress and the close-fitting natural straw cloche that is ornamented with appliqué work and peach and cream embroidery. The sight of that, my gloves and silk stockings, made me feel human again. She laid the items on the chair back and set my barred shoes by the hearth. 'Thank you! And Elisa —'

'What?'

'Derek was asking you about a cloak that had a stain.'

'What of it?'

'Did he give it to you?'

'He tried to. I wasn't having it.'

Monday. Today was washday. Elisa seems to me the most get-on-with-it person I have ever met. She would make quite a team with Mrs Sugden. 'I need that cloak, for evidence. Is it in the wash?'

'First off, do you think me or Mrs Pickup have had time to do a wash today? Second off, that's a thick woollen cloak. Only a fool would wash it. And you know my other reason why I won't touch it.'

323

'Where is it then?'

'You'll have to ask the young reporter himself. Happen he's writing a piece for his newspaper about it. "I am the cloak that covered the murder victim."'

Something like a chortle came from within the box bed.

'What do you mean?' I stared at Elisa. 'I don't follow.'

'I've seen him in the library, scribbling his little heart out and changing his mind. Wasting paper, screwing it up and throwing it in the basket. Well his scribblings will do nicely for the fire.' She went to the door. 'I'll leave you to change in peace.'

I began to dress, taking my time in front of the fire. I was halfway decent when the door in the box bed slid back. I paused. There was not another sound. I finished dressing.

'Is that you, Mrs Varey?'

'Who else are you expecting?'

I went to catch my first glimpse of her. She was sitting up against the pillows, wearing a white nightdress. The family resemblance was there in her square jaw and heavy eyebrows. She wore her hair in two grey plaits.

'Hello. I'm Kate Shackleton.'

'Hello.' She gave me an appraising look. 'You look dressed for a party. Mind you, it's a nice frock.'

'Thank you.'

'I was beginning to think I'd dreamed it. But now I know he's dead.'

'Tobias Murchison died on Saturday from a stab wound in the heart.'

'What heart?'

'You're a hard woman, Mrs Varey.'

'Not hard. I would have loved his child if it had come into the world. You can tell me one thing.'

'What's that?'

'Is any of my lot suspected?'

'I don't believe so.'

'Then you can put on your hat and don't mind me. And you can use my comb. I'll be getting up soon.'

As if in confirmation, she left the door to the bed open.

The room was warm but there was a fire, to heat the oven. A mixture of peat and coal gave off a smell of earth, smoke and Mrs Sugden's compost heap. I thought of apparitions, comings and goings, and disappearing umbrellas.

When Elisa returned, I saw that she had Mrs Blondell's cloak. She draped it over a chair, and went out again. I resisted the urge to tell her that by not putting the item in the wash and through the mangle, she may have saved Derek Blondell from the gallows.

I looked at myself in the brown speckled mirror by the kitchen sink, combed my hair and picked up my hat.

I was now ready to face Marcus, armed with telegram and cloak. 'Do you have a small pair of scissors handy, Mrs Varey?'

'Top left drawer of dresser.'

'Thank you.'

The drawer in question contained everything that a domesticated human being might ever need, and much that would never be called for. Fortunately, the scissors were on top. I would need to unpick the stitches carefully. Mrs Blondell would want her cloak back in one piece and in good shape. It was disconcerting to see the bloodstain, where the cloak had covered Tobias. What was also troubling was that

I could not feel a letter, no paper that crackled. Yet there was a spot near the hem where the fabric of the cape was slightly thicker.

I began to snip. It was a slow business, unpicking the neat, tiny stitches. My snipping was rewarded. Where the material had been folded over, an envelope had been wrapped in lining material and sewn inside. It took a great deal of care to release this item, holding it with a hanky to avoid leaving fingerprints.

The envelope, written in purple ink, was addressed to D. Blondell, Esq.

Once more, the voice came from the box bed. 'What is it you're looking for?'

'This and that.'

'Are you after knowing how to remove blood?'

'No.'

'Come close and I'll tell you.'

She must have thought I was trying to clear someone's name.

Constable Briggs was by the constabulary car on the dirt road. I gave him a note to take in to Marcus, who was still interviewing Carine. 'Just please hand it to him, Mr Briggs. It's important.'

I waited near the door.

Moments later, Marcus emerged, closing the door behind him and leaving the constable with Carine. I stood to one side, so that Carine would not see me, and handed Marcus the telegram from Mrs Sugden.

We stepped into a small laundry room. Marcus read the telegram and handed it back to me. 'Is this the cloak?'

'Yes. It was used to cover Tobias. Derek asked Elisa to wash it for him. Fortunately, she didn't.'

He drew on white gloves, examined the envelope and took out the letter.

I felt treacherous towards Carine, treacherous and wretched. I understood why she would have lied about not writing to Derek. It would be humiliating to own up to an indiscretion with a callow youth. Though perhaps I was misjudging her, and the passion was one-sided.

What the writing and purple ink confirmed was that the suggestion slip of Ponden Hall as a destination for a photographic outing had most certainly come from Carine. She had distinctive handwriting, not at all what was to be expected from an elementary education but the kind of hand one would expect from someone who had attended art classes. I realised that so many of Carine's accomplishments must have been hard-won.

I watched as Marcus read the single-page letter. And then, he read it aloud.

'"*Dearest Derek, You have done the right thing. I am so glad I have you to rely on. Come on Saturday at the usual time. As always, Carine.*"'

'It says nothing!'

He took an evidence bag from his pocket and slipped the letter into it. 'What do you think she means by "the right thing", Kate?'

'Ask her, and ask him. I don't doubt you will hear two different answers.'

'And what is your answer?'

'That she wanted him to burn her letters, and he did burn them.'

'Then why did she write the letters in the first place?'

'I don't know, perhaps as an encouragement to him. A

one-sided correspondence would be most unusual. She kept his letters as a token of his feelings, or reassurance, or enjoyment or . . . '

'Or what?'

'Derek's letters would be bound to cast suspicion on him. I hope this is wide of the mark, but Mr Sykes and I thought of the Thompson and Bywater case. It was Edith Thompson's letters to Freddie Bywater that sent her to the gallows.'

'Are you suggesting that Carine deliberately created a situation where Derek would be likely to feel jealous and enraged, and murder her husband?'

'It seems utterly unlikely. I'm simply saying the thought came to me, and to Sykes. You still have Derek in custody?'

'Yes. But what has made you change your mind about Carine? You were all sympathy.'

'I haven't changed my mind.'

'I can see that you have.'

'It's difficult to say. Lots of small things, and something that I can't quite put my finger on.'

'I have until tomorrow before Leeds CID tell her about what, or I should say who, was found in the cellar.'

'Carine's mother?' I asked.

'They believe so.'

'How have they identified her?'

'She had a dentist who never discarded records. The contents of her handbag were intact. It appears conclusive. But how did you know?'

'I know that she "went away" when Carine was five years old.'

'Once she knows about the body, she may be too

distraught to be interviewed. I have very little time, Kate. And now I don't want her to be alone.'

'Shall I sit with her?'

'Yes, stay with her. First, I'll ask her about this letter. Miss Rufus was tackling me earlier. If the two of you are with her, Carine may be more at ease.'

'You mean she may let down her guard.'

'That too.'

'Marcus, you do know that she is pregnant?'

He nodded. 'I spoke to the matron at Lindisfarne. And you were correct in saying that her husband could not be the father.' Marcus ran his fingers over an eyebrow, something he did when trying to solve a puzzle. 'Go on, Kate. Tell me what you are thinking. I can hear your brain ticking.'

'First, you tell me something. Did the special constables find the murder weapon?'

'They did not. We are still searching for the knife that went missing from the kitchen here. How did you know?'

'I didn't, not for sure, but it seemed the most obvious item to be searching for. Tell me, have you met the old woman in the box bed?'

'No. I'm told that she is sickly.'

'She's as sick as you or I. She will know who took the knife.'

'Will you ask her?'

'She wouldn't tell me, and I would lose her trust by asking, especially if the knife was taken by someone close to her.'

'Elisa?'

'She had motive. I don't believe she, her mother or your special constable Timmy Preston would have been happy to see Tobias Murchison return home hale and hearty.'

'I wish you had told me this before I charged Derek Blondell with murder.'

'You've charged him?'

'No, as it happens. Not yet. But it won't hurt if Miss Varey and Timothy Preston think that.'

'Going back to the knife, have you many places left to search?'

'Unfortunately, yes. It could be anywhere.'

'You have certain special constables who might be more than willing to have the truth of that murder hidden.'

'Kate, your mistrust of everyone and everything grows in leaps and bounds. Congratulations.' He indicated the evidence bag containing the letter. 'Thanks for this. By the way, I'm with Mrs Murchison in the big hall. There's a door at the back of that room that leads to what the family call their sun parlour. I have a plain-clothes man with me, and your Mr Sykes who has turned up some interesting information.'

Thirty-four

The Laying of Flowers

I went to sit outside on the bench. Not many minutes passed before Harriet and Rita returned. They brightened considerably at the sight of me. Sergeant Dog pulled on his leash, anxious to reach me. Harriet let him come running. He was wagging his tail and slobbering.

Rita followed and sat beside me.

'Have you brought Carine back?'

'Yes.'

Harriet showed considerable tact. She took Sergeant by his collar and hauled him into the house. 'Come on. Let's see if we can find you something to eat.'

'Where is she?' Rita asked. 'I must see her.'

'She is in the hall, talking to the chief inspector.'

'How is she?'

'Bearing up. She is going to need your support.'

'Kate, you could have stopped this.'

'Stopped what?' Did she think I could have prevented the murder?

Rita strode towards the house, calling back to me. 'Hasn't she suffered enough without being subjected to police interrogation?'

Harriet came out of the house. 'The old lady's got up. She's nice, Mrs Varey. She found a marrow bone for Sergeant Dog.'

I could not help thinking that the marrow bone must be Mrs Varey's reward for one of us having murdered Tobias.

'Did I do well, keeping Rita occupied?'

'Yes. How did you do it?'

'I asked her about crossing India and Africa. I told her I wanted to go there.'

'And do you?'

'I don't need to. She told me all about it. She told me everything.'

My niece was getting a more thorough education than her mother would have hoped for. 'I forgot to ask you, did you get the old umbrella mended?'

'Yes. What do you think I've been using?'

'Tell me again about losing the good umbrella.'

'It's gone! I'll never see that nice umbrella again. I didn't lose it on purpose.'

'I want you to tell me about how it happened, the queue, the crowd, people moving.'

She opened her mouth, took a sharp intake of breath. 'I think I know why you're asking.'

Elisa came to the door and rang the gong. 'I'm serving up afternoon tea, orders of Mr Charles.'

Afternoon tea was a subdued affair. Carine, Rita and I sat at one of the small tables. Harriet stayed in the kitchen with the dog and Mrs Varey.

Elisa put down a tray and placed a pot of tea, plates of sandwiches and a seed cake on the table.

Walking had made us all hungry, in spite of the distress.

Carine ate a ham sandwich. 'The police can't keep us here much longer. Does anyone know the train times?'

She believed she would be going back to her beloved studio. Even if she did, even if I were wrong about her, it could never be the same again once she knew that her mother had lain dead in the cellar all these years. How much longer could that information be kept from her?

The news would hit her between the eyes. After such knowledge there would be no way of living there as she had before. What would she do? How she would put one foot before the other, have a rational thought, or find a spark of hope?

So many details had flitted into my thoughts over the past hours. I must find a way of making sense of them before this great blow fell.

Rita was trying to be helpful. She suggested that we should go into Keighley to buy a mourning dress.

'I couldn't.' Carine slapped down her cup, spilling tea in the saucer. 'I don't want to go into Keighley knowing that Derek is being held there, under suspicion.'

'Haworth then.' Rita was not to be put off.

'Rita, I have a black dress with me. I'm in mourning for my father, in case you'd forgotten.'

'Then I should wear black too,' Rita insisted. 'Though I do have my white sari. In India that would be acceptable attire for mourning. I'll wear that. You should have a new dress.'

'Why?'

Rita gave Carine's arm a little squeeze. 'Because the one you have is too tight. You might be better in something that is not quite so well-fitting. That is what is so good about the sari. It leaves space for expansion.'

'I am not going to wear a sari.'

'Of course not.' Rita poured more tea and urged Carine to take another lump of sugar. 'You must keep your strength up.'

'I don't care about my strength.'

There was then talk about money, and who had cash.

The oddity of this conversation made me wonder if it was some kind of code between the two of them. Was the cash to make a getaway? Or were their minds befuddled by everything that had happened?

As I was trying to decide, Rita said, 'Tobias would want you to have a new dress. He will have brought money, in his wallet.'

Carine gulped and stared at Rita. 'I can't ask the police for his wallet.'

Rita put her hand over Carine's. 'Of course you couldn't, but I could. If they say no, don't worry. I have a guinea.'

'What would I get for a guinea?'

That was when I lost patience. I was about to tell them that none of this mattered when a thought occurred to me. 'Let us go into Haworth, anyway. Never mind about money and wallets.'

Rita brightened up at this. 'Let's go now, before the shops close.'

Surprisingly, Carine agreed. 'I don't care about buying a new black dress. But I want to lay flowers at the spot where Tobias fell.'

Rita clapped her hands together. 'That is such a beautiful idea. We should have a ceremony.' She stood. 'I'm going upstairs. I'll get my white sari.'

Carine pushed back her chair. 'I'll come up with you. I need to powder my nose. I must look a fright.'

'You look no such thing.'

When they had gone, I tapped on the parlour door. Marcus, Sykes, and a man I had not seen before stood as I entered. They had been looking at a pile of papers on a low table that was set between them.

Marcus introduced Cyril Hayes, a plain-clothes CID man.

'Mr Charles, we three, Carine, Rita and I are going into Haworth. Carine wishes to lay flowers where Tobias fell. Rita has a ceremony in mind.' I hesitated to say this. I did not want to say it. 'I think we should be followed.'

I expected to be asked why.

Marcus turned to the plain-clothes man. 'Job for you, Hayes.'

'Right-o, sir.'

I glanced at the papers that were on the table. Marcus said, 'Sykes, tell Mrs Shackleton what you've told me.'

As always, Sykes gave a crisp and precise report.

'You asked me to look into Rita's remark that Mr Murchison was seeing a woman at the Leeds Club – a cook – on a regular basis. According to my contact at the Leeds Club, there is no Molly the cook or any other woman working there. The chef has male assistants.' He consulted his notebook. 'On Saturday when Mrs Sugden was taking care of the studio, a property agent called to take particulars. I spoke to his clerk. Mr Murchison had put Carine's studio up for sale, with a view to buying larger premises in Boar Lane. As an afterthought, I went back to see the clerk, asking which solicitor Mr Murchison instructed, and I went to see him, as a friend of the family. He was tight-lipped, as you might expect, but I waited until his clerk came out on an errand and had a word. It seems that Mr Murchison was having his wife followed.'

At first, this seemed preposterous. True, there would be a child that wasn't his, but Tobias was quite capable of pretending that it was, if only for the rounds of drinks that would follow.

'Tobias would be mad to divorce Carine. She kept that business going. And everyone adores her.'

'Well not quite,' Sykes said. 'It could be an intention to start proceedings, or he may have simply wanted to know, or have something to hold over her as a threat.'

That made sense. She would not want to harm Edward, or have information come out that might risk his being dismissed from his job.

'Did he name a correspondent?' I asked.

Sykes shook his head. 'Couldn't get that out of the clerk. He wouldn't expand without I parted with more cash than I had on me.'

Marcus said, 'I've put someone on it.'

I looked at my watch. Carine and Rita would take a little while to get ready for going out, but Rita would be keen to reach Haworth before the shops closed. 'Did any more letters turn up, from Carine to Derek?'

Sykes allowed himself a smile. 'A search of Derek Blondell's desk and locker revealed only that he spends work's time writing speculative articles for submission to *The Mole of the World* and *Amateur Photographer Monthly*, oh and a novel and stories.'

336

Marcus intervened. 'Don't forget this little lot.' He indicated the newspapers on the table.

Sykes cleared his throat. 'When I cleared the old film from the studio cellar, I put all the rubbish in sacks and thought nothing of it. Credit where it's due, Mrs Sugden rescued these newspapers. She said it was a waste. She could make the newspaper into those twisty little cobs for the fire.'

Marcus said quietly, 'There are thirty-five cuttings about the Thompson and Bywater case.'

The newspaper items were dog-eared and creased. I did not look, not needing to. I remembered the case only too well.

'I'd better go. Carine and Rita must be ready by now.'

Marcus gave a nod to his plain-clothes man, Cyril Hayes.

Mr Hayes said, 'I'll stick close, Mrs Shackleton, but I'll give you a few minutes' start. Don't look back for me. I'll be there.'

Harriet had been so good. She was on the bench outside, with the dog.

'Have Carine and Rita come down yet?'

'Not yet.'

'Where are you going? Can I come?'

'Not this time. See if Elisa needs help.'

'I like Elisa, and I think that she's upset that Edward left without saying goodbye.'

'That's what I think, too. I have a feeling he will be back.'

At that moment, Carine and Rita appeared.

We were ready to go.

Thirty-five

The Click of the Shutter

We walked back to where we had stood on Saturday. The Parsonage Museum had not yet opened to the public. The little lane and the garden were as deserted as a church on a weekday. A paint-spattered sheet lay on the ground outside the front door. A decorator came from the house, bringing out a can of paint, putting it down and picking up another. He glanced at us.

We must have been a curious sight. Rita had wound her white sari around her silk pantaloons and top, and above that sported the Selfridges cardigan. Carine wore her too-tight black dress. Thanks to my encounter with the stream, and the choice of items brought from my trunk by Elisa, I was dressed for afternoon tea in good company.

We stood in a circle on the path where Tobias had breathed his last. Carine had brought three gladioli from Ponden Hall garden.

'I lay these flowers in memory of my husband, Tobias. We did not say goodbye, Toby. I say it now. I hope and pray you are in a better place.'

Rita murmured an incantation in Hindustani. She hummed in a rising crescendo, followed by a Monteverdi madrigal, so beautifully sung that three decorators came to listen, and gave a round of applause.

It was my turn. 'Farewell, Tobias. Justice will be done, and seen to be done.'

As we turned away, Carine said, 'Edward should have been here.'

After that, we walked down the main street. 'This is the way Mrs Hudson brought me,' Carine said, looking about her. 'She took me into the park to sit on a bench. I believe she thought I might faint. I didn't.'

Rita concentrated on the shops. We failed to find a suitable black dress. Rita took this personally. 'You'd think that in a place famous for untimely deaths, they would be a little more prepared for people who mourn.'

The one shop that might have stocked such an item had a sign on the door: CLOSED DUE TO BEREAVEMENT.

Carine did not seem to mind, though Rita minded very much.

I caught a glimpse of the man who was following us, but was careful to show no sign of having noticed him.

Part way down the hill, Carine came to an abrupt halt. 'I'm going buy a bunch of flowers and something for the children.'

Rita said, 'What children?'

'Mrs Hudson, the police sergeant's wife, was so kind to me.'

Rita entered into the spirit of this. 'Carine, you are so thoughtful. That is a lovely idea. Buy chocolate.'

'The children slept with their parents, so that I could have a quiet room.'

I wondered whether Mr and Mrs Hudson took the children into their bed to keep them safe from Carine.

At the flower shop, Carine again favoured gladioli. In the Co-op, she bought three bars of milk chocolate.

We continued down the hill.

A pair of wrought-iron gates, dated 1927, led to the park. Whoever forged the gates had been given an optimistic date. The park was as yet incomplete, with digging still going on, and men working on an additional path. Some beds were in bloom, with irises and delphiniums, and there was a small rose garden.

Carine thought she might not remember the way once she reached the other side of the park. 'I was in such a state of shock on Saturday.'

It was then that the thought occurred to me. She is precisely retracing her steps from Saturday.

'We can always ask,' Rita said.

But Carine did remember.

As we came closer to the police house, Carine said, 'Let me do this on my own. I don't want Mrs Hudson to think I have come with a delegation.'

Rita readily agreed. 'Look, there's a parade of shops. Come and find us when you're ready. There may even be a dress shop.'

Carine carried on walking.

The man following us dogged Carine's footsteps, keeping closer now than previously. He took something from his pocket. I guessed that it might be a tiny camera.

Rita and I looked in the draper's shop window. A translucent yellow blind created a golden glow, and more prosaically kept the items on display from fading. We went inside, inspected hooks and eyes, replacement suspenders, fancy buttons and balls of wool.

We walked about the hardware store with its sharp scent of metal and mops. We admired enamel basins and galvanised steel buckets.

We were in the newsagent's when Rita said, 'Carine is taking an awfully long time. She must have been invited in for tea.'

Slowly, we walked along the road.

'It's over there,' Rita said, seeing the blue lamp. 'Had we better ask?'

She did not wait for me to answer but hurried across the road in front of a Ringtons Tea van causing the driver to swerve and give a blast on his horn.

Slowly, I followed her. Normally, a privet hedge would not arouse interest. This one did. On the ground by the gate lay a scattering of leaves. There was a gap, where someone might have thrust an arm, while searching. So this was where Carine had dropped the knife – a place where no one would come to look. If she had not tried to retrieve it, it may have remained unnoticed for years. But she could not take that chance with the murder weapon.

I waited by the gate.

Rita was ringing the doorbell.

Mrs Hudson came to the door. She glanced at Rita, and then at me. Her look was grim and sorrowful. Perhaps she had shed a few tears. There would never be another time in her life when a polite young woman would bring flowers and chocolates, and seconds later be asked to account for her movements and held in custody.

She waited for Rita to ask her question. 'Is Mrs Murchison here?'

'I'm sorry, love. You can't see Mrs Murchison. She has an appointment with the chief inspector from Scotland Yard.'

If my guess was correct, Carine Murchison was in serious need of a solicitor.

The door to the police house closed.

Rita turned to me. 'Did you see that, Kate? She just shut the door on me.'

'Rita, go back to Ponden Hall. There's nothing you can do here.'

'What do you mean?'

I turned and began to hurry back in the direction we had come, feeling sure the police house was now closed to us. I must find another telephone.

Rita came hurrying after me. 'Kate, what do you know that I don't?'

'I know that Carine needs a solicitor. I'm going to make a telephone call.'

'I have a solicitor friend. You met him. Andrew likes Carine. He's sympathetic.'

'She doesn't need sympathy, Rita.'

The person Carine needed was Mr Cohen. I got to know him well a few years earlier. He was the man to go to if you needed a good defence, and an impressive barrister.

Rita grabbed my arm. 'I'm not going away, Kate. We mustn't abandon Carine. Stay with me and we'll take her home.'

'She'll need you, but not like this.'

'What are you saying?'

'I believe that Carine will have questions to answer about Tobias's death.'

'That's ridiculous. She wasn't even there. They've charged Derek. I couldn't have believed it of him, but it must be true. Carine wouldn't hurt a fly.'

I walked away, not giving voice to my thought that Carine had no reason to hurt a fly. She had reasons to hurt Tobias.

Very occasionally, I break into a run. I used to run a lot when I was a girl because I was often late. Or I'd run if someone had annoyed or upset me and I just wanted to be home as fast as I could.

I told myself that I was running in case the post office closed before I reached it, but really I was running from that house where Carine was being held along with whatever she had taken from the bush. The knife, I felt sure. I remembered, too, that on Saturday she had worn cream lace gloves. She did not have them with her when I collected her from the hospital. I stopped running, took some deep breaths and made myself calm down. There was a post office right here on Mill Hey. We had passed it earlier.

At the post office, I asked for the directories. My hands shook as I looked for Mr Cohen's telegraphic address. The hands on the post office clock ticked towards closing time. I would make a telephone call, that would be quicker and it would save me having to write a long explanation on a short form.

While the operator tried to connect me, I willed Mrs

343

Sugden to be at home, and took deep breaths as I waited. Thankfully, Mrs Sugden answered. I spoke so calmly that it was as if someone else had taken over this task.

'Mrs Sugden, we have the telephone number and address of Mr Cohen the solicitor, both his office and his home. Find out where he is. Tell him you are coming to see him. Give him the name of my friend whose shop you have been taking care of. Say that person is being held at Keighley station on a very serious charge and I want him to arrange her defence.'

'I'll do that right away.' Practical as ever, she added, 'He'll charge a bob or two.'

'Tell him it will be taken care of.'

'I'll do it now.'

I hung up the telephone. Mrs Sugden was right that a good defence for Carine would cost dear. By rights, she ought to be entitled to the proceeds of her studio premises and business, but her father had made Tobias his beneficiary. I suspected that the law might not allow a person accused of murdering her husband to inherit his estate.

In my garage, there is a white Rolls-Royce, kindly bequeathed to me by a grateful Indian princess. That splendid car sits there, waiting for the day when I might employ a chauffeur. Someone else would love it, I'm sure.

Rita was sitting on the wall of the police house. A familiar Alvis car was by the kerb, its driver at the wheel. So Carine was still inside. Out of breath from hurrying back from the post office, I sat down beside Rita.

'Where have you been? What's going on?'

'Something I needed to do. Who is inside now?'

'That Scotland Yard chap and a policewoman.'

The driver opened the car door. 'Off you go, ladies. No spectators please.'

I had no intention of moving. 'We're friends of Mrs Hudson, officer, invited for tea.'

Rita whispered, 'Kate, when they come out, we grab Carine and we run.'

'Rita, we have nowhere to run. And when Carine comes out, for heaven's sake, keep quiet. I have something to tell her. I don't want it to be lost in a commotion. The best thing you could do is start walking back.'

'And let her think I've deserted her? Never!' She ran her hands through her hair. 'Besides, I've lost my sense of direction.'

'After I've spoken to her, do whatever you please but just keep out of the way for now. Walk down the road. Give me a chance to speak to Carine.'

'All right. If you say so. As they set off, I'll throw myself under the wheels. That'll stop them.'

Rita moved a few yards off. I went into the garden, out of sight of the driver. A moment later, the house door opened. Carine was brought out, the woman constable gripping her arm, Marcus following.

I dashed across and spoke to her. 'Carine, a solicitor, Mr Cohen will act for you.' She turned to look at me as the policewoman hurried her to the car. 'Until Mr Cohen comes, say nothing except your name, address and date of birth. Not another word!'

The driver shut the door.

Marcus glared at me. 'Thank you, Mrs Shackleton.'

The car swerved to avoid Rita. She ran alongside the car, banging on the window. When it left her behind, she and I fell into step.

'Kate, if she did it Tobias drove her to it. But she can't have killed him, can she?'

'I don't know.'

'She wasn't there.'

'We need to go back to Ponden Hall, Rita.'

Thirty-Six

Harriet's Umbrella

On arriving back at Ponden, I was greeted by Sergeant Dog. He was delighted to see me and did much slobbering and tail wagging. Rita said that she would go sit under a tree in the walled garden, to chant. Would somebody join her? When Harriet heard that Carine had been arrested, she decided to join Rita, just in case the chanting helped. She took Sergeant Dog with her. He seemed happy to go, perhaps regarding Harriet and me as interchangeable.

It was the most beautiful mild evening, with a pale sun and a light breeze. The thought of Carine being locked up in a cell was almost unbearable. Sykes and I sat in the courtyard.

'Mr Sykes, I wish you had taken Harriet home on Sunday.'

'She insisted. She didn't want to leave you in the lurch. Besides, that dickey seat was a bit of a squeeze for her and your dog.'

'He's not my dog, and it's past time for Harriet to go home.'

'I'll take her back. But what will you do?'

'I want to be in the magistrates' court tomorrow when Carine is indicted. Rita will want to be there too. I've arranged for Mr Cohen to see Carine and arrange for her defence.'

He was silent for a while, but I guessed that, like Mrs Sugden, he would be thinking of the cost. Finally, he said, 'I'm glad. Would you have done that for Derek, or Edward?'

'I don't know.'

'Mr Charles said Derek will be released this evening.'

'Why so late?'

'I said I'd see that he got to his train. He's the age of my kids.'

'That's kind of you.'

'He's friends with Harriet, isn't he?'

'Yes. She sees him at the pictures. He walks her home sometimes.'

'Then how about if I suggest she comes with me to pick him up? I'll see Derek onto the train, and drive Harriet home.'

'You'd better take the dog, too. He won't be allowed in the magistrates' court, and I'm going straight home after that.'

The sound of chanting floated across from the walled garden, reaching a crescendo, augmented by the howling of the bloodhound, joining in most plaintively.

Harriet came back moments later. 'I don't want Sergeant Dog to think that howling is a good idea.'

'It's time that he went home, Harriet, and you must go with him. He can go to my mother at the weekend.'

Sykes chipped in. 'Mrs Sugden said the constable who

brought him says he's trained to be good with cats, so yours will be safe.'

I smiled. 'Sookie will soon put him in his place.'

Harriet did not object. It is a habit of hers to seem deceptively quiescent, and then to come up with an alternative plan. 'Do you know what I was thinking?'

'What?'

'I don't want to go until the murder has been solved.'

'I think it might be solved, Harriet, only we won't know for sure until much later, so really it's time to go home. I'll be coming back tomorrow.'

'So it was Derek?' Harriet's mouth opened. 'I know he was soft on Carine but . . . '

I glanced at Sykes, urging him to say something. He left it to me.

'Harriet, Derek will be released. He has his belongings with him because he thought he would go home on Sunday. He has been through a difficult ordeal so might you consider going with Mr Sykes to meet him at Keighley police station and see him onto the train?'

She thought for a moment, and gave a sigh that seemed far too old for her. 'I will meet him, just because if that were me, I'd want someone to meet me and go with me to the station. But do you know what?'

'What?'

'Derek wouldn't do the same for me. He's too selfish. He only thinks of what great things he'll do.'

'You could be right, Harriet.'

'I thought he used to walk me home from the pictures because he liked me, but he only wanted to hear what I had to say. I heard him talking to Rita about *Rin Tin Tin*.

He was saying exactly what I'd said to him, same words, everything.'

'Well then you're right about him. He's older than you, but you are more grown up, and kind. You'll be doing the right thing. That's what's important.'

I waited. I knew that she had another question.

Harriet was thinking. It took her a moment to speak. 'Edward has gone. Rita is here. No one is mentioning the camper. Derek is to be set free. Who did it? Did Mr Murchison stab himself?'

'No.'

Sykes moved to go. 'I'll just check on the car and bring it along. Harriet, you might need to ask Elisa for a dish, and a bottle of water, in case we have to stop on the way back for the dog.'

Harriet stared at me. 'You're not saying it's Carine?'

'We can't know for sure, but that is a possibility.'

She did not seem as surprised as I expected her to be. 'When I looked at Carine on the train, pretending to be asleep, and she reminded me of that doll in the County Arcade, I thought that she looked – I don't know, too good to be true, but I never thought—'

'Go get that water.'

Sykes helped Sergeant into the dickey seat. He sat still for half a minute and then jumped out and ran to me. 'It's all right, Sergeant. Harriet is coming.'

She appeared a few moments later, carrying a bottle of water and an enamel pie dish. 'I hope he won't be too disappointed when we take him home. Life won't always be so exciting for him.'

'Harriet, don't forget that he is not our dog.'

'He probably is ours. I forgot to tell you. I saw Auntie Ginny and Uncle when I was taking him for a walk. They're not moving to the country. Uncle won't be retiring. They won't be buying the house from Mr and Mrs Porter.'

'Even if you're right, that doesn't mean Mother won't have the dog.'

'I told her he pulls. I told her he'd break her arm. Besides, Sergeant Dog might want to have a say in the matter. He might decide that we're his home.'

Sykes once more helped the dog into the dickey seat. He climbed in and started the car. 'Right then – all on board!'

Harriet got into the passenger seat. She wanted one more word. 'There is a possibility for Carine, isn't there? That the worst won't happen to her? I do so like Carine.'

'Everyone does, Harriet, and there are always possibilities.'

I waved them off. She called, 'Say goodbye to Rita for me.'

Rita came from the walled garden, just in time to wave. She carried sprigs of lavender and handed one to me. The scent of lavender makes it hard to imagine that anything could be amiss in the world. I wondered how Carine would survive without flowers.

Rita and I sat by the fire in the main hall. It was not much of a fire, there only to keep something burning in the hearth. No one troubled to mend it. One often has a niggling doubt, but not this time. Carine had murdered Tobias. I could understand why. In some ways it must have seemed a perfectly reasonable act. He had married her under false pretences. She was pregnant by another man. He was having her followed. She was an attractive woman, with a good business. Perhaps she wanted to be a widow, with her child, a girl who might walk with her on Woodhouse Moor and sit for a photograph as she had done with her own mother.

Who was I to stand in the way of Carine's dreams?

The answer looked back at me from the fire. Murder is the most appalling of crimes, and yet there may be something worse. That something would be to watch another person, an innocent person, pay the price. Carine would have let Derek take the blame. Perhaps she thought someone else would kill Tobias, one of the Vareys, perhaps. Or he might have met with an 'accident' while walking on some precipitous path.

Elisa began to clear away the dishes. 'Mr Charles of Scotland Yard is here. He wants to speak to all of us. I'll show him in, will I?'

She asked us, her paying guests, for permission.

Of course, he needed no permission, and she did not need to ask. The evening teemed with courtesies, as we tip-toed around each other, each with a particular slice of guilt.

Marcus came in, hat in hand.

'I'm here as a courtesy, ladies. Miss Varey, would you please ask your mother to come in? It is better that you hear the news from me, rather than picking up rumours from special constables.'

'We already know,' Rita said. 'You are putting Carine before the bench tomorrow. It is the most appalling lie and it will be shown up as such. Tell him, Kate.'

'Let Mr Charles speak, Rita.'

'We'll wait until Mrs and Miss Varey can join us. They have a right to hear.'

Mrs Varey walked with a stick. We heard her tap-tapping across the corridor from the kitchen.

Marcus waited until the Vareys were seated.

'I will be brief. Mrs Murchison will appear before the Keighley magistrates tomorrow. She has been charged with the murder of Tobias Murchison. Mrs Murchison is represented by a solicitor who will provide her defence. The expected outcome for tomorrow is that she will be remanded in custody until the next session of the assizes.'

'On what evidence?' Rita came to her feet. 'She wasn't even there.'

Marcus ignored her. 'On behalf of Scotland Yard, I thank you for your co-operation. I extend condolences for the loss of Mr Murchison.'

'Where will you take her?' Rita demanded.

'That I can't say.' Marcus put on his hat and wished us good evening.

Mrs Varey, leaving her stick hooked onto the chair back, made her way into the family parlour. 'Good riddance to him and his condolences.'

Elisa went to sit beside Rita on the sofa.

Rita glared at me. 'Traitor! You think that by finding a solicitor, you let yourself off the hook.'

More than anything else, I wanted to be away from them all.

'I'm going to Stanbury, Elisa. Don't lock me out.'

'I won't.'

I left the house and walked towards the track that led to the mill, undecided as to whether I should cut the corner and take the scenic route or – given the hour – walk by the road. The choice was made for me when I saw the constabulary car, parked by the reservoir.

Marcus got out, and waited for me to reach him. 'I

thought you'd come in this direction. Sorry it's been such an ordeal.'

'I'm going to see my parents. My mother will be worrying.'

'Let me drive you there. Mr Hood and Mr Porter were very helpful. I said I'd call to say goodbye.'

We both got in the car. He did not start the engine, but lit a cigarette and offered it to me. I don't usually, but once in a while I smoke. This was one of those times.

'You're confident then?'

'Yes, Kate. I'm confident that Carine is guilty.'

'What was found in the police house garden?'

'A kitchen knife and a pair of bloodstained cream lace gloves. She was caught in the act of taking them from a bush near the gate. She had brought a pillowcase to wrap them in, and had a large handbag with her.'

'She had that same handbag with her on Saturday.' If Carine had left those articles where they were, and not taken the risk of trying to retrieve them, they may not have been found for months, perhaps never. But Carine dared not take that chance. 'How did she manage to take the knife and the gloves with her from the parsonage to the police house without anyone in the Sunday school noticing, or Mrs Hudson noticing?'

'There was a brown paper bag in the bush too, also stained with blood. Mrs Hudson left Carine by the gate while she took out her key. To hide the incriminating evidence was the act of a moment, less than a moment.'

'So it was all planned.'

'It was carefully planned.'

'You know she is mentally unbalanced, Marcus?'

'I thought that's what you would say.'

'Has she been told about the discovery of her mother's body in the cellar?'

'Her solicitor will tell her tomorrow, after the hearing in the magistrates' court. What age did you say she was when her mother disappeared?'

'Five.'

A flock of starlings flew across the reservoir.

When they were out of sight, Marcus said, 'Her solicitor tried to prevent my charging her on the grounds that when Tobias fell, Carine was not there. You'd thought of that, hadn't you?'

'Yes.'

'How did you know that she had done it?'

I hesitated to tell him how the thought had come to me. I would have preferred it to be some brilliant deduction based on abstract logic. 'Harriet told me something. It kept coming into my mind, and I couldn't think why.'

'What did she tell you?'

'She lost her umbrella.'

'What?'

'She was in a crowded cinema queue. Everyone was pressed tightly together, people wanting to keep their place. The queue began to move. Queues have a life of their own. By the time she missed her umbrella, she had been swept along almost to the entrance of the cinema. I asked myself why that scene kept coming into my thoughts when there was so much else going on, matters of life and death.

'On Saturday by the parsonage, waiting to see Lady Roberts present the deeds, we were in a similar position, barely able to move because of the crush as people pushed forward for a better view of the handover.

'Carine missed the handover of the deeds because she had slipped away, saying she felt unwell. She spoke to Tobias before she went. He grunted, which was just like him, typical of his attitude. So at the time it didn't occur to me that he should have answered, or gone with her.

'Of course, he couldn't have. Edward thought that Tobias bent his head for a kiss. His head fell forward because he was dying, from a knife wound to his heart. He remained standing because on all sides, he was surrounded by people whose attention was elsewhere, propping him up. I don't know whether Carine pressed the catch on the swordstick that released the blade, or whether Tobias did that as he slumped forward.'

'Slim, quick and charming Carine; people remembered making way for her.'

'By the time I realised he was dead, Carine was in the Sunday school room, recuperating.'

Marcus took my hand. 'Did Tobias Murchison hurt you when he fell?'

'Just start the car, Marcus. Let's go say goodbye to the Porters.'

Early on Tuesday morning, Elisa, Rita and I went to pick flowers. I chose rosebay willowherb, toadflax and cranesbill. Rita thought that a powerful scent would matter. She clipped wild thyme, basil and clover. Elisa wanted sunshine. She picked buttercups, daisies and marigolds that go to bed with the sun and rise with him weeping. We intended to be in the magistrates' court and sit on the front row with flowers. Rita said that we must show Carine we care, and believe in her. It was Rita's plan that we must rise at dawn and walk from Stanbury to Keighley in procession.

Elisa and I persuaded her that the flowers would survive better if Timmy Preston took us into Haworth on the cart, for the train to Keighley.

I was surprised to see Derek Blondell waiting to go into the courtroom.

'I'm here for my paper. What's been happening?'

'Nothing.' What a tiresome boy he is.

Edward was already on the front row, holding a white rose. It was a pity he did not put such a rose in his lapel ten years ago, for a wedding day.

Carine's case was the first to be heard. I wanted to sink into the floor when Derek took out his notebook and pencil. Carine was brought in, handcuffed to a policewoman. She looked tired. No, she looked exhausted and ill.

Carine glanced at the five of us, four of us with flowers, and Derek with his notebook and pencil.

The reliable and brilliant Mr Cohen was there. From the look on Carine's face, it seemed to me that she had already been told about her mother's body. Mr Cohen may have done that as a way of making sure she was too shocked to speak.

Sometimes the most dramatic episodes are over in a few moments and that was true here. Carine had to confirm her name, her address and her date of birth, and listen to the charge. Mr Cohen ensured that nothing else was said.

Derek suddenly called out, 'Carine, have you heard about your mother?'

She glanced at him with a look of confusion, as if he was

someone from another world. Before the usher had time to reach him, Elisa pulled Derek from his seat by his lapels, turned him round and marched him out of the courtroom.

Carine and her police escort were gone.

Mr Cohen is a small man, full of movement. You might picture him on a starting line, waiting for the call: On your marks, Get set, Go!

He spoke to me. 'I'm going back to Leeds. Will you come with me in the car? I want you to meet the barrister. He's here on another case.'

Rita was crying. 'I wanted to give her the flowers.'

'Can Miss Rufus come too, Mr Cohen?'

'Of course.' He patted Rita's arm. 'We will act most diligently for your friend, Miss Rufus.'

Marcus drew me to one side. 'I'll see you again soon, under different circumstances. Thanks to you and Sykes for your help.'

Thirty-Seven

The Spiritual Quality of Light

For several days after Carine had been transferred to prison to await trial, my dining room became the headquarters of her defence campaign. Mr Cohen decided that it would be better for him to come to the mountain of Headingley than to ask the mountain to come to him.

It was an encouragement to him, and something of a relief to me, that the tradespeople and residents of Headingley, with the exception of Tobias's cronies in the Oak, were generously contributing to raise funds for Carine's defence. I permitted myself the venal thought that, after all, I might not need to sell the Rolls-Royce.

Mr Cohen had begun to compile a dossier of his client's accomplishments, qualities and respected place in the community. Mrs Varey and Elisa Varey gave a sworn statement that early on the morning of Saturday, 4 August, Mrs Murchison borrowed a knife to cut lavender. An accomplished water colourist, she intended to draw a still life. The Vareys told her to keep the knife by her, in case she saw some other plant or flower in the fields or on the moors that caught her eye. A perfectionist, Mrs Murchison wanted to capture the exact texture and shade of her subject.

Carine's school friend's mother, Mrs Cleverdon, sat at my dining table admitting she had always worried about Carine after her mother disappeared. Carine had watched at the school gates, expecting her mother to come for her. For a year, she went on asking the other mothers if they had seen her. It was Mrs Cleverdon's conviction that there had been foul play. Carine had nightmares. The Cleverdons took her on holiday to Scarborough when she was eight years old. The landlady at the boarding house banged on their door when Carine woke up screaming and calling, 'Daddy, stop!' The landlady misunderstood and the family came close to being ignominiously evicted in the middle of the night. Mrs Cleverdon believed that the landlady, if still alive, would remember that vivid incident. On return, Mr Cleverdon reported the matter to the police because there had always been suspicions surrounding the disappearance of Carine's devoted mother, Geraldine Whitaker.

It was through Mrs Cleverdon's information that Carine's aunt in Otley was tracked down. Carine had stayed with her during her breakdown at the beginning of the war. The doctor who treated her was prepared to testify to the nature of her breakdown. He had advised a longer period of rest and recuperation, but she took up work on the Leeds trams as soon as the call came for women workers.

Mr Cohen was pleased with the witnesses Rita brought with her. The trusted pharmacist, Mr Norton, and the local solicitor, Mr Barrington, had each made a written note of what Carine said to them on the day of her father's funeral.

She feared her husband intended to kill her. She feared he intended to push her down the cellar steps to her death.

When the men had gone, Mr Cohen slapped his palms together. 'We have it: the father, no longer a threat; the husband to whom the fears are transferred. From the photographs I have seen, those two might have been father and son. Now there's a thought. Certain qualified gentlemen who deal in matters of the mind will be most interested in this case.'

Mr Cohen developed a strategy. He judged that Edward Chester would be of no use as a defence witness.

There was much that would remain unsaid. Derek Blondell was sufficiently chastened that he kept his counsel, and merely admitted a boyish crush. Carine's letter to him could be simply explained, if explanation were necessary. No one would hide evidence; it would simply come to light as required, and be presented in an appropriate way.

The trial, and Carine's committal to an asylum at His Majesty's pleasure, was widely reported, though not by Derek Blondell.

I jump ahead of myself. There was other news, of a lighter nature, that came as a great surprise.

During the time that Mr Cohen was instructing his barrister, an invitation to Rita's wedding popped onto our doormat. I was alerted to the arrival of the post by Sergeant Dog's happy bark. Harriet swears that our bloodhound is expecting a letter, and that he likes all correspondence to be read to him.

The invitation was printed in gold letters on high-quality card.

MR AND MRS BELLINGHAM RUFUS
INVITE YOU TO THE WEDDING
OF THEIR DAUGHTER RITA
TO MR ANDREW JOHN BARRINGTON
AT LEEDS REGISTER OFFICE
ON SATURDAY, 1 SEPTEMBER 1928
RSVP

There was a similar envelope for Harriet. I placed this on the shelf, in case Sergeant Dog decided to open it himself.

I walked up to Norton's Pharmacy and found Rita in her usual place behind the counter. 'Rita, what's this? You didn't tell me.'

'Can you come?'

'My formal reply is already in the post to your parents. I wouldn't miss it. Thank you for the invitation.'

'Will you take a photograph for us on the day?'

'Of course.'

'I'd like Harriet to be bridesmaid and you to be my witness. Mr Norton will be Andrew's witness.'

'You've taken me by surprise. I thought you and Andrew were friends, and not really that way inclined towards each other.'

'Please keep that to yourself, Kate. This is to be a bona fide marriage. It is not a marriage of convenience. There is nothing bogus about it. We are very fond of each other and have known each other for ten years. You might say friendship ripened into courtship.'

'And did it?'

'I said you might say it, and keep on saying it, especially in front of my and Andrew's parents. We are a perfect match. He is the kindest of men. All I have to do is dress soberly at public functions, and say very little while we are applying to adopt Carine's baby daughter.'

'How do you know she's going to have a daughter?'

'What else would she have? Child then, let's say child.'

'I wish you both much happiness, Rita.'

'No need for that tosh, Kate. We'll be happy enough. Is there any news from Mr Cohen?'

'He is confident that no jury with an ounce of humanity would return a verdict that would lead to the death penalty.'

Rita shuddered. 'Don't even say those words.'

'I don't know whether he was being too optimistic, but he seems to believe that in ten years' time there'll be doctors who will happily declare that Carine has regained her mental equilibrium.'

'Ten years!'

I went to peruse the shelves while customers came to the counter asking for Beechams Powders and tonic wine. We resumed our conversation when they had left.

'She will come back to us, Kate, I'm sure of it. You see, photography is all about the spiritual quality of light. Carine lived in the shadows for such a very long time. Now that those shadows have gone, she will be herself again. Wouldn't you say that is distinctly possible?'

'Everything is possible, Rita.'

It was from Mrs Porter that Mother heard that the Vareys were no longer tenants of Ponden Hall. When their lease was up, they did not renew. Elisa married a schoolmaster. She now lives with her husband in school accommodation. Mrs Varey went with her daughter and stays in the village nearby. I thought back to the day of the magistrates' court hearing, when Elisa lifted Derek from his seat by the lapels and marched him out of the building. She would be a far better match for Edward Chester than Carine.

I saw a slim volume of Edward's poetry in the bookshop. His latest verses, remembering a lost love, reminded me of the lamenting poems that Thomas Hardy wrote after his wife died. Hardy had stopped loving Emma and was afterwards overcome with remorse and longing. I had some sympathy for Thomas Hardy, but pass no comment on Edward Chester. They were young. As another poet once said, we are put on earth a little while to learn to bear the beams of love. The beams of love proved overpowering. In their different ways, Carine and Edward were courageous individuals, but perhaps not when it mattered most.

It was Harriet who solved the mystery of the anonymous writer of articles for *The Mole of the World*. After Derek Blondell turned up at Keighley Magistrates' Court, on the morning of Carine's appearance, it was not because he was 'there for his paper'. It was because he had been sacked. He went to Harriet to find out whether she had news about what might happen next. He asked her to keep him informed. She declined.

We now occasionally take *The Mole of the World*, to see what Derek is up to. Thankfully, he was not permitted to write about Carine until after she had been committed to an asylum. I will spare you Derek's staff reporter article, with photographs, headed 'I Loved a Murderess'.

It was a year before Rita and I were permitted to visit Carine in the asylum. Thanks to the defence fund and the generosity of an anonymous donor, who had fallen in love with her photograph, Carine was accommodated in a reasonably comfortable manner in an institution that believed in treatment rather than punishment. Being allowed to continue with her design of greetings cards, she had gained special privileges and earned a goodly sum for the institution, where she became a favourite. Everybody loved her.

She waited for us by the big gates, which cast a shadow across the grounds, like the bars on a prison window. Carine stood in a shaft of sunlight. It was a great relief to see that she had regained her former radiance.

She stood there often, another inmate told us. Occasionally, she said that she was waiting for her mother.

We sat on a bench near the lawn, with the flowers we had brought. Rita gave Carine the picture of little Geraldine Carine Barrington. 'Andrew is very good with her. We both love her, and tell her about you. We are in a big house in Far Headingley, with plenty of room for you when you are able to come.'

Carine smiled. 'I should like that.'

Since marrying Andrew and taking responsibility for Geraldine, Rita has changed in certain ways. She has developed a practical streak and is now willing to give advice, whether wanted or not. She took Carine's hand. 'What your friend over there said, about how you sometimes wait at the gate for your mother. The thing is, Carine –' Rita hesitated, and adopted her most gentle tone. 'I am sorry if this sounds cruel, but your mother died such a long time ago. She will never come.'

Carine looked at Rita as if she presented a puzzle. 'Rita love, I can't argue with you over that. But some things are best not voiced until I have been in this institution for the minimum term. Only then will I be considered cured.'

Carine was, after all, a perfectly reasonable woman.

Acknowledgements

It was a great pleasure to visit Stanbury and Haworth in the depths of winter, during a heatwave and times between. My first stay at Ponden Hall was some years ago when Brenda Taylor, now of Ponden House, was the owner. Brenda and the present owners of Ponden Hall, Julie Akhurst and Steve Brown, have been most welcoming and helpful. They and Ann Dinsdale, Principal Curator of the Brontë Parsonage Museum, and Haworth historian Steven Wood have generously shared their knowledge. Steven took me on a memorable walking tour of Haworth one rainy day.

Julie, Ann and Steven read and commented on an early version of the manuscript, as did my good friend Sylvia Gill. Any mistakes are mine.

This being a work of fiction, I have taken the liberty of creating Lindisfarne Clinic on Bridgehouse Lane and Laverall Hall in Stanbury village.

In *The Real Wuthering Heights, The Story of the Withins Farms*, authors Steven Wood and Peter Brears comment on the spellings Withins and Withens and on the spelling variations that have appeared in records since 1567. They jettisoned their preferred spelling 'Withens' in favour of 'Withins', largely because that is the Ordnance Survey's spelling. I have followed their example. Withins is also the spelling on local signposts.

Thanks to Eveleigh Bradford, author of *Headingley, this pleasant rural village*, the definitive history of Headingley; Peter Brears; Lynne Strutt and Ralph Lindley. I am grateful to the staff of Keighley Local Studies Library and the Leeds Library for their help.

As always, thanks to Dominic Wakeford and the team at Piatkus, and to Judith Murdoch and Rebecca Winfield.

The real Elisa Varey bid in a charity auction for the risky privilege of allowing me to use her inspirational name. Thanks, Elisa.

Kate Shackleton's First Case

My name is Kate Shackleton. At the time of these events I was thirty years old and at something of a crossroads in my life. On a pleasant and unseasonably warm March day, 1 March 1921 to be precise, Doris Butler and I were celebrating her twenty-third birthday in the spa town of Harrogate, Yorkshire.

We met on a crowded train to London, when Doris had just turned nineteen. I was nursing with the Voluntary Aid Detachment and due to report to St Thomas's Hospital the following day, where I would stay in the accommodation provided. Doris had been working on the land, until she broke her arm. While her arm was on the mend, she took it into her head to leave the land, and leave home. With the burning ambition to become an actress, the princely sum of two pounds in her purse, and not knowing a soul or having anywhere to stay, she caught the train to London. I thought her both brave and foolish. When we arrived at King's Cross, I took her to my cousin's girlfriend, begging a place for her to sleep on the sofa. Doris and I stayed in touch and became firm friends.

On that day of her twenty-third birthday, after window

shopping, and a stroll around the Valley Gardens, we made our way to the tea rooms on Cambridge Crescent.

The smell of fresh bread and cakes from the downstairs shop made me straight away think this was a good choice. Certainly there were lots of people taking afternoon tea in the downstairs dining room on our left. A sign informed us of additional seating upstairs. We made our way up.

An elderly pianist, with stiffly starched high collar and well-brushed black suit, played Tchaikovsky's *Waltz of the Flowers*. A waitress, neatly dressed in black with white apron and headband, took our coats.

Doris is something of a beauty. On that day of her birthday, she wore a long-sleeved copper-coloured dress, the bodice and hem embossed with leaf shapes. The outfit perfectly suited her auburn hair and creamy skin. I knew she would be dressed to the nines and so I had chosen a blue low-waist shift dress in Paulette silk, which was the latest fashion, at least for those of us who did not try too hard to keep up with fashions. My jet necklace goes very well with it.

'Kate, you look sleek, stylish and up to the minute. Love the dress, and blue suits your dark hair. I'm glad you had it bobbed.'

I was quite pleased with the hair style myself. 'It's easy to take care of. When a ward was busy, we couldn't snatch five minutes, much less worry about hairpins.'

The waitress showed us to our table. We knew that we wanted afternoon tea and so placed our order.

I glanced about the room. Ladies exchanged polite confidences over cups of tea and dainty sandwiches. There was a palpable air of refinement. I whispered to Doris, 'It's the kind of place where we must pretend we are in 1910 and King Edward is still on the throne.'

She giggled. 'Don't make me laugh or we'll be thrown out.'

This was the moment to give her my gift. She unwrapped the small package, and was delighted with the Eau de Cologne.

By the time the waitress brought tea and a three-tiered cake stand with sandwiches and cakes, we were engrossed in our chat. Doris was holding forth with the kind of conversation often heard among us young women at that time, especially those who were sufficiently fortunate so as to not worry about where we would find next week's rent. I was secure in that regard, being what they call comfortably off. Doris struggled.

'The thing is, Kate, one must find something to do with one's life, try and make a difference in the world.'

We had such conversations then. We envied courageous and clever women who were good talkers and pledged themselves to creating a world of peace and kindness. All the same, it surprised me to hear Doris showing uncertainty about her future.

'I can't bear to return to RADA. I want to do something useful in the world.'

Doris was a scholarship student in her final year at the Royal Academy of Dramatic Art. Previously she had seemed so confident and certain of her future. She would be an actress, not just any actress but one whose name would live forever in the annals of theatre.

As we ate our egg and cress sandwiches, the pianist began to play 'Happy Birthday'.

'Doris, someone else shares your birthday!' I looked about the room, to see who might have a cake on their table, or be singing along to the tune. All was quiet. I glanced at the pianist. He nodded his head and smiled in our direction.

It became clear that he was playing for Doris, but how did he know?

Doris laughed. 'When did you ask him to play that? I didn't see you do it, you sly minx!'

'I didn't.'

'You're joking.'

'No, honestly, I wouldn't have thought of it. Sorry, perhaps I should.' Personally, I would not want everyone in a café to know it was my birthday, but Doris has a very different personality. She is outgoing and would not mind the whole of Harrogate, indeed all of Yorkshire, knowing that it was her special day.

Doris's smile faded. She turned pale. 'He's here then.'

'Who?'

'I was going to tell you.'

'What were you going to tell me?'

'I would have told you later. That's why I suggested we walk through Valley Gardens. I wanted to tell you then, Kate, out in the open air where it might blow away.'

'What is it? Just say, for heaven's sake.'

'You offered to come to London and meet me there.'

'I did.'

She ran her tongue across her lips, and took a sip of tea, her hand shaking. 'I left London because I am being followed, pestered out of my mind. The police tell me such personal business is not a matter for them, unless a crime has been committed.'

'Who is pestering you?'

'Someone I agreed to marry. We met at a party. He had been at RADA and dropped out, though everyone said how brilliant he was. He wined and dined me, was so utterly charming and generous. How could I have known there is something seriously amiss with him? You see, I can hardly bear to say his name.'

'You didn't become engaged again!' Immediately I regretted the implied criticism. She became a picture of misery, suddenly anxious.

'You see, even you blame me. Let us get out of here.'

I reached out and put my hand on her arm. 'First tell me, what is the matter?'

It took several moments for her to compose herself. 'I've sworn off it now, getting engaged. You know it was a terrible weakness of mine. I hate to see disappointment. I like to make men happy if I can, even for a short time, especially if they have been through the wars – I mean properly through the wars not metaphorically. The others took it in good part. Charles Beaumont even insisted I keep the ring. Can't a girl get engaged and change her mind without a man turning nasty? Honestly, Kate, it lasted five and a half minutes and he has been following me ever since. That's why I came north.' She took out her powder compact, patted her hair and through the small mirror looked about the café. 'I can't see him, but believe me he is here. He must have followed me onto the train.' She shivered. 'I can't bear to think I was under his eye all this time, being watched, followed. I had a feeling he was lurking, when we walked through the gardens.'

'But what can he do to you?'

'He promised to kill me if I do not marry him. He says if he can't have me, no one else will.' All earlier gaiety fled, and the pastries lost their allure. The Earl Grey tea went cold.

She stood. 'I'll just ... I'll just wash my hands and powder my nose, and then we'll go.' She walked towards the stairs that led to the function room and toilets.

When she had gone, I surreptitiously looked about the café but could see no solitary male. Perhaps the pianist had played 'Happy Birthday' because he saw me give Doris the bottle of scent. I was just about to ask him whether this was so.

Suddenly, and he seemed to appear from nowhere, a man in a pin-striped suit crossed the room and began to take the stairs two at a time, the stairs that led to the toilets. Either the gentleman had been caught short and needed the lavatory in a hurry, or else he was chasing Doris.

Disbelief and foreboding struck me like a gale force wind. Foreboding won. I reached for something, anything, to have in my hand as a weapon, probably meaning to grab a knife or plate. As I made a dash for the stairs, I realised that I had picked up a pastry – a rock bun.

On the landing, I looked about. Where was Doris? Where was the powder room? Where was the man in the pin-striped suit? Perhaps I was over-reacting.

I spotted the door marked Ladies' Powder Room and hurried in that direction, vaguely aware of a sound nearby. I turned, but saw no one.

As I pushed open the door of the toilet, I believe I screamed. There was Doris and the man in pin-stripes, his hands around her throat, throttling her as she gasped for air and struggled to free herself, flailing her arms.

Wishing I held a rock rather than a rock bun, I hurled myself at him, screaming blue murder as I did. He was tall and I had to jump on his back. I grabbed a handful of oiled hair in one hand and squashed the rock bun in his face with the other, hoping the crumbs would choke and blind him.

He released his hold on Doris. She collapsed to the floor. I kept on screaming and trying to poke his eyes. He flung me off and made for the door.

Mercifully, my cries alerted a member of staff, although at the time I was not aware of that as I struggled to revive Doris. I do remember that moments later the elderly pianist arrived to lend a hand.

Within twenty minutes, Adam Kitchen had been arrested. The police advised Doris and me to spend the night in Harrogate. The constable explained that the magistrates, who would judge the case the next morning, might have questions for us.

Doris and I passed the night in a dingy hotel where even the cold water in the jug on the washstand was rationed. We were provided with a sliver of soap the width of a postage stamp, and a small towel that was so worn it let in the light. Being Harrogate, the owner was so genteel and polite that any complaint would have been an offence against decorum.

We laughed about it, as only you can with someone who has shared your history. Doris came to stay with me after the telegram arrived. My husband Gerald, an army medical officer, was missing in action and presumed dead. Doris was the only person who shared my hope that missing did not mean dead. Gerald might be injured, but alive. He might have lost his memory, but it would come back. He might be sheltered by kind people.

As it turned out, neither Doris nor I were to be called at the magistrates' court. The police had decided to press charges. However, naturally enough, we both needed to witness the outcome.

The case against Adam Kitchen was the last to be heard that morning. The previous offences had been minor, summary offences, punishable by the magistrates: taking a bicycle without permission; being drunk in charge of a horse and cart; stealing a box of matches. The offenders showed a mixture of defiance and contrition. The bicycle was 'borrowed'; the man with the horse and cart 'only had two pints, your honour'; the woman had simply 'forgotten to pay' for the matches.

And then came Doris's assailant.

Escorted into the dock by two policemen, he wore his own clothing from the day before: pin-striped suit, white shirt and tie. He looked surprisingly spruce, though something about him was different. I watched to see whether he might give away his disturbed state of mind by a nervous or guilty twitch. He neither straightened his tie nor stroked at his moustache. He stood gaunt, straight and tall. Was I the only person in the courtroom to feel a wave of arrogance emanating from him, and flooding the space between? Here was a man you would not want to bump into in a dark alley. The people in this courtroom, and indeed the magistrates on the bench, might view him differently. They would see a smart, respectable man, a returned soldier.

The pristine white shirt puzzled me. Also, yesterday he wore a plaid tie. Today his tie was black.

The question that pounded in my brain was this: Are

you mad or bad? Soon followed by the realisation that he could be both.

He had certainly proved dangerous to know.

He spoke to confirm his name: Adam Kitchen, his date of birth, 22 June 1891, and his address. He was twenty-nine years old. When asked his occupation, he hesitated before stating: salesman. His address was Clapham, London. When asked by the chief magistrate what brought him to Harrogate, he answered with a calm lie.

'I am in pursuit of my occupation, sir. I came to Harrogate to sell crystal wireless kits door to door.'

'And did you sell any crystal wireless kits?' the leading magistrate asked.

'No, sir. I had not long arrived and was seated on a bench on The Stray, admiring the daffodils, a host of golden daffodils.'

'There is no need for poetry, Mr Kitchen, simply answer my questions.'

'I had not yet begun my sales work, sir. I was consulting a Harrogate street map.'

'Liar!' Doris whispered. She pursed her lips, puffed out air and then took a deep breath. 'He has chased me three hundred miles.'

The distance between the capital and the spa town is a little over two hundred miles, but now was not the moment to prove myself a stickler for detail.

Doris shrugged her shoulders, almost to her ears, and then relaxed them, an exercise taught her in drama school. She had in the past given me several demonstrations of her theatrical exercises. I was glad that she was seated behind a rotund man. Adam Kitchen would not have the satisfaction of seeing how much self-control it took for Doris to compose herself. Neither would the perpetrator see any reaction from me.

A murmur of surprise and a frisson of interest rippled through the court when the charge was stated.

The newspaper reporter on the front row scribbled, glancing up to look at the man before the bench. Here was that most unusual case, a serious crime where the magistrates must judge whether there is a case to answer. If so, Adam Kitchen would be committed to the next session of the Assizes. Doris's former fiancé would be judged by a jury of his peers. The charge brought by the police was as serious as it could be: attempted murder.

Doris was once more pale with that haunted look I had noticed when she arrived at Harrogate station. I reached for her hand.

Bravely, she did not avert her eyes. As Andrew Kitchen stood to attention and faced the bench, she gazed steadily across the shoulder of the rotund man in front of us.

The arresting policeman read from his notebook.

'Yesterday, Tuesday, 1 March 1921 at 3.30 o'clock in the afternoon, I attended at Betty's Tea Rooms, Cambridge Crescent, after the manager reported an affray . . . '

'Affray!' Doris leaned forward. 'In that moment, I faced my own death.' She spoke with the subdued emotion and careful clarity that came with theatrical training.

Her words were absolutely true. Another moment and his throttling would have squeezed the life from her. It was my task, as the good friend, to try and help her remain calm. 'Shh, be patient, Doris. The officer will come to the point.'

Luckily for us, the leading magistrate must have been hard of hearing, or at the very least he would have asked for silence in court. At worst, we would have been ignominiously escorted out.

'Kate, why doesn't he say the blighter tried to kill me?'

'He has. That is the charge.'

'But he's not saying it.'

The policeman continued his report in that flat monotone that is somewhat soothing unless you are the person whose life may be at stake. 'The victim bore marks on her throat of attempted strangling. She had lost consciousness and had been revived by the friend who came to her aid.'

The three magistrates silently read the brief statements taken from Doris, me and the tea rooms' manager. The magistrates passed the statements between them and conferred in whispers.

A solicitor had been appointed to speak for the defendant. He recited Adam Kitchen's own account of his war record before setting out the defence. 'My client was merely attempting to remonstrate with his former fiancée, Miss Doris Butler, when he was set upon from behind by the fiancée's friend. He deeply regrets his hasty actions but denies the charge of attempted murder.'

The magistrates conferred again, leaning in close to each other. There was nodding, as well as shaking, of heads. A photograph was shown of Doris's bruising.

The leading magistrate asked for clarification. 'Constable, you have written in your statement precisely where in the tea rooms this alleged incident took place. Would you now repeat that for the benefit of the court?'

Whether through embarrassment or because he had

inadvertently skipped a line from his notebook, the constable had omitted to say aloud this part of his statement. He cleared his throat, bringing his hand to his mouth as if to unzip his lips.

He took a deep breath. 'The incident occurred in the Ladies' Powder Room.'

Silence in the courtroom was broken by a collective gasp. The sense of outrage became palpable. The rotund man in front of us gave a groan of horror and murmured, 'The bounder should be flogged.'

The leading magistrate adjusted his spectacles. His colleague to the left tapped his pen. The third magistrate opened his mouth wide enough to let in a number eleven tram.

Andrew Kitchen had broken a cardinal rule. No gentleman would enter the Ladies' Powder Room.

The magistrate expressed his sympathy for the victim and praised the courage of the victim's friend. By now, it had become clear to those in the courtroom that victim and friend were seated on the sixth row. Heads turned towards us. We must be sure to make a dash for the door the instant the case concluded.

The police constable begged leave to speak on a point of information.

The magistrates conferred.

The constable was urged to speak.

'Sir, Mr Kitchen says that he was in Harrogate in order to sell crystal wireless kits door to door and was consulting a street map of Harrogate. Mr Kitchen had no crystals, wires, sales material or a street map of Harrogate on his person when arrested.'

How I admired that constable. Here was a man after my own heart. It is so often the tiny details, the minutiae of life that reveal the truth of any situation.

Andrew Kitchen was committed for trial at Leeds Assizes on the charge of attempted murder. Application for bail was refused.

Kitchen howled. He flung out his arm, vaguely in our direction. 'Doris Butler is a trained actress, your worship, good at adopting piteous states. She painted those marks on her throat with iodine. I love her. I wish to countersue for breach of promise.' He was still shouting as he was led away. 'The other one tried to kill me. She came armed.'

Doris leaned forward, head in her hands. 'I'm going to be sick.'

I dragged her arm. 'Quick, come on! Let's get you out of here.'

The newspaper man was on our heels. We dodged in and out of shops, twice hiding in ladies' changing rooms. Finally we gave the man the slip and escaped to the railway station.

We showed our tickets at the barrier and crossed to the far platform. Doris had a ticket to Weeton. Her mother rented a cottage in Huby and managed a smallholding where she grew flowers and vegetables and kept chickens. Until Doris went to drama school she had also worked there, and was especially good at taking care of the hens.

A light drizzle started as we crossed the railway bridge for Platform 2. We hurried towards the shelter.

Doris was a few strides ahead. She came to such a sudden halt that I bumped into her. I saw why. The rotund man from the courtroom was seated on the bench, smiling up at us.

He raised his hat.

When he saw Doris's dismay, he said in a pleasant voice, 'Please don't be alarmed, Miss Butler. You have nothing to fear from me.' He stood. 'Gooch is the name. You were in the Youth Players with my son Robin. I was a friend of your father.'

'Mr Gooch, of course, hello.'

We all sat down on the bench, Mr Gooch, then Doris, and then me. There is something reassuring about a man who calls his son Robin, after the red-breasted favourite bird of Christmas cards.

Mr Gooch shook his head. His several chins waggled. 'I wish I had been in that café. I would have shoved the blighter down the stairs head first.'

'Thank you, Mr Gooch. This is my friend Mrs Kate Shackleton. She saved my life.'

We extended hands across Doris's middle and shook. 'How do you do, Mrs Shackleton. Congratulations on your quick-thinking rescue. I only wish you had done for the blighter. He claimed you were armed.'

'That was a lie,' I said. 'Do I look as if I carry a weapon?'

'Then it's a pity you couldn't have hit him with something heavy. I assume there are chairs and vanity tables in the Ladies' Powder Room.'

'Mr Gooch deals in furniture,' Doris explained helpfully.

Doris and Mr Gooch reminisced about his son Robin. Although it was not said in so many words, I understood from their conversation that Robin had been a casualty of the war.

When there was a lull in the conversation, I asked, 'How do you think the case against Adam Kitchen might go in court, Mr Gooch?'

He took a deep breath that puffed out his red cheeks. Pursing his lips, he let out a meaningful burst of air. 'I'm sorry to say that I know something about the bounder's solicitor. That man has a reputation to keep. He knows precisely which barrister to instruct and how to instruct them. If this Kitchen chap has money enough to pay for the best, then he will have a good chance of getting off.'

Doris closed her eyes. 'I can't bear it. I'll never feel safe again.'

It now made sense that Kitchen had worn a clean white shirt and black tie to appear before the magistrates. His solicitor had made sure that he looked respectable.

'Who is this solicitor?' I asked.

'His name is Septimus Peershaw, of Peershaw, Peel and Wellington. Anyone with a guilty conscience, sticky fingers, or found in possession of a plain brown envelope stuffed with used notes would go to him like a shot.'

A subdued silence followed, soon to be broken by the roar of the Leeds train drawing onto the platform.

Mr Gooch opened the door onto an empty carriage.

We clambered in. Doris and I sat side by side, Mr Gooch opposite.

He placed his trilby on the seat beside him and leaned forward. 'I notice there are calls for young women to go out into the Empire, particularly Australia. If I were young, I should consider that myself.'

We were all familiar with such attempts to solve the problem of 'surplus women', who after the war could not hope to find husbands in England.

Neither Doris nor I commented on his well-meant suggestion.

What lay behind his words was the belief that Adam Kitchen would be found not guilty. If so, Doris would need to flee, or spend the rest of her life looking over her shoulder.

As the train pulled into Weeton Station, Doris said suddenly, 'Get off here, Kate. Come with me.'

'Of course I will.' It had been my intention to do so.

She sighed with relief. 'Come and see our house and the chicks. You can catch a later train.' It was more plea than request. I thought perhaps she did not want to be alone when she explained to her mother everything that had happened, and why she had spent the night in Harrogate. We said goodbye to Mr Gooch, who assured us that he would follow the case and that if there was anything he could do, Doris need only ask.

As we walked from the station along the path, Doris talked about her father who had not returned from the war. 'I'm glad you're coming back with me. I want you to see the matchstick model of York Minster that Dad made. He was so talented, Kate. He sketched the Minster too, quite perfectly.'

Walking along the familiar path towards the cottage soothed her. Empty, ploughed fields stretched on either side. Bare bushes moved in the breeze, in a state of waiting. 'You would like it here in the spring. If worse comes to worst and I can't go back to RADA, I shall become something of a whiz at winning prizes for bantams and turnips.'

I could imagine that she might. She had amazed her friends by coaxing vegetables from the long narrow stretch of tired garden behind the shared and overcrowded London house. Dismissing warnings that she would spoil her hands, she kept on digging and planting until the harvest. But by the time she had harvested the vegetables and carried masses of flowers to the local shop for sale, acting had begun to absorb her very being. Her activity in the long garden ceased and the weeds rejoiced.

Doris grew more confident in her own talent and became ambitious to rise to the top of her chosen profession.

If that dreadful man had knocked the stuffing out of her, and undermined her confidence as an actress, he had a lot more to answer for than the charge of attempted murder.

'You mustn't let what Kitchen did keep you from going back to RADA.'

She came to a stop. A blue tit alighted on a nearby bush. It cocked its head, as if waiting for her reply.

'They will all blame me. They will side with him.'

'That's ridiculous.'

'No, it's true. Everyone who saw him perform admired him. He took a medal for his King Lear.'

'I suppose he did, especially the madness on the heath. That would be second nature.'

'It's thought a tragedy that he has not yet made his mark. I'll be expected to be ashamed at causing a scandal and giving RADA a bad name.'

I turned and faced her. '*He* tried to kill *you*, not the other way around. Do not take the blame.'

She nodded. 'Of course you are right, in one respect . . .'

'In all respects.'

As we rounded the bend, the cottage came into view. It was a small two-storey building made of local stone. Smoke curled from the chimney. Ivy threatened to cover the mullioned windows.

As we came closer to her childhood home, the colour began to come back into her cheeks.

We reached an outhouse, the kind of building that might be used for storing tools. The door was partially open. Hens and ducks pecked at the earth by the door.

'Come and say hello to my hens.'

When she opened the door farther, a fine noise ensued. The hens that had remained indoors were greeting her. She spoke to them, and then told me their social and medical histories. A cabinet on the wall held bottles of oil. She explained their uses as she applied oil from one of the bottles to a bird's beak.

'Mam is no good with hens. Fortunately our neighbour Phil is almost as good a hen doctor as I am.' She bent down to speak to a favourite. 'You were in good hands, my chicklet.'

This was another side to Doris that I had not suspected. Perhaps all actresses have it within them to be a hundred other people. That might be what makes a good thespian.

'Come on, Kate. You must meet Mother.'

We walked the few yards to the house. The outer door opened onto a small porch area with stairs directly in front. The open door on our right led to the kitchen-living room.

Mrs Butler was wiping crumbs from the deal table with her hands and did not look up when the door opened. She turned to the black-leaded kitchen range and brushed the crumbs from her palms into the coal scuttle.

It should not have surprised me that Doris's mother was attractive, and still relatively young. She had given birth to Doris, an only child, when she was just sixteen.

Mrs Butler's auburn hair was twisted into a top knot, loose strands falling across her high cheek bones. She wore a large pinafore over a wool skirt and baggy cardigan. 'Doris! What are you doing here? I thought you must've gone straight back to London after your tea party.'

'No, I told you!' She introduced me and had obviously talked about me because Mrs Butler said, 'Oh you're the one who was in nursing and might go back to it.'

'Yes I was, with the Voluntary Aid Detachment.' I did not answer her comment that I 'might go back to it', being unsure what I would do in the future.

It had been explained to me that the training that satisfied for wartime would not be sufficient for professional nursing. There would be additional mandatory courses and a probationary in-service period. The nearest hospital for such training was the Leeds General Infirmary, where my husband had worked as a surgeon before becoming an army medical officer.

Perhaps it was cowardly of me, but I could not bring myself to work and train in the building where I would hear the echo of Gerald's footsteps, or catch a ghostly glimpse of him turning at the end of a corridor. The hospital authorities had erected a plaque to commemorate the fallen. At the unveiling, I wanted to scream. I wanted to tear down that plaque, to demolish the wall, and tell anyone who would listen that Gerald would come home.

And then I was back in the present. Doris had shifted the conversation, saying, 'The hens are looking well. I expect that's thanks to Phil.'

At that moment, a man aged about thirty strode through the door. He must have padded down the stairs with the softness of a cat. 'And your thanks are accepted, Doris.' His shirt sleeves were rolled, braces dangling. He wore thick socks but no shoes, a man who clearly felt himself very much at home here. Under a shock of unruly black hair, his smiling weather-beaten face had the confident look of 'man of the house'.

Mrs Butler turned away. She picked up the poker from the hearth and stirred at the fire. Coals crackled. Ash made a gentle sound as it dropped through the grate onto the metal plate below.

Phil walked to the only armchair and sat down. He took out a cigarette and lit it from the poker that still glowed red.

Doris looked beyond him, to the corner of the room. On the wall next to the range, fitted into the corner, were four wooden drawers, painted brown. Above the drawers was a cupboard to the height of the ceiling, with a space of about eighteen inches between the top of the drawers and the base of the cupboard.

Doris was staring at this space. 'Where's Dad's matchstick York Minster?'

Phil stood. 'I'm forgetting my manners. Our guest must have a seat.'

'Where's the Minster? I want Kate to see it.'

Mrs Butler said, 'Then you should have fetched Kate last week. York Minster came a cropper.'

Doris continued to look at the space where York Minster must have stood. 'But . . . but how could it? It's been there since . . . '

She stopped, either unable to remember how long the matchstick edifice had been there, or realising that it would never be there again. Her mother sat down on the low seat by the hearth. 'It's a miracle it lasted as long as it did. Even the real Minster has scaffolding up.'

Phil chose that moment to own up. 'I'm sorry, Doris.

I'd had a drink. I fell asleep and the fire was out. I needed a match.'

'But it wasn't made of matches. It was whittled shapes.'

'Yes I know that now. The one I picked off didn't strike.'

'But it was so well made, how could you?'

The fire began to belch smoke, sending choking billows into the room.

No one spoke.

Mrs Butler coughed.

Phil picked up a sheet of newspaper and wafted it about. He placed a shovel in front of the fire and the newspaper over it, in an attempt to draw smoke up the chimney.

Mrs Butler said, 'Accidents happen.'

As if fate decided to confirm this fact, the newspaper caught fire.

Doris went upstairs.

I sat on a tall stool. No one attempted small talk.

Using poker and shovel, Phil pushed the remnants of the burnt sheet of newsprint onto the fire.

Doris came down several moments later. In one hand she carried a carpet bag. In the other she held a sketch pad. 'At least Dad's drawings are still intact. I'll take this with me. I want to keep something of Dad's safe.' She glared at Phil. Her bitterness overflowed. 'A certain person might need a scrap of paper to wipe their arse.'

Phil opened his mouth to answer. Doris's mother appeared as if she might chip in. But Doris's use of bad language had shocked everyone into silence.

Some people are born with the ingrained determination to set the world to rights. It is my curse to be one of them. 'Where are the pieces of York Minster?'

Immediately, I wished I had not asked. Such an item would make excellent kindling. Such an item had probably already made excellent kindling. But no, all was not lost.

Phil brightened. 'It's in a sack in the outhouse. I would have put it together but I don't have the skill or the patience.'

Mrs Butler came to Phil's aid. 'It's true. He doesn't have the skill for that, but he's very good with the hens.'

'I know,' Doris said, keeping her dignity.

For Doris's sake, I volunteered. 'Let me take the sack. My brother is a dab hand at carpentry. He'll reassemble the Minster.'

Doris, Mrs Butler, Phil and I walked to the henhouse. A small clutch of fowls followed us in to see what was going on. Phil retrieved a filthy sack from a corner.

Doris looked at it and froze. She sighed, such a plaintive sound that the sack might have contained her father's bones.

I took the sack.

Mrs Butler and Phil walked with us along the path, as far as the dirt road that led to the station.

Doris ignored Phil and spoke to her mother. 'You might see something in the papers, Ma.'

'We don't read the papers,' Phil said. 'Mrs Gooch brings them round when they're a week old.'

'I was talking to Ma. You might see that Adam Kitchen tried to kill me yesterday.'

Mrs Butler stared. She clutched her arms around herself as if for protection. 'I never liked the sound of him, but what got into him that he tried to kill you?'

'The devil got into him.'

'You didn't break off the engagement?'

'Yes, and gave back the ring.'

'Oh. It was a diamond.'

'He's a cad, Ma. I'm well out of it.'

'So what happens now?'

'I go back to London. He will come to trial.'

'When?'

'I don't know.'

I chipped in, having a little knowledge on these matters. 'It could be as soon as the Easter Assizes, or the Summer Assizes, depending on the amount of business.'

Rather unhelpfully, I thought, Phil had to put in his two-penny-worth. 'He'll probably plead provocation, since you broke off with him.'

Rather too gently, I corrected him. 'Provocation is not a defence.'

The man was a simpleton, but I could see that the small-holding would be difficult for Mrs Butler to manage alone, and Phil must have other qualities in addition to his prowess with hens.

Doris kissed her mother on the cheek. Phil stood by rather awkwardly, hoping for some recognition.

I shook hands with the pair and was about to say thank you for the tea when I remembered we hadn't been offered any.

I went with Doris as far as York and saw her onto the next train to London. She leaned through the window. 'Would you keep this safe for me, Kate? I feel nothing is ever going to be safe again.'

I took the sketch pad.

'It's Dad's drawings of York Minster.'

Feeling a great weight of responsibility, I placed the sketch pad in the sack.

'Thanks, Kate.'

'Don't mention it. Just try not to accept a proposal of marriage before the train leaves the station.'

The stationmaster blew his whistle.

She managed a laugh. 'I won't! Promise! I shall steadfastly refuse all offers until we arrive at King's Cross.'

'And Doris, try and find out everything you can about you-know-who. If he did this to you, he may have done it to other people. He mustn't go free.'

She called to me again but with the noise of the engine, I could not catch her words.

A young chap, saying goodbye to his sweetheart, ran the length of the platform waving until the train left the station.

After Doris's train had disappeared leaving a trail of steam, I looked about the station, half expecting something bad to happen. Perhaps some chum of Doris's assailant would push me onto the tracks. Until that moment, I had been so concerned with the shock my friend had suffered as to not realise how much this episode had unnerved me. It was partly the cunning and ferocity of Kitchen's actions that shook me. But there was something else. For years it was my task to minister to wounded and sick men. This was the first time in my life I had been forced to attack a man.

I took a seat on a bench and carefully set down the sack.

The porter wheeled luggage. A man in postman's uniform took off his cap and scratched his head. An old man, seated at the other end of the bench, opened his newspaper.

These men were harmless, or were they?

I was brought up to believe there existed an unwritten social contract. A lady would put an awkward young man at ease, would deal with a socially difficult situation, or soothe a troubled brow. A gentleman would show gallantry, coming to the aid of the party, whoever or whatever that party might be.

Adam Kitchen was the example that broke the rule, if indeed that rule ever truly existed. Yet to look at him, no one would know. By the time of the next session of the Assizes, Septimus Peershaw, Esquire, solicitor for the crooked and the wealthy, would make Adam Kitchen appear normal. He would twist and bribe and create a most plausible version of events that drew sympathy for his client.

I set my watch by the station clock. There were twenty minutes to wait until I could catch a train back to Leeds.

Stirring myself, I bought a reviving bar of chocolate and a newspaper. The young assistant kindly let me consult the local telephone directory.

Septimus Peershaw was not listed in the directory, either personally or as having offices. He was not the sort of man to be on a police or court list of duty solicitors. In any case, it seemed to me unlikely that the Harrogate police would suggest a solicitor from outside their area.

Adam Kitchen must have been allowed to make a telephone call. Someone had come to his aid and arranged for legal representation.

He was wealthy, witness the ring. He had contacts who were able to find the right legal assistance for the job in hand. Such men got off, usually scot-free, or with a rap on the knuckles.

The charge against him might be reduced from attempted murder to assault, or even self-defence.

I had seen the evil in his eyes when I thwarted him. If he were freed, he would take revenge.

Doris needed someone to fight her corner. That someone would be me.

With that less than happy thought, and with no idea how to begin, I crossed to the far platform to wait for my train.

My house is in Headingley, just a short distance from the centre of the city, yet a world away. Mine is a quiet street with a small wood behind the house, giving the illusion of being countryside. Gerald and I chose the house together, before we married, so that we would have somewhere to start our new lives.

Although I had received the usual wartime telegram, I did not yet quite believe I would never see him again. Officialdom makes mistakes. Bureaucracy moves slowly. My few enquiries have been discreet. I had not given up hope.

The square green-painted van on the road outside my gate was instantly recognisable as an ex-army ambulance. It belongs to my brother Matthew, the younger of the twins by ten minutes. I am adopted and my mother always called me her lucky charm because – having stopped worrying about childlessness – seven years after adopting me, she gave birth to twin boys.

Matthew was not in the van.

I let myself in at the front door and called his name. There was no answer but a scraping sound from the kitchen. I followed the sound.

Matthew was there with his tool box. He opened and closed the back door. 'That's better! It was sticking. You should have told me.'

'I was going to mention it.'

'Should be fine now.' He looked at the sack and sniffed. 'Been somewhere nice?'

'It's a long story. When did you arrive?'

'A few hours ago. Mother telephoned to you last night, worried that you hadn't arrived back from Harrogate. When you still weren't answering at noon, I was dispatched to look for you.'

'For heaven's sake!'

'I know, I know. I told her there was no need to worry, Dad told her, Simon told her, but it was no use.'

We sat down at the kitchen table. 'She wants me back home you know.'

He rolled his eyes. 'Don't do it, Kate! She'd have you playing bridge and visiting Wakefield Theatre Royal every week.'

'I'm staying put, Matt. I can't go backwards. Anyway, you and Simon are at home.'

'Even if we weren't, you're settled here now.' He sniffed, and looked at the sack. 'What is that pong?'

'It's a surprise, a job for you, from Doris and it's only the sack that smells. Now let me run a bath. Mix me a gin and tonic, and then you can go out and buy fish and chips for us.'

'That's a good plan, but for heaven's sake, telephone Mother first.'

I felt much better after a bath and some food.

Matt and I sat in my dining room. He had placed York Minster on the table and even begun a little of the repair work, while I told him about what happened in Harrogate.

'I don't understand why this latest fiancé took it so badly. Did he not know Doris's history?'

'He probably thought he was special.'

'We men have a habit of that, I suppose. I'm glad I'll be able to repair her father's masterwork.'

395

'She won't have anywhere to put it. She's in digs with a group of other RADA students, that is if they don't kick her out from loyalty to the imprisoned swain who tried to kill her.'

'Oh you know young people, Kate. They'll be so in thrall to her story that she'll be the heroine of the hour.'

'You talk as if you're ancient. You and Doris are the same age.'

'Twenty-three is ancient, for some of us.' He turned the pages of the sketch book, looking admiringly at Doris's father's sketches of York Minster. 'Mr Butler was so talented.' He ran his hands through his hair. 'We'll never get over the loss, you know.'

'I know.'

He stood and went to the mantelpiece, picking up the photograph of Gerald in his uniform. 'I've just had a message from the beyond. Gerald thinks you and I ought to go dancing tonight.'

I laughed, but there was a stab of pain in my heart at his assumption. 'Gerald might not be in the beyond. Besides, it's nearly midnight.'

'Well wherever he is, and whatever the time is there, that's the message.' He held out a hand. 'Come on! Out of that chair! You shouldn't be lounging in silk pyjamas. I know a place where we can dance.'

'Where?'

'In Chapeltown, down some steps, through a green-painted door, close by the judges' residence and so never raided for selling drinks after hours. I've brought my glad rags, just in case you said yes.'

'Then while I change, ring Mother and tell her you'll be

staying the night, or she'll have Simon coming to look for you, and Dad coming to look for Simon.'

'I'll get the togs from the van.' He went into the hall and opened the front door, calling back, 'I told Mother I'd stay here tonight. Besides, it's only you, her all-alone darling daughter that she worries about.'

This was not true, but I did not contradict him. Instead I went upstairs and changed into my Delphos robe, which isn't a robe at all but the name of my beautiful multi-coloured long silk dress, bought before the war in Paris by Aunt Berta, and passed to me. It is one of those pieces that may not be in the height of fashion, but elegant, timeless and always in style.

Matt parked his van on a side street. He led the way to a basement door where he knocked three times and gave a password to a burly man with cauliflower ears.

We followed the man along a corridor into a cellar room lit by candles, oil lamps and the red dots of sweet-smelling cigarettes and foul cigars.

Music came fast and furious. Three saxophonists formed a circle, playing to each other. A pianist bashed the piano in a way that ought to have made a racket but turned the room into heaven. Some of the men were black, some white, and they made a new kind of music.

We sat at a small table and the waiter brought drinks, without asking what we wanted. My cocktail was long and green. 'You've been here before, Matt.'

'Now and again.'

'How did you find it?'

'Word goes round.'

'What about Simon, does he come?'

Matt laughed. 'Simon likes his pint at the local. I'm the transgressive one.'

'You always were.'

'How can a chap not want to come here, and forget, and just for a little while . . . '

He did not finish his sentence. A tall slender woman with coffee-coloured skin and a dress that matched the colour of my cocktail began to sing.

We were mesmerised. No one spoke until the last note of her song faded.

Matt leaned across to me. 'Everything and everyone crosses the Atlantic. Music, dancing, anxiety, a new feeling.'

'I disagree, Matt. The anxieties and the loss are all our own.'

It was almost noon the next morning when Matt brought me a cup of tea.

I propped myself up on pillows. 'Shouldn't you be at work?'

'I've taken some time off. I'm ahead of myself, and I want to talk to you.'

'What about?'

'Come down and scramble some eggs and I'll tell you.'

'Have you lit the fire?'

'I have.'

By the time I went down, he had toasted the teacakes and was already stirring eggs in the pan. 'You'll make some lucky creature a very good husband.'

'No chance, not until I'm at least as old and wise as you.'

'Thank you for the backhanded compliment.'

It was not until we had finished our breakfast that he came to the point. We were out walking in that area just beyond where I live, wandering through the trees, looking for the stream, listening to the birds complaining about the slow advent of spring.

Matt kicked a stone. 'We young Hoods need a plan, you, me and Simon.'

'I don't feel a young Hood, and don't forget I'm Shackleton now.'

'Same thing. We're all for one and one for all.'

'What kind of a plan?'

'I told you, Mother wants you back in Wakefield.'

'You did and I told you that I already know.' Someone had made a makeshift swing on the branch of an oak. I sat on it, swinging back and forth.

Matt gave the swing a push. 'It's because she worries about you, being alone and at a loose end.' The twigs crunched under his feet. 'I don't think you're going to go back into nursing.'

'Don't know what I'll do. Something, that's for sure. I can't twiddle my thumbs forever.'

'You're all right for money?'

'Yes.' Gerald's investments and insurance had seen to that. Also, there was the obligatory and time-honoured legacy, from an aunt on my mother's side whom I hardly knew. I always wondered about this legacy and whether the elderly aunt had thought me a blood relation rather than an adopted creature whose pedigree might not stand scrutiny.

'Kate, Mother is really determined. You will have to take desperate measures if you intend to withstand her onslaughts.'

'What do you mean?'

'You should employ a housekeeper, and then you won't be alone.'

'I don't want a housekeeper.'

'Then you'll be in danger of becoming one – a glorified housekeeper for Mother and Dad.'

'Not so sure about the glorified. Besides, I've nowhere to put a housekeeper. Ours is a small house.'

If he noticed that I had said 'ours' and not 'mine', he let it pass.

'I've thought of that. I drew up the plans while I was waiting for you to come back yesterday.'

'What plans?'

'You can have an annexe on the back. There's enough room. The person can have her own entrance and a door into the kitchen.'

I climbed off the swing. 'There isn't a person who needs an entrance.'

A squirrel stopped to stare, and then made a dash for the oak tree.

'There will be a person. She is waiting somewhere not far off, hoping a charming and self-sufficient w–' He almost said widow but caught himself in time. ' . . . a charming and self-sufficient woman will offer this willing female a position that requires tact, discretion and the ability to keep a cupboard stocked with food. She will be someone who can concoct a hearty soup in winter and throw together a choice dandelion leaf salad in summer.'

'And what will I do?'

'It will come to you what to do. Travel for a fashion house. Take photographs and turn them into greetings cards. Take up a noble cause. You'll think of something.'

'Why this sudden interest in creating an annexe and finding me a housekeeper?'

'So that I'll know you are settled, when I'm not here.'

There was something so sombre in his mood. As we walked into a clearing in the wood, a cloud covered the weak sun and cast a shadow. 'Matty, what's the matter? What are you going to do to yourself? You're frightening me.'

'Don't worry. Nothing bad is going to happen. I have such a good plan that it deserves to be written in capital letters. It's a joint plan, mine and Simon's.' He took my arm. 'When we were little, you always looked out for Simon and me. You were such a good big sister. Now I'm going to look out for you. What's the use of having a brother who's a wizard at constructing if you won't let him add on a very nice attachment to your house? If you want a housekeeper, it will be perfect, or a lodger, or a guest. Just say yes. I've designed an annexe. You can check the plans when we get back. Two superb brickies are waiting to start.'

He won.

Slowly but surely an annexe began to take shape in the garden at the back of my house. While I watched this extension come into being, the feeling grew in me that when it was completed there would emerge something that I could do.

I looked in the newspapers for suitable employment, but saw nothing.

I exchanged letters with Doris, urging her to keep up her spirits.

With my police superintendent father, I discussed the case of the Crown versus Adam Kitchen. Matt's twin, Simon, is a trainee solicitor. He looked up legal precedents and took a professional as well as a personal interest.

The twins are not identical but unmistakably brothers. Simon is the more serious and sober. He and I were in my drawing room. I put on a gramophone record to drown out the sound of hammering from the rear of the house where Matt and his helpers were doing something involving roof beams.

Simon misunderstood my reason for choosing a musical accompaniment to our conversation.

'Good thinking, Kate, I don't want anyone to hear what I have to say. What's more, you did not hear it from me. Understood?'

My London cousins work in government and the civil service. I would expect such obtuseness from them, but not from Simon. 'What are you talking about?'

'Something I heard at work, and thought you should know.'

'Then whatever it is, perhaps you ought not to tell me.'

'It's to do with the court case.'

Both Doris and I had been notified that Adam Kitchen would be brought before the Leeds Easter Assizes. Easter Day fell on 27 March that year. The trial was set for Monday, 4 April.

I hated the thought of having to see that man in the courtroom. Poor Doris would probably be held to ridicule when the case was reported. The newspapers would relish the story of a glamorous actress who had been throttled by her third fiancé.

Simon sat on the sofa.

I took the chair opposite. 'Do I need a strong cup of tea before I hear this?'

He went across to the gramophone and increased the volume. 'You'll need a double gin and tonic.'

'Oh dear, get it over with then.'

'A pal saw your name listed as a witness in the case of the Crown versus Adam Kitchen. He gave me a nod and a wink.'

'And did he say anything, or just nod and wink?'

'Has there been any disclosure to Doris?'

'What kind of disclosure? She's dreading the case but has said nothing. If there's something unpleasant, she won't have let it sink in.'

'Listen carefully. I won't say this again, and I never said it.'

'You are sounding so like Cousin James. Just spit it out.'

'Adam Kitchen will plead not guilty to attempted murder. If a lesser charge of assault is brought, he will still plead not guilty.'

'But that's preposterous. He followed Doris into the powder room and attacked her. He admitted as much.'

'Not according to him. He will say that he did not have the opportunity to speak up for himself in the magistrates' court. He will say that he was protecting his former fiancée's reputation by his silence.'

'What a liar!'

'People do lie, sometimes to protect another person but more usually to protect themselves.'

What sent a shiver of apprehension to the marrow of my bones was that I could picture Adam Kitchen. I could hear him denying the accusation while pretending to be the gentleman. He would make out that Doris and I were the liars.

'But Simon, how will he explain that he was in the ladies' powder room?'

'He will claim he was attacked and dragged into the ladies' lavatory by you and Doris . . . '

'What?!'

' . . . and he did not resist for fear of hurting you. Any injuries you sustained were caused when he tried to defend himself.'

People say that their jaw drops when they hear something astonishing. It had never before happened to me. 'That's preposterous.'

Giving me time to recover, Simon went to wind the gramophone. 'Sorry, Kate, but you see why I wanted to tell you.'

'Does he say why we dragged him into the ladies' lavatory?'

'You were angry because he refused to let Doris, a grasping woman who had been engaged three times to his knowledge, keep his diamond ring.'

I felt slightly sick. I could imagine that Adam Kitchen had already persuaded himself of the truth of his own story. He would deliver it with such conviction.

In a land with so many 'surplus women' the worst would be believed of us. Doris would be thought mad to have refused a proposal of marriage from such a smart, presentable man. He had most probably lost his job as a salesman – if, indeed, he ever had such a job. Certainly he had lost his liberty since the attack and would be feeling vengeful.

'What on earth do we do, Simon? There's so little time between now and the trial.'

He lit a cigarette. 'You need a plan, and so does Doris.'

'Doris isn't very good at plans.'

The plan would have to come from me then, and soon.

My mother is a great lover of theatre. Coming to the aid of an actress was for her the most worthy of causes. She was happy to help me put my plan into action, and particularly since this involved a visit to Harrogate.

Mother brought her title with her. That might seem an odd thing to say. Most of the time, she is simply Mrs Hood the police superintendent's wife. She married my father for love, turning her back on the suitors from her London life. She had formally 'come out', having been presented at court. Expectations for a 'good marriage' were high. Those expectations came to an end when my father, then a young police inspector, enjoying a rare trip to the capital, came to Mother's assistance after a kerfuffle in Trafalgar Square. Warnings of marrying in haste and repenting at leisure went unheeded. The rest, as they say, is history – a rather romantic history.

On that day of our visit to Harrogate, Mother once more became an aristocrat, for the purpose of seeing justice done. She ought to have stepped from a Bentley or a Rolls-Royce. Instead, she stepped from my 1913 Jowett motor car, the elegant Lady Virginia Rodpen, daughter of the late Lord and Lady Rodpen. Had she married a titled gentleman, Mother would have assumed whatever title accrued from her husband. As it was, because she married a commoner, she retained her own title.

We entered the tea rooms, Mother dressed in mauve and gold silk and velvet and with combs in her hair that might be mistaken for a tiara. I wore a cream midi blouse, pleated pale green jersey skirt, a loose matching jacket and a darker hat.

The elderly gentleman pianist recognised me immediately, perhaps because I made a bee-line for him and thanked him for coming to my and Doris's aid on that fateful day. I also whispered that my mother, Lady Rodpen, would love to thank him, too, if he might be allowed to join us at our table when time permitted. He readily agreed, briefly adjusting his cravat and casting an admiring glance towards Mother. He flexed his fingers, rubbed his old hands together and asked whether Lady Rodpen had a favourite tune.

There was another half hour of playing. We ordered a fresh pot of tea and asked for an extra cup. At a convenient moment, Mr Lipton, for that was the pianist's name, carefully closed the lid of his piano and came to join us.

Mother played her part well. She had a genuine fondness for gentlemen of the old school. Rather charmingly, she reminisced about a piano teacher she had as a girl, a delightful person, someone she would remember with affection until her dying day.

This was not the story she had told me, concerning a martinet of a creature ready to rap his pupil's knuckles if a rendition of the scale was out of tune.

Mr Lipton wished he had been that piano teacher. He was sure she must have been a most apt pupil.

Mother demurred with a sigh. It was her constant regret that she had not kept up the good work, as Mr Lipton had so undoubtedly done.

There is a fine art in flattery. In those moments, Mother's was so extreme as to reach the height of sincerity. Mr Lipton took her warmly expressed praise as his rightful due.

With sad reluctance, the pianist cast his mind back to the day of my and Doris's visit. He remembered the man sidling up to him and asking for 'Happy Birthday' to be played. 'I thought it odd that the tune was requested by someone not at the same table, but he said that he wished to surprise the young lady.'

Mother was about to speak but I knew we did not have long and so asked, 'And did you notice Doris go upstairs, Mr Lipton?'

He nodded. 'I was playing "Come into the Garden, Maud" which is the closing tune of my flower and garden sequence. Your friend moved so gracefully, like a dancer.' He closed his eyes, as if picturing the scene. 'And then that dreadful man followed her and you were after him, in a state of alarm I thought, with something in your hand.'

I felt suddenly deflated. My going after Kitchen with a rock bun would support his claim that we attacked him.

Mother kicked me under the table. Her words to me, as I was growing up, were frequently: watch and learn.

I did so now.

She gave him her sweetest smile. 'I expect it was some impulse that led you to leave your piano and follow my daughter up the stairs.'

Mr Lipton sighed his agreement.

Mother tilted her head, waiting to hear more.

'That particular set begins with "The Last Rose of Summer" and ends with "Come into the Garden, Maud".' He dashed an imaginary fleck of dust from his left cuff. 'When I saw your daughter follow that man up the stairs, I took the opportunity to follow, on the pretext of taking a short break to blow my nose.'

I felt a growing impatience. I did not wish to know about the man's playing order or his nasal practices. I thought back to what Simon had told me, Kitchen's claim that Doris and I dragged him into the toilet. If Mr Lipton had followed me upstairs, he might give the lie to that claim.

Mother was more patient. She reached for the pianist's slender hand. 'You would have come to the young ladies' aid if you could.'

He lowered his head. 'You are correct, your ladyship. It is the lumbago that slows me down.' He turned to me. 'By the time I reached the landing, you were opening the door of the ladies' room and you screamed. The manager heard your scream and was there before me. He called to me to send for the police.'

'Thank goodness you did,' I said. 'Mr Lipton, it might be of interest to the police that you saw me enter the ladies' room when Kitchen was already there.'

'What a good idea,' Mother said, as though this thought had never crossed her mind.

Mr Lipton considered. 'I do believe your daughter is right, Lady Rodpen. No statement was asked for from me.'

Mother squeezed his hand. 'You see, Mr Lipton, we fear the fellow will try to turn the tables.'

'Surely that would not be allowed to happen, your ladyship?'

'We are living in changed times, Mr Lipton, sadly changed times.'

He nodded. 'You are right. But is it too late for me to volunteer my statement?'

'Absolutely not. Please do it!' Would I have to twist his arm?

Mother kicked me under the table. 'You are a credit to the nation, Mr Lipton.'

'I shall do it, as soon as I leave here.' He took a big sip of tea.

Mother refilled his cup. 'You were quick-thinking, Mr Lipton.'

'I was up those stairs quite quickly, you know, Lady Rodpen, in spite of the lumbago. I'm a sprightly chap for my age.'

Being married to a police superintendent has given my mother certain unwanted insights into the intricacies of the law's long arm. She sighed. 'You see, this will all be information after the fact, or is it after the act, I can't remember. They should have taken your statement then and there.'

'I thought so at the time but the manager insisted I return to my piano and continue playing so as to restore calm. Once the man had been apprehended, the police spoke only to our manager, a most estimable man, but one who forgot my part in proceedings. The only telling was to my diary that very night.'

'You keep a diary?' Mother leaned towards him.

He breathed in the scent of her hair. 'I do indeed, your ladyship.'

'I warm to men who keep diaries. Such documents occasionally provide the most valuable evidence in a courtroom.'

'A courtroom?' He looked alarmed.

Mother offered him a cake.

He declined. 'My teeth harbour too many crumbs.' He looked slightly embarrassed. 'My diary was not written for others' eyes.'

'Be assured, sir, for the courts, diaries are on a par with sacred documents.'

He stood to return to his piano. 'Then I shall do it, ladies. The police will have my statement, and my diary.'

We left the tea rooms with the satisfaction of Mother having gained an admirer and me being able to tick off the first item in my plan.

As we stepped into the bustle of the street, I asked Mother, 'How did you know he followed me up the stairs?'

'He is a gallant gentleman and he sensed your concern. What rankles with him is that he is old and hung back. But I knew he would have followed you.'

'How did you know?'

'He followed his instincts. It is exactly what my old piano teacher would have done.'

Mother had not quite finished. As we walked into her favourite Harrogate hat shop, she said, 'I am on good terms with the wife of the barrister who will prosecute Adam Kitchen. I shall find a way of ensuring that this extra information from our pianist friend does not somehow become lost in police files.'

Later, we discussed what else might be done to ensure that Kitchen did not wriggle out of the charge of attempted murder. We ruled out the idea that I should befriend someone in his solicitor's office and find a way of looking at the documents. That might lead to my being charged with perverting the course of justice.

'What is Doris doing by way of sticking up for herself?' Mother asked.

'I don't know, but I'll write to her and find out.'

An exchange of letter revealed that Doris was doing nothing.

My dear Kate,

What would I do without you? That is so very helpful of you to have enlisted the aid of the old pianist.

You will tell me off for saying this but I can't help remembering how very talented Adam was, or is — I told you about his Lear. Perhaps if some theatre manager had recognised his abilities and given him work, he might not have turned so very strange. He was briefly in rep at Chichester but was let go — why, I do not know.

There was also a girlfriend before me. I believe that ended badly. His former flatmate tells me that she was the daughter of a shopkeeper on the King's Road. The shop sold games and novelties and she helped her father run it. It's thought that her name is Alice. What do you think I should do about that? I can hardly go and see her, buy a jigsaw puzzle, and then say, 'Oh by the way did Adam Kitchen ever try to murder you,' can I? Besides, I don't have the cash for a jigsaw puzzle.

Things here have not gone as badly as I feared. Once I told people that Adam was charged with attempted murder, almost everyone had a tale of thinking him a little odd and wondering why I had taken up with him — even those who never knew him.

Must dash — off to the theatre. Will resume this letter tomorrow when I have had another think.

Here I am back again. One of my friends knows the stage manager at Chichester and will find out why Adam was let go. As to the former girlfriend connection, please tell me what to do!

Because I must come to the court of assizes, and am dreading it, may I stay with you? It is all very well the law

411

demanding my presence but no one offers to pay my fare.
I wish I had kept that ring, even just to pawn now and
again. I am not asking you for money, Kate, even though I
know you are not poor, as I am. My friends here will have a
whip round. Actors are so very generous when they are not
being entirely mean and self-centred.

   Please write to me soon.
   Your friend
   Doris

I answered immediately, promising to buy Doris's return railway ticket in time for the court case. I also set out the instruction that she must write to the theatre manager at Chichester, explaining what had happened in Harrogate and asking him to write to the Chief Constable of Harrogate if there was any information regarding Adam Kitchen's time at Chichester that might be thought pertinent to the present case.

It was time for me to make a visit to London. I arranged to stay with Aunt Berta, Mother's sister, in Chelsea. Having only sons, she makes a fuss of me. We go shopping together, take tea at Fortnum's and call at Hatchards to buy the latest novels.

My luggage went ahead of me. After taking an early train from Leeds to King's Cross, I caught the tube to Goodge Street Station. There is something about Bloomsbury that makes me want to walk along the streets singing its praises. Perhaps it is a special atmosphere that comes from the pavements having been walked by actors, artists, writers and musicians. The very air of the place hangs dizzily over one, challenging the imagination.

I had arranged to meet Doris at the Royal Academy of Dramatic Art on Gower Street. A light rain fell and so I mounted the few steps to that enticing entrance that is framed by two solid pillars.

Doris appeared after about ten minutes, with a couple of fellow students, a young woman in baggy trousers and tunic and an older chap in a velvet suit. The two friends were going to a little theatre nearby to sit in on a rehearsal. They asked if we would join them, but Doris gave our excuses. It was our plan to find the games and novelty shop on the King's Road, and to see whether Alice, former girlfriend of Adam Kitchen, might be behind the counter and willing to speak to us.

Doris and I walked back to the tube station. 'We'll get something to eat in Chelsea, Kate.'

She seemed so confident that Kitchen would be found guilty that I felt almost reluctant to share my misgivings. My main reason for being here was, of course, to try and ensure that Adam Kitchen did not manage to fool a jury into believing that he was the injured party, and that we two females were the cause of his grief and incarceration.

Doris slipped through the barrier at the station without buying a ticket.

'Doris! You should be careful. Don't invite publicity.'

'You're right, as always. I can see it now in the evening rag. "Fare Dodger. Young actress admits she was foolish." I'd have to wipe away a tear and throw myself on the mercy of the court.'

'It's the other court case I'm thinking of. You must be seen as an upright and honest person, beyond reproach.'

'This is all so tedious, Kate. I'll be glad when the whole

business is over and I can take risks again. They do over-charge for fares. It should be taken into account that one is a student of drama and will repay the taxman and his minions a million times over once one becomes a revered leading lady.'

'You won't be a revered anything if we fail to have Kitchen locked up. You'll be a nervous wreck, frightened of your own shadow.'

This interested her. 'I could play that sort of part very well. I do like portraying fear and trepidation. It would work so well on screen, too. A close-up.'

We alighted at Sloane Square and began our walk along the King's Road, looking for a certain shop. We spotted the only one that it could possibly be: Potter's Games and Pastimes. I had to draw us away, into a nearby doorway, to remind Doris of The Plan.

'Oh by the way, Kate, it might be that Adam actually helped out at this shop occasionally.'

'Who said that?'

'Edward Danby, his former flatmate.'

'I thought Kitchen had independent means, what with the ring and how well-dressed he was.'

'Well yes. Perhaps he did it as a favour, to ingratiate himself with Alice's people.'

'That's possible.'

We glanced through the window and saw a grey-haired gentleman behind the counter, speaking to a customer.

'Alice isn't there then.' Doris seemed almost relieved. 'Should we come back tomorrow?'

'No. We must make the enquiry now. Be brave, Doris.'

'Who will do the talking?'

'It ought to be you. Imagine it is a part you are playing.'

'But I have no lines. I should have written some lines for myself.'

'Ask to see Alice. Say you have a mutual acquaintance.'

We watched as the shopkeeper wrapped a large box containing a board game. He took payment, and handed over the package.

While we waited for the customer to leave the shop, I looked at the window display. There were model-making kits for cars and aeroplanes, all sorts of puzzles, and a kit for making a cat's whisker wireless set, advertised as highly educational and giving an ear to the world.

Next to the cat's whisker set, there was an intriguing framed portrait of an Indian gentleman.

'I've remembered something,' Doris said. 'It may not be important.'

'What?'

'When the wicked one and I were first engaged, a few of our crowd, and he, passed this store one evening. We'd been to see a very dull play at the New Court Theatre in Sloane Square, and we were walking down to the pub.'

'And?'

'Adam said something odd.'

'What?'

'He said, "Don't buy your cat's whiskers here".'

'Did he say why?'

'No.'

'Is that all?' I asked.

'That was all, but there was a look on his face, and I knew there was something odd, and I knew I mustn't ask why.'

'Come on. Let's just go inside.'

The clapper rang as I opened the shop door.

The shopkeeper greeted us in a pleasant way, with the sort of glance that lets you know you may look about at your leisure and he will not pester you to buy.

It would be unfair to pose as customers. I gave Doris a prod.

'I'm sorry to disturb you, sir,' she began, rather too politely, 'but is Alice here?'

His look changed. To say his face darkened sounds like a line from a novel because faces do not suddenly darken unless the person blushes. He did not blush, but rather looked angry.

'No, she is not.'

'Ah.' Doris was slow in thinking what to say next but responded to my prod. 'I was hoping to see her. We have a mutual acquaintance that I wish to ask her about.'

The man seemed oddly at a loss for words. He bit his lip. Finally, he said, 'My daughter is not here.'

It was my turn. 'Might we leave a message for her, or will she be here tomorrow?'

'I haven't seen Alice for six months. Are you friends of hers?'

It was the way he spoke, the mixture of anger and grief that alarmed me. 'We have never met Alice.'

Doris tugged at my sleeve as she spoke. 'Sorry to have troubled you, Mr Potter.' She was ready to leave.

'I'm not Potter,' he said rather glumly. 'I took over from Potter and kept the name. No point in paying for a new sign.' He put both hands flat on the counter and stared at Doris. 'If you've never met Alice and don't know her last name, why are you here?'

I had no intention of leaving without finding out more, if possible. 'Sir, I believe we ought to tell you why we have come.'

'I wish you would.' This was the moment when he should have turned the shop sign to 'Closed', and invited us into the back room. He did not.

He looked from me to Doris. 'Go on. Speak your piece.'

Doris was silent.

'My friend Doris here was engaged to be married to Adam Kitchen. When she broke it off, he took it badly. He is presently on remand on the charge of attempting to murder Doris. Since this happened in Yorkshire, and we fear there may be a possibility that he will get away with it, we wanted to talk to Alice. We were told he courted her before turning his attentions to Doris.'

I had blurted this out quickly because as soon as I mentioned Kitchen's name, he stepped back from the counter and looked as though he might have some kind of attack. He sat down on a high stool and took out a cigarette. 'I don't usually smoke in the shop.' He lit the cigarette, and then looked at Doris. 'When was this?'

'The 1st of March. He attacked me, at a tea shop in Harrogate.'

'I mean when did you become engaged to him?'

'On New Year's Eve. It was a mistake, but you know, New Year's Eve, midnight, and all the excitement of moving into 1921 . . . ' She trailed off.

When the shopkeeper spoke, it was so quietly that a hush fell over all of us, as if a spell had been cast. 'She went in November. I thought she had gone away with him.'

Possibilities of many terrible things raced through my head.

To Doris's credit, she found words when I could not. 'He began to court me in November. Perhaps she had run away to escape from him, Mr . . . '

'Clark. Our name is Clark. She is Alice Clark, you must ask all your friends about her. She left a note. I was angry and threw it on the fireback. I was so sure she had gone off with him.'

'Did she say as much in the note, Mr Clark?' I asked.

He shook his head. 'No, but she would not have. I had the measure of him, a dilettante, never done a day's work in his life, living on his reputation as an officer and a gentleman, wearing an old school tie.'

Doris took a deep breath and for an awful moment I thought she was going to commend Adam Kitchen's performance in *King Lear*.

Mr Clark spoke first. 'I knew he was no good when he denigrated Jagadish Chandra Bose.'

'Was Mr Bose a friend of yours?' Doris asked.

'He is a Bengali gentleman and the cleverest man alive. There would be no cat's whiskers if not for him, yet that Kitchen fellow reckoned he could do as well.'

We all waited. It was up to Mr Clark to decide what must be done.

He took a drag on his cigarette. 'I shall shut up shop now and report Alice missing. You had better give me your names and addresses.'

Doris took out one of her portrait postcards, printed for when she graduates and writes to theatre managers with a note of her capabilities. She wrote her address on the back.

I had no card with me and so wrote my details on the page of a notebook.

Mr Clark was looking at Doris's picture and at her. 'You have a look of my Alice. Auburn hair, high cheek bones, blue eyes. His type I suppose. I wish I could get my hands on him.'

Doris gasped. Her hand went to her throat.

'What did he do to you?' Mr Clark asked.

'Tried to strangle me.'

I felt the need to give reassurance, even if it were false reassurance. 'Mr Clark, it could be that knowing you had been right about Kitchen your daughter wanted simply to leave, without worrying you further. Was there somewhere she might go?'

'I'll tell that to the police.'

He went into the back of the shop and came back wearing a shabby overcoat. 'Will you come with me to the police station?'

I agreed that we would, and wondered whether our interference would be of benefit to the case against Kitchen, or the reverse.

If Alice Clark had simply left an overbearing father, then we should look foolish and culpable. But I would rather look foolish and culpable and face the truth than live in a mist of uncertainty.

Perhaps all three of us, entering the Chelsea Police Station, wondered how our story would be received. I certainly did.

We were taken into a side room one by one, Mr Clark first. Each of us gave a statement.

I was last. Mr Clark had waited for us. 'Where will you go now, ladies? Do you need an escort?'

'Thank you, Mr Clark, but my aunt lives nearby. We

will go there. I am sorry to have brought you such ill news. I hope that you may think of somewhere Alice may have gone. She should feel safe to return to London, once she knows that Kitchen is in custody in the north.'

He nodded. 'I will hope for the best and fear the worst. I am only glad my dear wife is not here to share this pain.'

During the days that followed, I hoped to hear some news of Alice Clark, but there was no word.

Neither Doris nor I heard from Mr Clark. I had his telephone number, but it seemed intrusive to ring him. Instead, I telephoned to my aunt.

She arranged for her son James to call at the shop and buy something, and mention me and Doris. Mr Clark had no news. It was as if Alice had vanished into thin air. Her photograph had been circulated to every police force in the country.

Alice Clark was traced to Devon, where she had taken a job as a waitress. She confirmed to police that she had run away out of fear of Adam Kitchen and for that same reason had told no one of her whereabouts.

Doris had arrived early, so as to spend Easter with me before the trial began.

Although my brothers and their friends had finished building the extension to my house in record time, it was still a shell, not yet decorated and furnished. Perhaps it was just as well that the annexe was not ready for occupation, because Doris had become nervous. She wanted to be in the house, in the room next to mine. She was not sleeping well and dreaded the thought of facing Adam Kitchen across the courtroom. She had been informed that he still intended to plead not guilty.

We went to stay in Wakefield. My parents and the twins made every effort to put Doris at ease. Dad gave us tips about how to remain calm in court, and how to deal with any tricks or bullying from the barrister.

On Easter Day, after church, we played that childish game of looking for eggs in the garden. For a time, that gave Doris something else to think about. We all laughed about where the eggs were hidden. Of course the twins and I knew the hiding places, but we kept this from Doris and congratulated her heartily each time she found an egg.

My family have a dog, a failed police bloodhound called Constable. Constable joined in the search for eggs and made a particular favourite of Doris, as if he sensed her distress.

Matt, Doris and Constable were searching the shrubbery when Simon and I sat down together on the garden bench.

'Is there any word from your colleagues about what's going on with the case?' I asked.

'I wish I knew, Kate. It looks as if Kitchen is determined to stick with his not guilty plea and put you and Doris through the ordeal of a trial.'

Constable came across, wagging his tail and putting an egg by my feet.

'Good dog!' I took the egg and patted Constable's head.

'There is something else going on though.' Simon stroked Constable who was demanding more attention.

'Something about the case?'

'We have had detectives up from London, questioning him about something else. I don't know what. It could be what you mentioned about the other girlfriend.'

'Alice.'

'Yes, that's all I can think of. I'm at the wrong level for

anything to be shared with me. And of course Dad is constabulary rather than investigation so they don't always talk to each other.'

'Dad wouldn't anyway,' I said.

Our conversation was cut short when Doris came dashing over to add an egg to her collection.

Dad came to the door and called us in for Sunday lunch.

Simon laughed. 'We're like a bunch of kids, out here hunting for eggs.'

He was about to go indoors when I stopped him. 'Simon, what is it that you and Matt are keeping from me? Ever since that day when Matt came over and announced that he would build an annexe for me, there's been something he wanted to tell me but he won't spit it out.'

Matt called us to hurry up or the Yorkshire pudding would be cold.

We made our way to the back door. Simon said, 'Oh it's just a thought, an idea we had. I'll tell you when all this horrible business with Adam Kitchen is over.'

On Easter Monday, Doris and I drove back to my house. We found a good way to keep busy and take our minds off what was to come. Doris claimed to be a dab hand at wallpaper hanging. The annexe had a bedroom that looked out onto the wood, and a sitting room with a view of the garden. My genius brother had even included a small fully equipped bathroom. It was all so grand that Doris assured me any housekeeper would pay to move in. Although a door led into the kitchen, there was a tiny scullery with sink and gas ring so that the occupant might be self-contained when it came to brewing a cup of tea.

The doors and skirting boards were of fine wood and had

422

been varnished so there was no need for any painting. I was a little disappointed at this as I had rather fancied myself wielding a brush and choosing colours.

We borrowed a trestle table from a neighbour. I had chosen wallpapers with fronds of leaves for the annexe sitting room and rosebuds for the bedroom. We measured, cut and pasted, and spoke not a word about the forthcoming trial.

Each day, we made lunch together. In the afternoons, Doris read Ibsen's *Ghosts*, rehearsing for her part as Regina and asking me to read in some of the other parts. She was determined to know the whole play by heart as this had been chosen for the final piece – the play which would be performed by RADA students as their showcase when term drew to its close.

All the while, that thing we did not talk about loomed large. I have a calendar on the kitchen wall. It was my habit each morning to put a line through the previous day.

I crossed out the last day of March and turned the page.

It was April Fool's Day, when usually there would be pranks, and silly stories in the newspapers to deceive the gullible. In three more days, the trial of Adam Kitchen for the attempted murder of Doris Butler would begin.

We had finished papering the rooms. Although we noticed that the first two corners we did were not quite right, overall we were pleased with our efforts. 'If I don't reach the heights as an actress, Kate, you and I will become decorators to the rich and famous.'

As a change from *Ghosts*, Doris asked me would I read Helmer. The part she really wanted was Nora in *A Doll's House*. But she could not settle to Nora either.

423

We went back to *Ghosts*, dividing the parts between us. Having only one copy of the play we sat side by side on the floor in the newly papered sitting room of the annexe.

'We must live for the joy of life,' Doris declaimed, rather mournfully I thought. Immediately, we both almost jumped out of our skins when there was a rap on the windowpane.

I looked up to see Simon peering through at us and mouthing that he had been knocking at the front door.

The annexe has its own door and the key was in the lock. I let him in, thinking he had come to see our handiwork.

He duly admired what we had done. Matt would have noticed the slightly faulty corners straight away. Simon did not notice.

We all went into the kitchen and I put the kettle on.

It was clear that Simon was working up to something, but what?

He dunked a biscuit in his tea. 'I'm not sure whether this is good news, but perhaps it is.'

'What are you talking about?' I asked.

Doris leaned forward. 'You've come to tell me something about the case.'

Simon let out a breath. 'Yes. And I think you'll be relieved. Kitchen has changed his plea to guilty.'

'Well thank goodness for that.' I turned to Doris. 'You'll be spared the trial. We'll be spared the trial.'

'There is something else, isn't there?' Doris asked. 'You said you have good news and perhaps not good news.'

Simon misjudged his biscuit dunking and the biscuit disintegrated in his mug of tea. 'His barrister will enter a plea of guilty but with diminished responsibility while the balance of his mind was disturbed.'

Doris let out a cry. 'They'll let him go!'

Simon shook his head. 'No. Absolutely not. He would not have changed his plea but there's more than we thought. The men from Scotland Yard questioned him about Alice Clark. A letter came from the director of the Chichester theatre, about his behaviour and the reason for his dismissal. One of the actresses had made a statement to the Chichester police about him, a very serious complaint.'

Simon is often thought of as something of a cold fish but he looked at Doris with great compassion. 'Dear Doris, you've had such a lucky escape.'

Doris began to cry. That set me looking for hankies, for both of us.

We talked but it was all in circles and there was so much we did not know.

Simon was able to tell us this. 'Kitchen was examined by two doctors, one from London and another from Edinburgh. There might be a third, from a local hospital.'

'They ought to tell one,' Doris said. 'They ought to tell one every little thing if one is the person at the centre of this . . . this drama.'

'They won't let him play the insane card unless it's true.' Simon stirred the stew. 'That's how it is with something like this. Be brave, Doris. Put it behind you. You will be an actress everyone has heard of.'

'For the wrong reasons.'

'People forget the reasons. They will just remember your name, and kindly.'

Doris went out to walk around the wood, and take it all in, and breathe some fresh air, while I set the table. I don't know why I started crying again – relief, I suppose.

We stayed away from the court that Monday, 4 April, seeing no reason to look at that man again. Both Doris and I expected to hear something definite by the end of Monday, but sentencing was reserved.

Doris went back to London. I promised that as soon as there was news, I would let her know by telephoning to my aunt and having a message brought to her.

It was not until Friday, 8 April that we learned of the judgement. I was able to telephone Aunt Berta and ask her to let Doris know the outcome, just in case the police did not tell her.

Adam Kitchen was found guilty but insane. He was sentenced to be held in a secure asylum at His Majesty's pleasure.

In such a case, His Majesty's pleasure invariably meant forever.

That summer, Doris graduated from RADA. There was a series of end of year performances where, in front of invited audiences, the students strutted their stuff and showed their talents. Dad and Simon were unable to take time off work but Mother, Matt and I went to watch as Doris gave a spellbinding performance as Ibsen's Nora. Aunt Berta and my cousins came too.

Aunt Berta was so enchanted by Doris that she immediately made a bid to have Doris's company for the summer, along with mine. We spent an idyllic month on the French Riviera, in Antibes. Uncle had hoped to meet King Nicholas of Montenegro, as he had the previous year, but Nicholas evaded him by dying in March. For the rest of us, no one was sorry to avoid formal occasions. We wanted to paddle, to swim, to read under huge parasols, and to be dazzled by the bright sky.

It was on a glorious afternoon as we sat on the balcony of the rented house that Matt finally told me of his and Simon's plan. They had decided to go to Canada. During the war they met Canadian soldiers and had kept in touch.

'But why do you want to go?' I asked. 'You are so settled here, everything seems to be going so well for you. You're in demand for your furniture. Simon has qualified. He has a job for life.'

Matt lit a cigarette. 'That's the trouble, Kate. It's all too settled. Simon hates that job. You know how much he loves horses. Almost the most awful thing for him about the war was that he couldn't bear to see the horses suffer. Don't laugh at this because it sounds ridiculous but he has an obsession about joining the Royal Mounted Police. I think it is the thing that would help him recover.'

'I thought he had recovered.'

'No. He needs a new start, away from old England.'

'What about you?'

'I want to be in a new country, Kate, one with opportunities, horizons. So few people can afford my furniture here, and I want it to be available to everyone who has a sense of beauty. What was the quote from William Morris? "Have nothing in your house that you do not know to be useful, or believe to be beautiful." England is exhausted. I have this urge to start again, in a new world.'

'Have you told Dad, or Mother?'

'No. I'm telling you first. I suppose I want your permission. You would be the one left behind.'

In that moment, I knew the twins' departure was inevitable. They had always had a Peter Pan quality, something of the 'lost boy' about them, even before the war. They would forever look for a home that may or may not exist.

The rest of us would stay put, and carry on, with uncertainty, and hope.

'When will you go?'

'Sometime in the New Year.'

I was glad that Doris was coming to spend Christmas with us. The whole family had grown fond of her and rejoiced in her well-deserved success as an actress. Not only had she been in work since leaving RADA, but her diary for the next year was full of engagements.

She arrived at Wakefield station, looking stunning in a pale cashmere coat with astrakhan collar, wearing a close-fitting red velvet hat, red leather gloves and carrying a red bag.

Success suited her. It was wonderful to see her looking so well and to know that the nightmare of the past was behind her.

It was Christmas Eve when we gathered for supper in my parents' dining room and I thought this few days of Christmas might be the last time we were all together. Doris, I felt sure, would rise meteorically and inhabit another sphere. My brothers were set to sail for Canada on the White Star Line in February. Mother and Dad had taken it much better than I had hoped, with Mother saying she would visit them, and Dad confiding in me that he didn't believe they would last out there.

We all attended the midnight service at Wakefield Cathedral and sang the hymns and carols. Matt and Simon were both choir boys and had fine voices.

It was on Christmas morning that the blow fell.

We were in the drawing room, opening presents from under the tree. Simon and Doris had just pulled a cracker and Doris read one of those silly mottos that are instantly forgotten.

Police officers have a certain unmistakable way of knocking on a door. It was that sort of knock, even though whoever was demanding attention had already rung the doorbell.

Dad went, assuming that it was some summons for him on an urgent constabulary matter. He shut the drawing room door behind him.

Moments later, he opened it again, bringing a young constable with him.

'Doris, there is nothing to be alarmed about. This is Constable Bodkin. He has some news that you must hear, but everything is under control.'

People usually say that everything is under control when everything is spinning out of control. Dad's words put us all in an instant funk.

Constable Bodkin did not help. 'Miss Doris Butler?' he asked – as if Dad would have made a mistake.

'Yes. What is it? Is it my mother?'

Dad realised he should have come straight to the point. 'No Doris, it concerns Adam Kitchen.'

It was Constable Bodkin's turn. 'Miss Butler, I'm sorry to say that Kitchen escaped from the asylum yesterday evening. There was a religious service and preparations for Christmas. Somehow it was not noticed until this morning that he was missing. There is an alert. He is sought, but you are advised to take all precautions.'

Doris ran her hands through her carefully arranged hair,

making a mess of it. She closed her eyes. 'It's starting all over again. I can't bear it.'

'He stole some money,' the constable added. 'The railway companies have been notified, his picture circulated. It's thought he will head for London. Given there is a skeleton rail schedule, we're not expecting him to get far.'

Doris shook her head. 'He'll think I've gone to my mother's. She has a smallholding in Huby. Someone should go there.'

Dad led the constable into the kitchen.

The sparkle had gone out of our Christmas morning. Mother asked Simon to refill the sherry glasses.

Doris drank her sherry and held out her glass for another. 'I'll come to Canada with you two. It's the only way I'll ever escape him.'

'That's too drastic,' Mother said. 'Your future is here, your career is here. The police will catch him in no time.'

'And if they do, he'll escape again. You don't know him.' She spoke into the sherry glass. 'He is cunning, and there's money in his family. I don't know how but he will get at it. He's an actor, don't forget. He can change his appearance, his voice and his mannerisms. They won't catch him.'

Matt put on a brave face. 'He'll have us to deal with if he comes anywhere near you while you're here, and by the time you go back to London, he will be apprehended. The judges, the law, they won't be thwarted. Aren't I right, Simon?'

Simon, conscious of his position as the recently qualified solicitor, confirmed Matt's sentiments, though somewhat unconvincingly.

None of us had a great appetite for Christmas dinner, but

we put on our best faces and tried to talk of other subjects, all eager to save the day from entire ruin.

The telephone rang as we began on the Christmas pudding.

Dad went to answer it.

We all waited.

'Now there is nothing to worry about but . . . ' he said when he came back. 'Kate, that was your neighbour, Miss Merton. There was a break-in at your house. She has called the police. As far as she can see there is no great damage. The cards and letters that were on your mantelpiece have been disturbed.'

Doris and I exchanged a look. There had been a card from her, asking had she got the right address for my parents as she wanted to send them a card. She also wanted to be sure of it in case there was a mix-up at the station, or a delay in the trains, and she might have to take a taxi.

She had quoted the correct address. If that break-in had been committed by Kitchen, then he knew where she was.

'Is Miss Merton still on the line?'

'No, it was a poor line and she wanted to go back to your house and wait for the police to come.'

'Was there anything else, any other damage?' I asked.

'She said that your model of York Minster had been knocked from the dining table onto the floor.'

Doris's present to Matt had been a jigsaw puzzle of York Minster. It was her way of thanking him for reassembling her father's model that had been damaged by her mother's fancy man.

'It will be all right, Doris,' Matt said. 'I can fix it again. There's time before we set sail. I'll make sure of it.'

Dad was still in the doorway. The gravity of the situation

was clear. He spoke to Mother, and then his look included the rest of us. 'It's Christmas Day and we ought to be doing our best to rejoice, but I'm going into the station. Doris, I will make entirely sure that everything possible is done to find and apprehend that man. Until that happens, you will be safe with us. Simon and Matthew will keep a look out. I'll have constables posted front and back for twenty-four hours.'

Whether it was police precautions or a failure of Doris's nemesis to find the house, we were not disturbed.

The next morning, St Stephen's Day, broke bright and clear.

It was Matt's idea, at breakfast, that we should go on an outing, and we all agreed. That is, Matt, Simon, Doris and I who welcomed the diversion. Mother said she would stay put and we young people must go off and have an enjoyable day. She insisted we should take a pork pie, ham sandwiches and bottles of water, just in case there was nowhere open for us to have lunch.

'Where will you go?' Mother asked.

We were not sure.

It was Doris's idea that we should go to York. 'I haven't been there since I went with Dad. I was just ten years old and he had begun his sketching of the Minster. I was impatient, just wanting to walk around the city walls. He wanted to go in the Minster, but when we went inside, I didn't like it. I felt afraid. Now I want to see it again.'

And so it was decided: destination, York.

We set off in Simon's car.

It was a long journey but that was all to the good because there is something about being on the move that gives the sense of leaving one's troubles behind. Simon had made the journey before. He had the Automobile Association's handwritten cards of instruction that he handed to Matt, our navigator.

I do believe that for long stretches even Doris forgot to worry as we sang 'The Twelve Days of Christmas' and 'Good King Wenceslas'.

At Tadcaster, Simon had to take out the petrol can and fill up. That gave us time to stretch our legs. The petrol station owner was grumpy about being disturbed but cheered up when we sang him a carol and gave him a chocolate. We set off again, bringing the stench of petrol with us.

It was a great relief to arrive at our destination, drive through Micklegate and find a place to park the motor. We wandered through the narrow lanes and alleyways until we came to a place where we could climb onto the city wall.

Simon was all for going to Clifford's Tower but I reminded him that Doris was our guest and wanted to see the Minster. If we had time later, we could go to the mound and the tower.

The organ was playing and the young choir in full throat when we entered the Minster. It was a children's service. I would have sat at the back and listened to the angelic voices, but the others were already stepping quietly across the church.

I caught up.

Doris whispered, 'Dad wanted to take me up the winding tower, to the roof, to look out across the city. Let's do it now. I might never come this way again.'

Without more words, we went to the winding staircase. A small sign warned us that there were two hundred and seventy-five steps.

Matt prompted, 'You go first, Kate, you're the eldest, that's what you always used to say.'

I was glad to go first. If the boys went first they would go racing up and I wanted us to stay together. The steps really did wind. They were uneven and bumpy too. We passed narrow passageways that may or may not have led somewhere.

We must have been eighty feet above the ground when the way led us out into the open air. This was not the very top of the tower but there was a ledge or walkway. I followed the people just ahead of us, and then turned to look. Matt and Simon must have been waylaid by investigating one of the passageways off the stairs, or admiring a gargoyle.

Doris and I ascended farther, to the top of the tower.

The area was a broad open space. The afternoon sun cast a warm light across the city below. The people ahead of us had walked as far as they dare to the edge, and had their backs to us.

I turned when I heard footsteps, thinking Simon and Matt had caught up. I began to speak, to say that I wished I had brought my camera. The words on my tongue became pebbles. It must have been my gasp for breath that made Doris turn her head.

There he was, Adam Kitchen, dishevelled and unshaven, walking towards us, leaning forwards, his intentions horribly clear.

He spoke so softly. 'I knew you would come here, Doris. You are so predictable.'

Somehow Doris found her voice. 'Adam, don't do this. I know you can't help yourself. It's not too late to . . . '

He paused, as if trying to remember his lines. 'You will

never be a good actress. You are too easy to read. But we'll be together now, in death if not in life.'

Doris screamed. I don't know what I did, tried to stand in his way I think. It all felt so unreal, like something that you would see in the picture house.

He shoved me aside as he ran towards Doris who stood as still as one of the worn medieval statues.

It was his shove that brought me to life and I got to Doris before him and threw myself at her so that we both fell onto the uneven roof and so did not see him fall, only heard his scream.

And then my lovely brothers appeared, and the other people who had walked up the winding stairs before us came over and said something.

There is always someone who is very matter of fact on any occasion. One of the other party, a stout gentleman with a red face said, 'That's a hundred foot drop, that is.'

His wife brought out smelling salts.

The other woman, who looked like her sister, said, 'My goodness me.'

Afterwards, we remembered. In the letter on my mantelpiece that Kitchen had read when he broke in, Doris had said she would like to visit the Minster. I had forgotten, and so had she.

We never knew how long he had lurked in one of those narrow passageways, waiting for his moment like a patient cat knowing a mouse will eventually appear.

Months later, Doris and I talked about that day again. She had come to Liverpool where we said goodbye to the twins as they set sail for Canada, having made promises to write, to visit, never to lose touch.

Mother, Dad and I put on our bravest faces. Doris did her best to cheer us, saying we would all go to Canada and see them, and then contradicting herself. They would miss home. They would be back within the year.

She stayed with me for one night before going back to London. Her reconstructed model of York Minster was, for now, in my safe keeping. I would take care of it for Doris until she had a home of her own.

That day should not be far off because she is so in demand.

We were in the sitting room of the annexe, the room we had decorated together. We agreed that there was something appropriate about the fact that the wallpapering in the corners was not perfect, because nothing else in the world was perfect.

We had glasses of brandy, toasting our future, and the twins' futures.

'I wanted to ask you, Kate, did you notice someone else on the roof of the Minster?'

'The three people who were just ahead of us.'

'Not them.'

'And the twins, arriving when it was all over.'

'The soldier.'

'I didn't see a soldier.'

'It was my dad. I knew him straight away. He came home on leave, in 1916, looking so tired, wearing his uniform, and he was just like that again, dressed the same, but not tired any more, just . . . just my dad. He came up behind Adam Kitchen, and he pushed him. That was what happened.'

'I didn't see him.'

'Then he only appeared to me.' She was not sad about

436

this, but took a sip of brandy and smiled. 'He always said I should go back to the Minster one day, and I should climb the steps, and think of him.'

'Well I'm glad, Doris. And I'll come to the opening of your next show. You'll be the talk of the town. And if anyone talks to me in the interval about the star of the show, I'll say, "That's my friend Doris".'

Late the next morning, there was a knocking on my front door.

I opened the door to a woman with a lined, careworn face. She was small and seemed almost to disappear into the brown wool coat.

'I'm sorry to call on you unannounced, Mrs Shackleton. It is Mrs Shackleton?'

'Yes, but I don't believe we've met.'

She twisted her mouth and bit her lip. 'I'm Mrs Gooch. My son Robin was in the Youth Players with Doris. I got your address from Doris's mother.'

I motioned her to come in. 'I'm sorry, Mrs Gooch, but you've missed Doris. She went back to London yesterday.'

She hesitated. 'Well, it was you I've come to see.'

'Then come in.'

'Thank you.' She stepped inside. I took her into the drawing room. She sank into a chair with such obvious relief that I thought she must be exhausted.

'The kettle has just boiled. You'll have a cup of tea?'

'If you're making some.' She glanced at the framed photograph on the mantelpiece, Gerald in his uniform. 'I've come to talk to you about my son, Robin.'

'Then I'd better make that pot of tea.'

I kept a steady hand as I poured water onto the teapot.

437

What could I say to a stranger who had lost her son? While I searched for words, and wondered why she wanted to speak to me, I opened a tin of shortbread biscuits and then took cups and saucers from the cupboard.

I carried in the tray and set it down. 'Milk and sugar?'

'No sugar, thank you.'

'Do have a biscuit.'

When she showed no sign of speaking, I said, 'I didn't know your son, Mrs Gooch. Doris and I only met a few years ago, when she moved to London. I'm sorry for your loss.'

'Did Doris say anything about Robin?'

Doris had never mentioned Robin, but it seemed unkind to say so. 'I knew his name because she and Mr Gooch talked about him. We met your husband in the railway station.'

Her lip trembled. 'I expect my husband told you he was dead.'

Her words gave me the shivers. Was she, like me, unwilling to accept the bad news that other people took as gospel?

'He did say that your son had not come back from the war.'

The silence stretched. I willed myself to stay calm and not to try and hurry her.

'Robin did not come back from the war because he never went.'

'What do you mean?'

'He was a conscientious objector. He refused to fight.'

I had heard stories about the foul treatment of conscientious objectors; 'conchies', 'yellow bellies'. They were imprisoned, sent to do hard labour, put before mock firing squads.

'Did he go with the Red Cross then?'

438

'No. He was what they call an absolutist. He refused any part in the war. War was murder, he said. Ever since he was a little lad he would never hurt a fly. When the time came for his conscription, he refused. My husband tells people he is dead. He says it would be better for Robin to be dead than to be a living dishonour to us.'

'And where is Robin now?'

'I have no news of him, no trace. That is why I have come to you.' Tears came to her eyes. She took out a hanky but simply clenched it in her fist. 'I hope you will help me find him.'

'Why me, Mrs Gooch?'

'Doris's mother told me about you, and so did a friend's daughter who works as a waitress in the tea rooms. You helped Doris. You found out about Adam Kitchen's other girlfriend. You pushed Doris into finding out that Kitchen was sacked from a theatre somewhere down south. You made sure he didn't get off when he went to court.'

'Mrs Gooch, I don't know what to say.'

'And Doris's mother told me how you tracked down an officer who didn't go back to his family when the war was over. And I know that you found an old soldier sleeping rough and knew where he was from by his accent.'

'I had help from the men's regiments.'

She took this as a judgement on her pacifist son. Once more she glanced at Gerald's photograph on the mantelpiece. She stood. 'I shouldn't have asked you.'

'Please sit down, Mrs Gooch. Let us think about this. I'll need to know more.'

'Will you help me then?' A light of hope came into her eyes.

'I'll do my best, Mrs Gooch.'

We talked for a long time. I asked her questions, and made notes about Robin's Quaker girlfriend, relatives, friends and the places Robin may have visited. I asked what kind of work he would have looked for. She gave me a photograph of Robin.

'It's the only one I have of him grown up.'

'I'll take good care of it.'

'I nearly forgot that I brought you some eggs, laid this morning.'

'Well that is really kind, and I fancy one now. Let's go in the kitchen.'

'I'm so grateful to you. I wish I could pay you for your time and your trouble.'

'How could this be about payment, Mrs Gooch? Don't even think in those terms.'

I found a tin of tomato soup in the cupboard and so with the eggs was able to provide a two-course lunch.

We sat at the kitchen table. 'I'm guessing you won't want Mr Gooch to know about this search for Robin?'

She shook her head. 'I might tell him when summat comes of it. I just hope Robin is well and that he'll find a life for hisself.'

'Will your husband ask where you were today?'

'He's out the whole day. If I'm back by six he'll be none the wiser.'

'Then you just leave this with me. I'll start today. There'll be someone at the Quaker Meeting House. They will tell me where to make enquiries. I'm sure they'll have information about conscientious objectors.'

'And shall I come back another day then, when my mister is out of the house?'

'I'll send word by Doris's mother and we can arrange to meet. Can she be relied on?'

'She can. Some say she's no better than she ought to be but I've always liked her. She's a good neighbour.'

When we had eaten our late lunch, I drove Mrs Gooch to the railway station and waited with her until her train came.

On the way back from the station, I realised I ought to buy groceries. I stopped the car by the parade of shops.

A postcard in the newsagent's window caught my eye. It was written in a neat hand.

RESPECTABLE FEMALE SEEKS
POSITION AS HOUSEKEEPER
PLAIN COOKING – EXPERIENCE –
REFERENCES
APPLY WITHIN FOR THE ADDRESS
OF MRS SUGDEN

I stared at the card. This seemed too good to be true. Matt was right. I needed a housekeeper, especially now that I had something to do, something important, helping another woman who was suffering, as we all were.

Although my mother's first choice would be to have me back with her, as a second choice she would relish helping to choose a housekeeper. I could hear her voice in my head telling me to call at a reputable staff agency and interview candidates. I could picture her going through the small advertisements in *The Lady* magazine, circling likely individuals. Finding a housekeeper would become a major and time-consuming task.

I stepped into the shop.

The newsagents know me. I have the papers and the *Photographic Journal* delivered.

We wished each other good morning.

'When was that card put in the window, Mrs Weatherfield, the one advertising for a housekeeping post?'

'Just this morning. Mind you, the person had several cards with her. She must be placing them roundabout.'

'What was she like?'

'She seemed right enough.'

'Then I should like her address please.'

Buying groceries could wait. Once I have made up my mind, I do not like to waste time. By the end of the day I intended to have a housekeeper. The housekeeper would have an annexe. Mrs Sugden and I were meant for each other, I felt sure.

I would help a mother find her lost boy.

From now on I would not sit twiddling my thumbs, waiting for a future. There was something in the world for me to do. I would start this very day.